Addicted After All

Addicted Series

RECOMMENDED READING ORDER

Addicted After All

KRISTA RITCHIE
& BECCA RITCHIE

BERKLEY ROMANCE
NEW YORK

BERKLEY ROMANCE
Published by Berkley
An imprint of Penguin Random House LLC
penguinrandomhouse.com

Copyright © 2014 by K.B. Ritchie
Excerpt from *Fuel the Fire* copyright © 2015 by K.B. Ritchie
Bonus Material copyright © 2023 by Krista & Becca Ritchie

Library of Congress Cataloging-in-Publication Data

Names: Ritchie, Krista, author. | Ritchie, Becca, author.
Title: Addicted after all / Krista Ritchie & Becca Ritchie.
Description: First Berkley Romance edition. |
New York: Berkley Romance, 2023. | Series: Addicted series
Identifiers: LCCN 2023018335 | ISBN 9780593639610 (trade paperback)
Subjects: LCSH: Sex addicts—Fiction. |
LCGFT: Romance fiction. | Erotic fiction. | Novels.
Classification: LCC PS3618.I7675 A64 2023 | DDC 813/.6—dc23/eng/20230512
LC record available at https://lccn.loc.gov/2023018335

Addicted After All was originally self-published, in a different form, in 2014.

First Berkley Romance Edition: September 2023

Printed in the United States of America
3rd Printing

Book design by Kristin del Rosario
Interior art: Broken heart on wall © Valentina Shikina / Shutterstock.com

To you, the reader:

When we originally wrote the Addicted series, we were in college with big, lofty dreams and hopes of Lily and Lo's story finding some people. It became so much more than just one romance between childhood friends, thanks to readers who wanted to see more.

It was about sisters, written by two sisters. It was about friendship, and the family you have and also make along the way. Rose's and Daisy's stories—the Calloway Sisters spin-off series—are woven so intrinsically into Lily's novels because we believe that one life does not stop while another goes on a journey. Every novel impacts every character. So the best way to read Lily's story and not miss a thing is by combining her series with the Calloway Sisters series in a ten-book reading order. It's the order we wrote the novels—all three sisters intertwined together.

This is the Addicted series. Ten books. Six friends. Three couples. One epic saga.

We hope these characters bring you as much happiness as they've brought us throughout the years.

As Lily would say, thankyouthankyouthankyou for choosing them and us. Happy reading!

All the love in every universe,
Krista and Becca

One

Loren Hale

In the pitch-black of night, I run as fast as rage will carry me. Gravel from the suburban road digs into my bare feet, February's cold biting my flesh. I had no time to slip on shoes, a shirt, or even grab a coat.

"*Motherfuckers*," Ryke growls through gritted teeth, using his full power, endurance   everything that made him a collegiate track star—to chase after dark-clothed figures that bolt down the street. I never thought I'd be able to match my brother's speed. No longer weighed down by self-pity and hatred, I can go farther than I dreamed.

And I do.

My legs pump forward in sync with his, our muscles sharpening in the same way. Our veins bursting and heating with blood-red fury. Because we thought these stupid fucking guys shot one of the girls through the window.

A minute ago, Ryke and I were upstairs and heard a few loud bangs, followed by Lily's and Daisy's panicked screams. As we rushed to the main floor, Daisy was ghostly pale. Lily was holding her little sister's hand, and my gaze dropped to Lil's stomach, a noticeable bump at eighteen weeks pregnant.

I fucking ran on instinct. Only this time, I'm not the one being chased.

Ryke was right by my side, no hesitation, no questions asked. He took one look at Daisy's horror-stricken face, and he just lost it. Our fame and notoriety shouldn't put *either* of the girls in harm's way. It's complete bullshit.

All six of us—Ryke, Daisy, Connor, Rose, Lily, and me—now live in a rich, gated Philadelphia neighborhood. Only these so-called "gates" surround the neighborhood, not our eight-bedroom house. Sometimes, the real shits are the ones right down the street, and for the past two weeks, they've egged our door, toilet papered the yard, and forked the grass.

This is the first time we've heard them scamper away, and so this is the first time we've ever tried to catch them.

We gain on them, and their muffled cursing becomes louder, their panic clearer in their hurried steps, and half of the guys scatter toward a brick mansion with floodlights illuminating a massive door. About three guys continue to sprint ahead.

Then they spin around and point their paintball guns at us. A series of *pops* split the air before a couple shots connect with my shoulder and ribs like a two-second punch.

Jesus. I want to shout until my throat bleeds and shake them until they get it. Until they realize that we're not board games they can play with—when they're sitting in their rooms with nothing to do.

We are people. Real. Living, breathing things that have breaking points. I want to scream it all, but I can't utter one single goddamn word. Everything is caged in my lungs.

The guys stop shooting at us when they realize we're much closer. "Go, go, go!" they scream at each other. One guy in a hoodie glances over his shoulder, and then he trips over his own feet. Right as he stumbles, about to eat the asphalt, I grip the back of his black sweatshirt. My pulse skyrockets with adrenaline.

Ryke slows to a stop with me.

"Let me fucking go!" the guy shouts, thrashing in my grasp. I feel my heart bang against my chest, and my brows furrow at his scrawny build. *He's young.*

In a matter of seconds, his friends leave him, racing further into the darkness. He notices his buddies sprinting away, and he redirects his anger. "HEY! YOU PUSSIES! YOU'RE GOING TO LEAVE ME HERE?!"

I rip the paintball gun out of his hand and toss it to Ryke, and then the guy whips around on me, swinging his fist haphazardly at my face. I easily dodge it, but he's squirming so much that it's hard to hold him upright without him slipping in my hands.

"Get a grip," Ryke growls at him.

He tries to elbow my ribs, and I grasp his arm, adding with a sneer, "You're the one who's been fucking with *us*."

"And you're the cuntbag who's called the cops like a little bitch," the guy snarls back. That's when the hood falls off his head, and I stare directly into his venomous gaze. Tousled brown hair and a young, soft face. He can't be any older than seventeen.

My blood chills. And I crane my neck at Ryke. "Do you see any cops?" I ask him with a mocking tone.

"No," Ryke says, his voice rough.

I turn back to the guy in my clutch. "See, it's just you and us—"

"That's great," he cuts me off with a short laugh, "let's have a fucking tea party and celebrate the new year. And then when I leave, you both can go *fuck* the same girl and knock her up again."

I shake, my heart slamming into my ribs. A million different insults burn my brain, the malicious ones trying to take hold.

Then Ryke charges forward, fists clenched. "You mother-fucking—"

"Stop," I tell Ryke, making sure to wedge my body between him and the teen. He can't *hit* him. Not even if this guy spouts off a thousand rumors that've been circulating the tabloids. Not if he knows more about us than we'll ever know about him. He's a bored teenager, fighting his own battles that we'll never see.

I get it.

I used to do this shit all the time. I was thrown in jail for vandalism more often than for underage drinking.

"What?" the guy feigns confusion, provoking Ryke. "Are you butthurt that you didn't get extra time with the slut—"

"You want to play this goddamn game with me," I interject, my voice so sharp that it physically pains me. "I can make you cry so hard, you bleed out of your eye sockets, so let's rewind—*you* fucked with us first, and all we're asking is for you to stop. We're not your prep school friends." I'm trying not to be condescending. I could have easily said, "We're not your little prep school friends, *kid*." But if someone said that to me at sixteen, seventeen, or eighteen, I'd spit in their face and tell them to eat shit.

He breathes heavily with a curled lip, hatred spreading across his features, like he can't stand to be here for more than a second longer. I stare right at him, not giving him an easy out. And he finally says, "We're just joking around."

Ryke steps forward and raises the paintball gun at the guy's face. "This is not a fucking joke!"

The guy huffs and says to me, "Is your brother a moron? It's only a *paintball* gun."

Ryke throws the gun across the road, and the casing shatters.

"Hey!" the guy shouts.

"My girlfriend has PTSD, you *fucking* idiot," Ryke growls. "You point something that resembles a gun at a window, and there are people who'll feel like it's one."

My ribs tighten. Daisy has been through more than Lily and I ever imagined, and it's these facts—the ones that I desperately needed—that make it easier to see his happiness with her. I never thought I'd pray to every fucking god to ensure that their relationship lasts. It's not even a selfish want.

I study the guy's face, and any remorse is drowned by anger, his voice shaking with it. "Which girlfriend is that?" he sneers at Ryke. "The one you *raped* when she was fifteen or your brother's fiancée?"

"Are you fucking kidding me?!" Ryke yells, his nose flaring. It fucking sucks. People will always know details about our lives before we even know their names. But I can't blame *him* for it. It's just the way it is.

I watch this teen glower at the ground like *let me go, let me fucking go.*

Not yet.

I grip his jaw and force his face to mine. "Great," I say, "you can believe those goddamn lies, you can spread them, whatever— but we see you around our house, scaring our girls, we'll do worse than call the cops." I release him with this threat, letting his own imagination frighten him. "I've met shittier fucks than you, so don't think you're something special."

His chest collapses as he breathes heavily, shooting me a glare that can no way match mine. And then he spins his back on us and sprints down the road, stumbling for a second before he regains his speed.

He shouts back, "Go suck cock, you pussies!" And he waves his middle fingers at us.

Ryke lets out a frustrated groan. "I fucking *hate* these guys."

"They're just bored." The neighborhood heard that "famous people" moved in down the block, and so these teenagers have been attracted to our house ever since. "We can't call the cops," I snap at him. "I hope you realize that." For one, that guy in the hoodie could've been me at seventeen. And every time I was thrown in jail, it did nothing but piss me off even more. For another, it only gives them reason to retaliate against us. To return with more eggs, more paintballs, and maybe something worse down the road.

I'm smart enough now to recognize the pointlessness of this kind of feud and revenge.

Connor Cobalt taught me that.

My lips slowly rise.

Ryke groans again, puncturing my thoughts. "I wish there was an easy fucking solution to this."

"Yeah." I nod. "Me too." We start walking back down the dark street to our house. I try to loosen my tense shoulders by rotating them. "Maybe the girls shouldn't come to the meeting tomorrow." Remembering my father's phone call this evening binds my muscles again. I rub the back of my neck, this familiar agitation festering. After tonight, I'd like to fucking cancel on our dad. "I just don't want him to drop more shit on top of us, not while we're dealing with this."

"I don't want Daisy there anyway." He extends his arms, and I can see splatters of blue paint on his shoulder and chest with reddish welts. "Why the fuck is he dragging the girls into his issues to begin with? It should be just you and me." He gestures from his lean body to mine.

"We don't know what it's about," I remind Ryke. "All he said was that he wanted to talk to the four of us." I lick my lips, my breath smoking the air. I try not to shiver in the cold, especially at the thought of how he left out Connor and Rose. Whatever our dad is up to—it only involves Ryke, Daisy, Lily, and me. I'm hoping it's not about the rumors in *Celebrity Crush*—that Lily might be pregnant with Ryke's kid, not mine. I hate even entertaining those lies.

I try to let out another long breath, but I feel my face contort in an irritated scowl.

"With Jonathan, that could mean fucking anything," Ryke retorts.

"Yeah, and take it from someone who's been to these 'impromptu meetings'—you have to be *prepared* for anything." I remember the one where he basically forced my proposal with Lily, right in his office.

I refuse to believe this is worse than that. So maybe that's why I'm not as freaked by it as Ryke. My brother revived his relationship with our dad—and this is what comes with it. I step into the lion's den every single time I enter Jonathan Hale's mansion, and I just fucking pray that I leave without a deep wound. I pray that I'm strong enough to withstand everything he throws at me. And for the first time, I believe that someone out there, some godforsaken thing or spirit or madman, is listening to a fuck-up like me.

I slow my pace as soon as headlights point in our direction. I raise my hand to shield the fluorescence. Ryke grabs my bicep and guides me toward the curb so we're not hit in the dark. I'm not surprised when the Escalade brakes beside us. The tinted window rolls down, revealing the driver.

Connor Cobalt, twenty-six, has one hand on the wheel, dressed in a white button-down. His wavy brown hair is perfectly styled like he just returned from a business meeting.

He didn't, by the way. I know for a fact that he was in a third-floor study with Rose, reading or thumbing through a dictionary—whatever they do in their spare time.

He can't hide his blinding grin, the humor palpable in his gaze as he scrutinizes our lack of wardrobe in the cold winter. Then his deep blue eyes meet my amber ones.

"Soliciting again?" he banters with an arched brow. "How much for a blow job, darling?"

"As much as you're worth," I reply, opening the passenger door.

"How about you, Ryke?" Connor asks as my brother climbs into the backseat.

"I'm not for fucking sale," Ryke says roughly, slamming his door shut.

I give Connor a look. "It's been a long night. What were you—reading?"

"Coming, actually," Connor says, putting the car into gear and driving back toward our house.

"Fucking fantastic," Ryke groans. "While we were freezing our asses off, chasing these idiots, you were getting off."

Connor doesn't even try to restrain his grin. "I'm the all-around winner here. It shouldn't be surprising to anyone by now." Neither is his arrogance. I actually smile and point the blowers at my body, the heat expelling.

Connor's eyes flit to the orange and blue splatters on my ribs and shoulder. Like Ryke, red welts lie beneath the paint. His grin fades. "I don't see how chasing them while they still had paintball guns was effective."

"It's called *intimidation*," I tell him.

"You mean stupidity."

"Yeah? What's the better option? Calling the police? We're not doing that, Connor," I remind him.

"I never said we should. The press would pick up the story, and it'd put more attention on everyone." He pauses. "You both realize that they could've accidentally shot you in the eye?"

"Fucking worth it," Ryke says, crossing his arms over his chest.

I add, "If you saw the girls, you would've wanted us to run after them, paintball guns or not."

Connor trains his gaze back on the road. "I did see the girls."

I frown as I scan his features. He's closed up again, which makes me nervous. "Is Lily okay?" I clench my teeth in fear of the possibility that she may not be. My back stiffens and my muscles tense. "Connor—"

"She's fine." He suddenly locks the car doors, and his eyes flicker to the rearview mirror at my older brother in the backseat, who grows more distressed. If Lily's okay, then that means—"Please don't jump out of the car," Connor tells him. "I've never injured anyone while driving, and I'd like to keep my record clean."

His nose flares. "What's wrong with Daisy?"

"She had a small panic attack."

Christ. I grimace, like knives slicing through my core, and it's mostly from sensing my brother behind me. I rotate to look back at Ryke. He pinches the bridge of his nose, his eyes tightened shut. I can tell he's swallowing a scream and restraining himself from punching the back of the seat.

"At least she's not pregnant," I throw out there. A silver lining.

Ryke drops his hand and cringes. His brown eyes rise to mine. "I fucking hate when people torment her."

I know that now. "But if we move to another neighborhood, it's just going to be the same thing in a different setting." We bring attention to ourselves wherever we are, and that won't change, not after Lily's sex addiction was publicized, not after *Princesses of Philly*, and definitely not after the molestation rumors with my father.

The reality is this: Lily is pregnant. Rose is pregnant. Daisy is hanging on to her sanity. And the media is as caustic as ever— spreading rumors, trying to snap photos of Lily's and Rose's bodies, and harassing Daisy about her relationship with Ryke and his relationship with *my* girlfriend.

I'm not the smartest one of us. Or the strongest. But I fucking know everyone has a breaking point. And sometimes I wonder if our limits are going to be tested now that Ryke is with Daisy, now that I'm about to be a father, and Connor will have a child with Rose. These things stretch us further than before.

A misstep will feel fatal. Because it's not just myself that I'm hurting. It's Lil. It's our kid. There's literally no room for mistakes anymore.

I wish I could be full of conceited optimism, but to be honest, everything just scares the shit out of me.

Two

Lily Calloway

kneel on the cold tile of Ryke and Daisy's messy bathroom, rubbing my little sister's back as she pukes in the toilet. "We should TP their front yard," I say with a nod. They deserve it for all the stupid shit they've done to our house this past week and then jumping out of nowhere and frightening us with paintball guns.

"Or we should rip out their ball sacs. Slowly," Rose says in a cold, threatening voice. She paces the bathroom with a Japanese paper fan, wafting cool air on herself half the time and Daisy for the other. She stops every so often to fold a crumpled towel on the floor or readjust the green bath mat. She's already reorganized the shampoo bottles and put away Daisy's tampons and hairbrush.

It's very weird, but I think I'm the most composed of the three of us right now. Sex isn't even on the brain yet. I internally smile. I make sure to file the rare accomplishment with a few others.

"I'm not touching their . . . stuff," I tell Rose, and just like that my face heats.

"*Balls*," Rose emphasizes the word, shooting me a death glare on an epic scale. I blame her hormones on the intensity of those yellow-green eyes. They're a lot scarier now. "Or *testicles* if that makes them any better for you."

I shake my head over and over, my face flushing. I've already been dizzy all night, a pregnancy symptom, and the red rash is not helping my spinning head any. "That's worse. And I don't have a problem with them. I like balls." I cringe. That sounds so bad. "I mean, I like *them*." An image of Lo's cock, hard and very erect, pops in my head, and my skin heats. *No. No. No.* I press my thighs tighter together.

Through Rose's intense glare, I see glimmers of sisterly concern.

I'm like a tortoise, slow and steady. I'm not one-hundred-percent able to talk about sex without flushing. I'm not sure if I ever will be *that* comfortable without feeling like someone's going to hurl a dildo at my face.

That happened two weeks ago outside of Lucky's Diner. Not fun. And I thought being pregnant would give me some sort of reprieve like: *don't throw sex toys at me and my unborn baby.* Not so.

"Regardless of whether you like them or not, their balls need to go," Rose says. She's so pissed at these guys who keep pranking us. I am too, but I don't have war maps and battlements planned in my head.

Daisy slumps down from the toilet, finally done puking. I flush the toilet and then press a cool washcloth to her forehead while she takes deep breaths.

We're all quiet for a minute, except for the *flap flap* of Rose's paper fan as she beats the air at Daisy. I have these painful flashbacks of what happened, and I'm more shaken up about my sister's reaction to the paintball guns than the actual guys.

She was polishing my toenails with a bottle of Lucky Lucky Lavender while I read pregnancy stories aloud from a "mommy-to-be" magazine. My back was to the window, but she looked up, pure dead-panic in her eyes, wide like saucers.

And that's when the bangs went off. I saw the blue and orange paint on the windowpane like neon bird crap, and we both sprung to our feet together, the nail polish spilling on the rug.

When Ryke and Lo ran down to us and out the door, Daisy muttered something and then stumbled up the stairs. She was a ghost, her breath sharp as she choked for air. Like she was gasping on dry land. I helped her to her bathroom on the second floor and tried to calm her so she'd breathe normally.

This all lasted for maybe twenty minutes, and it was only after she vomited that she was settling, more at ease. Her white tank top with the words—*kapow, baby*—is soaked through from sweat. She's not wearing a bra, which I understand. Neither am I. Free-boobing is the best. Plus, we're both very tiny up top.

"Can you talk?" I ask her, pulling a strand of blonde hair off her face. When she returned from Costa Rica with Ryke, she dyed the multicolored strands back to blonde and then changed the tips of her hair to pastel mint green. She's too cool for me, and she's my *little* sister. I don't even think she realizes the effect she has on people. When she smiles, usually everyone does too.

Maybe that's why Daisy's sadness hurts so much. It's like watching a Care Bear cry.

"I overreacted," she says in a morose voice, tears pooling.

My stomach knots. "I was there, Daisy, it was scary." I pull her closer to me so she's not clinging to the toilet bowl, and I wrap my arm around her waist. She's wearing Ryke's blue and red Penn baseball cap backward, and she rests her head tiredly on my shoulder.

"I'm sorry," she mumbles, wiping her eyes quickly. "I'm just disappointed in . . . myself." Her voice shakes.

I give Rose a look to *not* interject. She's not the most comforting human being in the world. And she knows this. So she mouths, *fine*, to me and stays out of it.

"I almost peed myself," I tell Daisy.

She laughs softly and looks up at me.

"I'm serious. I know I peed at least a little bit."

"It's because you're pregnant," Daisy says with a weak smile. "You can't hold your bladder."

"No, it was definitely from fear. I'm not *that* pregnant yet." Eighteen weeks and the baby bump is just noticeable. I've gained maybe five pounds or less, and my doctor wants me to eat more since I'm "underweight." I think "gangly" is a nicer word than "underweight."

Rose is twenty weeks along and a lot more pregnant-looking than me. She has a round bump in her black Calloway Couture dress that molds her body. She's been designing more maternity kind of clothes—just for herself. Lo called her vain last week, and she swatted him with her sketchbook.

I like that she's making sure she feels comfortable. That's important, especially when so many things are changing.

Daisy wipes the last of her tears with her sleeve, her other forearm wrapped in a bright yellow cast. No one was surprised that Costa Rica brought Daisy a bad compound fracture and a dislocated shoulder. When she has free rein of the wild, she goes hard.

I peel off the washcloth from her forehead.

"Thanks, Lily," she whispers to me.

My heart swells. I recognize that my addiction (and all the nasty media attention it brought) is the origin of her pain. But it's not guilt that makes me want to be here for Daisy. It's just purely out of love for my sister.

"Lily, your foot," Rose says with a scrunched face.

I glance down. Lucky Lucky Lavender is spilt all over my toes, and my left nails are half painted.

Daisy says, "I'll redo them."

Rose fans herself. "You won't have time. The minute Ryke barrels in here, he'll want to hold you." She rolls her eyes but adds, "It's sort of cute."

I picture that embrace leading to other sensual acts. But I don't think about it *too* hard. I squirm a little, clenching my thighs. "At least you'll probably get laid tonight," I say to Daisy and nudge her hip. That would be a definite perk in my book. But not *by* Ryke

Meadows. With Lo. Separately. I nod resolutely in my mind and avoid a dark red blush.

"I'm on my period," Daisy says, her cheeks still pale. "So that's out."

We're all quiet for a second, and I can't hold it in. "Just have sex in the shower." I'm surprising myself, more open than usual. Maybe all the sex talks I have with Ryke are subconsciously helping a little bit. I can share some tips without needing a desk to hide under.

"We've never done it like that. It'd be weird," she says.

My brows crinkle. "You've never done it in the shower?" *Wait.* I hold up my hands. "Ryke says he's done it in the *woods* before. But he's never done it in there?" I point at the glass doors of their giant shower with three different nozzles and spigots, plus fancy cobblestone wall tiles.

Rose looks fascinated by this talk, her back straightened and eyes alert.

"We've done it there, just not on my period." Daisy isn't shy about her love life with Ryke, which I really like. It makes it easier to talk to her about Lo. "Isn't it gross?" she asks.

"It's worth it . . ." I trail off. "Though I may not be the best source. I've been known to rank sex above food."

Daisy laughs softly. I'm glad I can joke about my addiction now. I even smile.

"How about a sleepover in the guest room?" Rose asks Daisy. "We'll redo Lily's toenails and sleep in the king-sized bed."

"I'll kick you," Daisy suddenly says. "If we sleep in the same bed, I mean. I move a lot and could kick you in the womb or something, and then you'll both miscarry because of me." She inhales sharply.

"Then you're doing me a favor."

"Rose!" I shout.

She rolls her eyes again, regret flashing in them. She's not filtering *anything* lately. "It's hot in here." She fans herself some more, sweat beading her forehead.

"Maybe you should sit down," Daisy suggests.

"I'll sit down after we've plotted our retaliation and our plans tonight. They're more important." She likes to pretend her pregnancy has *no* side effects on her, even though she was the one hit with bad morning sickness. I thankfully bypassed that.

"I vote sleepover and TPing." I raise my hand in the air just as hurried footsteps sound and the door whooshes open.

Three

Ryke bounds into his bathroom first, followed quickly by Lo and then Connor. As they stand towering above us, a new tension strains the air, and I think we all feel our dynamic shifting just a bit. It used to be Daisy and Ryke on the outside of the inner circle.

Now it's guys versus girls.

We scrutinize them while they do the same to us, measuring our well-being from afar. I notice the red marks on Lo's shoulder and ribs, splashed with blue and orange paint. Ryke has similar paintball imprints. It's safe to assume they were shot. My stomach tosses. *They were shot*. That phrase—no. I don't want to picture anything like that happening.

"I hope those guys look *ten million* times worse than the two of you," Rose says, slicing through the tension.

"They're teenagers," Lo says flatly. They must've let them go.

"Perfect, we'll just call their parents."

The guys are quiet, and Ryke hasn't taken his eyes off Daisy. I can tell that she's embarrassed by what happened and the extra attention that bears down on her. She lifts her legs to her chest, shielding her boobs (and see-through shirt) from the guys. I watch her pick at the white inside of her cast, and then she sets her cheek back on my shoulder.

"Hello?" Rose snaps her fingers at them and then zeroes in on Connor, his hands in the pockets of his black slacks. "*You.*"

"We're not tattling, Rose."

She glares. "Please. It's not tattling. It's *justice.*"

"It's both. Though the tattling will undoubtedly outweigh the justice."

Ryke and Lo approach us while Connor walks over to Rose by the sink.

"Dais . . ." Ryke whispers, squatting down, eye level with her. The concern in his face clenches my heart in different ways. I've always wanted my sister to find someone that cares for her, so deeply, but I never thought that someone would be related to Loren Hale. I will always love that extra bond I share with Daisy, for however long her relationship does last.

I'm rooting for them to go on forever.

She lifts her head up and finally meets his eyes. Tears spill off her lashes, cascading down the long scar on her cheek. "I . . ." Her chin trembles, and I have a suspicion she was about to say *over-reacted* but stopped herself short.

Ryke sits in front of Daisy and spreads his legs around her so when he draws her close, she fits right against his chest. It's a tender, gentle embrace that I would've never expected from an aggressive guy like Ryke. But he has a soft side when it comes to my little sister.

She twists the baseball cap frontways and lowers it, blocking her eyes from him and everyone else. Her body vibrates with heavier tears, and I'm not sure how to comfort her. She feels like she failed herself, upset that she had a panic attack over paintball guns and caused a scene.

Ryke holds her tightly, and her slender arms wrap around his bare chest. An impenetrable stone in a raging storm. That's what Ryke Meadows has always been.

"Lily." The sharp voice captures my attention. Lo stands above me. His amber-eyed focus is all mine to obtain. His features are deathly beautiful, the severely cut cheekbones and smooth Irish skin. I think: *his baby is in me*. It's such a weird thought.

But it sweeps me in an electric current, sparking each nerve and adding an extra beat to my heart.

"Hi," I breathe shallowly like this is the first time I've ever seen him. My neck heats, no doubt with a vibrant red hue.

His lips rise in a gorgeous smile. "Lily," he says again, huskily, in a deep, *sexual* voice.

My body tingles. "Don't do that," I whisper-hiss, flushing more.

"Lily," he repeats, subtly licking his bottom lip. Oh my God. I spring to my feet to pinch him or punch him in the ribs for teasing me with my *name*. Who does that? He didn't even touch me yet. As soon as I land on my feet, the world spins one hundred and eighty degrees. I teeter backward as my vision blurs with black and white blinding spots.

"*Lily*." Worry breaches his voice, but I feel his hands around my hips before I tumble and fall. He combs my short brown hair out of my face, and I blink a few times, his features clearing past the dizzy haze.

"That's . . . my least favorite *Lily*," I say under my breath.

He exhales loudly. "Don't stand up that quickly next time. Your blood pressure—"

"—is low," I finish. "I know." I've been taking lots of extra steps to ensure a healthy pregnancy: vitamins, eating less junk food, and reading books. But the more I try, the less I succeed. Rose leaves her doctor with an A-plus report and a pat on the back. I leave mine with a list of things to work on.

Lo said that they probably bribe the doctor to say nice things, just to one-up us. I doubt it. Though maybe the doctor is scared of

Rose's wrath. That is a likely possibility, especially since she went through four ob-gyn's before choosing Dr. Freida Dhar.

My finger skims the blue paint on his ribs, the place so red beneath that I wonder if it'll bruise. And I just hug Lo, my arms flying around his waist. The idea of a real bullet slicing through his skin nearly chokes the breath from my lungs. To lose Loren Hale is to lose my life. It's these moments—of catastrophic change and brutal, ugly fatality—that I recognize how deeply I love him.

He tilts my chin up with his fingers, reading my pained features well, and whispers, "We're okay."

I nod. *We're okay.* And then he kisses my lips, full of pressure and force that numbs my brain. *Yes.* I shut my eyes and drift with the bursting sensations, his hand falling to the hem of my leggings. *Yes.* I feel so wet and ready for that image of his cock to become reality. But maybe now isn't a good time?

I'm not sure.

And then he pulls away, my lips still warm from his touch. He mouths, *later.*

Later. I can do later. "What's later?" I ask.

He just smiles.

His teasing is killing me. In a good-bad way. I cross my ankles, spin around to face my sisters, and lean against Lo's chest. His hands settle on my hips, some of his fingers dipping below the hem of my leggings. He's sneaky.

I catch myself rubbing my ass against his crotch, and I stop when his fingertips dig into my skin like he's trying not to be *that* aroused.

Later.

I can hear Ryke whispering quietly to Daisy, but I can't make out any of the words.

Across from me, Rose pulls her silky brown hair in a pony while she speaks to Connor in French. And then her gaze drifts to mine, and she goes quiet.

"Talking about us?" Lo asks her, and I can feel his bitter half-smile behind me.

Rose's eyes narrow. "You're spending too much time with my husband," she says. Connor barely even balks at this, knowing exactly where she's going. My brows pinch in confusion with Lo's.

"Why is that?" Lo asks.

"You've acquired his narcissism. *No*, we were not talking about *you*." She snaps her hairband in place. "Get over yourself."

Lo's face sharpens. "Hey, Rose," he says. *Oh no.* "You want to know what karmic justice looks like? Your baby, *ripping* slowly through your vagina on its way out." He flashes another dry smile, and I punch him in the arm. He barely even acknowledges the attack. The *get over yourself* comment must have really eaten at him.

Rose straightens to attention and shoots him two middle fingers. "Fuck. You. Times two."

"I can count, thanks," Lo says.

Connor is leaning against the sink counter with his arm hooked around Rose's waist. His grin grows and grows the longer they go at it. That's great for him, but I'm starting to sweat profusely, scared their back-and-forth verbal fight will go down a bad, bad road. They've been there before, and it can easily happen again.

"They teach algebra in detention?" she says with a tilt of her head.

"Weak," he replies back.

She purses her lips.

I glance down at Daisy, still sitting on the floor with Ryke. He spins the blue baseball cap backward on her head again, her tears dry. She rarely wears makeup like me, so she has no mascara streaks. Ryke leans in to kiss her, and she swiftly turns her head.

The bottom of my stomach drops at the rejection.

Ryke is rigid and unmoving. And then Daisy says, "I threw up earlier . . ." *Oh . . . Daisy.* I cringe at how many moments she probably wishes she could alter and rewind. She rises to her feet and heads to the sink. Connor scoots over so she has room to brush her teeth.

Ryke stands and rubs his lips in thought as he wanders over to us. And then he whispers to me, "She threw up?"

I nod. "She was nauseous. She's better now, I think."

"At least she gave you a warning," Lo tells Ryke. "Lily would've just kissed me."

I gape and then think about it for a second. "Yeah . . . maybe." I probably would've forgotten that I threw up. I crinkle my nose. "Am I that gross?"

"No, love," Lo says and then kisses the outside of my lips like the biggest tease. I just realize that Ryke has already left our side and gone to Daisy's.

Rose clears her throat to rein everyone's focus.

"Hairball?" Lo questions.

Rose ignores him by clasping her hands loudly together. "We were holding a vote before you three showed up. We want to pay-back these guys—"

"*No*," Lo immediately says, surprising me so much that my mouth falls.

Rose crosses her arms, drawing more attention to her breasts, which have grown considerably since her first week of pregnancy. "I despise uninformed voters."

"I get it," Lo forces, taking a step forward and unlatching from me. "You want to scare them as badly as they scared your little sister. But you retaliate, and you're provoking them even more."

I breathe deeply. This is a new Loren Hale. One who has learned from all of his mistakes. One that understands right and wrong and every gray, messy part in between.

It's a better Loren, the version of himself he has been fighting for all along. I'm so overwhelmed by his proclamation that I have to quickly wipe tears before they appear.

"This isn't an autocracy." Rose points her folded paper fan at him. "You can't decide what the house is going to do."

"If it's a democracy," Connor cuts in, "then why were you voting without us, Rose?" Good points.

"You weren't *here*, Richard." She spins to him. "Now that you are, you can have your vote."

"A pity vote," Connor says easily. "You're giving me something you hate."

Rose's narrowed eyes actually soften at this blow. Her shoulders slacken for a second.

Daisy switches off the faucet, and I realize she's already rinsed the toothpaste from her mouth. Ryke is holding her hand, which is really cute. I try to contain a burgeoning smile. One second I'm near tears, and now I'm almost beaming. My hormones need to take a water break and let me be in a content stasis, for once.

"I don't think we should fight about this," Daisy says softly.

"We're not," almost everyone says in unison—everyone but Ryke, who just rolls his eyes at us.

"It's toilet paper," I suddenly pipe in. "We're reclaiming our . . ."

"Power," Rose proclaims, raising her chin.

Ryke shakes his head. "There's better fucking ways to feel safe than retaliating." His eyes ping from me to Rose, to Daisy, and then back to me.

I hesitate between siding with Lo, who I believe is right about not provoking our neighbors, or with my sisters, who need my support. "Daisy should decide," I realize. I want to do what Daisy feels is best. She's the one who's frightened the most.

Daisy wavers uneasily, all eyes pinning on her. Ryke stands behind her, his arms wrapped around her chest so no one can see her nipples. That's even cuter than the hand-holding. I catch my expression in the mirror. Oh my God, my smile is so dopey-looking.

"I . . . don't want to upset anyone," she finally says.

"You won't," Connor tells her. "Everyone has their own opinions, and we'll respect yours. Though there is a right answer and a wrong answer here."

Rose smacks his chest with the back of her hand. He catches it and kisses her palm.

"Can I have some time to think about it?" Daisy asks.

"Yes," I say before Rose shoots her down. "It's probably better if you think about it first."

Surprisingly, Rose nods in agreement, though I bet she's still plotting revenge scenarios in her mind. I wish I had a voodoo doll or magic where I could enact nonlethal punishment from afar. Like *Sabrina the Teenage Witch*. Though her spells usually backfired.

I hook my finger through the hem of Lo's sweatpants, and I lock eyes with Daisy. "Sleepover?"

"What are you talking about?" Ryke asks.

Rose's fingers are laced with Connor's. "We were considering spending the night in one of the guest rooms, just us girls."

Ryke's features darken like an incoming thunderstorm. He obviously would rather her sleep with him, but maybe he's afraid she'll kick us too. And I wonder what he does at night to make her feel safe and whether she'll even be able to fall asleep with us.

"Speak," Rose snaps at him.

"If Daisy wants to have a sleepover with you two that's fucking fine," Ryke declares. "I'm not going to tell her what to do. All I want is what she wants."

The corners of Rose's lips curve upward. "You are so much better than Julian."

Lo lets out a dry laugh. "Over half of the male population is better than Daisy's ex-boyfriend."

"Don't fucking remind me about him," Ryke says.

Daisy clears her throat. "I do know what I want to do about sleeping tonight." Everyone focuses on her. She inhales strongly and says, "I think I should sleep in my own bed. I really don't want to roll over onto one of you, and I'm afraid I'll be so freaked about it . . . and other things that I won't fall asleep."

I nod understandingly, as does Rose.

"Thanks for telling us your feelings," I say to Daisy with a smile.

She smiles back.

I would've liked either one she chose, but this one is a very good option. I'm getting Loren Hale tonight.

My most favorite thing in the world.

Four

Lily Calloway

The champagne-colored comforter bunches at the bottom of the king-sized bed, and neither of us wastes energy to tug them up. A thin layer of sweat coats my body, and despite the faint exhaustion swirling around me, I crave a repeat.

My fluctuating hormones have not helped my cause. At all.

Lo tilts his head on the dark red pillow beside me, lying on his back as his chest rises and falls in a heavy rhythm. Of all the places we've lived together, this room is the most spacious and suits our personalities the best. A black chandelier with candles (instead of glitzy diamonds) hangs above our bed. Two black armoires sit beside a comfy suede couch and dark purple chairs, red throw pillows and a champagne rug in addition. It actually feels like home.

I squirm, clamping my thighs together, while I watch Lo's breathing, and I ache to touch his abs.

He licks his lips and says, "Not good enough, I take it."

"What?" I squeak out, my eyes wide. It was *very* good. Stellar. Worthy of rocket ships and trips to the moon.

Dimples dot his cheeks as he tries hard not to smile. "You have that look."

"What look?" I turn to face him fully, my hip on the soft mattress.

"The one that says you want me to fuck you again," he tells me, so casually. But it has a way of lighting up my core with newfound eagerness and desire.

"Oh . . . *that* look." I try to clear my face. It barely works. I'm staring too hard at his lips, the soft pink ones that beg to be kissed. "You know, just because I *may* want to do it again, it doesn't mean the other time wasn't good enough."

"I know," he breathes. "I'm just teasing you, Lil." He draws me closer to his waist, and I think, maybe, his hand will descend to the very wet spot between my legs. Instead, his palm slides from my collar to my stomach.

I'm partly grateful that I'm not that big and round yet. Some positions will be harder during sex, and yeah, it's a selfish thought, one that I have been trying really hard to overcome. Because in about five months, I'll need to be completely selfless—or at least have a somewhat controlled sex life.

"Have you felt anything yet?" he asks softly, his fingers circling my belly.

I don't know if he's trying to distract me from sex or if this is a legitimate question. When he grabs the crumpled sheet by his ankles and pulls it over our waists, hiding his cock from view, I think it's probably the former. But I answer anyway.

"No," I whisper. "Not that I'm looking forward to it. It's going to be weird." I'll like knowing my baby is alive and active, but just the idea of something alive and moving inside of *me* has a certain creep factor. Remembering that the baby is a part of Lo lessens some of that.

"You'd tell me though, right?" he asks, his eyes flitting to mine. "I want to know when it happens for the first time."

It's my turn to try and contain my smile. Lo has been supportive since he found out that I was pregnant. The fact that he *never* wanted children—that this baby was an unwelcome surprise rather than a joyous one—has been shelved somewhere else. Somewhere too far to ever reach again.

"I tell you everything," I remind him. "Like how I dumped my Goldfish crackers in a bowl of mint chocolate chip ice cream. Which was so good but so gross." It's my favorite snack.

"It was disgusting," Lo confirms. He props his elbow on the bed, his fingers lightly brushing my hip bone.

I close my eyes, practically melting, and his hand drifts back up to my collar. *So mean.* When I open them again, I catch sight of the white envelope on the nightstand. "Maybe we shouldn't wait."

Lo follows my gaze and shakes his head. "Rose will kill you."

He's right. A few weeks ago, she was obsessively eating oranges while I dunked my Goldfish in an ocean of ice cream. As she ripped the peel off, she said that she wanted to be present when I learned the sex of my baby.

She was intimidatingly scary, but I would've said yes, even if she was all smiles. So after my ultrasound, we told the doctor to seal the news in an envelope. There it rests. I think I can wait until the morning.

"What do you want?" I ask him a question that we've both dodged for some time. "A boy or a girl?" Deep down, I know my answer, even if I wish I could be neutral and long for a boy and a girl equally.

"It shouldn't matter," he evades, his amber eyes searching mine, looking for my response to the same question. It's okay. I can admit it first.

I open my mouth to say the words, and they lodge in my throat, barred from exit by internal fears.

"Lily?" he murmurs, leaning over my small frame and combing the hair from my face. He's halfway on my body, semi-cloaked in Loren Hale.

I tangle my legs with his. *Better.*

"You don't have to say anything," he tells me.

I think I need to though. I'd rather let these things out. "If we have a girl . . ." I breathe softly, ". . . there's a good chance she'll be ridiculed." Her mom will be a sex addict. It'll be like Daisy, pegged as one just for being my sister. I can imagine my daughter having a bumpier, rockier road. And Daisy's is already horrible enough.

Lo finds my hands and intertwines our fingers together. My leg brushes his thigh, nearing his crotch, and my pulse speeds up a fraction. His hand lowers back to my hip bone, holding me still. And I relax in this position, the heat of his body warming me. It's effortless. Our normal.

"Maybe in the future, people won't judge girls differently than guys," he says.

"What do you mean?" I'm staring at his lips again, but I focus on his words.

He tucks a flyaway piece of hair behind my ear. "When girls sleep around—maybe they won't be called sluts and whores. Maybe they'll be treated like guys. Then no one will care about your addiction, not enough to harass Luna."

Luna. My heart palpitates at the name we chose if we have a girl.

The world he described seems imaginary. One made from fiction. Not a future.

"Doubtful," I whisper.

He stares down into me and says, "I'll keep her safe."

My eyes well with tears while my lips pull high. "Against the world, Loren Hale?"

"Yeah." He nods. "Against the world, Lily Calloway. I'm familiar with that battle."

I kiss him, lifting my head off the pillow to meet those pink lips.

He deepens the kiss, his tongue sliding sensually against mine before drawing away. "So you want a boy then?" he asks, figuring me out. I think I could raise a boy better than a girl. I think he'd like me as a mom. At least, I hope so.

"Yeah," I whisper, searching Lo's eyes now for his answer. "Do you want a boy?"

"If you want one, then yeah." He nods.

I punch him lightly in the arm. "That's not an answer," I refute. "Stop placating me."

His amber eyes narrow, and he blinks a couple times like I'm no longer Lily but some alien girl. "Since when do you use the word *placate*?"

"Since Connor gave me that thesaurus for Christmas." Rose said it was a rude present, but he took the time to scribble notes in the margins. Like the word *bastard*, he wrote: *the best-looking one is in your arms*. A literal truth. I run my hands along Lo's shoulder muscles. "He highlighted all the cool words for me."

Lo lets out a short laugh. "Connor's definition of cool isn't the same one you and I follow."

"Oh." That's probably true too.

He grins and then takes my face in his hands, kissing me before I realize what's happened. A surprise kiss. One that oozes my bones and rouses my soul. His lips suck gently on my bottom one, and his hand tangles in my brown hair. I moan into the next kiss, especially as his thumb rubs the soft spot on my neck.

He smiles just before his tongue flicks into my mouth.

My pelvis bucks up into his, and my legs spread on either side of him. *Yes.*

Breathless, he says, "That's what placating you looks like."

Oh.

I flush. "Can you do it again?" I wonder.

"You told me to stop," he teases. "My wish is your command."

I rap my fist on his shoulder once more, but his smile only intensifies, dimpling his cheeks this time. And then he suddenly says,

"I want a girl." His smile vanishes with his words. I want it to return.

"Why?" I whisper. I think I know.

"I don't want our kid to turn out like me," he says, the angles of his face more tortured-looking than before. "Spiteful and bitter—a complete fucking *asshole*." He shakes his head, his gaze dropping. "I want him to be like you."

"A sex addict?" I frown.

"No, Lil," he murmurs. "Kindhearted, loving . . . introspective."

"I'm not introspective."

He kisses the outside of my lips. "Yes you are, love." He's only a breath away from me as he adds, "I just can't make the same mistakes as my father did with me."

"You're not him," I say softly. Jonathan alienated one son and drove the other down a dark, dark path. Lo would never do that.

He kisses my temple and then slides out from under the sheet. "I'm going to take a shower." As he climbs off the bed, buck naked, he gives me a look that says *join me*.

My face brightens, and I'm about to run into his arms, when my phone pings. Lo's phone vibrates on the nightstand too. He checks his screen while I check mine.

> 7:30 p.m. at my house on Wednesday. This is mandatory, so if you're considering canceling, think again. —Jonathan

I look at who he group texted: Daisy, Ryke, Lo, and me. He's reminding us about the "meeting" he's called. "It looks like just a dinner," I say, though my stomach flips.

"Yeah." Lo's voice isn't as optimistic.

I'm trying to prepare for the worst—but at this point, I'm not even sure what the worst is anymore.

Five

Loren Hale

Heavy sleet and snow confine us indoors for the morning, but even though we can't run outside, I stop by my brother's room to see if he'll work out with Connor and me. My muscles pull taut, my chest bound tight, and I need to release this tension before I open the envelope, especially before we meet with our father.

When I try to turn the doorknob, it clicks locked. I sigh agitatedly. I've already tried texting him, and he didn't answer. Fuck it, I'm waking him up. I bang my fist on the white wood and wait for a response.

After a few seconds of hushed noises and footsteps, the door swings open. Ryke holds the frame with a rigid arm while I catch Daisy skirting into her bathroom behind him.

"What?" Ryke asks curtly, only wearing drawstring pants. It's not his lack of clothes or even Daisy sleeping with him that I have a problem with. Those facts I've accepted, no matter how weird it is at times.

It's his apparent exhaustion that bothers me. Even beneath his hardened, dark glare, I can spot how tired he is by his eyes. "Did you sleep last night?"

The shower squeaks through the wall. Ryke shakes his head

and speaks quietly. "She was terrified, and nothing I did helped . . ." He runs his fingers through his thick hair.

My older brother likes to insert himself in any situation, to fix it, so this is probably killing him. "She has to go to the meeting Wednesday," I remind him. "I know it fucking sucks, but we need to play by his rules." I don't want to find out what happens if one of us cancels on our dad. And I also fear pushing him to drink. He's been sober for this long—and he's different now. Sure he's still an asshole, not exactly soft, but he filters a lot of his comments.

It's easier to be around him.

Ryke pinches his eyes, and then rubs them wearily. "I'm going to call Daisy's therapist, and hopefully she'll see her before the meeting."

I listen to the shower water splash against the tiles, and a thought barrels into me, one that twists my face in a cringe. But I put it out there anyway. "Have you tried just having sex?" I ask.

Ryke glowers and his hand tightens on the door frame like he's going to slam it in my face.

I elaborate with an edged voice. "I'm not saying it's a solution, but she'll be exhausted if you go at it long enough, and then she'll fall asleep."

"Is that what you do with Lily?" he asks tensely.

I grind my teeth. He's not spinning this back on me. "It's one fucking time, you asshole," I tell him, "Daisy won't be addicted to it. So go fuck her, so she can shut off her brain and sleep."

Ryke's shoulders slacken. "She's on her period, and she's not excited about the idea of being fucked right now."

Jesus Christ. I rub my mouth and try not to think hard about who we're discussing. "She's in the damn shower. Stop talking to me and go have sex. And when you're done, I'll be at the gym with Connor." I start walking backward as I talk. "Come with her, don't come with us, and I'll see you later."

He flips me off, but I catch him nod as he shuts his door.

I descend the stairs and round into the kitchen—twice as large as the one in the Princeton house. The expensive silver appliances, granite countertops, gray walls, and leather barstools are all thanks to some interior designer Rose hired. Every time I notice the mansion décor, modern and classic and more adult than I am, I realize that I'm supposed to have my shit together.

That I'm no longer in my college years.

I'm twenty-four. *Time to grow up.*

I'm trying.

God, I'm trying.

By the marbled sink, Connor grabs a blue mug from a glass cabinet. "Morning, darling," he says. He's dressed in Nike athletic pants and a navy blue T-shirt, so I don't have to ask if he's still on for the gym.

I nod to him and rest my forearms on the cold counter. "Boy or girl?" I ask, the question already jailing my muscles in an uncomfortable vice. I decide to do sit-ups in the kitchen while I wait for him. I walk in front of the island and lie on the floorboards.

"Is this what I want or what I think Rose will have?" he questions.

"What you want." I watch him pour his coffee, and then I rest my hands behind my head and use my core to rise to my bent legs.

Connor walks over and steps on the tops of my shoes, keeping me stationary. He cups his mug. "I want many children, so I don't really mind which one is first, as long as there's a second."

It surprises me, and I freeze midway to my knees. "Why?" He's arrogant, conceited—really self-absorbed, not in a bad way exactly. It's just a fact. And none of those things say *I want a big, loud family.*

He grins into his sip of coffee, towering above me at six-four. "The challenge is worth the reward, and I'm ready for a new one."

At least one of us is confident. I scowl, my back touching the floor again.

"You're going to do fine, Lo," Connor assures me.

I want to believe him, but if anyone is good at *placating* people, it's Connor. I can't put faith in every word he says when I know it's designed to calm me. I love it. I need it. But my past history says I'm more likely to fail than succeed. So I tell him, "We'll see."

Feet patter against the floorboards, and I turn my head, first noticing a hemp ankle bracelet. Long legs hidden beneath sweatpants—*Ryke's* sweatpants—and a yellow cutoff top with the words: *flower power.*

What the hell. "Where's your boyfriend?" I ask Daisy as she opens the fridge. There's no way they had sex. He'd last longer than one minute with her. I stifle a worse cringe. *Don't think about it.*

"Huh?" She plays dumb, grabbing a Lightning Bolt! energy drink.

I rest my forearms on my knees, and Connor watches her closely, still drinking his coffee. She has dark rings beneath bloodshot eyes.

"You look like shit," I tell her flatly. "Where's your *boyfriend?*"

She dips her baseball cap low, shrouding her gaze. That's annoying. "Your dad won't care how I look, right?"

I don't know. "If you're worried about it, you can put on makeup," I say, my sharp tone cutting my eardrums. "Lily won't, so you don't have to." I exhale, and Connor steps off my shoes to refill his coffee. Something tells me that we're not going to make it to the gym today.

"Ryke's right here." She motions past me and takes a swig of her energy drink.

That's when my brother rounds the island corner, entering the kitchen. He beelines straight for Daisy and snatches the baseball cap off her head, her damp blonde hair soaking her shirt.

"Hey, bro," I say, not adding anything more since Daisy's here. It's normal for the three of us to talk about the girls and sex, but not when they're around. And I have a pretty good feeling they do the same to us.

Ryke turns his head, and I give him a look like *what the fuck happened?* I thought he had a plan in motion.

"She's not Lily," he suddenly tells me.

My eyes narrow, my blood heating. "What is that supposed to mean?"

"Yeah?" Daisy asks Ryke with a frown.

Ryke lets out a frustrated groan. "Just drop it."

"No," I snap. Now my mind is reeling. "You started it. You finish it."

"Words to live by," Connor smiles. He's completely at ease with no information about this argument, but maybe he has everything he needs by observing us.

"All I fucking meant," Ryke says, extending his arms, "is that Lily will do almost *anything* in bed." The fact that he talks to Lily about sex *often* still unnerves me. "Daisy won't, and I'm not going to force her to have sex when she doesn't want it."

Daisy's mouth has dropped, her face reddening in embarrassment. She glances quickly at Connor and blushes even more. "This is not happening," she mutters.

"It's happening," I tell her with a sardonic smile.

"Don't be a fucking dick," Ryke snaps, trying to close the subject now.

I could wait to ask Lily about whether or not Daisy has used sex to fall asleep—therefore, not being a "fucking dick." Or I could wait to ask Ryke after Daisy leaves. But frankly, that sounds like too much work. Plus, Ryke frequently talks to *my* girlfriend about sex, so guess what? This is how it feels. "Daisy," I call to her, stretching my leg while I sit on the floor.

Ryke shoots me a look. "*Lo,* fuck off."

I ignore him while Daisy acknowledges me. And I ask point-blank, "Have you ever tried to sleep by having sex?" It takes more effort to keep a straight face, not cringing, than to say the words.

"You don't have to answer him," Ryke tells her. And he mouths to me, *shut the fuck up.* Too late for that.

Her face stays red. "Not on purpose, no . . ." She opens her mouth to add more, but she hesitates.

"Don't be afraid to hurt my feelings," I tell her. "I can take it." That's why she always holds back—why everyone walks on eggshells around Lily and me. Afraid they'll fracture us like we're glass dolls. I'm past that. All the damage has been done. You can't break something that's already broken.

". . . I didn't want to use sex like that." She adds quickly, "Not to say that what you do with Lily is wrong, I just . . ." She lets out a breath. "Maybe I should try . . ."

"No, you don't want to," Ryke interjects.

"But Lo says—"

"Lo, I'm going to fucking kill you," Ryke growls at me, his glare murderous. "You don't have all the fucking answers."

I raise my hands. "Calm down, Chewbacca, it was just a suggestion." I nod to Daisy. "He's right. You obviously don't want to do it, so don't do it."

"Don't do what?" Lily suddenly plops down on my crotch, straddling my lap. Her hands lie flat on my chest. She puts her face close to mine and whispers, "Why are you on the floor?" Her cheeks are glowing with this euphoric happiness that causes me to smile almost immediately.

She's wearing long johns and her white fuzzy Wampa hat, and I'm swept in a flashback: she was seventeen, standing outside my childhood house in that same camping underwear. Just as adorable as she is now.

My nose brushes hers in a featherlight touch, and I hear her breath sharpen. My lips to her ear, I murmur, "I was prepared for you to straddle me."

She shoves my chest playfully, and I laugh, grasping her hips, so she realizes that I want her right here, not any further away. Not a foot or a yard. She subconsciously digs her pelvis into me, and I swallow a groan as the pressure builds in my cock. I'm used to it.

I'm even used to the red flush that grows from her neck to her forehead. She catches herself mid-grind and freezes. I tug on her Wampa earflaps while she notices everyone staring.

"Hi," she says. ". . . what'd I interrupt?"

"Nothing," Daisy says quickly.

"That's not suspicious," Connor announces as though he expected better from her. Like she's a goddamn master of deception. I mean, she hid a lot from us, but she's not *that* good.

Lily's gaze darts from Ryke to Connor to me. "You guys aren't ganging up on her, are you?" She pauses with a sharp inhale. "I mean not like that!"

I wince, suddenly realizing that she took "gang" to a sexual level.

"Lily," Ryke groans, his hands on his head in distress. He looks how I feel. Connor is still complacent. I wish I could be like that, but my mind needs scrubbed.

"Sorry!" she shouts, covering her eyes. "I thought everyone was thinking it." She peeks out at me. "You were thinking it, right?"

"Sure," I lie.

She moans into her hands, catching my dry tone easily.

"Lily, it's okay," Daisy says. "No big deal."

Lily blows out a long breath, and I massage her shoulders. Then a pair of heels clicks across the floorboards. Here we go.

"Is everyone ready?" Rose asks, an envelope between her fingers.

"I thought we were waiting till the afternoon?" I say.

"Everyone's together right now." She actually withholds a spiteful retort. And it's clear how nervous she is, the fear flickering in her yellow-green eyes. Connor must sense it too because he instantly draws her to his chest and grips her waist firmly. Her black dress shows off her baby bump, which is much bigger than Lily's small one.

It scares me.

I know every girl's body is different—but sometimes I wonder whether Lily may lose our baby, just in comparison to Rose's size. And that frightens me even more . . . that I'd fear losing something that I never wanted to begin with.

These feelings are crazy. I get to experience every fucked-up emotion without a crutch. No Maker's Mark. No Macallan or Jameson.

I think I'm okay with that. Even when it hurts.

Lily unfurls her crumpled envelope, and my back straightens, leaning against the lower cupboards while she's still on my lap.

"Are you going first?" Lily asks her sister, craning her neck over her shoulder.

Rose shakes her head, her collarbones protruding as she holds in a breath. "No, you go," Connor speaks in French, not caring that Ryke can eavesdrop, and Rose replies in a hushed voice.

"Should I get my camera?" Daisy asks with a bright smile. It almost distracts me from the dark circles under her eyes.

"Use your phone," Lily says, her hands shaking with nerves. "But don't post anything on Instagram."

Daisy mock gasps. "I already did."

"Ha ha," I say dryly.

Ryke looks like he could fuck her against the cupboards, an expression I don't like catching from him. And then Daisy struggles to hop on the high counter with one good hand, the other in a cast.

Without hesitation, Ryke easily lifts her up. She swings her legs and holds out her smartphone. Instead of a photo, she begins recording us. Even narrating, "It's Saturday, February seventh. Lily Calloway is about to find out the sex of her baby. Will it be a boy or a girl? Predictions?" Her phone whips to Ryke.

"Girl," he deadpans.

"One smile," Daisy says.

His lips barely rise.

"Pathetic," I tell him. "You can't even smile for my future kid."

"Yeah, Uncle Ryke," Daisy jokes.

Ryke gives her a hard look. "Don't say that again." And then he actually smiles, not a full-blown one with teeth, but it's good enough. This video recording actually lessens the tension in my muscles.

Lily even perks up with more excitement, her worries fluttering somewhere else. *Thanks, Daisy.*

"What's your prediction, Connor and Rose?" She points the camera phone at the couple by the coffee pot.

Rose stiffens. "Girl."

"Boy," Connor says, setting his mug on the counter.

Rose rotates to face him. "You *have* to disagree with me?"

"I don't *have* to." He pauses to grin. "Though I like to."

Rose is suddenly quiet, and his hand slips beneath her hair as he kisses her forehead.

Then Daisy whips her phone lens at us. "Lily and Lo, predictions?"

Lily's green eyes flicker up to mine, and they tumble with so many fears and hesitations that I wish we were alone. In this solitary moment. So I could hold her. Shut out the rest of the world.

Just us.

No more noise.

"A girl," Lily breathes. It's not what she wants. It's what I want, but it's going to hurt either way.

"Boy," I whisper.

Her chest collapses, and she shakes her head at me like it won't be a boy. It may be. Half of me will be happy for Lily. The other half will be scared shitless again. The parts of me that I love the most are the parts that belong to her.

"Hurry up," Rose says, her voice abnormally high-pitched. I cringe. She's nothing short of petrified because she's going next. And no matter how much Rose aggravates me on a daily basis, I'm not a fan of watching her like this.

Connor whispers quickly in her ear, and I notice how she rubs her hands anxiously. He clutches one so she stops making her skin raw.

"You open it," Lily whispers to me, rerouting my attention. She pushes the envelope into my hands.

My stomach tightens, but somehow, I force my joints to work. I tear the seal and unfold the white paper. My pulse races like I'm about to jump off a building and make a speech in front of a packed stadium. I can barely read the typed letters at first. They blur together, and it takes a few extended seconds to piece them apart.

She studies my expression for a long moment and says, "It's a boy."

I am flooded with temperatures below zero, and I pass the paper to her, so she can verify what she already knows is real.

Her eyes travel eagerly over the words, and then she delicately folds the paper.

"You can smile, Lil." *Please smile.*

A tear rolls down her cheek.

No. I lean forward and cup her face in my hands. "Lily. *I'm happy.*" Somewhere. In all the good places that belong to her. There, I know I am.

Her lips are chapped as she licks them, and she glances back at the paper to reaffirm that we're really having a boy.

I wipe her tears that fall. "Say something," I breathe. *Smile, Lil.*

"I'm . . . really, really happy." Her voice trembles. And then she laughs into a smile, one that's half-pained. For me. On the precipice of two polar opposite emotions.

"It's better this way, with a boy," I whisper, her glassy eyes flitting between me and the paper. "You have to believe that I believe it." All I want is to sense her joy and rid the tar that's seeped from me to her. I ruin most things I touch, and she's the best thing I have left.

She nods repeatedly, trying to accept this as truth, and then I kiss her, desperation drowning my veins, my bones, my very fractured soul. A noise ripples through her throat. She clutches to me the way I do to her—our bodies promising things that our words can't.

I inhale sharply into a deeper embrace, my tongue tangling with hers. Her chest merges with mine, my hands disappearing in her short hair beneath her hat.

There are moments with Lily where I feel like we're one person. Where we share every sensation that bites our skin.

No one is in the kitchen but us.

And yet, they are. I become aware of this fact the moment Rose shouts something loud in French.

Lily and I abruptly part.

Rose is pointing at us while she yells, and Connor is quick to shout back. The seriousness of the conversation illuminates when Connor grips her wrists, clutching her so she stops flailing around.

Lily and I rise quickly to our feet. "What's going on?" Lily asks the only person who would know besides the couple fighting.

Ryke has a hand on Daisy's thigh while he watches Rose, his brows hardened. "She's saying that she can't do it," he translates. Daisy clicks off her phone and sets her camera aside.

"Do what?" I frown. She can't be that scared to have a boy.

"See the gender," Ryke clarifies. "Connor is telling her that she needs to stop acting like it's not happening."

Lily's mouth falls, and her head whips between her sister and Ryke. "And?" she prods. Having a translator is nice, which begs the question . . .

"Why haven't you done this before?" I snap.

His hand rises on Daisy's thigh, who swings her legs, which

dangle off the counter. "Because it hasn't been fucking important before now. You don't want to hear the things they say to each other on a daily basis. Fucking trust me."

Yeah, I do.

Lily rocks forward on her feet. "What did Rose say?"

Ryke listens for a second. "That it doesn't matter if they find out the gender now or when the baby is born."

Connor breathes heavily, more emotions coursing through his features: anger, concern, determination—things that he usually conceals. He speaks again. In French. They're in their own world. Kind of like the one Lily and I were just in. Blocking out our surroundings for one serious moment.

Ryke continues to translate, "He says, *don't you want to prepare in any way that you can?*"

Rose jerks in his grasp and snaps back.

"She says, *I can't prepare for a baby, no matter how much I read and study. I'll never be ready.*" A weight drops in the room with that truth. It's a fear I think we all share, but Rose has never liked kids, so it's different for her, maybe. I don't know. I shake my head. It goes beyond having a boy, having a girl—it's just having a child at all.

Ryke sighs like this translating thing is frustrating him. "I can't hear Connor." Because he's whispering in Rose's ear.

And then Rose tries to untangle out of her husband's strong grasp again. "Let me go, Richard," she says, finally switching to English.

"*Rose.*" He forces her name, his voice so cold that the hairs on my arms rise.

"Connor," she says just as icily. "*Stop.*" Her yellow-green eyes assault him.

He releases her arms, and I notice the white envelope clenched in her fist.

"We're having a girl," she states like it's a fact. It's definitely not one. And then she starts opening and closing kitchen drawers, searching for something.

"Rose," Connor says again, his tone more even and temperate. "It's okay. Just stop and breathe for a second." She's tuning him out. "*Rose.*"

I shake my head as I watch Rose slam the fourth drawer shut. "She's lost it."

"Shut up, Loren!" Rose shouts.

I flinch. I honestly didn't think she was listening to me either. And then in the fifth drawer, she finds a packet of matches.

"Rose!" Daisy and Lily scream in unison, but Connor is beside his wife before her sisters can swarm her. She's already lit a match and holds it to the paper.

The flame eats the document quickly, and Connor steals it out of her hand and tosses it in the sink. He holds her from behind, his arms wrapped tightly around her waist, and as he murmurs in her ear, her rigid body starts to uncoil like he's expelling every volatile, toxic emotion and leaving her bare.

My face is stuck in a permanent cringe again. Her breakdowns happen more often since her pregnancy.

Connor spins her around and then presses her head into his shoulder. His eyes flit up to mine, and I read them well enough. He needs privacy.

Daisy hops off the counter and leaves for the living room with Ryke. Lily and I follow close behind, my hand in hers. There's no way anyone is finding out the sex of Rose's baby. We're not going to know until the day he or she is born.

When we're out of earshot from the kitchen, Daisy walks backward, and she says, "Maximoff Hale. He's going to have the coolest parents alive." She holds her fist out to Lily, who actually smiles brightly now. It falters only a little when she glances at me—to make sure it's okay.

I hate that she worries about upsetting me. For *smiling*. I nod to her and try to relax.

Lily fist-bumps her sister.

Then Daisy raises her fist to me with a sunny expression that makes my life seem better than it is. I look up at my brother, who meets my eyes. I get it. Why he loves her.

She's a light in a dark place. Even when she's going through deep shit too. Daisy and Ryke are the definition of selfless. In comparison, I'm the monster, the asshole, the villain. But in Lily Calloway's eyes I'm the hero.

That has to count for something.

Six

Loren Hale

My best friend, my girlfriend, my someday wife is insatiable.

I'm drenched in sweat, my hair slick while I push inside of Lily, my hands gripping her wrists above her head on our mattress. I kiss her deeply and rock my pelvis harder. She tears away from my lips to cry out, her mouth permanently open, gasping. I watch her eyes shut, her limbs trembling for release, and my body lights on fire. My cock screams to come.

Right now.

I ignore its demand. With shallow breaths and a groan aching my throat, I thrust rhythmically against Lil and try to make this good enough for her. I let go of her wrist to reach down between our bodies, my fingers brushing her swollen clit.

She loses it, her back arching, her pelvis digging right into mine. "Lo!" she screams.

Don't come, I force myself in my head. Even as I feel her pulse around my dick as she hits a climax. I don't want to peak. Not yet.

Still hard and full inside Lil, I keep moving, and her free hand massages her tender breast, her chest much larger since her pregnancy. I lightly push her hand aside and pinch her erect nipple with my fingers. She buries her cheek into the pillow. "_Yes_," I hear her breathe.

Christ. I'm going to come soon. I press my lips to her temple. I hit a spot that blinds me for a second, and I grunt, "Lil."

She whimpers, her legs vibrating around my waist.

My body is welded against hers. No separation between us. At fourteen, we had sex together and it felt wrong, even if I begged for it to be right.

Ten years later, I fit inside of her like we've never been apart. And maybe it's still not the "right" that every other couple has— but this isn't a wrong kind of love. It's just the kind that belongs to us.

I push hard, and I come, my nerves firing and my skin blazing. I keep her full while my chest falls and rises for air. She stretches her arms across my shoulders and squeezes her thighs tighter around my waist. I'm almost rock-hard again. I stifle a groan and study her expression. The only exhaustion lies in her eyelids that sag. Just slightly.

"Again," she whispers, trying to thrust up against me with what energy she has left.

Pregnant Lily is the horniest Lily I've ever encountered. She was hard to please before. But I always managed to. Now it's literally impossible.

I roll onto my side while she's still tucked against me. I don't pull out. I comb her damp hair away from her face, and she eyes my lips like they're calling out to her. And then she kisses me hungrily, rocking her hips while we lie on our sides together. The sheets are bunched at the foot of the bed, the comforter hanging off. The dim lights illuminate her features perfectly for me, and every inch of her skin is just flooded with arousal that I can't squash.

"Lil," I breathe, breaking the kiss to whisper in her ear. "Shhh."

"Just one more . . ." she says, and one of her hands dips down like she's going to touch herself to get off if I don't help.

I seize her wrist again and pull her arm to my shoulder, forcing her clutch there. "Look at me, love."

She tilts her head, but her eyes pin to my lips.

"Higher," I say. I recognize that my body for Lily is the equivalent of me being tucked in bed with a bottle of bourbon.

Her green irises finally flit up to my amber ones, her lips parted in need. She subconsciously rocks forward, especially as she trails my jawline.

I place a firm hand on her hip, and I have to shut my eyes not to harden all the way. When I open them, she's staring at *me*, not my lips or body. *Good job, Lil.* I lean closer so that my arm is behind her head, nestling her to me.

"Once more," she says with wide eyes. "I promise it'll be the last time. Cross my heart."

I hate rejecting her, especially when her hormones are fucking with her body. "My cock belongs to you, but you can't fuck it all night, Lil." I might as well be her personal sex toy, which, honestly, I would have no problem with if she wasn't addicted to *sex*.

She flushes, and her breath shallows. I watch her gaze descend to my shaft, the rest of me disappeared between her legs, one thigh draped over my waist.

She starts, "I can blow—"

"No, listen to me, Lil," I say forcefully. "We're going to sleep, and later . . ." I check the clock. 3 a.m. ". . . in the morning, we'll have sex again. But you have to wait." I'm not even going to fantasize that she can last twenty-four hours without another climax.

"Okay," she breathes, and I go to pull out. But she grips my biceps, her fingers digging deep. "Waitwaitwait."

I hesitate and then ease back into her.

Her big green eyes look up at me. "I just . . . want you inside of me."

My skin heats at her words. I'd love to stay inside of her, but . . . "You can't move."

"I won't!" she says, her chest lifting in eagerness. "I'll be really still, I promise."

Any giddy promises that she makes during sex are adorable—but completely unreliable. I skim the length of her body for a second, her skin beaded with sweat, her lankiness and bony hips actually healthy, feminine and delicate.

"Let me try," she pleads.

And this does it for me. I won't steal an accomplishment from her, even if I think it'll end in defeat. "You can try, love." I kiss right outside of her lips, as a small test. She restrains herself from kissing me more, but I feel her pulse around my dick, a sensation that almost causes me to grow inside of her.

I let out a deep breath, and train my body to cooperate with me. For her. I can't be hard, or else she'll start thrusting, and I won't be able to control my wants either.

"Close your eyes," I remind her. "Sleep."

With her cheek on the pillow, she finally shuts her eyes. "I still see you in my sleep," she says, her lips rising in a smile.

I'm smiling too. "Try to imagine an ugly version of me."

"No," she says with this adorable pout.

I kiss her quickly on the lips, my palm pressed to the small of her back, above her ass. I'm familiar with every inch of her body, and that knowledge likes to grip my shaft harder than Lily's best hand job. I whisper in her ear, "Dream of a mutant war with dozens of superpowers at work and even more casualties." It's the least sexy thing I can think of right now.

Her shoulders relax, and she exhales strongly.

Exhaustion starts to unwind my muscles. But concern for her binds them back again. I want to make sure she falls asleep before I do.

Mere minutes pass before she bucks up into me. *Goddammit.*

The pressure causes me to harden, and she lets out the most breathless, pleasured cry. I almost come in seconds.

"Lil," I chastise while her eyes snap open. "What happened?"

She grips my shoulder. "I pictured . . ." Her cheeks roast. ". . . Hellion screwing X-23. It'snotmyfault!" she slurs. "They were a part of the mutant war that you said I should imagine."

"No more mutants for you, love."

"*Nonono*," she says quickly. "I can handle them. And you. And your . . ." Her eyes drop to our pelvises. Her legs and arms tremble, willing herself not to move. Right now, I just want to grind deep against her until I fill her full of my cum.

But we're straddling a bad line.

"You're going to move, right?" she whispers. "Please, Lo. You're hard, and it feels . . ." She bucks up again.

Jesus Christ. My nerves light up. "Easy . . . easy," I whisper. I rest my forehead on hers and take a long breath. "What'd you imagine?" I run my hand up her belly to her breast, and I rub her nipple with my thumb.

"Hmm?"

"With Hellion and Laura?" I ask, bringing up my favorite *X-Men* couple.

"His hardness . . . between my legs . . . I mean *her* legs," she says softly. "*Please . . .*"

I dip my head down and flick her nipple with my tongue, and she hits another high that rolls her eyes, her mouth frozen open. I clutch her ass and push her up, much harder into me, while she contracts around my cock. *God*.

Dammit.

Even though my mind bursts with my veins, I somehow don't come with her. Force of habit. I held back.

"*Again*," she breathes.

Insatiable.

No matter how many times we fuck, she will keep saying *again*.

"Later," I tell her.

"You're hard," she notes, her eyes on my lips for the thousandth time.

"Ignore my cock, Lily Calloway."

She gawks. "Never."

I shouldn't smile, but I do. "Guess what, Lil?"

"What?" Her eyes light.

"I'm going to fuck you slowly, and then I'm going to stay right inside of you. You come again after that, and I pull out." I literally cannot handle Lily contracting and pulsing and clenching against my cock. The intensity and pressure are too much for me.

Her brows pinch. "That's not very nice."

I lean close, my lips a breath from hers. "You must be the last one to hear then . . . I'm very . . . very . . . *mean.*" I kiss her so strongly that her head rises off the pillow when I draw back, inhaling her body.

Then I grind right against her. She's so tight around me that I can hardly pull my shaft back and ram in. I just dig forward, now on top of her instead of side-to-side, and I taste her with my tongue, my lips stinging and swelling above hers. The whole bed rocks with my movement, the wooden posts thudding into the wall.

She's small beneath me, like a ravenous tiny girl, aching for carnal things. I'm aware that she's carrying our child, and it only heightens the sensations that heat me.

Two more thrusts and Lily moans into the pillow again.

I rest my forearm on the bed, an edged noise slicing my throat. I hold still in her warmth, pooling my mind with exhaustion. We're both caked with sweat, our hair doused like we've been running a marathon.

We're back on our sides, and I inspect her features.

Even if she doesn't say it, her eyes do. *Again.*

No.

This has to be it. I kiss her lips lightly. "No more."

She nods, understanding, but her limbs quake like they long for another round. "I'll go to sleep this time. I *promise*." She nods determinedly.

My lips brush her temple, and I stroke her damp hair.

It's going to be a long night.

Seven

Lily Calloway

My orgasms are out of this world amazing.

Which is the best and worst thing. I just want more and more. "I think it's like you tasting the most delicious whiskey ever," I tell Lo while he pulls me onto my feet, the morning after we've fooled around for a long, long time with naps in between.

I'm sore all over, and I can barely even shuffle forward without feeling an ache in my joints and my sweet spot.

I won't let my mind believe this is a regression, not when it's a symptom of pregnancy: great orgasms and higher libido. What's not normal: the uncontrollable, compulsive beast inside of me. But the Lily beast is at bay, hibernating in a cozy cave. I'm sure of it. She's not ever supposed to come out again. She's *very* aware of this.

In black boxer briefs, Lo's amber eyes descend from my head to my toes. I stand completely naked, my skin reddening the more he grazes me with his sight. "Are you drunk off me, love?" he asks, those intoxicating eyes flitting back to mine.

Maybe. "Just not addicted." My metaphor was a bad one, I realize.

"Good." He tugs me to him and playfully bites my neck. "You bath. Me shower." And then he kisses my nose.

I frown. "Why can't we both take a bath or shower together?"

He suddenly lifts me in his arms, a cradle. "Because," he says with a playful tone while he walks, "boys and girls don't bathe together. Everyone knows this, Lil."

"We broke that rule a long time ago," I mention. He sets my butt on the cold edge of the white marbled tub, and he turns the silver handles to the bath.

He tests the temperature. "Did we?" he feigns confusion and stares at the ceiling. "I don't remember bathing with a Lily Calloway." He glances back down at me. "What does she look like?"

How do I even describe my features? "Brown hair . . ." I have a hard time concentrating when Lo's gaze drops to my breasts that have grown much larger in the past weeks. "Really tiny boobs, a bony butt—"

"You mean the most *adorable* ass, the cutest boobs, and the prettiest brown hair?" He mockingly gasps and says, "I do know her." He snaps his fingers. "She does this thing . . ." He lets out a trained, playful laugh.

I smile. "What thing?"

"You wouldn't understand. It's between me and her, an inside . . ." He trails off as he looks back at me, his face sharpening a little. "Put your feet in the bath, love."

I realize that I'm straddling the edge of the tub. Oh my God. Am I grinding? I lick my dry lips and set my soles into the warm water. To erase this horrible awkwardness that I've caused, I just say, "I understand inside things," I say. "Not in like a perverted way." Oh my God.

I climb into the half-full tub so I can drown beneath the water and never surface. As soon as I plop down, Lo must sense my plan because he laces his fingers with mine, holding me upright. I reach for the bath foam ball in a basket of beauty products that Rose set out for me.

"She does this thing . . ." Lo continues, his voice lighter. ". . . with her nose."

I frown. "What?"

"There it is." Lo smiles. And then he pretends to be shocked. "Jesus Christ, you're her!"

I splash water at him, but it hits the side of the tub pathetically, not high enough. "What do I do?"

"You crinkle your nose," he tells me, "when you're thinking hard or when you're confused."

My mouth falls. No. "I have the 'who farted' face? All the time?" I groan and sink into the water. It's betrayed me, barely rising to cover my breasts. Spigot, work faster! I need a water shield to hide under.

"It's painfully adorable," Lo assures me. He rises to his feet and then drops his boxer briefs. "Eyes up here, Lil."

Sure. I focus my gaze on his face and not his beautiful package down below. I expect him to share the water with me, but instead, he heads to the shower. "Don't forget to wash your pretty hair."

"You're still not going to share a bath with me?"

"Not this morning."

"I promise I won't touch you," I say, feeling good about this proclamation. I can withstand Loren Hale. I know I can.

"It's more than tempting. Trust me, Lil." He opens the glass door and disappears inside the tiled shower. Once the water gushes, I can't hear him any longer.

Am I that bad that he can't take a bath with me?

I drop my hands in the water and clench my thighs together, the soreness still present. I crave touch, I do. A part of me wonders if I can clean with a washcloth down there without rubbing my clit.

I can. I find a purple washcloth, do a quick little rub, and then toss it aside, not allowing myself to go further. See, I'm not that bad.

I lower into the water as it rises, and after I dunk my head and scrub some shampoo, I relax a little, and drowsiness takes over.

Very gently, I begin to fall asleep.

Eight

Lily Calloway

Today is a big day. Not delivery day. I'm many months away from that. But it's the one where we find out what Jonathan Hale wants.

I send the Superheroes & Scones store manager, Maya, a quick text about purchasing the new editions of *Deadpool* while I wait for everyone to meet me at the kitchen bar. I suppose I'm early, the oven clock reading 6:30 p.m. Lo should be back from Halway Comics in a few minutes, breezing through the door.

"You don't have to come, Dais," Ryke says adamantly, his rough voice echoing from the living room. I crane my neck to try to spot them, but they're blocked by the wall.

"Your dad said it's mandatory," she tells him, "and I want to be there."

"*I* don't want you to be there because you're in fucking pain right now."

What? I spring off the barstool and rush into the living room.

"I feel *amazing*." She says the word like she could run five miles.

I step into the room as Ryke tells her, "I would believe you more if you weren't doubled over, Calloway."

Daisy is hunching, her hand on the back of the couch like a support. Her cast hangs by her side, and her head dips down low.

"I'm standing upright," she says. "I'm taller than tall." And then I notice her casted wrist curving to her stomach like her abdomen hurts.

"Fuck this." Ryke picks her up and cradles her easily in his arms.

"What's wrong?" I ask.

Ryke spins toward me, and Daisy turns her head into his chest, clearly wincing in pain now. "Cramps," Ryke answers.

I frown, and I feel myself crinkling my nose like Lo mentioned. I try to wipe away that look.

"Are you about to fucking sneeze or something?" he asks in that mean, blunt way.

"No." I flush. "I'm just confused . . ." I scan Daisy, who fists Ryke's plain white tee, her discomfort clear.

"I don't see how this is fucking confusing," Ryke deadpans.

Afraid to embarrass Daisy, I hesitate delving into the subject, but he started it so . . . maybe he already knows everything. She seems to be open with him since they're dating anyway. "Daisy?" I say softly.

"Huh?" She won't remove her face from his shoulder, refusing to let me see her in pain.

"This is kind of long for a period, isn't it?" I try to count the days since she said she started. It has to be about nine.

Ryke stiffens, but he stares down at Daisy, not speaking for her.

"It's been a while," she says slowly. "But I've had ten-day periods before . . . you know, I have this theory . . ." She grimaces. ". . . that it's my body's way of saying it loves me." She almost climbs higher onto Ryke's body as the cramps most likely return with a vengeance. Ryke wears this hard concern that's nothing short of masculine and kind of scary and cute at the same time.

For her, not me. Just to be clear.

And then it clicks. "You still have irregular periods?" She used to have them during her extreme dieting phases. I blame modeling.

"They're not as bad as they were," Daisy says.

Ryke doesn't seem as optimistic. "Four months of nothing and then this?" he tells her. "I can't imagine what they were like before you met me."

"Heaven," she says sarcastically.

"And now you're in hell, fucking around with me."

She laughs, but it dies quickly.

"Do you need Midol?" I ask.

"I took some already. It'll pass if I don't think about it. That's what Rose always says about cramps."

Mental power. That's a smart person trait that I'm not so sure I have. With bad cramps, I just curl on my side, cling to Lo and have a Marvel movie marathon. I usually can't concentrate on the films, just focused on the clenching in my abdomen.

I have faith that Daisy can do it though. She's strong.

Shoes suddenly clap against the hardwood, and Lo appears from the kitchen, entering through the back door. "Hey," he says to us, first scrutinizing my well-being, then his brother and Daisy. "We should leave now in case there's traffic."

I spot his nervous anxiety from his locked shoulders and cut jawline. His hand even shakes a little, but he balls it into a fist when he catches me watching.

Lo approaches me while Ryke carries Daisy out the front door, still cradling her. "I'm fine, Lil," Lo assures me. "Come on." He wraps his arm around my shoulders.

"How was work?" I ask.

"Boring," he says, rubbing his lips, another giveaway that he's anxious. I reach out and hold his hand. His shoulders slacken by a fraction.

He shuts the front door behind him. "What's up with Daisy?"

"Cramps," I say.

His face scrunches like, *what?*

"I questioned it too, but her periods are still out of whack." What's strange is that discussing Daisy's periods has been the norm for some time. I wonder if she realizes that Rose spreads this news like wildfire, and it becomes a topic among the guys too. I hope she's not that embarrassed by it.

We descend the short stairs and walk to Lo's matte black Audi, parked by the fir tree. Growing up, Lo always bummed rides with me, but when he first started Halway Comics, Jonathan removed the monthly cap on Lo's trust fund so he had enough to buy a car.

Ryke always tries to drive the Audi when he's with Lo. Really, his love and obsession with the two-door car are grounds for cheating on his silver Infiniti.

This time, instead of asking Lo to drive, Ryke climbs in the backseat with Daisy, ahead of us. He'd rather take care of his girl-friend than drive a cool car. If I was allowed on social media, I'd document this moment and upload it, literal, cute *proof* that Raisy is meant to be.

Say that was me in Daisy's position, Ryke wouldn't crawl in the backseat on my account. In fact, he'd *beg* Lo to let him drive so he didn't have to withstand my moaning and groaning. Our families' publicists can't see how useful this evidence is against the three-way rumors.

Lo lets out a short, amused laugh. "Ryke has to be dying."

I have a feeling this isn't about the car. Since Daisy is on her period, Ryke probably hasn't had any action in a while. "He went *four months* without sex," I remind Lo. "This has to be easy."

"So easy that he's most likely jerking off, counting the days until he can get laid again."

I don't know.

Ryke is a guy, but for some reason, I got the impression that he'd rather Daisy have periods than none at all.

"You know that I can't have sex for weeks after I give birth, right?" I suddenly blurt out. I never thought it'd be an issue with him, but I forgot that he has needs—ones I've built to extreme levels. Ryke even said it: Lo fucks the most out of all the guys.

And I'm going to take that away from him.

Lo says quickly, "I know, Lil." He rests his hands on my shoulders and guides me toward the Audi. And then his lips nestle against my neck and he groans, a not-so-good one. "Your hair smells like Rose."

"I think it's the stuff in the basket she gave me."

He kisses my temple. "I'm burning that shit."

"It was a present."

He grimaces. "Fine, whatever. It can stay as decoration."

I crane my neck over my shoulder to catch a glimpse of him, and I notice his muscles have unwound a lot more.

"Lily."

"Yeah?"

"Move faster." He pats my ass, and my breath hitches. I've stopped about ten feet from his car. With this incentive, I quicken my pace. And the reality of where we're headed sets in.

To Jonathan Hale's we go.

He changed the location to the country club," Lo tells us, as he drives out of our gated neighborhood. Oh. So to Jonathan Hale's we don't go?

Lo passes me his iPod that's connected to the stereo system. This is the best part of being the side passenger. I have complete control over the music. That and I'm in touching distance of Loren Hale.

I cross my legs on the black leather seat and glance back at Daisy, her head on Ryke's lap while she curls in a ball. "Theories?" she asks everyone about what's going to happen with Jonathan.

I scroll through the iPod. "I think he's just lonely."

Lo taps the steering wheel. "He says it's important."

"He thinks brunch and golf are fucking important," Ryke says roughly, his arm stretching along the black leather seat. It looks like he's giving the Audi a little hug. His eyes suddenly land on me. "Why are you smiling at me like that?"

"Can't a person smile at you?" I say.

"No," he deadpans.

I flip my hair at him as I turn around, feeling cooler than I know I look, and I find my favorite song in the whole wide universe of brilliant tunes. The moment the electronic beats start blaring through the speakers, I turn the volume way up. It's the only way to listen to Skrillex's "Bangarang."

Lo's lips rise the moment he hears the song, as though memories and sentiments flood him. We've had good bedroom dance parties to this one. And epic sex against the wall.

Ryke groans while I start head-bobbing and shoulder-dancing. If I wasn't in a car, I'd be grinding up on Lo. This song deserves some body contact.

"This song fucking sucks," Ryke declares.

I immediately freeze, and my jaw drops.

With one hand on the wheel, Lo uses his free one to shoot Ryke the middle finger. Ha! I stick my tongue out at him, a very immature slight, but I feel younger again with Lo. Like when we were teenagers, drowning out everything else.

Daisy is laughing so hard, her medicine probably kicking in.

Ryke says, "If your kid inherits your musical taste, I'm going to fucking rip my hair out."

I smile. I kind of hope Maximoff does.

"Shit," Lo curses, his jaw muscles twitching. Through his window, I notice a tan minivan in the next lane, matching the Audi's speed. I highly doubt the van is full of preteens and a soccer mom.

The paparazzi must've either seen us leave the neighborhood or they were tipped on our whereabouts. I have battled a lot of my "going out in public" phobias, but having a van tucked so close to Lo makes me nervous.

I bite my nails, and I shift so my heel is pressed to the spot between my legs.

"Try speeding up," Ryke suggests while Daisy lifts her head off his lap to peek at the paparazzi. The van window rolls down, and a cameraman points the lens at the Audi's tinted glass. I doubt he'll have any good shots, but he snaps photos anyway, flashes blinking.

Lo shifts the manual car into another gear, going about twenty over the speed limit on an uncongested two-lane road.

I lower the volume of the song so he can concentrate.

"Turn it back up," Lo tells me, his voice only slightly edged. He doesn't look panicked and neither does Ryke, so I increase the stereo volume once more. He switches into the left lane and then checks the rearview mirror.

"My theory," Daisy says to lessen the tension, "is that Jonathan wants us to host some kind of charity function for him. Like PR stuff."

"That's a pretty good theory." I nod. I can see that happening. My finger stings . . . I nibbled the nail to the bed. Shit.

"Lil, put your feet on the floor," Lo tells me. He must notice the position of my heel.

"You should be watching the road," I say as I set my soles on the floor mat, but I clench my thighs together, kind of hoping for a stronger pressure, just to take away this anxiety. A climax sounds nice.

Stop, Lily.

"I can multitask," he says, checking the rearview again. "Connor Cobalt didn't patent that skill—goddammit."

The stupid van has caught up to our car, and I squirm uneasily in the seat. Lo looks to me for a second. "*Lil.*"

I flinch at his reprimanding tone. My hand is creeping like a criminal between my legs. *Nonono.* I raise my palms in the air, surrendering. "I'm fine. I promise."

His concern has elevated to extreme proportions. "Maybe we shouldn't go to this meeting—"

"Nonono. I can do this. Lo, please." My eyes widen like *believe in me.*

He studies my state of being, his gaze flitting from the road to me. And then he nods. "Hey, bro," he calls back to Ryke. "I'm going to pull off the side of the road. Lil and I are going to switch with you and Daisy."

"Fine with me," Ryke says, actually looking happy about driving.

Lo is *this* worried about my anxiety. "I'm okay," I try to convince him.

"I lied," Lo tells me, slowing down onto the emergency lane. He parks the Audi and snaps off his buckle. "I can't multitask."

Oh. I lick my dry lips. "Okay."

I unclick my seatbelt. The van parks ahead of us, the doors already opening. We're on public property, so they have every right to take photos. By the time we all step out of the Audi, two cameramen have left their van to snap pictures.

"Lily, look right here," one of them calls out.

I've learned not to take the camera bait, focusing on Lo's car and nothing else.

As Ryke passes his brother, he flips off both camera guys, and the flashbulbs blink repeatedly.

"Is Lily pregnant with your baby?" one asks Ryke.

"Daisy, how do you feel about Ryke sleeping with your sister?"

My stomach somersaults. I hate that she's still being affected by my mistakes.

Except for Ryke's middle fingers, none of us answer the paparazzi. We slip into our new seats, and Lo immediately wraps his arm around my waist, his hands in mine. It's affection and touch that calms my nerves by a few degrees.

Ryke and Daisy buckle their seatbelts, and then Daisy reaches *deep* into Ryke's *front* pocket . . .

Uhhh . . . I grow unexpectedly hot, and I can't tell if it's from embarrassment or something worse. I try to convince myself it's the former.

I look around to see if anyone notices what she's doing, but Lo is texting, probably his father. And Ryke is adjusting his seat and mirrors.

Daisy retrieves Ryke's smart phone and plugs it into the stereo. I relax a little. My mind is a dirty, dirty place.

"You two . . ." Ryke rotates to look at me and his little brother. "Put your fucking seatbelts on."

"Just don't kill me," Lo says as we both buckle. "I'm too young to die." He flashes his signature half-smile.

Ryke reverses the car, even with one hand on the wheel. He drives with much more precision than Lo, but Ryke succumbs to road rage the fastest out of everyone. In my opinion, it's not a very good tradeoff.

Daisy chooses a song I vaguely recall, and I spot the title on the dashboard screen: "Dark Center of the Universe" by Modest Mouse. I bet it's more of a "Ryke" song since she usually goes for upbeat tunes and less angsty ones.

The moment Ryke shifts the car out of reverse, we go from zero to I'm-gonna-die. I wrap my arm around my belly and then clutch Lo's leg.

"He's gonna kill us," I whisper-hiss to Lo.

He's too busy watching the cameramen jump back into their van to reply.

"There aren't any cops in twenty miles," Daisy tells Ryke.

I frown. "How do you know that?"

She waves her cell. "An app."

My daredevil little sister *would* have an app alerting her of nearby policemen.

"Bonnie and Clyde," Lo says dryly, "we're not robbing a bank. And really, I don't want to know what gets you off. K, thanks."

Ryke leans forward to look out the window. "Motherfuckers."

Yep, they've caught up to us.

He steps on the gas, and my lungs suddenly rocket to my throat. "OhmyGodohmyGod." This is like one of those theme rides in amusement parks—the ones where I end up peeing a little bit because I'm terrified of heights.

Only this is worse because Ryke is operating the machinery.

He slams on the *brakes*. "Hold on," he tells us, the warning coming way too late.

I think I just peed. I check my crotch. Not that much. Thank God.

Lo clasps my hand while the van speeds ahead, and Ryke swerves through the grassy median into the lanes going the *other* way. Now we're headed in the opposite direction of the van. And the country club.

Daisy is not only smiling like this is the best experience she's had all week, but she lowers the window and sticks her hand out.

They are really meant for each other.

"You both are insane," Lo says matter-of-factly. "You shouldn't worry about children because I don't think either of you will live long enough to have any."

Daisy mock gasps. "Too late. I'm already pregnant."

"Cute, Calloway," Ryke says, speeding up and pulling off the nearest exit so he can go a new way. He's still speeding.

"Should we start praying?" I whisper to Lo. "Or maybe if we concentrate hard enough, our teleportation powers will kick in, and we can blink away." I pause. That's really selfish, leaving Ryke and Daisy to fend for themselves. "Or maybe we'll be able to stop time."

And that's when a giant white Trailblazer merges into our lane and hits our Audi, crashing into the driver's door and the one nearest Lo.

The side airbags pop, and little bitty pieces of glass rain down on both Ryke and Loren, crunchy like gravel.

"*Fuck*," Ryke curses. We must've been in their blind spot.

The seatbelt has dug hard on my belly, and I feel more wetness between my legs. I solidify, wondering if it's something worse than just pee. Ryke has to pull over into a nearby gas station with the Trailblazer, especially since the Audi is driving strange.

"I think the wheels are fucking bent," Ryke says. Daisy turns off the stereo and brushes some of the glass out of Ryke's hair.

I should do the same to Lo, but my eyes are just too wide, transfixed on one issue. I open my legs and peer down, but I can't see much since my leggings are black.

"Lil?" Lo says, worry edging his voice. I can't move.

Ryke tries to open his car door, but it's jammed. Daisy climbs out of the Audi first, then Ryke crawls over the middle console and exits. I'm next.

I can't move.

"*Lily*," Lo forces my name and cups my face, turning it to him. "What's wrong?"

"I either peed or . . ." My eyes burn.

Lo glances down at my lap. "You're bleeding?"

"I don't know," I say in one tight breath.

He lifts up my sweater and tugs at the band of my leggings to peer down. After pulling at my panties, we both see a few droplets of blood.

"Lo . . ." I say, tears welling.

"It's probably nothing . . ." But he already has his phone out, dialing a number. I'm guessing 911. He kisses my temple and then whispers, "Climb out. I'm right behind you."

I swallow a lump and step out of the car. Police sirens blare in the distance, and glass sprinkles the pavement. The Trailblazer isn't as beat up as our smaller car, but the driver is still inspecting his bumper.

"Daisy," Ryke says, his voice full of concern.

My head whips to the side, and I spot my little sister leaning against the Audi's hood. She stares faraway, lost in her mind it seems. Ryke keeps waving a hand at her, but she's not even responding.

"*Daisy*, fucking look at me."

"What . . ." She blinks in a daze, and her arms tremble. It's like she's somewhere else entirely, maybe back in Paris, in the riot, where her face was scarred. The sirens and wreck could've triggered the trauma from that night.

Lo emerges from the Audi and immediately places his hands on my hips. "Lily," he whispers, "an ambulance is coming. I just want to get you checked out. As a precaution, okay?" He tucks a piece of hair behind my ear.

I bite my gums to keep my watery gaze at bay. "What about the meeting with your dad?"

"I've texted him." He hugs me to his chest. "It's probably nothing," he says again.

Yeah. It's probably nothing.

I feel a hot tear escape. I'm at the mercy of fate. It's a cruel thing. To be in the hands of the universe.

Forces that are rarely on our side.

Nine

Loren Hale

I just wish I could feel him," Lily says.

She rests on the hospital bed, one of her palms on her lower abdomen. I hold her other hand, standing beside her while we wait for the ER doctor to return and do an ultrasound.

"I mean, I know I haven't felt him before. But now I just really wish he'd kick or move, just to let me know that he's . . ." Tears build in her green eyes, her cheeks splotched with red.

I squeeze her hand. "He's fine," I say, my voice more edged than I like. My pulse hasn't slowed. *I don't want to lose him*—it's a realization that crushes my lungs.

I don't want to lose this kid that I never even wanted.

He's a piece of me and Lily, and most people would consider that a tainted, damaged thing. But the more I think about it—and the longer she carries *our* child—I recognize all of the good parts of us.

They fucking exist.

And there is a hope, a chance, that he could be more than what I am. That he could be better than me.

Lily sniffs, and I wipe beneath her eyes with my thumb. I turn my head to check on my brother.

By the door, Ryke sits hunched over. A cell phone on his lap. His face buried in his hands. He's apologized about a hundred times.

Once for my totaled car, ninety-nine times for Lily.

"It's not your fault," I say for the fiftieth. The car hit *us*. It was just a freak accident.

"I was speeding," Ryke says, dropping his hands. His eyes are bloodshot. Mine remain dry and continue to burn, so I'm guessing they mirror his.

"Not by much." He'd slowed down by that point.

His phone buzzes, and he quickly picks it up. His face contorts. "She's getting fucking psych evaluated." He tried to follow Daisy to her hospital room, but a nurse told him *family only,* and so he was shuffled to ours.

Now we know why they kicked him out. "Maybe that's a good thing," I tell him.

Her eyes didn't look right. The Paris riot—it's still with me. Ryke's eyebrow is slit in the corner, a literal scar from that night like Daisy's cheek. I have no external wounds to show for, but I remember the fear, the complete lack of control, and I never want to experience that again. It's panic so deep that death feels close. Suffocating.

Inside out.

Today was a very small taste of that, and I think we all know it triggered something in Daisy that we can't see.

Ryke runs his hands through his hair, distressed, and then he scans Lily on the hospital bed. "I'm so fucking sorry, Lily."

"It's okay," she says in a soft voice. Her chin quakes.

"Shh, love." I lean closer to her and hold her face between two hands. "*He's okay.*" My chest collapses at the pain in her eyes.

"I can't feel him," she cries, tears leaking.

My heart is torn to shreds. "You could never feel him," I remind her. "It doesn't mean he's dead." The moment I say the word, she bursts from a cry to a guttural sob. I can't explain this hurt that courses through me—it's like being submerged beneath water. "Shh, Lil," I choke out her name. I end up stroking her head, wishing I could just crawl on the hospital bed and hold her in my arms.

The door suddenly opens, but it's Ryke. Leaving. I catch him pinching his eyes before he disappears. After a few minutes of silence, Lily breathes out trained breaths, her eyes shut as wet trails streak her cheeks.

When Ryke enters the room again, so does the doctor, and I wonder if my brother tracked him down. I have a feeling he did.

The man with combed blond hair and blue scrubs does a small double take, recognizing our faces from the media, probably. He snatches a chart off the wall. "I'm Dr. Adams. I'll be taking your ultrasound."

"You seem young," I say.

"I'm a first-year resident."

As long as he can read the machine, I don't really care what year he is.

Dr. Adams sits on a stool and lifts Lily's sweater to her ribs. While he squirts gel on her stomach, his gaze pings between me and Ryke, deep in thought. "So, who's the father?"

Ryke crosses his arms, and I glower. He can't be serious.

"Loren is," Lily answers softly.

"I may have lost my kid, and that's what you ask me?" I say to this guy.

Dr. Adams switches on the ultrasound monitor. "If you need a paternity test—"

"She doesn't fucking need one," I cut him off. My throat is too closed up to add anything else. I can't even flash a dry smile. I just glare.

Ryke adds, "You have the worst fucking bedside manner I've ever seen."

"I'm working on it," he says unenthusiastically. And then he presses the probe on her stomach, smoothing the gel out as he runs it across her skin. The sonogram pops up on the monitor, and Lily's fingers tighten around mine, her collar protruding as she inhales.

And slowly, I hear the *beep, beep, beep* of another heart.

The relief almost buckles my legs.

He's okay.

I rub my lips as my body asks me to exhale, to breathe, to cry. I bottle every sentiment that normal people let out. *Why are you fucking crying, Loren?* I hear my dad's voice in the pit of my ear. And I shut down any tears. Just like that.

"He's looking good," Dr. Adams affirms. "Vitals of both mother and child, no internal bleeding, everything in check." He quickly stands up, wiping the gel off her stomach with a towel. "I suggest consulting your ob-gyn within the week, just as routine, but it all should be fine. I have to do some paperwork, and I'll have a nurse release you when you're free to go."

He speaks so fast that he's out the door, and the weight of this *good* news hits me harder.

My life wasn't rerouted again. Not this time. I sit on the edge of the hospital bed, and Lily immediately flings her arms around my shoulders, her forehead to my chest. I hug her closer, my heart pounding so hard that I wonder if she can feel it.

I want him.

Goddamn I want this kid more than I've wanted a lot of things in life.

And I know it's because he's a part of us. I'd never want to destroy a piece of Lily. No matter if the road ahead will be rougher. Without her, it'd be unbearable. We've crossed a point where losing our son would hurt more than actually having him.

"Lil," I whisper, my lips brushing her ear. "I love you." My hand slides across her neck, and she lifts her head and kisses me, so tenderly that I understand she wants it to be one kiss and nothing more sexual. I open my mouth to ask if she's okay.

But she speaks before I can. "You're relieved."

I shake my head and tilt her chin up.

She frowns.

"I'm *happy*," I clarify. Despite all of my fears, I'm happy that he's alive.

She kisses my cheek and then I can't hold back any longer, I kiss her full force, my breath becoming hers and hers mine. One of my arms wraps along her back. When the door creaks open, we instantly part.

"Thanks," Daisy says to a nurse who must've led her here.

"Do you need anything else, honey?"

"No, I'm good." She has stapled papers in her hand, and she waves to the nurse as she leaves. When Daisy spins around, Ryke approaches her without hesitance or caution—he kisses her on impact with deep concern. And she holds on to his waist, her body curving toward him in acceptance and want of that embrace.

I'm about to look away, but he pulls back and says, "You fucking scared me."

"I scared myself," she whispers, searching his eyes. "Don't make me cry."

"It's okay to cry, Dais."

My stomach knots.

She nods and stands on the tips of her toes to kiss him once more. Then she says, "I love you."

His shoulders almost relax, but his face stays hardened. He whispers in her ear.

After I give him the time to say *I love you* back, I clear my throat, and they both turn to look at us.

Daisy steps forward, her eyes widening. "Lily—"

"The baby's fine," I explain. Lily still holds on to me like she's learning how to breathe again. "What's with the papers?" I gesture to the stack in Daisy's hand.

"Oh . . ." Daisy pauses for a second, and she glances between me and my brother. "Guess what?" She waves the papers theatrically in the air and outstretches her arms. "I'm pregnant." Then she bows.

The room is dead silent.

My brother's face falls.

I go utterly still.

"What?" Ryke says, his hands resting on his head.

Lily's jaw has dropped to the floor.

And then Daisy straightens up with a playful smile. "Just kidding."

Ryke lets out a long breath that turns into a growl. "Fucking hell, Daisy. I've had about five heart attacks in the past fucking hour."

"It was a joke," she says quietly. "You know, the ones where you laugh at the end."

"I'm not fucking laughing."

"Wrong crowd," she says. "I must've missed the room with the boyfriend who would've laughed."

"Must be the boyfriend who doesn't know you that well." He grabs the papers out of her hand and flips through them. She used the "I'm pregnant" announcement to deflect whatever those papers are about.

Ryke's features turn grave, and I understand how serious it must be.

"What is it?" Lily asks Daisy.

She shrugs weakly. "They want to put me on some medication again."

Ryke folds the paper, which must be prescriptions that she'll need to pick up, and he stuffs it in his back pocket.

My phone buzzes, but so does everyone else's.

We all check the group text.

Please, one of you, fucking call me.
We'll reschedule the meeting. I just
want to know if my grandson's
alive. —Dad

He'd probably be here if traffic wasn't gridlocked from the wreck. I'm the first to text him back.

Yeah. I hesitate on what else to add, my body binding with more emotion. I try to smother these feelings on instinct. I swallow and type: *he's okay.*

Ten

Loren Hale

With a grocery bag in hand, I slowly open the door to my bedroom. I hope Lily is either asleep or watching *Thor* from where we left off—right before she craved apples and cream cheese icing. Both of which weren't in the house. I had to take Lily's car—since mine is out of commission—to make a run to the store.

When I walk through, I see Lil on our bed, my tablet cupped in her hand while her brows furrow. The moment I shut the door, she flinches and hides the tablet beneath the comforters.

Not porn, is my first and only thought.

"Hiding something?" I ask her.

She holds out her hands for the grocery bag, her eyes widening. I stand at the foot of the bed. She looks ridiculously adorable dressed in red Spider-Man onesie pajamas that she bought in college.

"Did you get the icing?" She perks up and reaches for the plastic bag.

I retract my arm, keeping a hard demeanor. "How about we trade? Give me the tablet, and I'll give you the food?"

"I wasn't doing anything wrong," she says, but makes no movement to grab the tablet.

I suddenly seize her ankle and tug her to the edge of the bed quickly. The breath rushes out of her, and her eyes land solely on my package. I put my face very close to hers so she stares right into my gaze. "Lily Calloway, are you looking at porn?"

"No," she says. I don't detect the lie.

"Were you on Tumblr?"

She presses her lips together.

I give her a no-nonsense look. "Lil."

"Lo."

I shake my head at her. "What could be so goddamn interesting that you'd risk your precious apples and icing?"

She raises her hands. "I can explain." Her mouth stays frozen, wide open, and no words escape.

To cut to the chase, I rest a knee on the bed, lean forward and steal my tablet back. She doesn't even attempt to retrieve it. She just buries her face in the comforter, her cheeks reddening in embarrassment.

I'm more confused. I type in my password on the lock screen. And what pops up is an article, not on Tumblr, titled: *Best sex positions during pregnancy.*

It's not even close to being bad.

She mumbles something into the comforter that sounds like, *I was just curious.*

I take the tub of icing and the tray of sliced apples out of the bag and then roll Lily on her back. She shields her face with her hands.

"I couldn't help it. I mean, I could, but I just wondered what would feel the best and . . . and I'm going to stop talking now."

I straddle her, my knees on either side of her hips, and she peeks out of her fingers, inspecting the icing and the apples in my clutch.

"Am I dreaming?" she whispers.

"No, love."

She crinkles her nose. "This seems an awful lot like one of my fantasies." She pauses. "Only you're supposed to be naked."

"In time," I tell her, snapping open the tub of icing.

"So you're not mad at me?" she asks, propping her body on her elbows.

"I trust you, Lil." I'd rather her be comfortable when we sleep together than panicked and anxious anyway. I recognize how unfair it must be when I can read all of these sites, have all of this knowledge, and she's supposedly not allowed any of it—for the sake of not arousing her. We're going to fuck regardless.

She reddens even more as she whispers, "Are we going to have sex right now?"

"Why are you whispering?" I say. "Are you hiding someone under the bed?"

"No," she says, watching me dip an apple in icing.

With my other hand, I cup the spot between her legs, and she writhes beneath me, a breathless sound leaving her lips. My cock throbs a couple times. I'm about to put the apple between her lips, but the moment I lean forward, our window suddenly shatters. I flinch as a projectile *thuds* hard on the floorboards.

What the hell?

Lily goes rigid in fright, her fingers gripping my biceps.

Climbing off her body, I instinctively position her behind me. "Lil, stay back." My command is muffled through shouting outside, alarmed voices that echo into our bedroom.

"Come on, go, go!"

"Run. Run! He's going to see us!"

My pulse is racing with blood-red heat as I start to piece together this incident. A prank. I grind my teeth. A *stupid* prank. I immediately stand off the bed, and Lily crawls to the edge.

I give her a warning look. "Lily, stay *back*." Too much glass litters the floor, and I don't want her near it. My eyes fall to her abdomen. I have someone else to look out for too. This must trigger a maternal impulse in Lily. She remains still, not following me.

With a pit in my stomach, I step around the sharp shards and pick up a brick, a note attached with a rubber band. I head to the window before I read it, my muscles in taut strands. Right outside, I spot about five teenagers in black hoodies sprinting across our yard. Floodlights still illuminate the grass.

Only one of the guys turns to look back. And his eyes meet mine. Dead on. I feel how severely sharpened my face is—I sense the malice in my eyes. But it all bleeds away the moment I see the same exact expression in this teenager. The same guy that I grabbed in the street during the paintball prank.

I shake my head at him.

He inhales heavily. And then he sprints away, following his friends. My gaze falls to the cold brick. I snap off the rubber band and unfurl the white paper.

"What does it say?" Lily asks.

> *Roses are red.*
> *Violets are blue.*
> *Fuck your slut.*
> *We all know your brother will too.*

With white knuckles, I crumple the paper, my veins on fire. I suppress this irritation. I hate the three-way rumors, but what I hate more are the ones about our kid belonging to Ryke.

"Lo?" she says.

And what I can't stomach—is Lily's reaction to these things. It tears her down, and I want her to rise above it all. But it fucking hurts. I know it. So I'm going to do my best to shield her from this shit.

I pull the velvet purple curtains closed, a lie already concocted in my head. "It's a bad joke about small dicks. It's not even funny."

She nods, probably not even believing me, but she lets it go anyway. Her gaze travels to the glass, the broken window already concealed behind the curtain.

"I'll clean it later," I say the moment our door blows open without a knock.

"Hey," Ryke says. "I heard a . . ." He sees the glass and then the brick in my hand.

"Here." I step around the shards and hand him the brick and balled note. "Do what you want with this. It's nothing to me."

His shoulders tighten, and he unfurls the note, reading it quickly. His voice lowers so Lily can't hear him. "This is fucking wrong."

"We've heard it all before," I say. "I can deal with it." I don't need Ryke to threaten these guys on my behalf. I have a louder voice than him anyway. I've always been capable of lashing out. This is the route I've never taken before.

Wait and see. Be calm. Try to put my emotions aside to find the better option.

"Are you sure?" Ryke asks me, his eyes flickering to Lily on the bed and back to me.

"They're not going to break our fragile hearts into little pieces," I say dryly. "So no one needs to contact a realtor. We're not moving." Everyone's lives have changed too many times because of outside forces. This house is supposed to be *our* stability, and these teenagers aren't going to take that away.

We've lost way too much already.

"You feel like you need something, and you come to me, okay?" Ryke suddenly says. He means booze.

I play dumb. "Sure. Next time I need a shoulder to cry on, I'll make sure to blow snot on your shirt."

He flips me off, but we both end up smiling weakly.

I rub the back of my neck. "Can you just let everyone else know what happened? I want to be alone with Lily right now, and Rose hasn't learned how to knock either."

Ryke rolls his eyes. "Yeah, I'll tell everyone to give you an hour—"

"Longer," I say.

Lily inhales in surprise and partial arousal.

Both Ryke and I turn to look at Lil, her skin nearly blending into her red onesie. She flings a blanket over her head so Ryke can't see her embarrassment. I can't hold back a smile. Goddamn, I love her.

"I already fucking saw you, Lily," my brother says like she's being ridiculous.

Lily mumbles out a response that sounds like, *no you didn't.*

I pat Ryke's shoulder. "See you later."

He takes the hint and exits the bedroom, shutting the door on his way out. I climb back on the bed, straddle her and yank the blanket off her face, her hair frizzing with the static. Her lips part while her gaze trails my body.

"In my fantasy, you're naked," she reminds me.

"Do you want this to last longer than an hour, love?"

She nods with wide, desirous eyes.

I kiss her lips tenderly and then whisper, "Then we're going to go really, really *slow.*"

She smiles and kisses me back, agreeing to this plan. She pauses for just a second, and I sense the hesitation in her body, which is unlike Lily.

"Do you think they'll stop?" she asks me seriously.

I realize she's talking about the teenagers. "Maybe," I say. "I don't know." I frown. "Are you scared?"

"Not really. We dealt with worse assholes in prep school, right?"

Me, I think. I was worse. I poured pig's blood on a guy's front door and did countless other things. "Right," I breathe.

"They can't come *in* the house . . ." she says with unease.

"No," I say forcefully. "They wouldn't. Plus, we have a security system."

She nods repeatedly, and then *she* kisses me quickly and deeply. I rest her back against the mattress again. I just try to forget about the interruption, the teenagers, and the sharp look of the young guy down the street—the one that simultaneously said *fuck you*.

And *kill me*.

Eleven

Lily Calloway

How could I have slept through a fucking car accident?" Rose says, aghast for the umpteenth time. She sits on a leather barstool with a winter recipe book cracked open.

"Queen Rose, it's been ten days," Loren says with little amusement. "You weren't even *there*, so let us peons reflect on the situation, and you can let it go." He gives her a bitter smile and dusts flour off his hands with a towel. That was one of his nicer comments of the day.

Baking, I have found, makes Loren Hale mean. Almost like smiling, *happy* gingerbread men frustrate him. He already put frowny faces on the second batch of cookies, just to ensure that they all share in his irritated state of being.

"I can't let it go," Rose says in a huff. "No one even *called* us." She angrily flips a page in her recipe book. They found out about the car accident from *Celebrity Crush* before we could tell them. We'll never live it down.

But I know it's more than not calling. Rose is scared that she's now part of the *outer* circle. Connor isn't happy either. They both like to know everything before everyone—so this stings.

I watch Daisy and Ryke man the blender in our stainless-steel kitchen. Measuring cups, cupcake trays, sugar, and butter are splayed on the countertops.

I'm not wandering around, but I eat chocolate chips out of the bag next to Rose, which I'd like to think helps in some way. I'm taste testing the food.

It's edible. Just in case someone out there is wondering.

"I would've liked a text message, at least," Connor says, opening a carton of eggs. He stands closest to Lo on the other side of the bar counter.

Lo leans against the cupboard. He snaps back, "I'll send you one right now if it makes you feel better." He doesn't even add *love* on the end of it, which he reserves only for me and one of his best friends.

Connor's eyebrow arches, and he stares blankly at him.

I say to Lo, "Baking makes you mean."

He grips the counter, takes a deep breath, and his narrowed amber eyes flit up to me. "My dad texted me about the meeting."

The kitchen goes quiet except for the whirling blender.

"And?" I ask, caging a breath.

"And *nothing*. He just keeps saying he'll explain in person, but now he's not even saying when that'll be." He straightens up as he exhales again. "It's annoying as shit."

Ryke says, "He's just messing with us. It's what he fucking does."

Lo shakes his head again in disagreement. "It's like he's scared or something . . . I don't know. I don't want to think about it, honestly."

Rose points to a photo of peppermint cookies. "Whole Foods sells this *exact* cookie."

Lo looks grateful for the digression, even if it's coming from Rose. My older sister is ready to hop off the barstool, grab her keys, and go shopping.

Her shopping skills far outrank her cooking skills.

And I agree, this sounds like a brilliant plan. I perk up. I'm about to call quits on our attempt at baking. I'm known to be lazy, so I have a perfect excuse.

But Connor rips the recipe book out of Rose's hand and skims the ingredients. "You can make this easily, darling."

Her yellow-green eyes pierce his forehead. "I don't cook. The smart thing, Richard, would be to save time and buy all of this." She gestures to the tray of misshapen gingerbread men (Lo's), burnt snickerdoodles (Daisy's), and perfectly brown oatmeal raisins (Ryke's).

"It's the efficient thing," Connor says. "But Maria asked for homemade cookies, not store-bought ones." Poppy's daughter is having some sort of baked goods sale, and my oldest sister enlisted our help.

"Maria also knows that I *loathe* baking." Rose stretches over the bar to talk to Connor.

Oh, this is good. I eat the chocolate chips like popcorn, my lips rising in entertainment. The nerd stars are sparkling. Lo is watching too, and he joins my side and sticks his hand in the chocolate chip bag.

Connor is practically grinning. "Are you really implying that she's doing this on purpose?"

"Yes." Rose pulls back her shoulders like a cat ready to pounce.

Connor grins, full-on now. "She's six."

Lo whispers to me, "Burn."

"Rose has this," I whisper back. "Watch." I'm Team Nerd Stars, but if I must choose an allegiance, I will go with my sister, every time.

"All kids are devils in disguise," Rose retorts, her forearms on the bar, "and apparently I'm the *only* one who sees them for what they really are."

"And what is that?"

"Small, tiny gremlins."

Lo chokes on a chocolate chip. I pat his back and keep eating mine, my eyes widening with delight. This is better than a summer blockbuster.

Rose's butt rises off the stool as she continues, "The kind that will suck up all of your time and energy, and before you know it, you're an old hag with *nothing* but saggy, disgusting cookies."

"Your hyperboles are nothing new," he tells her. I think he only likes them when they come from her.

She scoffs. "I speak the truth."

"If anyone here is a truthteller, it's me, darling." He winks.

She glares. "Next time you wink at me, Richard, I'm going to scratch out your eyeball and set it on fire."

He leans closer to her, their lips a breath apart. "Go ahead and try."

Her gaze falls to his mouth, the sexual tension heightened, but it doesn't stir me to bad places. Their intellectual love is always more amusing to me than erotic. "If you're a truthteller," she says, "then what does that make me, Richard?"

"A storyteller. The world needs those, so don't feel bad." Ohhhhh.

"Double burn," Lo says. He looks to me. "You were saying, love?" He's Team Connor, all the way.

I refuse to concede. My sister will come out on top.

Rose's cheeks are flushed though—half in anger and half in arousal, her breath shallow. And she glowers. "Don't smirk at me." Her eyes flit to his lips again and back to his deep blues.

Connor's grin only overtakes his face, arrogant and—

"I married an egomaniac," Rose says. "What is wrong with me?"

Okay, so maybe she's going to come out on bottom, but I think that's a place she likes to be in the bedroom. In my book, she won. I nod definitively.

Connor leans forward, his wrists on the counter, fingers skimming her arms. "Rien du tout." *Nothing at all.*

I flinch in surprise with the candy bag in hand, chocolate chips sailing through the air. Everyone turns to me, and I redden. Still, I point at Connor. "I understood you! Ha!" My French translation book is *finally* paying off.

And Connor gives me one of the most genuine smiles, and then he claps, not in sarcasm but real applause for someone who aced a test and deserves an A-plus.

It fills me with more confidence than I think I've ever had. I can be on the same level as the two smartest people in the house. It just takes a little work and dedication. Things they excel in—things I'm learning.

Lo kisses my temple, his hands swooping around my waist from behind. My body warms at his touch, and I purposefully avoid his features, not able to stare too long. His gorgeous jawline and amber eyes will send me on a one-way ticket to the bedroom, and I've been doing . . . not so hot these past few days in the sex department.

It's just difficult being so aroused all the time.

Lo even reads me well, no teasing. He just keeps his one loose arm around me and stays by my side. He says to Rose, "It's funny how you're bitching when we've done most of the baking." He gestures from his chest to Ryke to Connor.

"Daisy helped us," Ryke reminds him, popping the lid off the chocolate icing.

"And Daisy," Lo amends.

"I'm bitching for Lily too, not just for myself." She raises her chin to me. "You're welcome." And then she folds her hands on the counter and sits straighter. I do love Rose, even when she's standing on the opposite side from Lo.

He flashes her a half-smile and then walks back to Connor. He pats him on the shoulder. "She's all yours, love."

Connor grins a billion-dollar grin, and his eyes never waver from Rose's, and hers never detach from his, like they're speaking in their brains. Mind reading—a smart person superpower.

I smile and scoop some chocolate chips off the counter while Lo checks the oven. When I look up, I catch Ryke and Daisy flirting, *two* of his fingers dipping into the chocolate icing.

My body actually reacts, my skin warming in places it shouldn't. I stiffen, remembering a similar icing situation in the past with them. When they weren't together. But I never heated back then. I definitely didn't break into an aroused sweat. I wipe my arm over my clammy forehead, cursing myself for feeling *anything* at all.

Daisy faces her older boyfriend, holding on to his belt loops, and then Ryke sucks the chocolate off, his fingers deep in his mouth, and his eyes roll back in a fake orgasm.

Holy shit.

I need to look away. Ryke Meadows *cannot* be arousing me. No, no, *no*. If there is one constant it's this: Ryke Meadows is my mood killer, my go-to image to make me *dry*. My hormonal body doesn't realize how annoying Ryke can be.

As soon as Ryke drops his fingers, he kisses Daisy so deeply, with skilled tongue action. Her hands grip his thick brown hair.

I grow wet and force my gaze anywhere else.

That was not *hot*, I try to fool myself. I want to crawl beneath the barstool, hide and disintegrate into the floorboards.

This is too awkward to even talk about, let alone ponder in my dirty, messed-up mind. Now my elbows are even red.

Great.

I hear a tray clatter on the stove, and I realize Lo not only saw me squirming, but he may have caught the source of my arousal.

Oh God. My face contorts in humiliation. I'm not turned on by his brother—he can't believe that. Not when Mr. Clean on the Febreze bottle made me hot and bothered the other day. And he's old and bald and very two-dimensional.

But Lo's features have marbleized in this *I hate the fucking world* expression that he carries almost twenty-four-seven. "Your cookies are burnt," he snaps at Ryke, breaking my gaze.

Wait, come back.

Ryke detaches from Daisy in an instant. "Fuck," he curses and checks the tray on the stove. His brows pinch. "They look fine to me." He flips one over, the bottom light brown.

"My bad," Lo says dryly.

I open my mouth to call him over, but his back suddenly spins like he's icing me out. My heart lurches. *Turn around.* I need to know I didn't upset him . . . or offend him. I usually have the best read on Lo, and I have no superpowers of mental persuasion or any magic like Connor. I am too much of a squib to fix this.

Turn around. Nothing.

Lo whispers with Connor, and a pit wedges even further in my lungs.

And then Daisy's phone rings while Ryke washes his hands.

"Who is it?" Rose asks.

Daisy's face falls a little. "Mom. She's trying to convince me to go to a plastic surgeon for the scar again, on top of planning my birthday." She lets out a tired breath and rubs her eyes. "I'll be a couple minutes."

"I'll talk to her," Rose says, outstretching her hand to snatch the phone as Daisy passes.

"No." Daisy hugs the cell to her chest and walks backward to the basement door. "You don't need the stress. It's all cool. I can handle her." With this, Daisy disappears. The last thing I hear her say is, "Hey, Mom."

I try not to worry about Daisy or Lo, and instead focus on Ryke, who chucks some dirty bowls into the sink. Maybe I can squash this and convince Lo that *nothing* is happening. I'm repelled by Ryke. We're *so* platonic it hurts.

In a nonsexual way.

I cringe. I really need to stop thinking. I ask Ryke, "What are you getting her?"

He rotates to me, his features all dark. All stone to his brother's ice. "For what?"

Rose lets out a not-so-surprised half-laugh. "Her birthday," she says flatly. "Tell me you've already bought her something."

"For fuck's sake, it was *just* Valentine's Day." And he canceled his plans of camping under the stars with Daisy that day, the paparazzi just too rabid after the small car wreck. Any time we pop up in the tabloids like a newsworthy blip, our photos start selling for more money. So February 14th, Ryke just cooked Daisy dinner and spent the night indoors like Lo and me.

Connor and Rose were the only two who ventured out, and Rose called the evening "hellish" since they were late for their dinner reservations in New York. Even though their whereabouts were tipped to the media, Rose returned home with an uncharacteristically giddy smile and a limo *full* of red and pink roses.

They were from her fans, who showed up to see her, just to say *I love you, Rose Calloway*, and give her a present on Valentine's Day. I love our short-lived reality show for bringing this type of unexpected joy into our lives, and it verifies why these kinds of fans should rule the world.

"So what if it was *just* Valentine's Day," Rose snaps, redirecting my thoughts to the present, "it's still her birthday on the twentieth, and she'll expect a gift from her *boyfriend*."

"I'm working on it," Ryke says, nearing the bar counter while Lo and Connor share furtive whispers a few feet away.

I tuck a piece of hair behind my ear, my palms sweaty. I wish I wasn't on the outs.

"Look," Ryke continues, "a lot is going on . . ." He trails off as Rose snatches the nearest utensil—a whisk—and points it at him threateningly.

This would be scarier if it was something sharp. Like a knife or a fork.

"Do not tell me that you forgot her birthday," Rose says in her icy tone. Oh no.

But I remember that Ryke isn't Lo. He holds his hands up defensively. "Daisy is not the type of fucking person to remind anyone about her birthday. It's not my fault."

"That was directed toward me," Rose says like she caught an insult midair with a baseball glove.

Ryke frowns in confusion. "What?"

"Because I emailed you my birthday itinerary in advance . . ." Off Ryke's scrunched gaze, she adds, "Do you even *check* your email?"

"To be honest, I don't even know my password," Ryke tells her. "And who plans their birthday *six* months in advance?" Solid points. I look to Lo, wondering if he sees how cordial this conversation is—how unsexy we all are.

My heart just keeps sinking the longer I stare at his back.

Rose drums her fingers on the bar counter. "I'm not ashamed. It's the one day of the year dedicated to *me*, so if three hundred and sixty-four days fail to live up to my standards, I still have this one."

"You sound like Connor," I point out with a small smile.

She glares. "If Connor appreciated the narcissism in his own birthday that'd make sense, but he refuses to believe they're anything more than meaningless."

I wait for Connor to pipe in about how he won't celebrate his birthday, but like Lo, he's not paying attention to our discussion.

I find myself scratching my arm, and I immediately freeze in slight panic. I haven't done that in a while. Ryke's face hardens in that masculine concern—something I do not want to see right now. In fact, I need to stop making eye contact with him altogether. I have a new tactic: avoid Ryke Meadows.

Rose is still drawn to the birthday topic, thankfully not noticing my strangeness. "Buy her diamond earrings," she says.

"She'd fucking hate that."

I stare at the bar counter while I mutter, "She'll like anything you get her." Daisy is pretty much the easiest person to please.

"Is there something interesting about the counter that we don't fucking know about?" Ryke suddenly asks me.

I squint at the granite, speckles of gray, white, and black. "I think if you close one eye like this . . . you can see a bunny rabbit."

"Everyone is so fucking weird."

Rose dismisses that comment with the swat of her hand. "Just wait until you have your first fight with Daisy." She says it like she's expecting the moment to happen. Why is she putting that thought into his head?

I lightly elbow Rose. "Don't say that. They don't fight." I can't see Daisy being *that* upset over a present.

"Everyone fights."

I point my finger at Ryke, and it accidentally pokes him in the eye. Oh my God! When did he get that close to me?

"Fuck, Lily," he curses, his hand flying to his face.

I wince. "Sorry . . . I was going to tell you not to fight with her."

"I fucking got that." He sighs with a heavy growl. "I didn't mean to say it like that." He drops his hand, his eye a little reddened from my attack. He glances at the basement door and then back to me. "You okay?"

"Yeah?" *Do I not look okay?* My heart is racing with anxiety.

If I shift a little, I can feel how soaked my panties are, and I hate, hate, *hate* that he was the cause. I'm not even attracted to him right now.

He suddenly walks around the bar counter, his nearness alarming me, especially as I notice Lo watching us and my reaction. Ryke clasps my wrist, prying my hand from my arm, half-moon nail indentions by my elbow. I was scratching again?

I can feel his body heat, and I instinctively hop off the stool and push him away with two firm palms, a little more aggressively than I intended.

"What the fuck?" Ryke swears.

"Just stay back," I say, breathing heavily. I shuffle into the kitchen.

"Lily—"

"Shh. It's better if you don't talk about this," I tell him. *Let's just forget my weirdness ever happened and pretend that everything is okay. Nothing is happening between Ryke and me. Nothing.*

Ryke glowers. "Are you reading the fucking tabloids again?"

"Yes." I nod. "It's important that I'm up-to-date on all the rumors." The three-ways, the *I'm having Ryke's baby* ones are out of control. Lo says it doesn't bother him, but at the hospital, I could tell that comment from the doctor dug underneath his skin. It hurt me just as much.

"That's the stupidest fucking excuse," he tells me. "We're friends, Lily. That's *it*. You know it. I know it. So what if the fucking world doesn't believe us?"

"I care!" I shout. I can't turn it off like he can. After a while, the ridicule hurts.

"You're fucking stronger than that!" he yells back. I don't feel it. Not today. I think Ryke just wishes I was at his level. If all of us didn't give a shit, then he'd never have to watch us crumble.

I feel tears crest my eyes. I wish, so badly, that I could be more like him. Doesn't he understand how much we'd all replace parts of ourselves just to have a little of what he possesses?

"Hey," Lo cuts in, his tone not as sharp. "Leave her alone, man."

My heart skips, and even though Lo sticks up for me, I still can't read him. It frightens me. We're out of sync, and I can't remember the last time this happened. Maybe in college, when we went without talking for a whole week and our addictions overtook our lives.

Ryke breathes heavily. "I don't want the fucking tabloids ruining my friendship with her."

Rose pipes in, "That's what they're hoping, for all of us to break apart. Little assholes . . ." She stares off like she's plotting someone's demise.

"We're still friends," I tell Ryke.

"Then why can't you fucking look at me?"

I'm scared of you. It's an awful truth. Really, I'm scared of myself, but the weight on my chest lessens when I place the guilt somewhere else.

I raise my head, but I only meet Loren Hale's gaze. He stares straight through me like he is reaching right into my soul and piecing apart all of my intricate fears. What frightens me most: not knowing what my best friend feels.

I'm about to approach him in the middle of the kitchen and collide with his hard, rigid body. But I don't have to lift a foot.

He walks to me. And he pulls my small frame to him, embracing me with two strong arms, a warm cocoon where my heart begins to slow. I rest my cheek on his chest, his body pressed along mine, and I shut my eyes.

His hand lowers to the small of my back, and he dips his head. His lips to my ear, he whispers, "I'm not going anywhere." He pauses, an extended one that stops my pulse. "Lil . . . how aroused are you?" He would've checked without asking if we were alone.

I flush and tilt my chin up. I whisper quickly, "I'm only aroused by you."

His face sharpens and he says, "Shhh."

Why is he shushing me? "It's true." My voice shakes.

He kisses the outside of my lips, really tenderly. Where is his head at?

"Lil," he warns like I did something wrong. I concentrate and realize I'm pushing my pelvis right up against him, his bulge edging toward my wetness as I *hike* my leg around him.

I drop my foot, my whole body flaming with embarrassment. I cover my face with both my hands. This is one of those days I wish I could erase. Dr. Banning, my therapist, says that everyone has them, but I always play my bad days on loop, tormenting me for eternity.

"It's okay, Lil," he breathes. "Look at me." He grips my wrists, tearing them away from my face. Still, I tighten my eyes closed, too ashamed . . . I'd like to vanish again.

Invisibility, kick in. Please.

"I love you," he says so empathetically that it tears open my heart. "I understand you. Please hold on to that, Lil."

He should be angry at me. He should hate how disgusting I am—what my body is craving. It's not right.

"*Lily*," he forces, cupping my face in both his hands. "Breathe, love."

I take a deep one, and then I sense a tall masculine body a couple feet behind me. Most likely Connor. He's not too close, but the longer he stands there, the more my body reacts in ways I dislike. Lo studies all of my muscle tics and spasms. Diagnosing me. I cross my ankles and shut my eyes again, snuffing out every perverted image that I should not have in public or at all.

Why? Why do I have to like things that I shouldn't?

The heat of two bodies stimulates parts of me that my brain has abandoned. The sensual parts that care little about names, relations, and faces. Just the high of a climax.

Not Connor. I can't grow wet from him.

This is so wrong.

I cling to Lo, shaking, afraid of myself. I haven't felt this gross in a while.

His lips fall to my ear at the right moment while he rubs my back. "Shh, Lil." He pulls me even closer to his body. No space between us. "I'm going to take care of you, love."

With sex? I wonder. The guilt sinks to a low, hollow place.

"Not with sex," he says, as though he can read my mind.

"I'msorry," I mumble together, burying my face in his arm and refusing to acknowledge Rose, Ryke, or Connor.

Today is a not-so-good day.

I could have reined myself in, but I slipped off the diving board and belly flopped in the deep end. I know addictions are up-and-down kind of things, but the downs really, really hurt. At least Lo was wading in the water, there to keep me from drowning this time.

He hasn't given up on us.

It's silly to think that's a possibility anyway. It's an irrational fear that I should never let cling to me. He is my soul. I am his. The moment we give up on each other is the moment that neither of us exists.

Lo lifts me in a front piggyback, and he carries me toward the staircase while I clutch him like a koala bear to a tree.

As we leave, I hear Daisy enter the kitchen. "Mom has already planned my birthday." A long pause before she adds, "We're taking the yacht out, and everyone's invited."

I can barely even concentrate on that future drama when my mind has zeroed in on Loren Hale and only Loren Hale. I need him.

I want him.

I just can't let myself have all of him tonight. *No sex.*

But it will be enough. It has to be.

Lo climbs two more stairs before the front door bursts open and bangs against the wall.

He cranes his neck over his shoulder, and every muscle in his arms and abdomen tenses against me. I peek from the crook of his bicep and make direct eye contact with a stern, severe man. Dark brown hair that's grayed by the temples. A jaw as hard and intimidating as Ryke Meadows' and a glower as deathly as Loren Hale's.

Jonathan Hale is the scariest parts of both his sons.

"Meeting," Jonathan Hale says roughly, his voice husky and foreboding. "Now."

My arousal still exists. I can't just extinguish it because of Jonathan's worst timing. So I recognize that I'm in serious trouble.

Twelve

Loren Hale

I want to fucking scream.

At no one in particular.

If I could, I'd disappear into my bedroom with Lily and try to get her to a better place than the one she's at. I hate that she's anxious, and I hate that she's scared of herself. And I recognize what just happened—that she became aroused from someone other than me. It's not a new development. Since she's been pregnant, she's gotten hot from almost everything.

What's different is that she's starting to let her addiction fuck with her mind. Affect our relationship. I won't let anything tear us apart. Especially not something we've both been fighting for so long.

"Loren!" my father calls.

I stand on the stairs uneasily, about to drop Lil on her feet, but she spiders my body, terrified more of herself than of my dad in the living room. After years of dealing with her sex addiction, I know how to help her, but I can't respond to him and her at the same time.

"Lo," she breathes.

"Lil," I say, cupping her face with one hand and her ass with the other. I force her gaze to mine, and she cuts me off before I can speak.

"I'm only attracted to you. You know that, right?" Fear spikes her voice.

I can feel my face sharpen in aggravation. Not at her. Just the situation. I wanted time to take her upstairs and talk to her. "I know, Lil—"

"Loren, come here, *now*," my dad interrupts again.

"One second!" I yell back. This is my only moment to get her on the same page as me. "Lil, you know how much you love porn?"

She nods, and I wipe some of her silent tears. My stomach twists the longer she's upset.

"That's all this is. You're turned on by a lot of stuff, love. We live with two other couples, and one is into PDA . . ." I watch her face scrunch as she tries to understand. I figured out that she'd be aroused by the PDA quickly, and I mentioned to Connor that I was concerned she'd become scared of Ryke and him.

It's a small regression, a speed bump.

So we tested it out. He stood behind her for a few seconds. Not even that close. I've seen Lily freak, but never about Connor—someone she used to think was gay.

Lily shakes her head repeatedly at me, confusion seeping into her green eyes. "I'm *not* turned on by your brother," she whispers with wide eyes, her fingers digging into my shoulders.

"He could've been *anyone*, Lil. Do you understand?" The pain in her eyes—pain for *me*, thinking she's hurt me somehow—breaks my heart into too many goddamn pieces. I just want to hold her tightly until it's just us left. No one around us. Drown everything out.

She rubs her eyes. "Ryke is like a porn star?"

I almost laugh, but her chin quivers. "Lil?" My lungs drop.

"I'm not allowed to watch porn," she says with worry. "So . . . if everything is like porn, then . . ."

No. Christ no. "Lil, don't be afraid of the fucking world, please." I can't have her scared to go outside again. I'm screwing this up, really badly. And this isn't like a failed grade on a test. I am holding my girlfriend's well-being in my hands right now.

"I just . . . how do I fix this?" she asks me.

"LOREN!" my dad calls like a knife in my gut.

My fingers slide into her straight brown hair, and I say, "You just have to accept that what you feel is okay."

Tears squeeze out of her eyes. "Lo . . ." Her throat bobs. "It doesn't feel okay."

I kiss her cheek, and I whisper, "After we get done talking to my dad, I'm going to show you that it is."

"LOREN!"

"Give him a fucking break," Ryke retorts downstairs.

My veins pulse hard. I trust that if I leave her alone, she won't touch herself. But at this moment, I don't want her to face a challenge that she's already hurdled fifty million fucking times. It's one that's never easy, and she doesn't need to prove herself after an agonizing hour.

I'd rather her not be in pain at all. That means I enable her and have sex. I can't do that. I have to settle for somewhere in the middle of pain and ecstasy. Between a high and a low.

It sounds easier finding that place than it really is.

I bring her downstairs with me, carrying her in a front piggyback. When we enter the living room, the fireplace is lit, and outside the fogged windows, snow falls. The air is strained, especially as Ryke and my father stay standing while Daisy fidgets on the suede love seat, crossing and uncrossing her long legs.

I sit on the couch with Lily, and my father scrutinizes her for too many seconds.

"You could have called," I tell him, "or texted me." None of us needed a spontaneous meeting with him. Before, we had all worked up to it.

"But I didn't. Shit happens every day that you can't prepare for, Loren," he says, as if I'm not familiar with that.

I've walked through life with a blindfold, hoping I didn't crash into things, sometimes praying that I did. Preparation has never been my thing. My life is a "toss this dart at me" kind of random. Let's see which body part it pierces.

My dad disinterestedly inspects hardbacks on a tall wooden shelf, all belonging to Rose and Connor. "Think of this as a life lesson," he says.

My jaw tics in irritation. "Like I need any more of those."

I wait for the, *don't be a little shit.*

He buries his fists in the pockets of his black slacks, no whiskey in hand. And he faces the couch. "You're probably right." No insult for me. I lean back in surprise. He's been sober for almost four months. It still seems like a dream, but these moments make it more real.

I rub Lily's shoulders, but she squeezes her thighs around my waist. I'd rather not move her off my lap, but I'm afraid she's going to grind on me. I scoot her onto the cushion, and I toss a purple blanket over her. She adjusts so her heel digs into the spot between her legs.

Christ, Lil.

My dad's gaze drifts over to the foyer. "This is just between the four of us."

"I've never fought with you about anything," Connor says easily, Rose by his side. "Let's not change that." It sounds like a threat.

I've never seen anyone really hold the same power in a room as my father. Lily's dad is submissive toward Jonathan. *Soft* is what my dad calls him. And Connor has always played their game with a fake smile and a firm handshake.

This is different.

My father sizes him up, a literal once-over from head to toe.

Ryke says, "Let them fucking stay."

Rose has already settled in a Queen Anne chair next to me, crossing her ankles, Connor standing beside the armrest.

My dad keeps his attention on Connor. "I understand why you like Ryke. What'd you call him the other day? Your *attack dog*."

Ryke flips Connor off without meeting his eyes, but it's in jest. He's said that plenty of times to his face.

"I like him all the same," Connor says.

"But what's Loren to you?" my dad asks. He thinks he's poking at a weak spot of Connor's, but he's doing a poor job. He can't break the guy. He's built of titanium or some sort of indestructible alien material. Like Superman.

I open my mouth to tell my dad to leave him alone.

But he continues, "Lo's a college dropout, has failed at every athletic sport he's ever tried." My blood runs cold, and Lily suddenly clutches my hand, trying to comfort me. I can't move. "He's not smart or strong. Frankly, he's a goddamn *liability*. So what use is he to you?" Through all these statements, I want to believe my dad is trying to protect me from Connor. Right? Like Ryke once did.

Connor is a user, he's saying.

My brows knot. Yeah, I know this about Connor.

"He's my best friend," Connor says without a beat. "I enjoy his company."

"Do you?" My dad glares, one that could shrivel a man.

Connor never backs down. "I know what you're implying, and you should stop."

"Is that a threat?"

"Yes," Connor says, poker-faced. Honestly, it's terrifying—not being able to see his emotions.

"I'm not here to ruin you, Connor, but if you stand in my way, I will. Unlike you, I'm a man with very little to lose."

"Jonathan," Rose suddenly says, her eyes fiery. And it's like my dad just recognizes her sitting right there. "You bring my husband down, you bring me down. We're staying right *here*." She might as well have said: *we're in the inner fucking circle, bitch. No one is pushing us out.*

My dad grinds his teeth in distaste.

Connor won this.

Rose is related to Greg Calloway. Greg is Jonathan's best friend. As a result, he'd never hurt Rose.

His eyes flicker up to Connor. "You aligned yourself fucking well. If I had a glass of bourbon, I'd cheers to you."

"I'm glad you don't," Connor says. I wait for him to add a smart-ass response, but he holds back this time. Or maybe it's the literal truth. I'll never know. With Connor, it's hard to discern these things unless you're in his head.

Ryke stays standing with Connor, and my dad addresses the entire room, though his gaze lands on me, and Lil the most. He starts pacing in front of the fireplace. His hands now on his hips. Then on the back of his neck. He rubs his fingers together like he's missing his glass of liquor.

My thoughts scramble. I just don't see what this could be about—

"You four." He suddenly stops pacing and motions between Ryke, Daisy, Lily, and me, appraising us. Like he's tallying our worth. When his eyes land on me, they actually redden. "One of you needs to grow the *fuck* up. I don't care which one of you it is, but it has to happen."

A noise between pain and laughter catches my throat. "What are you even talking about?"

My dad says, "Open your goddamn ears, Loren."

I grimace. "Right, I don't understand *anything*. Because I'm not smart enough or strong enough, because I can't hit a home run or make a touchdown, I can't comprehend sentences and words." I give him a half-smile that hurts my face.

"Clearly you're not stupid. You just like being a pain in my ass." His broad shoulders lock, and he fixes his suit and checks his watch. Like he's running out of time. He addresses the four of us again. "In the media, you all are represented about equally heinously. Now *I* think you're all beautiful little shits, but my opinion really doesn't matter." He digs into his pocket and pulls out a creased paper with coffee stains.

The only one who doesn't look confused is my dad—the one with all the answers.

"There are some people whose opinions *do* matter." He reads off the paper. "In a group of fourteen—ten men and four women, average age forty-two—every single goddamn female found Ryke Meadows, my eldest son, vulgar, aggressive, threatening, and I quote, 'a hazard to children everywhere.'"

"What the fuck are you reading?" Ryke asks.

Our dad flashes the paper at us, and instead of typed sentences, all I see are pen scribbles. "My notes," he clarifies. "Five men labeled you as a work in progress. The other five saw no silver lining with you. And a seventy-five-year-old said, I quote, 'If he spits in the face of a cameraman, what's to say he wouldn't spit in our faces?' A wise statement."

My pulse is racing. I keep shaking my head.

No one interrupts him. He focuses now on my brother's girlfriend, Lily's little sister, someone who I wish was far away from my dad. "Daisy Calloway, daughter of a respected entrepreneur. Every female said you're too young, too immature, and too reckless. The men, however, found you to be charming, alluring, and presentable." My dad looks up from the paper. "I don't take stock in their opinions since they were swayed by their dicks."

Daisy's mouth falls.

Ryke is fuming, steam practically rising off his skin.

I'm too stunned and caught off guard. I scratch the back of my neck that heats.

Before my brother actually charges forward—which is nearing

a possibility—our dad raises his hands in defense. "Moving on to Lily Calloway." Shit. I clasp Lily's knee beneath the blanket. She's unmoving.

"You don't need to read what the public thinks of her," I snap at him. "She gets it." We've all heard everything before.

He pushes his finger at the paper. "These fourteen people aren't the entire public. It's a fraction, and they're important." He continues reading from his notes, "Lily Calloway has sexual relations with two of my sons at once—as stated by five of fourteen. The women like that you're pregnant, but they find you shy, impersonal, and awkward on camera. Three men appeared to admire your Princeton undergraduate degree, while the rest thought it was insignificant. One woman said, and I quote, 'She is the most popular Calloway but also the most unpopular,' which is ridiculous but true."

Lily has the most negative press, but as a couple, we have the biggest fan base because of the way *Princesses of Philly* edited us. So I get that comment. What I don't understand is *the point* to this whole charade.

My father suddenly spins to me. I freeze as he says, "Loren Hale, my second-born son . . ." His shoulders slacken, and when his eyes flicker to mine, I see more admiration in them, more love. ". . . all fourteen were first scared to criticize you in front of me, but I goaded them into doing it."

"Wait." I frown. "You know these people, personally?" For some reason, I thought they were a random test group. Like someone asked pedestrians on the street their opinions about us.

"Of course, I do," he says. "All fourteen make up the board of directors for Hale Co."

I stare off, suddenly realizing what this may be about. *No, it can't . . .*

He continues while my head rolls, "Loren Hale is not as big of a hothead as Ryke Meadows . . . They were really going easy on you at first." He skims the paper. "The majority found you to be 'angry-looking,' which is a stupid little adjective. The women thought you came across thoughtful and caring toward your girl-friend, but they were worried if you were a team player. You are generally sympathetic in the media, being my bastard child, though you appear standoffish when it concerns Hale Co.—which worries all of them. It's why I'm here."

His eyes flit up to mine again.

And the answer that we've all wanted is about to finally come.

"I'm socially and corporately *tainted* since the . . . rumors about you and me."

He can't say it.

The *molestation* rumors. False accusations about my dad touch-ing me when I was a kid. There will always be skeptics believing they were true, no matter how much evidence crops up advocating against it. No matter how hard we scream, people still won't be-lieve us. It's what makes me sick most of the time.

"Stocks have dropped. Hale Co. isn't looking good, and the board is pressuring me to not only name an heir but to hand the company off. I can't represent it anymore. But I refuse to pass Hale Co. to some random, white-collared little shit. It's going to one of you four *beautiful* little shits and staying in the family."

He's been sitting on this for weeks, months, maybe. The board is forcing him to step down, and I can't even wrap my head around stepping up. I have a comic book business. I'm about to have a baby. Lily is hormonal and starting to regress. I've been sober for only *four* months since the last time I relapsed.

Hale Co. is a multibillion-dollar company. And I still feel like a little kid playing grown-up.

"If no one is going to say anything," my dad starts again, "then I'll go on. You need to impress the board, not me. They can vote you out at any time, so you have to earn their respect. But they will accept one of you, guide you, train you. This, I know. Hale Co. is a family company, something my father passed to me, and they appreciate that. It's a goddamn good marketing tool."

Ryke points at Daisy on the love seat. "She's not my fucking wife, so keep her out of this."

"I needed to give the board some options. She was one of the names brought up due to her affiliation with Fizzle. And if she means something to you, then she means something to me and the Hale legacy. If you don't fucking marry her, then she's still a goddamn Calloway."

A rock is in my throat, but I somehow clear it to ask, "Is the board choosing who takes over or are we?"

"The board will decide. You'll attend functions with them, meetings, and when they choose, you have to be willing to sign the papers and commit. If you don't, the company is no longer in our family's control, and we'll lose a *substantial* number of shares."

I didn't think that my dad would turn my world upside down again. Not like this. It's a life change for one of us.

Ryke just keeps shaking his head over and over.

"Ryke, I'll be fine," Daisy tells him. "It could be fun."

He towers above her while she's on the love seat. "You spent years doing things for your fucking mom. I'm not letting you do the same for my dad." He turns back to Jonathan. "I'll go through with the meetings, whatever. Just leave Daisy alone."

"That's not how it works," he says. "She can sabotage herself so they won't pick her, but she's still required to attend the meetings."

Ryke's eyes flash hot. "You can't just *promise* people things without asking us if it's fucking okay."

"Do you ever look at the name beside all the deposits in your checking account, Ryke? It's Hale Co.—every penny in your trust fund is from that company, and so I don't believe I should have to ask for your permission."

Ryke sets his hands on top of his head. "This is fucking unbelievable."

"I'm losing my goddamn company, and *you're* throwing a hissy fit. You've never even had a real job. You're *all* privileged and lucky. Every day *you* take it for granted."

Shit.

It's like he busted something in Ryke. My brother charges forward, and I shoot to my feet and grab his shoulder.

"Come on," I whisper to him, trying to force him backward, but he's like a brick wall, and his target is on Jonathan.

Ryke glowers. "I grew up *pretending* to have no real fucking parents. I'm an alcoholic. *Both* of your sons are alcoholics. There is no amount of privilege and wealth worth what's been fucking done to us and said about the people we love." And he ends it with, "I'm lucky to be alive, but I am not lucky to be your son."

My ribs bind around my lungs. The fact that they're on speaking terms, after years of silence, is progress enough.

"Please, tell me what you really feel," my dad says dryly.

Daisy jumps to her feet and stands between Ryke and my dad. She places her hands on my brother's chest. "Ryke, it's okay."

I glance back at Lily. She's staring off in a daze, but her palms are flat on top of the blanket. She's not touching herself. That eases some of my worry.

"Stay *the fuck* out of this," Ryke tells her. "I don't want you in it."

"I'd rather be picked to run Hale Co. than watch you take it over," she says honestly. "You've told me a million times how you've never wanted to be a part of it. And you always say to never do things that you hate, do the things you love. So don't change now."

His nose flares. "*You'll* fucking hate this job too. You'll be inside a building, in a cubicle, all fucking day, Dais."

"It's an office," our dad interjects, "with one of the best views of Philly. There are plenty of windows for her to jump out of."

Ryke looks like he could strangle him.

I grimace because it's a bad comment—one that I could've easily made instead.

"Ryke." Daisy clasps his arm, drawing his attention to her. "How about you let me decide what I hate and what I love, okay?" Her voice is sweet, but her words pack a punch.

He relents, right there. "I fucking hate this," he says lowly.

And I realize that she's not going to sabotage her chances. Because she doesn't want Ryke to be chosen. Ryke is probably going to try harder—because he doesn't want Daisy to live this kind of life. I think we all know there's a two percent chance she'd enjoy it.

As much as I would like to get off free, damage my own chances, and leave Ryke or Daisy to follow my father's dreams and not their own—I'm not that guy anymore. The hard things are usually the right things.

I know that now.

"I'll do it," I say. *I have* to do it, but I'm telling the whole room that I'm going to try. My chest constricts with the weight and pressure of this statement. Of the things and responsibilities that will become mine. It all rests right on top of Halway Comics, Superheroes & Scones, my child, and our addictions.

"No," Connor and Rose say in unison, both of them *glaring* at me for even offering.

But my dad is on cloud nine. I've never seen him smile like that, his pride overwhelming, and the foreign sentiment sits strangely inside me. He's always wanted me to take over Hale Co. Not Ryke. I may be the bastard and the second-born son, but I'm the one he raised.

I understand. This is my legacy—what I was always supposed to do in the end. Everything has led here.

Lily suddenly chimes in, "He has a business already. He doesn't have time for anything else."

It's true.

"Managers, *staff*," my father emphasizes. "He can leave Halway Comics in good hands, and Superheroes & Scones is practically running itself."

I shoot him a sharp look. "Lily does a lot—"

He cuts me off, "I expect Lily to put her best effort in the running too."

He can't be serious. "She's *pregnant*," I say with edge.

He outstretches his arms. "It's a *baby product* company. There is no better time for her to be involved than now. And when she gives birth, she can bring Maxof to some product testing."

"Maximoff," everyone corrects him.

"Get used to that." He scowls and searches the living room with his daggered gaze. Still no liquor cart. *Sorry, Dad.* "Not everyone will understand the things that you do."

Lily sits straighter. "I'll do it."

"Lily." I shake my head. "*No.*" The last thing that she needs is more anxiety.

She says, "Better me than you."

"No," I cringe, realizing exactly how Ryke just felt. I clench my teeth harder than before, more pissed now. I don't want the girls at Hale Co. I don't want this life for them.

They were free.

Weren't they?

"Both of you are self-sabotaging," I snap at Daisy and Lily.

"No," they reply adamantly.

I'm lying on the tracks of a train—letting it speed over me and just hoping that I'm not swept up in the momentum. It's now that I recognize what will happen.

We're all agreeing to my father's proposition *for* each other. No one will back down anymore.

I was indebted to my dad the moment he chose to let me live and enter this world. I thought I proved myself to him, but this future has been here all along, a path I knew I'd meet at some point. The suit and tie, the briefcase with the Hale Co. logo.

It's mine to take.

No one else should.

But everyone will fight for it. I can already see the wheels spinning in my brother's mind. His constricted muscles and the shake of his head that says *back down, let me have it*.

Ryke would endure hell for eternity if it meant that I could go to heaven.

Once upon a time I think I would've let him. Not anymore.

He deserves his paradise. So I'll fight against my brother. I'll fight against Lily and Daisy for this position. The winner is the loser.

And this cage has my name on it.

Thirteen

Loren Hale

"This is it?" I ask Ryke as he carries down Daisy's duffel bag. Rose has a five-piece suitcase stacked by the door along with the rest of our luggage for the yacht trip.

"That's it." He tosses the duffel on the pile. The girls are eating breakfast while we haul everything to the car. "How's Lily?" Ryke asks me in the foyer.

Connor abruptly finishes texting and straightens up off the wall.

"She's fine," I say vaguely. It's been a couple days since my dad unleashed the news about Hale Co., and afterward, I held Lily in my arms all night and tried to distract her with a Harry Potter marathon—something that wouldn't arouse her.

I think I said *no* only two times before she rolled away from me and tried to fight her compulsions. I have my fair share of ups and downs, but it'll always be harder watching Lily hit a low than going through my own. Watching someone you love in pain—and not being able to fix it—it's agony that I don't wish on anyone.

"Have you had sex?" Connor asks, while Ryke slips on his shoes, about to go for a short run with me. He bends down to tie the laces.

"Have you?" I retort. Connor knows the rules now. I'm not sharing details about my sex life without something in return.

Connor cups a mug of coffee. "She woke up to me thrusting inside of her. So I'd say yes."

My brows rise at *that* image. Jesus.

Still crouched, Ryke gapes at Connor. "You didn't really fuck her while she was asleep."

"She woke up a couple seconds after I pushed into her, which is the point." He sips his coffee and watches Ryke's expression darken. "Heel, boy," Connor banters.

I smile wide, even as Ryke stands an inch taller than me. Now he's closer to Connor's height than before. "Fucking hilarious."

"I thought so," Connor grins and sets his mug on an end table by the door. "I just know what my wife loves. If Daisy was into it, you'd do it too." I've never had sex with Lily like that—and honestly, I don't want to put the idea in her head. It's better if she doesn't expect it.

We've taken small steps throughout the years, like public sex. Her therapist actually approved of it—though she scolded us for lying in the first place and not admitting that we'd been doing it long before.

We were in the wrong for the lies. I think we both recognized that.

Now we're free of them again.

Ryke stretches his arm over his shoulder and lowers his voice. "Daisy would freak out if I fucked her while she was half asleep," he tells us. "She'd think I was someone who broke into the house . . ." He can't finish the rest, but his face twists. She'd think he was raping her.

I cringe. "She has some issues."

Ryke glares at me.

I raise my hands. "I meant that in a *nice* way." Though my sharp tone didn't help.

"Did you have sex last night?" Connor asks again, reverting back to the original topic. Me. Lily. Her addiction. It's an every week conversation. It doesn't aggravate me as much as it used to—not when they share too.

"Yeah," I say. "We waited twenty-four hours after she was really bad." She only came once, and then she stopped herself, a level of control that I worried she'd never reach.

"You're smiling," Connor notes.

"Must have been good," Ryke says, dropping his arm.

"It was." But for a different reason than they might think. "Ready?" I ask Ryke, opening the door. He nods, and as the February cold blows through, I pull my jacket hood over my head, snow lightly falling from the sky.

Ryke steps out of the doorway first, and a squishing noise freezes my bones. "Dick*fuckers*," Ryke curses.

"I thought we were banning that curse word from everyone's vocabulary?" Connor asks as he pushes the door further open so he can see what happened.

"Shit," I say and then laugh. *Literally*. My older brother just stepped into a pile of crap in a brown paper bag.

Connor laughs as Ryke shakes his foot like that'll get it off. "There are just too many responses to this."

"Shut the fuck up, Cobalt," Ryke retorts.

"Please, this can't be the first time you've been intimate with shit." Connor rubs his lips to keep from smiling so much, but he can't stop laughing. I hold on to the door frame, my side cramping while Ryke flashes his middle finger.

"Fuck off," Ryke groans and lifts his foot up with disgust. "Fucking A. I'm going to kill them." The sole of his shoe is most definitely covered in shit. And it must've been the teenagers down the street. They aren't finished with their pranks.

Great.

My laughter fades as I remember what happened with the paintball guns and the note attached to the brick.

Ryke is about to scrape his shoe on the brick stairs, and Connor grabs his shoulder to stop him. "Just toss your shoe in a doggy bag."

"Connor, I'm not—"

"Jokes aside, I'm serious," he says. "Don't smear it on the stairs." He cautiously looks over his shoulder and then back to us. "Rose doesn't need the stress before the trip."

"I'll clean the porch," I offer, just praying that they really did use dog shit.

"I got it," Ryke says, taking off his running shoe and disappearing inside for cleaning supplies.

I crane my neck and try to spot any sprinting teenager, but the long road is deserted this morning. Quiet and slick with a layer of snow and ice. I see my breath plume in the chilly air.

No one has brought up Hale Co.'s future since my dad was here. I try to mentally put it on the back burner so this trip won't be brutal. I should do the same with the teenagers down the street, but doubt enters me.

"What if they don't stop?" I ask Connor. *What if it gets worse than this?*

He's silent, and I turn my head to catch his features. He's staring through me, into me, seeing my fears because I spot them in his deep blue eyes, reflecting back at me.

"Then they don't stop," he says easily. Like it's nothing.

It is something though. "We're going to have children in this house soon."

"They're bored teenagers," he reminds me. "The more attention we give them, the more likely they'll return. We just have to be patient. I know it's hard for you . . . but you have to ignore the impulse that says *confront them.*"

I nod, staring fixedly at the ground. He's right.

It's a waiting game.

Fourteen

Lily Calloway

The swell of the ocean sways the yacht unstably, and I clamp on to the dresser in our cabin, steadying myself. Puerto Vallarta, Mexico, has been nice to me up until now. No sunburns on day one, no seasickness, and very little judgment from my parents.

Though I took a tiny peek at the tabloids.

They weren't kind.

The last poll was a blow to my confidence. *Is Lily Calloway fit to be a mother?* The gossip site accompanied this headline with a picture of me bending down on the yacht deck. I'd dropped my sunglasses earlier, and a stealthy cameraman on a tugboat caught me at the worst angle. Ryke was behind me. Lo was in front of me.

It looked bad. And the poll results aren't much better:

Yes: 36%

No: 64%

It's hard to stay positive when the world doesn't even have faith in you.

Good things have an expiration date.

Now the ocean has decided to rebel against gravity. The boat teeters, and I throw my gangly arms around the dresser, hugging an inanimate object for dear life.

I. Will. Not. Fall.

I shut my eyes tightly. What if we're sinking? I forgot to read about emergency exits and life jackets and things that Rose would've most definitely prepared for.

Maybe I do deserve that sixty-four percent skepticism.

I already suck at being a mom, and the baby isn't even *out* of my body yet.

A hand brushes my back. "Lil, the boat isn't rocking that badly," Lo coaxes.

My eyes snap open. Oh. We're *seemingly* level. "It's an illusion," I tell him. "A trick. Next thing you know, a boggart will come out of these drawers." Boggarts are kind of cool in the Harry Potter world. It's definitely an excuse to use a Patronus spell.

Lo is trying hard not to smile, but his cheeks dimple. "There's a problem, Lil. Neither of us are wizards."

I frown in distress. "But we have some sort of superpower," I say. "They just haven't kicked in yet." He opens his mouth, but I really can't handle any cynics right now. I want to believe we're magical. "Shhh, it's going to happen this weekend. I can feel it." And then the boat wobbles, and I cling harder to the dresser. "I forgot to read about emergency exits," I tell him. "If the boat sinks—"

"I have you, love." He slices through my panic, swooping his arm around my hips in the coziest Loren Hale embrace. He leans my back against the hardness of his chest, and my pulse begins to slow, my head whirling.

My fingers slip off the dresser in a single breath, and then he spins me around, confidence in his hypnotic amber eyes. His gaze relaxes any alarm, and my bones melt to a content stasis. He cups my face, and my body responds by curving into him.

I skim his features with meticulousness, etching the sharp lines of his jaw, those cheekbones. And the way his chest falls in a heavy, languid rhythm. My soul swells at the look behind his eyes, at the resolute, unbending expression he carries.

Loren Hale is ice.

Resilient isn't a word attached to him. Beneath fire, he loses. Ryke is the one who outlasts him. He's stone.

But there is something within Lo right now that defies this. I reach out, my fingertips grazing his smooth skin along his cheek, brushing his parted lips.

A feeling swirls inside of me—one where you know someone all your life, but in a singular moment they look strangely different. Like you're unearthing a fragment of them that has never surfaced or been touched before.

I see it—a piece of him uncloaked and unburied that has been hiding all this time. Strength that he never realized he had. My hand is magnetically drawn to his features, drifting to his neck.

He smiles through his eyes. "You don't look unsteady anymore."

Softly, I say, "You're a man."

His lips rise. "You're just now realizing this, Lily?" He licks his bottom one. It blazes my skin.

"It's just . . . you seem older," I breathe. *Stronger.* Able to withstand things that the world throws at him.

"Time will do that," he murmurs, his mouth so very close to mine. *Kiss me.*

"No," I whisper. "It's not time. It's something else." I inhale like our bodies have bound together, melded to him with no plan to separate.

His eyes glow with realization, sensing what I mean. He's not frightened of me or my addiction or his own. He has rebuilt every ounce of self-worth that his father took from him.

He leans close. *Kiss me.* But his lips breeze past my cheek and stop at the hollow of my ear. "You remember how it all began?"

His hands descend to my hips, diving toward my thighs. My fingers scrape along his toned shoulders, a sound tickling my throat.

I gather my breath to ask, "Me and you?" How we began. He guides me somewhere, my feet dazedly following his lead. And the backs of my legs hit the edge of the bed. A nautical comforter with tiny anchors printed across.

"You and me," he confirms.

I wrack my brain for the time, place, and date, my brows scrunching. "We were five . . . or six, right?" I should know the moment, but there are just so many that belong to Loren Hale. Picking out the first one would take decades.

"No, not as friends, Lil." He lifts underneath my arms and sets me perfectly on the bed. He leans my back against the soft mattress, and he hovers over me, his legs tangling with mine. Those amber eyes puncture straight through my skin and into my heart. "You remember how *we* began? *Us*."

Us . . .

The memory strikes me powerfully, and tears suddenly begin to brim. We were on my parents' yacht. *This* yacht. *This* room. Almost four years ago. We were both twenty and broken and struggling to find a semblance of peace. And then he uttered the words that changed everything.

Let me try to be enough for you.

"You remember," Lo breathes, his thumb brushing a stray tear.

"It was here." My voice is a whisper.

He nods. "It was here." His hypnotic expression pulls me into him, my pelvis bucking against his. He never breaks his soul-baring gaze from mine. "Back then," he says, "I was so addicted to you." He truly smiles, a very, very rare one. "I still am."

I am crying, flooded with emotions that cannot fit within my body. They explode outside of me—and I don't care to wipe them away. I just float through this bliss and let Loren Hale take me.

His fingers dip beneath my stretchy sweat shorts, and he tugs at the elastic, lowering them to my calves and burning my core with the slow, slow movement. "Back then, I asked you to be my girlfriend."

My heart hammers in my ears. To think of a time when we weren't even together, when I was no one's girlfriend—it's an ancient, dark era.

"And then I fucked you," he states matter-of-factly.

He spreads my legs open and stands at the foot of the bed. Then he pulls me so my bottom is half on the mattress, half off, and his semihard cock, through his jeans, puts pressure on a pulsing place of mine. My legs in his possession. I wonder if he can feel how wet I am—or if he can feel my heat drumming against him, craving him.

"I . . . I remember," I stammer, losing control of my vocabulary.

He pauses for a brief second, his eyes traversing across my body in hot waves. "This is going to be a million times better than that."

"Whaa . . ." I can't even finish my statement. The declaration arches my back, and I try to grind against him. *Closer.* But he has my legs hostage, my cheeks salty and tear-streaked. I am a mess, and the way Lo is staring at me, I might actually be a *sexy* mess too.

He suddenly drops to his knees. *Oh my God.* And then he lifts my legs over his shoulders. *Yesyesyes.*

I have no strength to prop my body, but I tilt my head at the right angle, gaining a visual. His eyes lock to mine as he places a tender kiss on the inside of my thigh. My mouth is permanently ajar, and a breathy sound emerges.

"Lo," I cry.

The featherlight kisses continue, nearing the aching spot. He has to be only an inch away when he draws back. *No!*

He takes his sweet time lowering my panties to my ankles, shifting my legs again, and then he fishes them off my feet and tosses them aside. He hikes my legs back over his shoulders, and the image makes me squirm. I need him.

I want him.

Right inside.

"*Lo.*"

"I'm going to make you come," he says with that Loren Hale sharp tone, deathly and alluring, "*so slowly.*" *Yes.* I cry in want, so ready, and his lips skim my leg, his breath warm and his teasing toxic. In the best possible way.

His hands rub against the soft flesh of my thighs. I reach out, placing my palms on top of them, hoping to guide them between my legs, but instead, they rise up to my ribs. Underneath my cotton shirt, up to my breasts.

Oh my God. He squeezes, his thumbs flicking my tender nipples. "I need you," I tell him, tears creasing my eyes again. Only these are from pleasure that he stretches out in infinite frequencies.

Kiss me right there. But he waits longer. He says, "I have a present for you."

Orgasms, I think. The gift is the best orgasm of my life. "I've been good," I remind him. In my recent hiccups, I came back strong and never drowned in the compulsive deep end of sex.

His smile pulls his lips. "You've been *great.*"

My mind dizzies. "Great is better than good." The spot clenches, my head tilting back. I'm going to come before he even gives me anything. "Lo!" I grip his forearms for support, my feet curving and my legs squirming on his shoulders.

He clutches my waist now, holding me steady. "Relax for me, Lil," he says in a sweetly edged voice. "No clenching."

I want to see how hard he is. I want him inside of me. Nothing else computes in my brain.

His head dips out of sight, and I feel his tongue, my legs twitching in response. He tightens his hold on one of them, still firmly in his care.

Oxygen whooshes from my lungs as he sucks and licks, caressing the most sensitive of nerves with his mouth. My eyes roll back, and no sound leaves as I come. Higher than high.

I don't even sense my body descending; I stay suspended in this climax. *More.* The response is normal for me.

I always want more.

And Lo knows this silent plea.

He gives me oral almost every day, but I recognize the difference the moment something hard presses against my other entrance. *Oh my God. Please, yes.*

My eyes burn with tears. "Lo," I cry. *Pleasepleaseplease let this be true and not in my mind.* I constrict in excitement and impulse, and then I wince at the pressure. *Oh God.*

His lips leave me, and I groan into the comforter.

"Relax, love," he reminds me.

We've had anal sex enough that I should know not to tighten so much, but my body responded on its own. Lo massages my thigh again, stirring my arousal. My mind is a mixer right now, blended with lust and longings.

Our doctor advised against anal sex while I'm pregnant, a restriction that's left me more than bummed. Which is why I ask, "Are you using your fingers?"

"No," he says. And his eyes carry the answer.

My eyes widen, my jaw unhinging. *Sex toys.* Oh my God. I tingle all over, imagining something long and hard inside of me, even though it's most likely just a small plug. "Are we allowed?" I whisper.

"I asked your ob-gyn. She said yes."

"Don't move," I blurt out. "Or I mean, move but . . . don't take it out, okay?" Fear surfaces—fear of this ending too soon.

"Shhh, Lil," he says. "Breathe slowly."

I can feel my rib cage jutting out with these sporadic inhales. I lie back more and shut my eyes. *He's going to fill me both places, at the same time*. It's a craving that I've wanted satiated for a while.

I try to relax my muscles, and his kisses begin again, soft and sweet, building up my need. I throb for a harder, deeper entry. And then he pushes on the toy, the pressure and sensations blind me. *Yes.* "Lo," I plead.

He rises to his feet, and seconds pass as he steps out of his jeans and black boxer briefs. He's harder than I even pictured, erect and as wanting as me. He pauses while I stare fixatedly at his long cock. *Inside now*, I mentally command. *Inside now.*

"Lil," he chokes, his arousal sweeping over his features.

I am full behind. I can't even imagine being full in the front too. I just haven't had it in so *so* long. Years. "Harder," I murmur. He hasn't even pushed into me yet.

He's too far away to hold. He's standing with my legs wrapped around his waist, my bottom off the mattress, while I'm lying. So I clutch the comforter in one hand and my breast with the other.

"Harder," I plead, his cock right there. I'm too exhausted from climaxing once already to thrust forward into him. He has most of the control, and that thought bridges me to a hotter, sweltering place. "Lo."

And then he pounds right into me, filling me hard. I am a goner. My body quakes, and he thrusts in melodic, deep rhythms that bring me to a new planet. A high-pitched gasp escapes my lips every time he slams *in*.

He rests one knee on the edge of the bed, and then another, climbing onto it and pulling my body up toward the pillow. His forearm sets beside my head, and he kisses the outside of my lips. Then he says, "Open."

I understand his request. I open my eyes, and he stares right into me as he thrusts. I can't corral the noises I make. I'm happy he's closer, nearer, so I can clutch onto his back and hold him to me.

I clench so hard that he only can go *in* and not out. It's a long-lasting euphoria. My head lolls and my eyes flutter as the high hits me. My spine arches, toes curling. A shiver runs through the length of my legs, and all the blissfulness in the world rains down on me.

I feel like I've just experienced sex and all its glory for the first time.

A sheen of sweat coats his shoulders, chest, and forehead, our breath ragged. He is grinning, his eyes full of knowing.

Yes, Loren Hale.

You are enough for me.

Fifteen

―――――

Lily Calloway

Daisy passes me the sunscreen in the living room area of the yacht. Our parents, Jonathan Hale, and his plus-one seclude themselves on sofas in the bow. I've noticed some uncomfortable tension during breakfast between them and us. My dad silently grabbed a bagel and went to the bow without a word. My mom followed quickly after.

"What happened last night?" I ask everyone. Daisy rubs sunscreen on her long legs while Rose flips through a magazine, Poppy sipping a mojito next to her. Rose shoots her looks for drinking a fruity alcoholic drink in her midst. I'm not so sad about the lack of alcohol during my pregnancy. I never drank much before it, but Rose does like her bloody marys, mimosas, and red wine.

"Didn't you hear the yelling?" Poppy asks me, adjusting her floppy straw hat.

"There was yelling?" My eyes cartoonishly pop out of my head. My orgasm was so supreme that it blocked out all other surrounding noises. Wow.

Pregnancy has its perks, but my horniness is both amazing and terrifying. Case in point, just remembering last night throbs my clit, blood rushing down there.

"Everyone should just forget it ever happened," Rose says uninterestedly.

"That's easy since I have no idea what it is," I mutter, squirting sunscreen on my palm. It makes a farting noise, and I whip my head around in embarrassment, hoping no one heard.

Daisy is smiling, though it's the kind of smile that makes me feel better. "Dad just got mad at me," she says. "It's my fault, anyway."

Rose snorts. "That's inaccurate."

"Rose is right," Poppy chimes in. "He's let you model in New York for years. He can't be upset now just because he *sees* how grown up you are."

"It's rude," Rose adds icily.

"It's not fair to you," Poppy rephrases in a warmer, softer tone.

Okay, the older sister support system is in check—minus me. I raise my hands, one of my arms still white with sunscreen. "What happened? Really?" I wonder if this is bad. Sex left me out of the loop again, but maybe this is different. That kind of sex was the best kind I've ever had. It can't be wrong.

Rose fans herself with her magazine, but Poppy beats her to the answer. "Dad learned that Ryke and Daisy were sharing a cabin. He said they weren't married or engaged, and he wanted them separated."

I frown. "Wait . . ." I shake my head. "That doesn't make sense. They've let Lo and me share a cabin since we were teenagers."

Rose tilts her head at me like I need to tap into my brain.

Oh. "It's Lo," I realize. He's always the exception. Well, Connor was too. Poppy's husband, Samuel Stokes, never got away with anything at first. He had to earn his way into my dad's good graces, and apparently Ryke does too.

"Ryke was angry," Poppy provides more details.

"He was *pissed*," Rose clarifies. I imagine his blood vessels ready to pop, his veins protruding in his biceps and forearms.

"Doesn't Dad know that you two live together?" I ask Daisy.

She tightens the straps of her neon green bikini and shakes her head. "No. He assumed we were staying in different rooms, like during *Princesses of Philly*."

Oh my God. My eyes are like saucers. This is really bad then. I picture my docile father growing horns toward Ryke. He probably thinks Ryke "deflowered" his youngest daughter. Not . . . exactly the case. "Did Ryke back down?"

"He tried as much as he could," Daisy says. "But Dad was basically attacking him."

The boat sways a bit, and Rose loses focus on the conversation, her skin paling. She shuts her eyes for a long, unsteady moment. It's hard to tell when Rose is sick, but she's been making frequent trips to the restroom. Her morning sickness is combating her seasickness in a not-so-nice way.

"This boat . . ." Rose says, drawing out her proclamation. ". . . is killing me. I am going to slaughter it by the end of this vacation. And if anyone has anything negative . . . or *rational* to say against me, I will push you overboard."

I'm not even going to tempt it.

Poppy reverts to the subject at hand. "I thought Ryke did a great job sticking up for himself and Daisy. He told Dad what everyone else wanted to say." I'm guessing that bit about Daisy being grown up. "With probably too many curse words," Poppy adds. "But Dad started yelling first."

My mouth drops. "What . . . ?"

"He was really mad," Daisy reminds me.

"Yeah, but . . ." That's crazy. I try to recall a single time when my dad raised his voice.

Off my confusion and shock, Poppy says, "He used to get so worked up over Sam that he'd start yelling. He's just worried about guys taking advantage of us."

Oh. My relationship with my dad is so dissimilar from my sisters'. He treated me more like his son than his daughter, letting me do what I pleased since he trusted Lo so much. I don't think he ever felt like he had to protect me like he does them.

My dad and I communicate in head nods, shoulder shrugs, and brief smiles.

Since my sex addiction, it took him a while to acknowledge me again. By not telling him my problems, I somehow broke our silent bond, something I didn't even really see until my therapist pointed it out. But we're okay now.

The smiles are back. The shoulder shrugs and shoulder pats happen more often. We haven't had any sort of emotional heart-to-heart, but I'm not looking for one.

"We're trying not to be disrespectful," Daisy explains about her situation with Ryke. "It's really fine if we stay in separate rooms."

It's her birthday. She deserves the orgasm that I had last night. That and more. I wish I could trade with her, but it's not looking possible.

Color returning to her cheeks, Rose eyes our oldest sister as she sips the mojito. "I hate you," Rose tells her, her glower drilling holes all over Poppy.

Poppy wipes her mouth with a napkin. "I remember you drinking *margaritas* while I was pregnant with Maria. So now you know how it feels."

Rose purses her lips, glaring now at the minty drink. "I bet it tastes horrible."

"It could be better," Poppy says nicely.

"I like you a little more."

While they talk, I spot a magazine on a rack by the wall, a shirtless Zac Efron on the cover. I throb again, an ache that grows at the sight of two-dimensional abs. When did the star of *High School Musical* look like that? Jeez.

I swallow hard, cursing my body. I had to even stop watching *Teen Wolf* this season for *this* very reason.

It makes me nervous. Lo tried to explain to me that the world isn't a porn-filled playground. I don't need to be frightened of my surroundings, even if everything turns me on. I just need to take deep breaths . . . I blow one out . . . and train my mind on different things, avoiding carnal fixations.

My mantra this trip: *I refuse to act on my arousal. Unless it's from Loren fucking Hale.*

I nod resolutely.

Now I must disappear and hide this red flush. "I'm heading out," I tell my sisters. All lathered in sunscreen, I exit through sliding glass doors and step onto the deck that overlooks the yacht's pool.

I stretch my arms, the afternoon rays beating down on my pale shoulders. Looking at the deck below, I skim the row of lounge chairs absentmindedly and then land on a supreme eight-pack with long masculine legs.

I freeze and do a literal double take at the toned body, with muscles that point toward his navy blue swim trunks, the guy's face blocked from view thanks to the bar.

My hormones do not care about my sanity.

I squeeze my thighs together, hot from more than just the sun. *Oh my God.* I know every ridge of Loren Hale's body, and this is not him. I burn with guilt. *I would never cheat on him*, I remind myself. I need a cold dip in the pool. Stat.

"His body is infuriating," Rose suddenly says beside me. I jump in fright.

"When did you . . ." I trail off as Daisy joins us, shutting the sliding door. Her yellow cast, with the words *Fuck Off* scrawled in Ryke's handwriting, is wrapped in plastic so she can get it wet.

Rose is focused on the guy below, resting her forearms on the railings, maybe in part to battle her seasickness. She shouts, "I hope you get a third degree burn and drown!"

What? My brows crinkle, and that's when the body stirs. Oh

no. Oh no. He sits up, bare feet dropping on either side of the lounge chair, and then he leans forward in plain sight.

Connor Cobalt.

I just got aroused from my sister's husband.

Someone I've never been attracted to like that. I'd like to say that pregnancy is awesome and beautiful, but this part is doing a number on me. I roast in embarrassment, unmoving, a statute on deck.

Connor wears classy sunglasses, a paperback in hand. And his grin widens at Rose. "You're wasting your hopes on the impossible, darling."

Rose straightens up and white-knuckles the railing. "I waste nothing more than you do."

"That's entirely false . . ." His gaze falls to her breasts, much larger, even in her black two-piece and sheer cover-up dress. ". . . but I'll let it go, this time."

"Watch out, Rose," Lo says, walking onto the pool deck below us, a towel slung over his shoulder. I scan his sculpted torso from hours in the gym, the view more pleasing and less humiliating. I wish I could send my body an *SOS: Loren Hale only!* signal. "I heard Connor likes spanking, *hard.*"

"Just heard?" Connor banters, his grin blinding.

Lo snaps his fingers in mock realization. "That's right, love, I forgot about last night."

"Impossible," Connor says. "I'm unforgettable." He winks at Lo, and I exhale loudly at the whole flirty male banter. An exhale that belongs to ravenous bedroom Lily 1.0. Not Lily 3.0.

Rose has completely zeroed in on her husband, but her face is clammy with sweat, her skin almost ashen. "Your hand is getting nowhere near my ass." Her threat sounds weak as she queasily rocks back.

Connor's grin vanishes in a second. "Rose?"

She puts a hand to her mouth and quickly spins to the sliding door.

Connor jolts to his feet, no longer humored. He sprints out of the pool deck toward the staircase. Rose darts inside the cabin where she came from. To go puke, most likely.

I can barely process my seesawing emotions, not when Connor runs across the second-floor deck. More concerned about his wife than anything else. He passes me and Daisy without a glance and disappears after my older sister.

The worst part: I still feel hot.

I take a quick look left and catch Daisy scrutinizing my beet-red expression. I try to play it cool, relax my arms, and offer her a small smile. She returns it and lightly hip-bumps me. "I know everyone didn't really have a choice, but I'm happy you're here," she says. "Thanks for coming."

Coming. I am on fire, paranoia heightening with the idea that *everyone* is reading my perverted thoughts. "Happy nineteenth," I tell her, which I should've this morning.

"Thanks." She smiles brighter. "I'm going to go get a drink from the bar. Do you want a water or anything?"

I shake my head. "I'll follow you down there though." We stroll along the skinny outside walkway. I just now recognize the muscle shirt she's wearing. I bought this one for her birthday: a print of a unicorn prancing in a field of daises with a rainbow. It reminded me of her, and I was too excited to wait until this weekend to reveal it. The white fabric covers her bikini.

"What'd Ryke get you?" I ask.

She shrugs and fixes her hair into a high bun. "He's not the gift-giver kind of guy."

Noooo. He did not forget. Rose texted him twenty different threats if he failed to remember Daisy's birthday present. I only know this because Ryke showed me a picture of a chopped, burnt hot dog that Rose sent him.

Thank goodness produce and meat products haven't turned me on. I'd be headed to a new horrible low if that happens.

"Ryke would make an exception for you," I tell her.

"It's okay." She shrugs again. I really can't tell if it bothers her or not.

And that's when Ryke climbs the stairs to our walkway, the stairs that we must descend. I've been successfully avoiding him since we baked cookies. I don't want to feel like a gross monster around Ryke, and until I figure out how to alter those feelings, I've decided to put myself in situations where I *can't* have them at all.

Which makes this run-in very, very awkward.

I go silent with Daisy, and we come to a sort of standstill. It's ten times worse because Ryke is very tanned and very shirtless. Another set of abs. More muscles that point to swim trunks, this time black ones with blue trim.

I find a solution, planting my gaze on his feet. Safe. There is nothing I can do about my embarrassed flush at this point. I just have to ignore it.

Ryke breaks the uneasy silence. "I left my sunglasses in the cabin."

Daisy lets out a mock gasp. "You mean these sunglasses?" She waves his black Wayfarers in the air and puts them on.

I take a peek, a mistake because he gives my little sister the longest once-over in history of once-overs. My breath feels shallow, and the shame starts rising like molten lava.

"Cute, Calloway."

I have to get out of here. I'll submerge my whole body in an ice-cold pool. Maybe it'll rewire my brain. Plan concocted, I step forward to dart away, my concentration back on the deck.

And then my chest instantly collides with Ryke. I flinch back. "Sorry!" I shout nervously, hands raised. I catch a glimpse of him, confusion knotting his eyebrows.

"Why are you fucking red?"

Oh my God.

"It's hot out," Daisy covers for me. She knows very well that this is a different sort of hot. And yet, she's on my side, sticking up for me—it's kindness that I love and cherish with all my heart. But guilt sinks low because I'm flushed partly from *her* boyfriend.

It's all screwed up.

I shield my face with a sweaty palm. "Yeah, it's really hot. Imheadingtothepool," I slur quickly, spinning on my heels to go to the stairs.

"We're right behind you," Ryke tells me.

And I suppress a shudder that borders fear (of myself) and something worse.

"*Not* like that, Lil." I hear the concern in his voice.

"IknowIknow," I mutter. I skip a couple steps on my way down to the main deck, and I round the corner toward the pool, tugging on the fabric of my one-piece that molds a very tiny baby bump. When the cool blue water comes into view, I ignore Lo on a lounge chair, and I'm prepared to just spring in.

I channel my inner dolphin.

Here I go.

I hop and splash into the pool, expecting the cold to breach my lungs, steal my breath, and fix everything.

Instead, the water warms my bones.

What. In. The. World.

I ungracefully surface, spitting chlorine water out of my mouth, the temperature of a *bath*. This did not go as planned. I comb my wet hair out of my face and eyes, and I try to heave my body out of the pool. I don't struggle for too long. Lo squats in front of me and effortlessly lifts underneath my arms.

I graze his features, lusting after his sheer masculinity. *Snap out of it, Lily.* I blink quickly, hoping he'll morph into a monster.

Not so. Loren Hale is striking and gorgeous through and

through. If he possesses any monstrous qualities, they're layered with beauty.

"Why are you so pretty?" I say.

His amber eyes penetrate me. "Just think about how awful I look in the morning."

I let out a small laugh. "You're still beautiful."

He lifts my chin so I stop staring at his lips. "Lily Calloway," he breathes, "you're doing really well. I'm proud of you." My heart swells.

He knows I'm aroused. He knows how hard it is to snuff out these feelings that pop up from almost anything and everything.

Dripping in water, I kiss his nose quickly, showing that I'm able to control this. Somewhat. And I choose the lounge chair next to his, lying down. "If I Jedi mind trick myself, all will be well," I tell him with a nod. I shut my eyes to attempt this.

I hear the legs of his lounge chair scrape along the deck. The frame touches mine, and he lies on his towel, close to me but not too close. A perfect untempting distance.

"You should know, Lil," he says in a low voice, "that every guy on this yacht has the hairiest goddamn feet. It's nothing but hobbits."

I smile, my eyes still closed. Although Frodo is cute, I'm pro-elves. "Are they all short too?"

"Oh yeah, they barely reach your waist."

"Except you," I say, licking my lips.

"I'm not an elf," he reminds me.

I pop one eye open and turn my head. He's lying on his back like me. "You're a wizard—"

"No, Lil," he whispers. "I'm human."

I shift on my side, my legs crossed together. I reach out to hold his hand, and he lets me, not scared of enabling. "Do you think our baby will have powers though? Even if we're human, he could be magical?"

Lo nods determinedly. "Definitely. He'll be the strongest guy ever."

"Like Professor Xavier." I smile at the image. But it fades quickly. "Do you think . . . do you think he'll forget about us, if we're just human and he's something more?" Beads of water roll down my temple.

Lo's hand rises to my arm, and he rubs my skin soothingly. The embrace comforts me more than it arouses. "I don't know," he says honestly. "I guess we'll see."

Yeah. I guess we will.

I've drawn closer to Lo, I realize, my ankle hooked over his, but it's not a sexual action. It's just a natural one.

While Lo grabs waters from inside, I decide to wade in the pool for longer than a couple seconds this time. I've been scrolling through his cell phone. Not the best idea since that picture of me bent over, reaching for sunglasses, has turned into an internet meme. My brows crinkle at the dozens of photoshopped images. There's one where Ryke grabs me from behind instead of just standing there.

Where I'm reaching for a dildo instead of sunglasses.

Where Loren and Ryke are cropped out and replaced by hot dogs.

It's awful. Though their photoshop skills are pretty good. I have to give them credit for that.

"Connor," Rose says, her lounge chair scooted next to his. A paperback perched on his lap, his hand has yet to leave her bare neck. He massages her while she clutches an empty ice bucket. Rose risked vomiting again to join me outside.

It takes a solid second to realize that Rose commanded him to do something since she's out of commission. Connor needs no more info to read her well.

He just stretches forward and *steals* the phone right from me. And then he settles back, his hand returning to Rose like nothing just happened.

"That was mean," I tell him. "I was doing important research."

"If I didn't do it, she would've tried," Connor explains, passing the cell to my sister. "And I don't want my wife moving around."

Rose searches through the phone's history and gives me a cold look.

I raise my hands out of the pool. "They were hard to avoid."

"The more you stare at these, the more paranoid you become. If *anyone* is jumping overboard, it's *me*." She went from slaughtering the boat to drowning herself. I take it that she's feeling pretty lousy still.

Connor flips a page in his book and says something in French.

She replies back, shutting her eyes tightly. He pulls her closer to his side, his arm sliding around her shoulders. Hugging her in comfort. He whispers another French word and then kisses her forehead.

I frown, wishing I could understand them. Even with my studying, I can only pick up a few words here and there. I block the sun with my fingers and scrutinize the spine on Connor's book. A smile replaces my frown. It's C. S. Lewis' *The Voyage of the Dawn Treader*.

For Christmas, I gifted Connor the entire Chronicles of Narnia series. Normal people ask for things *they* want for Christmas, but Connor asked us to gift him things we like. He consumed Lo's present—George R. R. Martin's Song of Fire and Ice series—in a matter of three weeks. Now he must be working on my gift.

In a happier mood, my gaze drifts and lands on Ryke and Daisy, both sitting on the silver railing near the stern. We're anchored, so the yacht doesn't wobble too badly. Daisy takes off her shirt, and Ryke wears her hairband around his wrist. Her blonde hair and dyed green tips are tangled and slightly frizzy.

I'm too far away to pick up their conversation, though Ryke smiles and that says enough.

"They're a good couple," I say aloud. And then I turn back to Rose and Connor, leaning my arms against the ledge. "Why does the media insist on destroying something beautiful?"

Rose slips her Chancl sunglasses on, her knee curved toward Connor, almost lying on her side. She seems more relaxed though.

Connor glances at Rose, his hand placed on her thigh. "Is this a rhetorical question?"

"I think so."

It wasn't, but maybe there isn't an answer.

Connor ditches his book to scroll through his phone, glimpsing at Rose every half minute to check on her. And when his eyes fix back on the cell, he suddenly frowns. "Lily, did you . . ." Even though his chair is propped up, he sits even straighter. "You joined Twitter?"

"Just for two seconds," I say, raising my hands again. It was really hard finding a username since variations of "Lily Calloway" were already taken by fans. I ended up with @lilycallowayX23, and I sent a total of *three* very important tweets.

"Right now?" he asks. "You joined Twitter five minutes ago, while we were all sitting here?"

I squint. "Is this a rhetorical question?"

Rose snatches his phone to confirm. "I don't understand why you always use that OTP thing."

"Because it's awesome," I say like it's the most obvious thing in the world. "I had to let the Twitterverse know that I am one-hundred-percent in support of Team Raisy." Our publicists should've thought of this strategy months ago. I'm only helping.

And these should clear up my stance on the matter. Tweet 1: *This is the official Twitter account of Lily Calloway. Hooray!*

I had to announce myself.

Tweet 2: *#Raisy is my favorite OTP. I ship it.*

Tweet 3: *Ryke & Daisy are cuter than cute right now. #Raisy is alive.*

I will make this trend. No more stupid "Raisy is dead" anymore.

"I know I didn't pass it by the publicist," I say, "but it really can only help."

Connor and Rose suddenly go quiet and very still. They exchange a few words in French to each other, and she delicately passes him his phone back.

I frown. "What?"

They're holding hands now. Like a united force.

My heart thuds.

Connor actually removes his sunglasses, his blue eyes very calm. It makes me less nervous. "Lily," he says, "it sort of seems like you're trying too hard. Does that make sense?"

"She understands," Rose tells him. "You don't have to talk down to her."

I don't understand though. "I'm just expressing myself."

"You need to tweet more then," he tells me. "Because the way this comes across—it makes it look like you're trying to cover up something."

I shake my head fiercely. "That's not what I was trying to do."

"I know," he says quickly. "I know, and other people will believe you."

"Okay good." I swallow a lump that's risen. *Where's Lo?*

Daisy is laughing, full-bellied laughs that pulls my attention over to her. Ryke has a brooding expression, but his lips curve upward too.

In two seconds flat, Ryke purposefully shoves Daisy's shoulder. With force.

She plummets off the side of the boat, a larger laugh echoing. It looked mean, not nice or friendly, but I'm sure my wild, daring sister loved it.

"Ryke!" A strict voice booms across the stern. My father—with his salt-and-pepper hair, pressed khakis, and polo shirt—storms over to this side of the boat. He looks ready to throw Ryke overboard.

Connor and Rose straighten, on alert.

My nerves swarm my belly, and I glance over my shoulder, waiting for Lo to appear. He's nowhere in sight though.

"You can't just push my daughter off the boat!" my father yells.

Ryke stands, but he's still outside the railing. His muscles are all strained, and his jaw locks, which isn't the only sign that he's frustrated and angry. It's all over his face. "No offense, but everything I fucking do annoys you."

"Then maybe you should change that," my dad retorts.

Ryke instinctively shakes his head.

"No?" my dad says with distaste. Their voices are much louder than Ryke's previous conversation with Daisy. I can hear most everything.

"Look, can we just fucking start over?" Ryke asks. "I'm *trying*—"

"The most you've done is bring my daughter back from Costa Rica with a broken arm and then write a profanity on her cast. And *no*, we are not starting over. I'm not going to forget how you lied to me about your relationship with her or about living together. I can, however, weigh that against your actions now. Do you understand?"

Ryke restrains himself from rolling his eyes.

Even though I've been distancing myself from him, I can still cheer him on. Internally I'm holding up a Team Ryke sign. *You're doing great, Ryke.* This really is hard for him. He's so unchanging, unbending. Unlike Connor, who's able to conform to any situation with fluidity.

Ryke takes a controlled breath, and he glances over the boat, checking on Daisy, before he looks back at my father. "I fucking realize that I'm the reason she broke her arm. I take full responsibility for that, but it was also an accident. She's been in a lot of those that don't even involve me."

In Costa Rica, Ryke dared Daisy to jump off the top of a waterfall. After he did it. Halfway up her climb to the top, she slipped on the wet rock and landed badly on her arm. Apparently Ryke didn't even know she broke a bone. He said that he was about to go after her, but then she jumped off the bottom ledge into the lagoon.

When she swam up to him, he figured it out. And I could tell— just by his recount of the story—that he blamed himself. He said that if he was spotting her, she wouldn't have broken a thing.

On the yacht, I don't hear my dad's response. A splash sounds in the pool, the water spraying my already damp hair. I spin around and see a figure swimming underneath the water toward me.

I recognize Lo's black swim trunks, and my world lights up. He nears me, his hands skimming my thighs, and his teeth playfully nip my flesh. My breath hitches, and for a dangerous second, I wonder if he'll move to another spot. One that calls for his attention.

Cool yourself, Lily.

I repeat the mantra again, and his head pops out of the water, his hands sliding to the small of my back, away from the aching places. It's better like this.

He brushes his light brown hair out of his face, pretty sexily, and I have to start thinking about hobbits. With large hairy feet. "Did I miss much?" he asks.

I avoid the subject of Twitter and just motion to his brother, who's gone on the defensive again. Ryke stays silent while my dad lectures him about protecting my little sister.

"Yeah, that was bound to happen again," Lo says with a cringe like he wishes it wasn't written in stone. I do too. "I'm going to go help him . . ." Lo is about to climb out of the pool when Ryke shakes his head at my dad, turns his back on him, and literally springs off the side of the boat into the ocean.

It's either incredibly dumb or by far the coolest thing he's ever done.

I think my father was in the middle of a sentence.

My dad's face turns bright red. No one says anything. Except for Lo. "My older brother just took *shut the fuck up* to a whole new level." He lets out an amazed laugh. "I would slow clap but your dad is walking this way . . ." My father glances at us with a huff, and Lo and Connor smile at the same time. A trained fake one that Ryke has yet to learn.

Lo waves, and my father waves tersely back before disappearing inside.

Connor leans against the lounge chair. "This is what happens when you bring dogs on boats. They jump off."

"Greg is still hoping Ryke can be trained." Lo kisses my cheek, a random kiss that surprises me. I cling to his side and rest my head on his chest, water droplets rolling down his skin.

Connor goes quiet before he says, "Some people are better as they are."

My eyes grow in shock.

Connor doesn't want Ryke to change. Not that much at least.

I don't think any of us do, but there's no question that he's going to have to follow some of my father's rules. If he doesn't, I'm afraid it'll put an irreparable strain on his relationship with Daisy.

And they just have to last.

Raisy is alive. I won't believe in anything less.

Sixteen

Loren Hale

E ven on vacation, to a country I love, my dad never lets me forget reality. He emailed me profiles of every Hale Co. board member with their likes and dislikes. He's trying to give me an advantage over Lily, Ryke, and Daisy. I rarely attempt to change people's perceptions of me, to kiss ass. I'm afraid the minute I step through the Hale Co. glass double doors, they're going to say, *what is this fucking kid doing here?*

He's an alcoholic.

He was expelled from college.

He's a loser.

I'm a natural-born failure.

But I don't want my son to grow up and have these same impressions of me. I want to be known for more than all of that. I just don't know how. Part of me believes it's impossible. I can't move mountains, no matter how hard I push.

Stop thinking, I tell myself. My mind won't shut off. In the yacht's cabin, I lie on the bed next to Lily, who's in a deep sleep. I check the clock: 4 a.m.

Four years ago, I'd go grab a bottle of Jameson. Take more than a few swigs. Call it a night after an hour.

I let out a heavy breath and quietly climb off the bed.

The moon bathes the room in blue, and I see a direct path to the door. I sneak out, gently shutting it behind me. And then I proceed down the hallway, knowing my course and destination.

I stop in front of another cabin, lamp light glowing beneath the door. No hesitation or second-guessing, I just open it.

Ryke leans against the headboard, in only sweatpants, a paperback folded in hand. His eyes meet mine with questioning and concern. He's alone, so I close the door and walk farther inside.

"Hey," he says while I take a seat on a wooden chair that faces his bed.

I'm not surprised that he's awake. If anyone has a fucked-up internal clock, it's my older brother. He'll alternate between 5 a.m. mornings to 5 a.m. nights, depending on who needs his help and if he's going climbing.

I rest my forearms on my thighs, slightly hunched. My fingers vibrate, and my leg jostles more than I like. I rub my lips, but it's clear that he sees my anxiety.

I let out another breath and look up at him. He has his arms on his bent knees, and my eyes fall to the paperback, loosely hanging by his fingers, a picture of a bull on the front cover. "What are you reading?"

His eyes flit to the book. "*The Sun Also Rises.*"

I frown, making out the title from here. "That's not what it says."

He tucks the novel away, underneath his pillow. "It's in Spanish."

Right. I try to smile but it's a bitter one. He's fluent in more languages than I can ever learn. "Is it good?" I ask.

He shrugs. "It's okay." He studies my expression for too long, and my gaze drops to my shaking hands.

I breathe out, the strain bursting my lungs. I imagine my nonconformist brother in a suit and tie, pretending to be something he's not. Entering this bullshit world that he's purposefully escaped. It's wrong, and I suddenly say, "I don't want you to change." It's not all selfless. I need him the way that he is.

"You know me," he says—three words that weren't true for decades of time. "Do you really think I can fucking change?"

I never thought he could. "The board will never choose you, you realize that?" I snap, my voice more edged. Remorse twists my face. "Not as you are, I mean." He curses too much. He's late to everything, even his own birthday. He shelters his intelligence from every fucking person—so they just see this aggressive, unfiltered guy. But all of this is why he's Ryke Meadows and not me, not Connor.

It's part of why I love him.

"Fuck them, then," he says. "But I'm still trying."

He also never gives up.

I'm scared because I always do, in the end. Pitted against each other—I lose. Every time. I put my fingers up to my lips, my palms pressed together. My foot still taps the ground. And I say, "Just give it to me."

His features darken, and he slides to the edge of the bed, sitting closer to me as his bare feet hit the floor. "No," he says, one word that tears a fucking hole inside of me.

"No?" I glare, grinding my teeth. "You don't even *want* it."

"Neither do you," he refutes. "How many times do I have to fucking tell you, Lo, that you don't owe *him* one fucking thing?" He points at the door.

I swallow hard. "I'm alive because—"

"Because Dad said *yes* to keeping you? Decent people don't use that to blackmail their children. You had *no choice* in coming into this fucking world. You should have a choice on what you do with your life afterward. And he's taking that away from you."

I shake my head on impulse, but I catch myself and stop. I rub my eyes with the heels of my palms. He's taking that choice away from Ryke too.

My brother leans forward. "Lo, *please* drop out of this. It's going to make you fucking sick."

I tug at the collar of my crew neck with a cringe. For once, I want to be the strong one. I want to save my brother from this hell. And he's saying that I'm too weak for it. That I'll destroy myself before I ever have the chance.

I'd like to believe that I'm better now, but it's easy to say that I am. It's harder to prove it. *I want to.* God I want to. "I think . . . we're both in agreement that neither of the girls should take over Hale Co.," I say.

Ryke nods adamantly.

Lily is about to have a baby. Daisy should be outside or whatever she likes to do. They're only trying to win this because they know that neither Ryke nor I want to live this life.

They're trying to protect us as much as we're trying to protect them.

I ask, "So why don't we just work together at the beginning?" If we help each other, maybe the girls won't even have a chance. It's a compromise, but in my mind, I see myself taking more of the burden from him. I will, in the end. I'm going to carry his weight for once. "Us against the girls."

Ryke considers this for a second, his fingers combing through his disheveled hair. And then his brown eyes flit up to mine. "I thought you said the board would never take me as I am." It'll be hard. But we'll still have a shot. We're Jonathan's sons. "Why would you want to work with me?"

"Because you're my brother," I say without pause, "and I'd rather be with you than against you."

I can't fight with Ryke. I need him on my side until the very end, until one of us is chosen. Maybe one day Connor and Ryke will pull away from me, and I'll no longer lean on them for support.

But it's only been four months since I last drank alcohol, and their fears have become mine. Of relapsing. I need him.

I need my brother.

I sit up and pull my shoulder back. "So how about it, Ryke Meadows, you want to be miserable with me?"

This is difficult for him to accept.

I see it in his eyes. By agreeing, he's willfully subjecting me to a certain torture. He'd rather beat me. I'd rather beat him—but I'm not sure I can at the beginning: when I first walk through those glass double doors, when I meet the board's judgment.

Before I run on my own, I need a crutch. It's either Ryke Meadows or a bottle of booze. And I can't let it be the latter.

So this is what I have to do. *Please. Say yes.*

He rises to his feet, and I do the same, my heart thrashing in my chest. And then he grabs my hand and hugs me, setting a palm on my back. "Okay," he says. "Let's do this together, little brother."

My muscles finally loosen for the first time that night.

When we break apart, something bangs into the door. We both flinch, and the sound happens again, a softer *thud* this time.

I step forward, but Ryke holds out his hand and says, "I got it." He cautiously heads to the door and cracks it open. Then he quickly swings it open.

Daisy stands on the other side, her eyes dazed and far off.

"Daisy?" Ryke says, concern all over his features. He waves his hand at her face. She doesn't even blink. "Fuck," he curses.

"She's sleepwalking," I guess.

"Yeah." He moves out of the way as she shuffles forward. "She's done this a couple times since her new meds." He gently places a hand on her shoulders and sort of guides her toward the bed without being forceful about it.

I hang back. "Need help?"

"No, I'm good," he says as Daisy sits on the navy comforter. He's able to lift her legs up on the mattress, and then he tucks her underneath the blankets while she shuts her eyes. "Fucking fantastic," he mutters and glances back at me. "I bet you Greg will notice that she's not in her bedroom in the morning."

"I'll tell him that she spent the night with Lily."

Ryke rocks back in surprise.

I head to the door. "You don't have to do everything on your own," I remind him. "I can help you too, you know." I hear my biting tone again. I wish I could wash it away. But maybe that's impossible.

He nods a couple times to himself. "I appreciate it."

"Just don't ask me for sex advice. I gave it to you fucking once, and you rejected me. A guy can only take so much."

Ryke flips me off with a weak smile, and then his attention falls back to the blonde girl in his bed. Tomorrow we're going onshore to Puerto Vallarta—Daisy doesn't know about what Ryke planned. Neither do the girls.

It'll be a surprise for her birthday.

Hopefully a good one.

Seventeen

Lily Calloway

Virgin margarita," I emphasize for the tenth time. The Spanish translation can't be that far off from my English. I have a feeling the thirty-something bartender understands this phrase. Especially as he laughs like I should be "living it up" and drinking tequila straight from the bottle. My stomach is blocked by the bar, so it's not like he can physically see my reasoning.

He speaks in Spanish a little bit and then begins pouring shots.

My eyes bulge. "Nonono." I wave my hand like I have a superpower to reverse time. If only that were the case—but I'd find better use for it. When I acquire my powers, I won't waste them on things like this.

The nightclub slowly amasses with people, multicolored strobe lights swirling and Latin music booming over the speakers. Even though it's not electronica, it's extremely danceable. A-plus-plus.

"Pregnant," I tell him, pointing to my belly that's hidden behind the bar.

He pushes the shots to me, and then his gaze rises behind my shoulder. "Is that your boyfriend?" He speaks English?!

Internally, I fume. But outwardly, I probably look like a

washed-ashore jellyfish. I check over my shoulder, and Garth, my two-hundred-and-fifty-pound bodyguard, stands behind me with his hands cupped. He's more gut than brawn, his bald head shiny in the light. But he looks intimidating to me.

And old enough to be my *dad*.

Which is why I spin around and try to set a withering Rose Calloway glare on the bartender. "No, he's *not* my boyfriend."

"What about that one?" He points over my shoulder with an amused smile. He's busting my balls. I look anyway and see Mikey— a blond, shorter bodyguard with a Hawaiian shirt—and Dave, who wears black sunglasses indoors. Dave is Poppy's middle-aged bodyguard. Mikey is Daisy's. And I suppose, in effect, Rose's bottle of pepper spray is hers.

Right on time, my three sisters appear, swarming the bar around me, and I exhale in relief.

"Are you seriously trying to serve a pregnant woman shots?" Rose says icily.

The bartender not so subtly ogles her breasts.

"Also pregnant," Rose snaps, "and even if I *wasn't*, I'd throw salt in your eyes." She actually reaches for the salt shaker, and Daisy snatches her arm.

"No fights on my birthday, remember?" Daisy says, bouncing on her toes to the music.

"It's the day *after* your birthday," Rose reminds her. "That window has closed." She's still angry that Ryke pushed all of the plans for Daisy's birthday to the twenty-first without mentioning it to her. She's out of the loop once again.

I didn't know about it either. It's another indication that the guys are teaming up. Or maybe they thought we couldn't keep a secret from our little sister.

Regardless, it was a good thing Ryke chose today to really celebrate Daisy turning nineteen. Our mom wanted to spend time with Daisy, so Ryke scheduled ATVs and bungee jumping this morning and afternoon. Not that Rose or I could join in—or that she'd want to.

Now we're topping it off with some drinks and dancing. Sans the alcohol for me.

Rose is having a stare-a-thon with the bartender, who is not necessarily lusting after her anymore. He's just trying to enrage her—something Connor does better than anyone else. *Where is he?*

My head whips around, and I meet Poppy's warm gaze. "The guys aren't back yet," she tells me.

My stomach knots, worried they got lost or something worse happened. I check my texts, no new messages from Lo. The guys split from us after dinner. They said they wanted to go to a cigar shop, but I've never even seen Ryke or Lo willingly smoke before.

"Who's *not* pregnant?" the bartender asks us with a sexy lilt. I'm not staring at him too hard—keeping my hormones at bay. My sisters and I are actually standing in a row, oldest to youngest.

"We aren't," Poppy announces, motioning to herself and Daisy on the other end.

"Rub it in," Rose snaps.

Poppy smiles, used to Rose—as we all are.

Daisy wraps her arm around my shoulders, and I tell the bartender, "It's her birthday." I gesture up at my five-foot-eleven sister.

The bartender zeroes in on her like I said *she's the one you should fuck*. Not my intention at all. I open my mouth to refute, but instead of a yearning gaze, he cringes, unable to hide his reaction to Daisy's scar that runs along her cheek.

Daisy just smiles politely, but she falls to the flats of her feet. I nudge her hip, but she gives me a weak smile too, like *it's okay*.

It doesn't feel like that.

He's already splitting up the shots between Poppy and Daisy.

"We'd like two virgin margaritas," Rose tells him, and she touches the top of my head to demonstrate that one is for me. "And if you poison my baby with alcohol, I will severely harm you."

The guy laughs.

"I wasn't joking," Rose says.

"Who's the father? The bald one?" He nods to the bodyguards again. Why does he keep saying that Garth is the father of our children? It's disturbing.

"That's rude," Poppy says before Rose can annihilate him with her glare and manicured nails.

"They've been following you throughout the club," he explains.

"They're our bodyguards," Daisy clarifies, fixing the hair underneath her baseball cap before she wears it backward again. Her blonde locks now shroud her scar.

"He knows that," Rose says, her yellow-green eyes never leaving his.

I have a feeling he's going to spit in our margaritas. Not that I want anything from him anymore.

But Rose is right on one account. He should know they're bodyguards, even if he's not sure *who* we are. We've brought more attention to ourselves in the club, especially by being together. I already see some people snapping photos of us with their cell phones and whispering to their friends. I've been approached three or four times by fans, asking for an autograph and selfie.

It always surprises me that people beyond the United States are interested in us. *Princesses of Philly* made my family more famous than I can even process sometimes. We're now internationally recognized. It's easier living in our own bubble of normalcy. When we step out—that's when it's crazy.

Poppy and Daisy clink glasses and then down their tequila shots while the bartender starts making our drinks. "Have the guys texted you?" I ask my sisters.

They all check their phones.

"No," Daisy says, slipping her cell in her short's pocket. She subconsciously touches the green and yellow hemp bracelet that

Ryke made for her birthday. A simple present that has more love in it than anything store-bought.

He did well.

"None from Sam," Poppy says.

Rose shakes her head, though she's the only one who sends a text back.

The bartender pours tequila into more shot glasses. He slides another one to Daisy. "For the birthday girl." He's sweet to her now, but I wonder if it's because she hid her scar or because he pities her.

Either way, it hurts to think about.

"Let me guess your age," he says with a smile.

I check my phone again. No texts. I bite my nails and then drop my hand quickly. Rose caught me though, a fiery glare scorching me.

"Only if you let me guess yours," Daisy replies, twirling a drink napkin on the bar.

His face lights up, and he rests his forearms on the counter, peering over it. He scans her entire body, lingering on her long legs. "Just making sure you aren't pregnant."

Rose mutters a violent curse under her breath. I only heard *penis*. Poppy is holding Rose's wrist in a maternal vise, one that also says *cool your jets*.

My jets are too cold. They're frozen to a statue-like posture. Our trip really has gone smoothly thus far. Not too much drama besides my father. It's bound to take a wrong turn somewhere, and I think tonight is the night. I'm just waiting for it, watching the storm clouds roll in.

"No baby in the oven," Daisy says easily, though she concentrates more on the napkin than on the guy.

"You're twenty-five," he guesses.

Daisy mock gasps. "How'd you know?"

"I'm good with faces." He smiles.

Rose snorts.

I laugh once, but it fades as he soaks in Daisy's slender, athletic frame.

"Your turn," he tells her.

Daisy takes the shot, licks her tequila-wet lips, and says, "You're eighty-nine, or maybe seventy-four."

"Nice try," he says, pouring her another shot. "I'm thirty-two."

She gasps again. "I wasn't right? I thought for sure you were a little blind in your right eye."

His lips downturn.

"I'm *nineteen*," Daisy retorts. "Nice try."

My smile overtakes my face. That was awesome. I raise my hand for a high five, and Daisy smacks my palm.

The shock passes through his features quickly. "That doesn't mean much to me," he says, "other than your pussy being tighter than your sisters."

All of our mouths simultaneously drop, except Rose, who is about to punch him. But she can't. Hands swoop around her waist from behind.

Connor.

And Ryke suddenly appears beside Daisy with a murderous glare, directed at the bartender. Oh shit. "Lily," Lo says my name in my ear.

My chest rises. They're all back. Unharmed it seems. Even Sam, Poppy's husband, his jaw unshaven like Ryke, and his features just as masculine as the rest of them.

Ryke has a paper bag in his clenched fist. *Cigars*, I think. To the bartender, he growls, "I don't even know what to fucking say to you."

"I do," Lo sneers; then he motions between Ryke and Daisy. "They're together, you dumb fuck. So swallow your tongue. And consider yourself lucky that only three out of eight people pray you choke on it." I'm guessing that's Ryke, Lo, and Rose. The hot-tempered triad.

I smile again, even though this is not the time to be smiling like a dopey fool. I just never really saw the three of them as a team like that until now.

"I say we cut it off," Rose threatens.

Connor, standing behind Rose, puts his hand to her forehead like he's checking her temperature. She swats his arm away. He says, "I'm just seeing if rage can boil a brain."

"My brain is working perfectly," she says. "I see a disgusting human being and it says *die*."

Connor is grinning from ear to ear. "Your brain has no mercy, darling."

She can't reply because the bartender interjects and points at Daisy accusingly. "She was flirting with me. I had no idea that she had a boyfriend." Oh my God.

Daisy pales. "I was not—"

"*Let me guess yours*," he says in a high-pitched tone that sounds *nothing* like Daisy.

"Fuck you," Ryke cuts in, his hand on Daisy's shoulder. "Come on, Dais."

The bartender can't let it go. "I'm just telling the truth."

Ryke growls, "And I'm telling you to *fuck off*."

I interject (yes, me of all people) and say, "You can keep the margarita." Out of principle, I won't drink anything that has been touched by his hands. He threw my sister under the bus, which I do not appreciate.

I spin around, and I'm shocked to see not only Rose following suit, but also Poppy and Daisy. I was the leader of this movement, heading toward an open leather couch by the wall. The trek involves being the center of attention, with camera phones pointed at us. But we all make it safely and settle there.

I sit between Lo's legs, leaning back against his chest so we all have room. I like it best here.

I look up and whisper to him, "You were gone for a while."

His eyes are daggered sharp, and something tells me it's not because of the bartender. "There were a lot of tourists out."

I don't believe that. It's February, and for the most part, the nightclub is sparse with mostly locals. "Are you lying to me?" I breathe, my face plummeting. Is it really guys versus girls to this extent?

He winces and dips his head closer to mine, his lips beside my ear. "All day, we've been followed by three guys, and we were trying to ditch them."

I frown. "What kind of guys?"

He explains quickly, "They're not paparazzi. They're either on vacation or they live here, but they wouldn't leave Ryke and me alone at the ATV park. They were trying to get a reaction out of us." His jaw is all ice tonight.

Cold rushes down my arms. "Did they say anything in particular?" I mentally recall all the rumors involving me, Lo, and Ryke.

"I don't know," he says in frustration.

"But . . . you heard them, right? They were close?" Or were they out of earshot?

Lo grinds his teeth. "They only spoke in Spanish."

Oh.

Oh. That means that Ryke hasn't translated everything for Lo. And neither has Connor, who's also fluent.

"It's aggravating," Lo says under his breath. They're censoring Lo, afraid that he'll be hurt and react poorly, like by drinking.

I hug my scrawny arms around his chest. "I believe in you."

I feel him inhale strongly, and then he kisses my temple. "I love you, Lil." His arms tighten around me.

I love you too, Loren Hale. He suddenly kisses me again, this time on the lips. Since he doesn't have telepathy (yet), I have to assume my eyes did all the talking.

"What's in the paper bag?" Daisy asks Ryke. My thoughts re-route. Ryke acts like it's nothing, just clutching the brown paper bag. He scrutinizes her hair that's draped over her scar, and he ends up stealing her baseball cap (really, it's his). And he wears it backward on his head. They're scooched together near us, and the other two couples are squashed on the opposing couch.

Sam is whispering in Poppy's ear with a huge smile, and she's laughing like he's telling the funniest story ever. It's what Rose would call "nauseating" and her eye roll right now expresses that.

"Can you tone down your *happy*?" Rose snaps.

Lo drapes his arms over my shoulders and holds me close. "Rose is allergic to happiness and kids. It's what gives her horns."

"Then you must be suffering from the same affliction," she retorts. "Look in the mirror."

I hold my breath, hoping this ends at that.

"My horns aren't encrusted with diamonds," Lo says. "So we're not the same."

Rose's lips slowly rise. Loren Hale made Rose Calloway *smile*. This is a first if there ever was one.

Connor is subtly massaging his wife's shoulder, and if she could see his overwhelming grin right now, she'd probably combat him with even more fiery passion. Nerd stars combusting—but not in a bad way or permanently. That's *never* happening. I nod to myself.

"Everyone," Connor says, gathering our attention with one word. I follow his gaze that has shifted to Ryke, who's removed the contents of the paper bag already, in his own world with Daisy.

It's a plastic carton. He pops the lid, places the carton on her lap, and then reaches into his pocket, pulling out a lighter.

My heart swells at the realization, and I peek into the carton to confirm.

Inside lies a slice of molten chocolate cake.

Connor's grin has nothing on Daisy's bright smile, a contagious one that causes our lips to lift just as high. Even Rose is showing off her pearly whites.

Chocolate cake.

That is what all four guys had been searching for. Not cigars.

It's possibly one of the sweetest, kindest gestures I've seen, because it's something that Daisy loves.

Ryke lights the waxy candle, and then he messes her hair with a rough, caring hand. And we all start to sing "Happy Birthday."

Daisy looks around at us, and her eyes begin to glass with tears. We've celebrated her birthday before, but this time it's different. We're all closer. She's finally with Ryke. It's like the puzzle pieces of our lives have begun to fit together just right.

When we finish the song, I have to wipe my eyes quickly.

I catch Rose wiping hers too, and I point a finger at her and gawk. She told me to *suck it up* last week when we were watching a movie and I cried at the end.

She mouths, *shut up*. And then she adds, *hormones*. Fine. I'll let her throw out the hormone card, especially because I use it all the time.

Daisy blows out the candle. Not long after, she dips her finger in the chocolate, and instead of sucking it off—*not dirty like that*—she draws a line of chocolate down Ryke's lips.

"Lil," Lo breathes in warning. I've scooted back up into his crotch. It's not my fault. The way they are staring at each other—this is *eye fucking* if I ever saw it.

A second later, they attack each other with carnal desire, the kind that you search for in good porn. I squeeze my eyes shut at my perverted thought. This is bad.

When I open them, their kiss is front and center, spotlighted, but no one else seems to be watching. There is serious *tongue*. Tongue that is done right. His hand envelops her face as he deepens the kiss, and she breaks from him, just to let out a pleasured cry.

Holy shit.

This is so physical and explosive that it really does deserve a fireworks show.

The other couples are talking and flirting, and Lo suddenly stands. "Follow me," he whispers in my ear.

"I'm okay," I tell him quickly, whipping my head *away* from the PDA. *Do not watch, Lily.* I try to bury any gross, guilty shameful feelings. *They do not exist*, I chant over and over.

Lo's brows rise and he says, "I know." He smiles to show me that he's being honest.

I believe him.

"Follow me, love," he repeats.

I throb in good-bad places. *Yes.* I rise to my feet like a dream. He has a head start, exiting the little couch area and onto the dance floor. He walks backward, beating his head to the music with very good rhythm. It's a song that you salsa to, one that is full of fire, smooth vocals, and a melodic beat.

Lo's dark gray crew neck fits him snuggly, an arrowhead necklace against his chest: a present I gave him for his twenty-first birthday some time ago. I can see the lines of his abs tightening beneath his shirt, especially as he begins to move his body to the song. Girls record him with fangirling giggles, their cell phones directed at my best friend. But his gaze is solely planted on me.

When we were younger, Lo was the one who taught me how to dance.

He's always been able to move like no one is watching, like no one can harm him in this brief expanse of time.

In his last year of college, before he was expelled, he refused to dance with me. Every single time. He sat at the bar and said *dance by yourself* when I asked.

It didn't always used to be like that.

So seeing him, right now, dancing in the middle of the club, with no alcohol in his clutch—it possesses me in ways that I can't express. It's like my soul is alive. Like I've woken up from a long, long sleep.

I slowly walk toward him, and he holds out his hand, waiting for me to near and take it.

I do.

And he draws me swiftly to his chest, my breath escaping. His hips begin to move with mine, so sensually that a heat builds across my skin.

I flourish beneath his intoxicating eyes, drinking him in completely.

He twirls me, and I hit his chest again, my feet following his in a steady pace. It's our bodies, melded together, that stirs every part of me.

I'm not letting go.

After a few minutes, the song dies down, and we ease to a slower sway. I want to hear his answer, even if it doesn't make much sense now that we're moving to the music. I grow the courage to ask anyway, "Will you dance with me?" For some reason, I still fear that rejection, the familiar response that always comes.

He cups my round face, his fingers lost in my hair, and his lips curve. Very softly, he says, "Yes, love. I'll dance with you."

Eighteen

Loren Hale

Husbands can't choose wives; boyfriends can't choose girlfriends and vice versa." Poppy sets out the parameters of the game as she sips a rum and Fizz. After claiming the leather couches by the wall, we decided to pay for VIP bottle service for Poppy, Daisy, Connor, and Sam. Anything is better than dealing with the shit bartender. Even playing truth or dare, which usually ends with someone throwing a fit.

Lily sits on my lap, her skin coated in a sheen of sweat from dancing earlier. It was a really good time. I missed it more than I realized.

I hold her to my chest, satisfied with the fact that we can't disappear and ditch our friends and family. This, right here, feels close to perfect.

Sam cautiously glances at all the locals who snap pictures of us, some even film us from their barstools. "Can we play this game some other time?" he asks us. "I really don't want to have to call Fizzle's publicists in the morning to clean up whatever happens tonight."

He's the head marketing guy or whatever at Fizzle. "Sammy," I say with the tilt of my head, "I get that being a chaperone is so deep within your pores that no facial strips can remove it, but we're not *ten*."

Connor rephrases, "We're all used to being filmed. Some more intimately than others." His voice is conversational, not bitter. I'd be causing *hell* if sex tapes of Lily and me were circulating through porn sites. I get that Connor has taken the publicity to his advantage, but this type of invasion of privacy has to be eating at Rose. It's been over a year since the first tape was released, and last I heard, there are now *five* online.

At his comment, Rose tenses and crosses her arms. "No one is allowed to mention the sex tapes until I can have a glass of wine." Her head whips to her husband. "That includes *you*."

"I was making a point," Connor says casually.

"Make it when I'm not in the room," she retorts.

They start bickering in French, and I tune them out. At the other end of my couch, Ryke slings his arm around Daisy's waist, and she rests her cheek on his shoulder. When Lily and I finished dancing, both Daisy and Ryke were missing. Poppy explained how they snuck off to the bathroom. To fuck.

Clearly.

It's not as uncomfortable with them returning as I thought it'd be. Maybe because they're not on top of each other—like Lily is with me. We'll forever take the PDA championship title, I realize. What's scary is that when we were just friends, we were always touching too.

It's hardwired into us. I pull her further against my chest, and her breathing shallows. I watch her take a trained inhale and exhale to control her urges. I rub her arm in comfort. She's doing well.

Sam clutches a vodka soda. "Let's just try to keep it classy."

Connor says, "Truth or dare by nature is juvenile. If you're looking for a posh game, we should break out chess or Scrabble.

However, you won't beat my wife, and you certainly won't beat me. So the level of fun, for you, isn't that high. I'd enjoy it though." He grins.

I whistle at his conceited statement, but I'm smiling.

"Truth or dare is fine as long as no one takes it too far," Sam says, his gaze landing on me.

I give him an invasive glare. Seriously, he doesn't need to treat me like I'm twelve years old. I swallow a biting retort that's about as nasty as what I said to the bartender. I don't want to put Sam on that level, but he's beginning to irritate me.

Connor fills the silence. "Some zebras can't change their stripes."

"Cobalt, are you calling me a fucking zebra?" Ryke interjects.

"Don't be offended," Connor says, not denying it. "Almost every animal plays a role in the kingdom. Even zebras."

"Yeah?" Ryke says roughly. "If I'm a fucking zebra, then what's my brother?"

Connor's deep blue eyes pin to me, full of clarity, something I desperately crave. His face becomes a complacent blank slate. "What animal do you want to be, darling?"

My eyebrows rise. "I have a choice?" Something tells me that he would've picked an inferior animal if he was truthful. He tiptoes around me. It's old knowledge by now. My muscles tighten, wishing he just called me a zebra like my brother.

Ryke groans. "I call fucking bullshit on this."

"It's called *favoritism*," Rose chimes in, her hand clasped firmly in her husband's.

"Favoritism *is* bullshit," Ryke says.

"I agree," Rose announces. Though infrequent, I hate when she teams up with Ryke. It's like two bulldozers headed in your direction. Having them on opposite sides is easier.

"Bullshit aside," Connor says, passing through this discussion quickly. "Who's starting the game?"

"Lily should," Poppy says, gesturing to Lil, who's been really quiet for the most part. In group discussions, she's more like the observer, not as loud or as brash. Her cheeks flush red at all the attention placed on her.

"Uhh . . ." Her head whips around, trying to find a person to ask a question to. Her back straightens as she grows more confident with her thoughts.

"Rose," she says.

Rose crosses her ankles, alert like she's about to answer some collegiate quiz question. Of course she's happy to be participating.

"Truth or dare?"

"Truth," she says instantly.

"Unsurprising," I add, just to tick her off.

Her yellow-green eyes drill into me.

"Umm," Lily says, and her face just keeps reddening and reddening. I can't read her mind, but I have a suspicion about what's rolling around her head.

I whisper in her ear, "It can be a sex question." That's the point of this game. It gets dirty.

Lily's eyes flicker nervously to Sam. Yeah, she's known him for a long time. It's like speaking to an older brother, slightly estranged since you don't know his likes and dislikes or the other side of his family. What makes it more awkward: he's close with Greg since they work together.

Sam checks his phone, as though he's hoping this will end soon so none of us embarrass ourselves.

"Oh noble Captain America," I say dryly, "cover your ears."

Sam pockets his cell. "Why?"

"You're like her older brother, and you work with her dad."

Confusion blankets his face.

Jesus Christ. "Do I need to spell it out for you?"

Still blank.

"S . . . E . . ." I start.

"Got it," he says, avoiding Lily's gaze. "Should she really be talking about that at all?"

Lily's chest collapses.

"Yes," I snap. "She's a human being and human beings ask sex questions during truth or dare."

Sam shakes his head at me. "I don't."

"Then you must be a reptile, Sammy. Go slither away."

"Lo," Poppy cuts in. "Be nice."

"Yes, Mother," I say back. I look at Sam. "Father. Are you going to ground me too?"

Sam is as unamused as me. I won't let anyone shame Lily. I get that he's confused about her sex addiction. Most people are, but their doubts plant something in her head. He can say that shit out loud when she's not around. Fine. But she's not in a good place to be welcoming comments from the fucking peanut gallery.

Daisy adds to the group, "I think anything should be game. It usually is."

"I'm just more reserved around you girls," Sam realizes.

"Which is why I told you to cover your ears," I say with less edge.

A light bulb goes off in his head like *I get it now.* Most of us are too comfortable with each other, and he's starting to understand that. So he nods but never plugs his ears, taking the risk.

"Okay, I have it," Lily cuts in, her hands on my knees. She clears her throat. "Rose, what position do you like the best?" Lily smiles more, able to ask this without stumbling over words.

Rose clutches Connor's hand so forcefully that his skin begins to turn purple. Lily bringing up the sex tapes would've been worse for Rose and way more awkward, so Lily went easy.

"My favorite position is Connor's least favorite position," she says.

"This isn't called lie or dare, darling." Connor fixes her hair over one shoulder, her neck bare.

Rose purses her lips, her collarbones protruding from her black dress. "Fine . . . my favorite position is missionary." She pauses briefly. "With a few alternations."

And just like that—Connor looks ready to fuck her across the couch.

I can't shut my mouth. Habit. "Meaning handcuffs, whips, and *yes sir*s."

Rose lunges for me—what the *hell*.

I instinctively flinch back while Connor seizes her around the waist—right before she catapults across the fucking table. She's incredibly pregnant and acting like she's a pole jumper in the Olympics.

I give her a weird look. "Way to sacrifice your baby for payback." It was such a low blow that I regret it the moment it leaves my lips. My heart clenches like it's skipping five beats at once.

Connor shoots me a single expression that says *drop it*. He's holding the back of Rose's head, and she says something fiercely to him in French.

I look to Ryke.

My brother sighs but ends up ratting them out, "She doesn't call Connor *sir*, ever."

Connor lets annoyance cross his face. He's not a fan of Ryke understanding their private French conversations. So I'm not surprised when Connor says something in *Italian* to Ryke. When Ryke responds in the same language, gesticulating like he's just as pissed, Lily's eyes grow big.

She extends her arms, almost whacking me in the face. "I thought we said no secret languages?"

I cut in, already sorry I started this string of arguments. "I got it wrong," I tell Rose. "I accept that. For Christ's sake, I wouldn't be surprised if I only got one out of three right."

Rose stares at me with more confidence in her stiff posture and focused eyes. "Two out of three were right," she says honestly, owning up to her sexual preferences.

I nod. "I'm not such a loser then," I say dryly. "Shocking."

She eases down a little. Look at that, I calmed the ice queen. Who would have thought this day would come?

Lily turns her head and whispers to me, "Maybe you're inheriting some of Connor's smart person powers." She noticed the same thing as me.

I give her a smile. "Yeah, maybe."

"Or you could've had them all this time and you never knew," she says, her eyes brightening at that idea.

"The former is more probable," I tell her, expecting her to frown. Instead, she clings to me harder, as though saying she loves me all the same.

I take a deep breath, one that releases all kinds of strain.

Seconds later, a server appears, passing out a new rum and Fizz to Poppy, a tequila sunrise to Daisy, and a glass of wine to Connor. Poppy twirls her stir straw in her drink and says to Rose, "Your turn."

Rose tugs at the hem of her dress and then rotates to Connor. "Truth or dare, Richard?"

"You can't choose him," Poppy reminds her. "We're not letting couples choose their partner."

Rose rolls her eyes dramatically. "For this absurd rule . . ." She targets her older sister. "Truth or dare?"

Poppy's muscles are relaxed from the booze, and she leans into her husband's chest. Sam and Poppy hug more than they kiss in public, and whenever they start to have an argument, they usually take it to another room. They're so normal that having them here reminds me how the rest of us ride these extremes of life, rarely wading in the "okay" content state.

Connor is too conceited.

Rose is too high-strung.

Daisy is too wild.

Ryke is too aggressive.

Lily is too awkward.

I'm too hateful.

Sam and Poppy are just right.

And I wonder if they're the ideal we should all be striving for. Or if we should just accept our nature and continue as we are.

After brief contemplation, Poppy says, "Dare."

"I dare you to give me a shoulder massage." Rose snaps her fingers like *hurry up*.

Of course she'd find a way to benefit from the dare.

Poppy scoots closer to her sister on the couch and starts kneading Rose's shoulders with her fingers. Rose looks at peace, as though everything worked in her favor.

"Loren," Poppy says. "Truth or dare?"

I tense. "Truth," I say, even though dare might be easier for me. I selfishly don't want to move Lily off my lap for any reason. I like her where she is.

"How many people in this room have you seen buck naked? Name them too."

I tilt my head. "And I was just starting to like you, Poppy."

"You always tell me that," she says warmly.

I do? I mentally pass through her comment while I calculate my answer. *Christ.* "Four people. Lily, of course. Ryke."

Ryke raises his brows quickly like *guilty*. This happens when we're undressing for events in one room. We all just don't care.

"Connor," I add.

He raises his wineglass to me.

"And unfortunately, Daisy." I glare at her for streaking in our house. I caught a small glimpse, and it was enough to imprint an image that I've tried, desperately, to erase.

She playfully winces. "Sorry."

Ryke shifts uncomfortably, but he doesn't say a word about it. I highly doubt he's that upset. But then I think about Ryke spotting

Lily undressed, and it almost twists my face, gross sentiments invading me.

There's a lot there that I don't like to imagine or talk about. Starting with *who's the baby daddy?* rumors and ending with Ryke and Lily discussing sex. The in-between—Lily being aroused by his make-out sessions with Daisy—is temporary and only fueled by her hormones. So I can live with it fine.

It's the other stuff that's attempting to unravel me.

"What about Rose?" Daisy suddenly asks me. "Didn't you see her naked with the leeches . . . ?"

Rose's mouth drops. "*Loren—*"

"Holster your broomstick," I tell her. "I didn't even *try* to look at you. For one, *no.*" I cringe. "For another, I was focused on Lily." I remember the road trip where the girls skinny-dipped in a pond. We were all trying to remove the leeches, not catch a peek of each other's girlfriend, wife, friend—whatever.

Rose relaxes back into Connor.

I nod to Daisy. "Truth or dare?" I'm betting she'll pick dare.

But she hesitates for a second, her cheek still on Ryke. Her eyes are glazed, which means she's tipsy, maybe verging on drunk. I haven't craved alcohol that severely tonight. It's easier when there are more people staying sober than just me.

Daisy raises her head and surprises me by saying, "Truth."

A question lights up in my mind. An asshole one. For Daisy, I would normally *try* to soften my spiteful, slightly vindictive nature. But it's a knee-jerk reaction. And I let it out faster than I can rein it in—forgetting in a moment that she's not Rose.

"When Connor walked in, and Ryke came on your face—how embarrassed were you?"

All of Daisy's sisters' jaws unhinge. Daisy slumps down into the couch, her eyes wide in complete horror. I may have unleashed one of the few secrets still kept in the group.

I hear Sam mutter to Poppy, "Where am I?" He's shielding his eyes with his hand. He's known Daisy practically forever.

Connor is smiling into his wineglass, and Ryke looks like he wants to tear off my head—or maybe Connor's.

"You fucking told him?" Ryke growls at Connor.

"Maybe a month ago," Connor admits. "It was a good story. I felt guilty for keeping it to myself."

"Fuck you," Ryke curses.

Rose smacks Connor's chest. "You walked in on them?"

"It was unintentional," Connor says easily. "Though the timing was bad—or perfect, depending on the way you look at it."

"There's no good fucking way to look at it," Ryke retorts.

"Had I not walked in right then, I don't think you would've come on her face at all."

Ryke groans. "Just stop fucking talking."

"Daisy?" Lily says, reaching out to comfort her little sister, which instantly makes me feel like a dick. Well-deserved, I know.

"It's cool," she says softly and then winces. "I mean, what happened wasn't cool. It was . . ." She meets my gaze. ". . . almost as embarrassing as this."

Ryke pinches his eyes like he wishes he could go back in time.

Yeah, now I feel like shit. My muscles constrict in taut bands. It's like every time I open my mouth, I eventually feel this pain. It's regret too shallow, always finding a way to surface. Yet still, I'd rather keep it there, right on the brink.

This guilt is what differentiates me from my father. I know this.

I watch Ryke lift Daisy onto his lap so she's not slumping in humiliation. He wraps an arm protectively around her collarbones, above her chest, and keeps shooting Connor and me an *I fucking hate you right now* look. It's weak in comparison to our dad. And Connor is hardly even perturbed, just casually drinking his wine.

"Truth or dare?" Daisy suddenly asks Lily.

Lily goes rigid. "Truth?" she says unsurely.

I wait for the *how many inches is Loren Hale?* That's the vindictive question I would've shot back in her position. Rose would've too. Anything to embarrass *me*. That question doesn't upset me though—but it's not something I would want to willingly advertise.

Daisy plays nice with me and asks Lily, "What's your biggest pet peeve about Lo?"

Lil tilts her chin up at me, and I stare down at her. "When you won't let me hold the comic book because *you* think that I'll crease the pages."

I almost laugh. "That's your biggest issue with me, love?"

She says, "It's much more annoying than you realize." She nods adamantly about this.

I'm possessive over my comics—that hasn't changed since forever. "I won't even let anyone else but *you* borrow seventy-five percent of them."

"I appreciate that," she says. "But some of them are *mine*."

"This is also true." I realize I'm possessive over *all* comics then.

Lily has another turn to ask a truth or dare, and she focuses on Ryke this time. Only she's avoiding his eyes. Great. She's still scared of him after being aroused by basically the entire male population. Fictional and real.

"Truth or dare?" Lily asks, her voice quiet.

"Dare," Ryke says, even more pissed by her cagy attitude. "Can you look at me?"

"No."

He groans. "Why do you keep acting like I have a disease, Lily?"

I cut in, trying to make this easier for her, especially as she turns bright red again, "It's not your turn to ask questions."

Ryke glowers. "I really don't want to fucking talk to you right now."

Fine. I'm mostly to blame for his sour mood anyway. I nudge Lil, and she straightens up.

"I dare you to . . . do a handstand for thirty seconds."

Sam finally drops his palm at this chaste dare. I wonder if there's a possibility that fatherhood made him more conservative.

My hand falls to Lily's abdomen. *Kick*, I stupidly command our son.

Yeah, he does nothing, and I end up rubbing circles with my thumb on Lil's stomach. She places her hand on top of mine. I exhale the restraint in my lungs.

I can't even fathom how much I may change after having a kid. I wonder whether it'll be a better me or a worse one.

To follow through with the dare, Daisy slides off my brother's lap, and then Ryke rises to his feet. He places his palms on the ground and uses his upper-body strength to force his legs erect. Camera flashes from cell phones go off in waves.

Lily isn't even watching Ryke, but Daisy leans over the couch armrest and whispers to her boyfriend. She must say something funny because his dark expression brightens a fraction.

When he finishes, easily landing back on his feet, he returns to the couch and holds Daisy again.

"I hoped you would roll over," Connor quips. "I didn't even get to rub your belly."

Ryke is not amused. He doesn't even flip him off this time. Shit.

Connor acts like he's not intimidated, but the look in my brother's eye—one that says *attack*—is not usually directed at us. I recoil as he says to Connor, "Dare or fucking dare?"

Connor finishes off his wine and sets the empty glass on the coffee table between the two couches. "I know in your own made-up language, adding a curse word changes the definition of the subsequent word, but to the rest of us, it's all the same."

"Dare or fucking dare?" Ryke doesn't back down.

Connor takes his hand off Rose's and rubs his lips, as though trying to hide his irritation. But I can't tell for sure. "I pick the only choice you're giving me."

And then Ryke says, without missing a beat, "Kiss Loren. For thirty fucking seconds."

Yeah.

He got us both back in one strike.

My stomach has caved.

And my eyes flit up to Connor, who is studying me, mostly. I can't read his expression, but he's definitely not uncomfortable like most people would be.

I'm confident in my sexuality enough to do the dare—I just worry about the cameras pointed at us and how this'll affect his reputation more than my own. He has more to lose, being the CEO of Cobalt Inc.

I notice that Sam has covered his eyes again, acting like this is not happening. It may not.

"Can't fucking do it?" Ryke challenges Connor, who I doubt has ever quit a game, even a "juvenile" one.

Without removing his gaze from mine, Connor says, "I'm just weighing my options." He's not Rose. Ryke's phrase would've egged her to do it, too prideful not to—but Connor is more logical about his actions.

And then he rises. "Stand up," he commands to me.

"Are you sure—"

"I can handle the backlash," he says, and his eyes briefly flicker to Ryke. I get it. He values his friendship with Ryke *this* much—that he's willing to risk criticism or a new headline in the tabloids just to even the playing fields again. "*Stand up.*"

Jesus Christ. I'm going. I'm going. I set Lily on the cushion beside Daisy, and then I rise, facing him, a coffee table separating us.

How does this even fucking work? He's two inches taller than me, and I have no idea who is going to go for it first. I lick my lips nervously, and I wonder if this looks more sexual than anxious. I wipe my mouth with my hand and glance back at Lily. "Don't look." *God fucking shit.* I don't need her to be aroused from *this*.

She hides her eyes behind her fingers, and I turn back to Connor.

Rose has said a few words in French that I can't understand, but Connor never replies. I have a feeling it's because Ryke can understand him. And then Rose huffs and switches to English, "Loren, you look scared. Maybe you should sit down."

Her voice is nicer than usual. I eye Connor. *I look scared because your husband is domineering as hell.*

She suddenly adds, "You're an antelope and he's a lion." I picture a lion chasing an antelope. And killing it for food.

My shoulders tense at that truth. "Yeah?" I say to her, looking past Connor at Rose. "Are you an antelope too?"

She says, "I'm the same breed as him."

"Toujours," Connor tells her. I understand the French word because he says it all the time.

Always.

Right as I turn to Connor, his hand cups the back of my head. And his lips touch mine.

My muscles solidify, and instead of just being awkwardly pressed together, he truly kisses me—with more confidence than I could ever possess.

I shut my eyes while his lips close over mine, and I try to follow his lead to the best of my ability. But Connor controls the action—and I'm grateful for that. His hand falls to my neck, and I find myself gripping his bicep. My lungs thrashing for air as I cage all oxygen elsewhere.

"Fifteen seconds," I hear Poppy say.

I've never kissed a guy before, which has to be really apparent. In the last three seconds, I feel Connor grinning against my lips. I swear he's entertained by the weirdest things.

"Time," Poppy says.

We break apart at the same moment. My lips actually slightly sting from the force. I wonder how many guys he's kissed before. After that, I highly doubt I'm the first. There are just too many clues for me to believe otherwise.

Connor rubs his bottom lip with his thumb, winks at me, and then spins to Ryke. "We're even."

Ryke nods, his brows raised in surprise.

"Did anyone else think that was hot?" Daisy says with a loopy smile, past tipsy.

"It was okay," Rose says flatly, which prompts Connor to study her with intrigue. I expected her to charge at me or him—since she hates me and loves him, and we just *kissed*.

But she doesn't care. I can't wrap my head around those two most of the time.

"Waitwaitwait," Lily slurs, and alarm shoots into me. My attention diverts to Lil, her fingers still shielding her eyes. "How hot was it? I need to know this!" My shoulders drop in relief that she's okay.

"A solid eight," Daisy declares, though she is staring only at Ryke right now. They're giving *fuck me* eyes to each other. This is all wrong. "It's masturbation worthy."

I grimace. "Stop."

"You're stroking Connor's ego," Rose tells her sister.

Lily is another color entirely—solid red. *Stroking*. I'm cringing more *now* than I was during the damn thing.

"All of my sexual encounters are masturbation worthy," Connor says. "This is nothing new." He does, literally, have millions of people jacking off to his sex tapes with his wife.

I slow clap, and Ryke joins in.

Connor smiles more.

The funny thing—other people in the club start clapping too. I can feel my smile. Fans can be really cool, despite a few hecklers here and there.

"An eight," Lily repeats, astounded. "I can't believe I missed it."

I reclaim my seat on the couch. "It wasn't like that, Lil."

Poppy adds, "You'll probably be able to Google it online."

"She's not allowed to look at porn," Rose says.

"This wasn't porn," I announce to everyone.

"So I can watch it?" Lily asks, her hands still shielding her face. She's picturing it right now. Probably further than anything that actually transpired. "Was their tongue?" she whispers to me, confirming my suspicions.

"No to both." I pull Lil's palm away from her eyes. And her gaze darts to my lips, as though imagining them against one of my best friend's. It's not a fantasy I want imbedded in her brain.

Connor sits beside Rose, and he kisses her forehead. She seems at ease.

Everyone does.

How could *that* break the tension in our group? Strain that *I* accidentally built from a dare.

And then Connor's deep blue eyes meet mine, and he smiles at me, a genuine one that he only reserves for friends.

He can slice through arguments, lower boiling points, and keep our friendship intact—not even remotely awkward after we just kissed.

And he's a part of my life.

Thank God.

Or rather, thank him. *Yeah*, I smile, *he'd want me to rephrase that.*

Nineteen

Lily Calloway

After the nightclub, we amble along the sidewalk, heading toward the dock so we can return to the yacht. "Spill," Rose says to Daisy, who is being supported mostly by me and Poppy, our arms around our little sister's waist.

Rose wants details about the sexual escapade that the guys knew before us. I kinda want more info too. All things involving blow jobs interest me, maybe a little too much.

Instead of answering, Daisy dodges Rose's request and inhales like she's breathing in tonight's full moon and glittering stars. She raises her fists sloppily into the air and shouts, "HELLO, MEXICO!"

The four guys, sauntering twenty feet ahead of us, all turn their heads in unison. *Damn*. That was sexy. I can admit that without flushing, right?

I check my arms.

Nope. Still red.

Ryke is the only one who remains spun around. He rotates fully, walking backward with an aluminum-foiled taco in hand. Most of the guys are eating them after we passed a food stand. I chose to go with dessert and eat a churro as a late-night snack.

Daisy focuses on her boyfriend and almost trips over her feet.

"Watch it, Calloway," he tells her.

"You watch it," she says, her retort not as good with her drunken state. Poppy and I hold her firmly to our sides.

"I am watching it," Ryke says, his eyes right on hers, "and she looks like a hot fucking mess."

"What are you going to do about it?" Daisy says in a smooth voice. Her smile radiates, but her eyelids droop.

Rose points an accusatory finger from Daisy to Ryke. "No flirting. We're having girl time."

Ryke ignores her and says, "I'll show you later, sweetheart." And then he spins around, walking with the guys. Ryke places a hand on Lo's shoulder, and they talk amongst themselves. Laughter emanates from their huddle, and Lo's is the loudest, the most full-bellied and jam-packed with true happiness.

My eyes sting with emotion.

Loren Hale is laughing.

It shouldn't be a rare phrase. But it is.

I am most happy when he is happy. The same, I know, applies to him.

Poppy stares off into space before saying, "He has good lines."

Daisy's brows furrow. "Ryke?"

Poppy nods. "It was a cute one." She smiles kindly at her.

"It wasn't a line," Daisy refutes with a deep frown. I sway, slightly shocked that she actually spoke her mind. I like this Daisy more than the one keeping the peace. It's easier to tell when she's having a good time and when she's just appearing to for our sake.

"I didn't mean it like that," Poppy says, giving her a side squeeze that unsteadies me. I gain my balance, thankfully. If I fall, so does my baby. It's a thought that tickles my brain like a nervous spasm.

With only one free hand, I bite into my churro that melts in my mouth. The long, fried donut is a little phallic-looking, but I try to employ the Ryke Meadows attitude of "not caring what other people think." An audible moan even leaves my lips. *I don't care.*

My cheeks and elbows do though, burning with disgrace.

I chew slowly to prolong the next bite. Even though I crave it. I swallow way too soon.

"He came on your face," Rose says bluntly.

Back to this. I join in. "And you didn't even tell us."

Poppy adds, "It's obviously an embarrassing moment for her."

Rose adjusts her handbag on her arm. "And if she told me when it happened, I would've bought her jewelry and a 'fuck you' dress."

Daisy smiles. "What do those look like?"

Rose waves a finger at her. "No, no, you're not going to distract me. I need more details than Connor."

Daisy scrunches her nose. "That's not possible. He was *there*."

My eyes bug at all of this. I've encountered some pretty awkward moments in my life, but nothing like this. "Did you like it?" I ask the least important question, probably. I'm just curious if that's a fantasy she'd repeat again.

"No," Daisy says softly, actually starting to open up. Her arms like jelly, flopping by her sides. The liquor has just loosened her joints like a limp . . . thing. I cough on my churro.

Rose pats my back with a stiff hand. "I told you not to eat that."

I smash the churro into her chest since the dessert is obviously not nice to me. Disgruntled, she tosses it on the sidewalk.

Poppy gapes. "Rose, you shouldn't litter." Our oldest sister leaves our side to pick up the churro and find a trash can.

"I'm feeding the birds," Rose calls after Poppy, who is already on an environmental mission.

Daisy is much harder to keep upright on my own, but I manage somewhat, resituating my clutch around her hip. Rose must see my struggle though because she replaces Poppy, hooking her arm with Daisy's and leisurely strolling along.

"I hate giving blow jobs," Rose suddenly opens up. She rarely talks about her sex life with Connor, so my lips part in shock.

Maybe she thinks it's only fair to offer some info when she keeps prodding Daisy. "I mean . . ." She sighs and rolls her eyes. "The first time wasn't awful, but it's my least favorite thing. I'm not good at it, and Connor is huge—do *not* mention that I complimented his dick. Please."

I am soaring with these tidbits. "My lips are zipped." No they are not. My mouth is permanently hung open. Though I can keep a sisterly secret. Rose has entrusted me with some before.

"Do you like them?" Daisy asks me with a tipsy smile.

"Yeah," I say without blushing. Ah-ha! Success. "I like the control and watching Lo . . ." *come*. I can feel my ears heating. Damn.

"I've never really liked them," Daisy says honestly. "And with Ryke, I can sometimes tell that he'd rather be pleasing me instead of me pleasing him. So he usually stops me before I get him off."

"Aww," I say. I've never made this sound out loud before, but this is an *aww* moment if there ever was one in my book. Some would call it a perverted book, but I think I'm going to rename it The Lily Calloway Sexy Times Book.

It has a nice ring to it. And it makes me feel less like a creep.

Daisy tries to hide a bigger smile. "You know the dare?" She's going to give us details?! Rose and I listen closely, very intrigued. "I was giving Ryke a blow job for the *very* first time, and that's when Connor walked in." She tucks her hair behind her ear, and the crowds that follow us (yes, people are trailing us, along with our bodyguards) grow in octave, so Daisy has to raise her voice. "I heard the door open, and I jerked back the same exact moment . . ." She trails off.

"He ejaculated," Rose finishes without balking.

I wince. "Do you have to use that term?"

"Yes," Rose says with confidence. I wonder if I'm making Daisy feel more ashamed by being all ashamed myself. It's a nasty cycle that I want to break.

"Lo has come on me before," I state. Wow, it kinda felt good.

Daisy smiles. "Really?"

"Yeah, my face too. But not that much anymore." I frown deeply, thinking about our current stasis of being. I feel healthier, and I like that Lo has spaced out all these steps with sex over months and months. It's better to go slow.

Fast is not the right speed for me.

Daisy looks a little lost in her head.

"What is it?" I ask.

She takes a deep breath. "Do you ever just want to run? Like strip all of your clothes and speed down a street, using all of your strength, no one stopping you but yourself?"

It sounds freeing, but I can't say it's a thought that's ever crossed my mind. After two minutes of pathetically running, I'd face-plant or grow out of breath—baby or no baby.

"No," Rose says definitively. "I don't run. I walk quickly." This has been her motto since she discovered high heels.

To Daisy, I say, "In theory it seems kind of nice."

She springs on her feet like she's ready to take off. "All theories should be tested, at least once."

"RYKE, STOP!" Lo suddenly screams ahead of us.

My heart is in my throat. Ryke has charged some random guy wearing a surfer graphic tee and frayed shorts. Lo restrains his brother by the shoulders.

Ryke spits out nasty words . . . all in Spanish. We walk faster to reach the guys.

"Go!" Rose shouts at the bodyguards and motions them like she's herding cattle. "They need your help."

Mikey says, "We're contracted to protect Daisy, Lily, and Poppy, so we're not leaving their sides."

Rose glares and then mutters curses while she searches for her pepper spray in her handbag.

Poppy has fallen behind, fixated on a vendor's booth selling porcelain sugar skulls, and Dave, her bodyguard, hovers over her.

She seems highly unaware of what's happening, and Sam is sprinting toward Poppy, leaving Connor, Loren, and Ryke alone.

"Traitor," Rose calls at him. "They need you!"

"So does Poppy!" he shouts back.

Rose purses her lips, and I focus on the surfer-tee heckler, who follows our guys for every step they take. He's not alone. With his two buddies, they jeer in Spanish. I can tell by the way they pump out their chests, their muscles flexed and their arms gesticulating.

Three guys. Maybe these people aren't random. Lo said that three guys have been pestering them all day, wherever they go. Maybe they found them again.

"Should we . . . ?" Daisy hesitates to run to Ryke, but I hold her jelly arm in a firm grip.

"No, let's stay out of it." Though I want to be closer. So we keep our pace.

Ryke yells in Spanish so loud that my ears blister. There is pain in his voice, beneath the anger, and Lo struggles to detain him as he thrashes. "Connor," Lo says, looking for help. Connor is listening intently to these three guys, not intervening.

We're only five feet away. Surfer Tee yells at Ryke and Lo with just as much venom, and then laughs mockingly like he's won a battle. Our lives are open to the public as if we live in a glass house, and people enjoy tapping on the walls, waiting and waiting for a reaction, for that little bit of entertainment. Forgetting that we aren't performers or mannequins put on display.

Forgetting that we can feel all the same.

"CONNOR!" Lo screams for help again, Ryke tearing through his arms. He's stronger than Lo. This has always been fact.

"Let him go," Connor says in a stoic voice.

"What?" Lo breathes out the word. It pains me. I'm so close to him now. I reach out like I can touch him, but I feel a large hand on my shoulder. Garth.

He draws me to the side so I'm not smacked by flailing limbs. Daisy slips out of my grip, and Rose leaves her to strut toward the fight. Daisy stays upright on her own, swaying only a little.

"Connor, *help me*," Lo pleads.

"I won't," Connor says like he wants Ryke to fight these people. "Just let him go, Lo."

Then Surfer Tee creates a V-shape with his fingers and obscenely sticks his tongue through it. His eyes have shifted. And they land right on me. Chills race down my spine.

Lo glances over his shoulder, finding the source of the ridicule.

It was me.

All of it, I realize.

Maybe they're saying my vagina is too big. I'm gross. I've slept with hundreds of faceless men. I'm diseased and disgusting. I am not fit to be a mom. I am and will always be a sex addict. Nothing more than that. I have heard it all and read it on social media. Though never have I witnessed it in Spanish.

I take another step forward, and Lo screams at me, "LILY, STAY BACK!"

My heart stops. The wrathful, pained look on his face plants me here as much as his voice. And his eyes flicker to my belly. I didn't mean—I *wouldn't* put my baby in harm's way. I wasn't going to. It's just . . . Lo.

He breathes raggedly and nods to me like, *please, Lily.*

I nod back.

When he ensures that I won't risk my safety, he spins back to his brother. In a single instant, Lo removes his hands from Ryke, and this is when I think Ryke will lose all self-control and throw a fist first, tapping into his aggressive side. He's snapped. Long before now. But he doesn't even have his fists barred yet, not even raised for a right hook or a sucker punch. He steps forward, then stops.

It's so quick. The tallest of the hecklers charges him, his eyes set on Ryke. In three lengthy strides, he nails his knuckles into Ryke's jaw. I can feel my heart beating out of my chest.

That is a sucker punch, one that lands Ryke on the cement ground.

The other two hecklers jump on Ryke, which causes Lo to snatch their arms and land a punch or two.

I flinch as a pair of knuckles connects with Lo's face. "Stop!" I shout at the hecklers, finding my voice with Lo's pain. The dark ocean water is on our right, shops on our left, the moon overhead, the dock in view. We're not *that* far away from the tugboat that'll bring us to the anchored yacht.

"This is not happening," Rose says, heading even *farther* forward with her pepper spray in hand. The moment she passes Connor, he seizes her wrist.

"What do you think you're doing, darling?"

"I'm fighting for my sister," she says seriously. She's pregnant too. And while I love having a sister that'd be willing to insert herself into a fistfight on my behalf, now's not a good time.

Even Daisy has enough sense to stay put—

Just as I think it, she sprints forward, and Mikey catches her around the waist. She kicks out. "Let me help him."

"No, Daisy," Mikey tells her.

"This is . . . sexist," she says, her arms flopping around with her legs.

"Agreed," Rose says to Connor.

"Hun," Connor tells her, "do I need to remind you that you're a vessel for our unborn child?"

"Are you trying to infuriate me more?" she retorts. "Now I just want to punch you."

"I'm a truthteller. If you don't like what I have to say, take it up with the liars of the world." And then we're all distracted when Surfer Tee kicks Lo *hard* below his chest.

"Lo!" I scream, especially as Lo crumples to the ground. My stomach caves, remembering his preexisting injury: broken ribs from the Paris riot. Hot tears squeeze through the corners of my eyes.

"*Please* don't do anything rash," Connor forces to Rose. And then he inserts himself in this fight, to defend Lo and pull him out of it. Connor ducks an incoming right hook and then protectively stands above Lo so no one can touch him. I watch Lo cough hoarsely on the cement.

He was laughing only minutes ago.

This is wrong.

I jerk forward on instinct, to hold Lo, to hug him. To wrap my arms around him. But Garth keeps me put.

A fist pounds into Connor's cheekbone as it becomes two on one, as Ryke turns his attention to Surfer Tee and lands a solid blow in his stomach. It's reciprocated with knuckles to Ryke's lip. They're all beating the shit out of each other. I hate this. I glance back at our bodyguards, trying to express every sentiment and plea in my eyes.

Please, help them.

Garth and Mikey exchange a look between each other, and that's all it takes. They release their holds on Daisy and me. Not so we can join the fight, but so they can.

It's like adding a couple of trump cards. The minute they step in, Garth pries Ryke off Surfer Tee, and Mikey assists Connor, keeping the other two at bay. The intensity drops by a million degrees.

Ryke spits blood on the cement and says something volatile at the hecklers in Spanish. It's such a scary fight that I didn't realize I was shaking until Rose reaches out and clutches my jittery hand.

"They're okay," Rose says softly.

"I can't believe that just happened," I murmur. I watch Ryke throw his palms in the air like *I'm done, I'm done.* He wipes his bloody mouth with the back of his hand.

I've conquered my fear of facing daylight, of standing among fans—now excited when they approach for selfies. I'm no longer crippled by the constant attention. No longer a scared little hermit who hides in her house. But I don't want to come out to find Lo beaten on the ground, accompanied by more people that I love.

"What if they had a knife?" I realize this could've been easily worse. "What if they had a gun?" I freeze.

Rose says, "We can only tolerate so much until we snap. Ryke's easy to enrage, but Connor's not, and he was upset. So you have to know that whatever they were saying must've been verging on a threat." She raises her chin. "If I wasn't pregnant—"

"You would punch back?" I presume.

"I would impale their gross, little black hearts with my heels."

Thank God she's on my side and not against me.

The hecklers have separated from our men, and they weakly stagger back, blood staining their shirts and a few shiners swelling their eyes.

Lo, Ryke, and Connor only appear minutely better, blood still splattering their clothes. All of them have taken hits. Connor is crouched over Lo, talking to him quietly while he nods like *I'm okay.*

I try to exhale a tight breath in my chest.

Ryke finally turns toward us, and he locks eyes with Daisy, who is all alone, a few feet ahead of me and Rose. Her chest rises and falls in a heavy, uneven rhythm like she's suffocating beneath a brutal wave.

Ryke assesses her as much as she assesses him.

She tugs at her tight shirt, and I remember her earlier thought about stripping and racing ahead and being held down by nothing at all.

Go, I want to tell her. She can sprint to the dock. The hecklers have disappeared down a side street, out of sight. She's safe.

But her feet stay on the ground, in place. "The full moon makes you crazy, you know," she tells him softly.

"No more fucking crazy than you." He steps nearer to Daisy and then draws her to his chest. His hand disappears beneath her shirt, as though stretching it so she's not as claustrophobic. The gesture is sweet. "And it's not the full moon, Dais. It's just people who want to shit on the ones I love. I can't fucking take it."

My shoulders lift with that proclamation. Lo is still hurt and my stomach won't unknot until he's in my arms and I'm in his.

So I head over to him as soon as he stands, wincing and favoring his ribs. I almost start shaking again at the flash of agony in his features. "Lo?" I whisper.

He stares down at me, his lip busted. Connor's cheekbone is red and will probably bruise. But just by sight, Ryke has the worst of it: both cheeks and his lip beat up and bloodied.

"I'm fine," Lo says.

"So fine that I can hug you?" I ask skeptically. He's putting on a good front.

"Go ahead, Lil," he nods.

I gently wrap my arms around him, keeping distance between our bodies.

His warm breath touches my temple as he whispers, "That's not how we hug."

"I'm not hurting you," I tell him adamantly. "I know you're in pai—"

He squeezes me to his chest, a common embrace for us, one where our bodies meld together with no beginning and end. It's like we're one. I feel his heart *thud, thud, thud* against my skin.

I'm not sure how long we stay like this, frozen in time, shielding the world from us. It's a moment that eclipses the rest of the day and shortens my lifespan to a single solitary snapshot. My belly flutters, a literal movement that causes me to straighten like a board.

"Lo . . ." I whisper.

"Lil?" He scrutinizes my expression.

It happens again, only this time, stronger, like a foot . . . I touch my abdomen, my heart quickening.

"Is he . . ." Lo trails off.

I nod. "I think so."

Lo places his hand on my belly, and after a few quiet seconds, the faint movement happens again. Lo's eyes smile so much that I laugh into one.

And then he kisses me, so suddenly. His lips right on mine. My arms right around him, his around me. Where they're meant to be.

Twenty

Loren Hale

S hut the door," Ryke orders, flipping on the faucet. I close the yacht's bathroom door behind me and sink on the tiled floor against the porcelain tub.

I wrap an arm around my ribs that shriek in pain, maybe fractured again. I try to ignore it. I've had this injury before, and all I can do is wait for it to heal. Since I'm an addict, they always advise to forgo medication. I won't take anything to numb this.

"Fuck." Ryke winces as he rinses his bloodied knuckles beneath the water.

Connor inspects his own bruised cheekbone in the mirror and says something in French to Ryke, who replies back.

"Stop," I tell them, each large breath stabbing my lungs. "I have to know." The girls are trying to calm down their parents, woken up after a text from an overly concerned Poppy. All I want to know is why the hell these guys have been following us and what they were saying about Lily.

Ryke and Connor share hesitance, and it's like someone kicks me again in the ribs.

"I can take it," I say with everything I have.

I can take it.

No one is going to bury me. I have to trust myself more than ever. Because I picture a life where I *never* stand up on my own, where I'm stuck leaning on Ryke and Connor, and it *hurts*. I want to take those first steps by myself again. For one turn of fate, I'd like to be the kind of guy that braces them from falling.

It's always felt impossible.

But it's a goal that's been keeping me moving.

"This won't push me over," I continue. "I won't drink. I just need to know."

Ryke turns back to the sink and washes his face.

Connor sits on the toilet lid and stares at the ground, haunted almost.

"Goddammit," I sneer with burning eyes. "Someone say something." It's killing me.

"I'm trying . . ." Ryke presses a towel to his lip and then leans against the wall. His eyes are also on the ground.

I sit higher up, but the pain shoots through my body, and I stay slightly slouched. "I know it's about Lily." My tendons sear.

"It's not just because I don't think you can handle it," Ryke suddenly tells me. He pulls the towel away from his lip, focusing on the damp cloth. "It's that . . ." His face twists. ". . . I don't know if I can translate it without screaming."

"Just give me something," I choke out the words.

Connor is quiet, looking concerned for me.

"I can handle it," I remind him.

"I know you can," Connor says. I can tell that he's placating me, saying what I want to hear.

Ryke balls the towel in his hand. "I'm just going to let some of it out as fast as I can."

I nod.

"*How many guys have pounded into that slut?*" he says at first. It's another swift kick.

I squeeze my eyes shut. *Don't think about it.*

"*Is she still full of their cum?*"

I shift, pain intensifying in my gut, but it's not from my ribs anymore. I can feel the type of torment Lily would experience if she heard these exact words. And the part that belongs to her is sunken with agony. The part that belongs to me is rattling with rage.

"*Bring her here . . .*" Ryke's voice breaks.

I open my eyes, and my brother is covering his mouth like he wants to scream and punch someone again.

My eyes are on fire, holding back. *Why are you fucking crying? Stop crying.* I'm not crying. "Keep going," I prod.

"I can't," Ryke says, shaking his head. He runs a hand through his hair.

"You have to," I tell him.

Ryke cringes at me like he sees into me.

"Just say the rest," I almost yell.

"No." He shakes his head again and steps away from the wall. "I'm fucking done torturing you. You're in fucking pain right now, and you want me to put you in *more* pain."

Is that what this is? Masochism. "I can take it," I remind him.

"I can't!" He points at his chest, his eyes bloodshot like mine. He breathes heavily, staring down at me, and he says, "*Bring her here, we want to see how many cocks can fit inside her . . .*" He trips up, and his voice cracks again. "I can't."

I'm crying.

I only realize it when the sound of a sob breaches my lips. Wet tears slide down, and I bring my knees up, resting my forearms on them. I hang my head. *Stop crying.*

"Keep going," I say in a choked whisper.

I'm surprised that Connor hears me. He takes over and speaks clinically, "*How many cocks can fit inside her giant cunt. You better have a leash on your bitch; we plan on riding her tonight.*"

The pain rips through my chest.

Ryke is beside me on the ground while Connor keeps talking. I sit idle between rage and grief, my emotions at war. I want to shut it all out, but then I want to feel the coldest, harshest parts of it. Maybe then it won't hurt me anymore.

After five minutes, my hands balled into fists, my shoulders shaking, and my cheeks slick with tears, I whisper, "Stop."

I reached my limit. I understand why Ryke snapped a fuse back in the street. It's just too much.

I want to protect Lily from this type of ridicule, but I can't. And I think that's the hardest thing to grapple with—that people would come face-to-face with us and say this shit outright.

And there is *nothing* we can do but sit here and bear it.

Get thicker skin. Don't be so sensitive, Loren. I am in love with Lily. To be unfeeling from someone hurting her—no rage, no grief—I'd have to be a fucking robot.

No armor can block out this pain. No booze this time. And I remember—almost one whole year ago, I heard defaming words about me and my father. I slid to the floor. I reached into a cupboard for a bottle of Glenfiddich. I broke my sobriety for the first time. And I never got off the ground that night. Not on my own.

Being in the media, I've learned to live with this hurt, stand up, and move on.

It's what I'll do now. It's what I'll do tomorrow and the next day. For however long this fight goes on.

Just stand up.

And I rise slowly to my feet. Heavy and shackled with weight. I still move.

Twenty-one

Loren Hale

S o let me get this fucking straight," my father says in an edged voice, "the four of you attacked three guys who've been harassing you all day. In the middle of the goddamn street?"

We couldn't avoid our parents for long. As soon as we left the bathroom, Greg and Jonathan called us into the yacht's living room. I stand between Ryke and Connor while Sam is on the end, the only one of us not beat to shit.

"Technically, they punched Ryke first," I offer.

"But it doesn't take away from the fact that you all responded the way you did," Greg says, facing us with my dad. All the girls, including Lily's mom, are situated on the couches behind us. Watching. Like we're testifying in an informal hearing or something. Like we're little kids about to be grounded.

"I'm not a boy," Ryke says, somehow not cursing.

"Did hitting someone make you feel like a big man?" our dad taunts. I focus on the crystal glass in Jonathan's hand: clear liquid with ice cubes.

Not vodka, I want to believe. I wish I trusted him, but a lot surrounding my father has pissed me off this trip, most notably the "date" he brought. I'm surprised she's not even in the living room right now. She's been glued to his hip since we left port.

"Fuck off," Ryke says, not in the mood for an interrogation. I don't think any of us are.

Greg interjects, "Settle down. We're just trying to understand what happened." His gaze traverses across all of us, inspecting our wounds, and my expression only says *I want out of here, now*. My emotions still grip my muscles like a vise. Every malicious word that Connor and Ryke translated blinks back into my head. *Don't think about it.* I'm trying.

God. I'm trying.

Greg's gaze stops on Sam. "Why aren't you all torn up?"

"I stayed out of it, sir," he says. "The fight really shouldn't have started in the first place. If we'd all just ignored them like I had suggested, I don't think they would have attacked Ryke."

I grit my teeth, and I turn my body, about to step toward him. Connor blocks my path, but I can't shut up about this. "Hey, Sammy," I say with ice in my eyes, "why don't you go be a hero on another boat." I lash out at him, even though I'm angry at the situation. "No one cares about your self-righteous bullshit." The guilt doesn't even tear a big enough hole inside of me. Maybe I'm already split open.

"Loren," Poppy defends her husband, about to spring up from the love seat. Samantha Calloway grips her shoulder and forces her back down.

"No." I'm not done. I point at Sam. "He *left* us, and now he's acting like he's the goddamn peacekeeper, like he knows best." No one knows. Not me. Not anyone. I meet Sam's narrowed eyes that blaze with hatred toward me. It's a look I've received almost every day of my life from people that I've barely met. "You don't know what's best, Captain America. You don't even know what's right. So stop pretending like you do."

Connor Cobalt, of all people, said *yes* to a fight by refusing to restrain Ryke. He wanted these guys to be punched in the face. That has to count for something.

"I left you to help Poppy," Sam retorts. "Otherwise, I would've been there."

"Poppy has a bodyguard," Greg replies, fear in his voice like she was in trouble. She wasn't. "She should've been taken care of." He turns to Dave, a bodyguard with dark shades on. He sits at the breakfast table with Mikey and Garth.

"She was fine," Dave confirms.

Sam shakes his head repeatedly. "I'm not seriously being reprimanded for looking after her."

"You look after the family," Greg says.

"My family *is* Poppy and Maria."

Greg quiets, silently upset. Truthfully, I've only ever heard him yell at Sam and Ryke, but this time he enacts his usual *I'm disappointed in you* look and stays still.

Jonathan takes over. "Your family is everyone in this fucking room," he retorts. "We're all bound together one way or another, and there will be a time when you need him." He points at Ryke. "Or him." He motions to me. "Just as they needed you tonight. So you want to be a selfish little fuck and paddle out on your own little lifeboat and leave everyone else to drown, so be it. You go do that, Samuel. Because when the rest of us are carrying life jackets, we won't throw you one."

It's harsh. But nothing about our lifestyle is smooth or easy or uncomplicated. It's always been us versus everyone else. And it's hardest when we turn on each other. We all know it. I'm even to blame for causing rifts, but it's better to stay together than be apart.

"I'm trying," Sam says slowly, "to grapple with this concept. I'm not used to these kids—"

"I'm not a kid," I say heatedly.

"I remember you as one," Sam says. "And if you were grown up, you wouldn't have given those guys a reaction or a reason to start a worthless fight. You're about to have a *baby*—"

"Shut the fuck up," Ryke suddenly interjects, protecting me from Sam's words.

I can take it.

I can take it, I believe.

Connor finally speaks. His voice is temperate in a room of combustible personalities. "I understand where you're coming from, Sam, but before you cast judgment on Loren, you don't even know what the fight was about. Unless you can suddenly speak Spanish?"

Sam shakes his head and quiets. Then he says, "I'm sorry."

I realize he's looking at me.

I frown deeply, confused. It's like Connor has some sort of hypnosis over him. But I take it with a nod. I can't fathom what it's like to have a kid to protect, but in his position, I doubt we'd choose what he did. There is a difference between us and him. We're all loyal to each other. He was right—we're younger than him. We grew up together experiencing monumental moments at the same time.

Sam doesn't know us.

Not really.

His allegiance is blind, based on relationships set out in paper and ink. Not in emotions or blood. Maybe that's why it's harder for him.

"What were they saying in Spanish?" Greg asks, looking between Ryke and Connor.

Everyone goes quiet, and my ribs flame. I'm rigid and unmoving.

"Someone speak," my dad cuts in, his fingers tightening around his glass.

"It was about Lily," I let out, though I can't say anything more than that.

The room grows silent, and I crane my neck over my shoulder. Lily clutches the armrest of the couch and produces a weak smile for me. *Lil.*

She knew it was about her. This whole time.

She knew.

The bottom of my stomach drops and then constricts.

"I have a question," Greg chimes in again. I expect him to ask specifically what the hecklers said, but his gaze sets on Connor. "Where was Rose if you were in the fight? She doesn't have a bodyguard." I'm selfishly thankful that he's redirected the conversation onto someone else.

"I trusted my wife," Connor says easily. "I had to make a choice, and I made it."

My father takes a swig of his drink, and I hone in on the liquid again. "At least we all know where your priorities lie."

Connor stays impassive at the insult. "I'm not a knight in shining armor, and I've never insinuated myself to be one. I leave that to the men who like to straddle horses and prance around in meadows."

Ryke actually laughs beside me, knowing it was a lighthearted shot at him.

I smile too. God, how the hell am I smiling right now? It fades pretty fast.

"You're spineless," my father says into his next gulp. My face contorts in a grimace.

"If I'm spineless, then every man in comparison is an annelid."

My father's brows shoot up. "An anus?"

Rose cuts in, "A *worm*."

Connor is grinning, loving that his wife understood him. "Jonathan," he says easily, "the fact that Rose is completely unharmed, sitting right there"—he gestures to Rose behind him—"suggests that I chose right and you're wrong. So please, continue to argue against evidence."

Greg interjects before my dad can speak, "The real issue here is the fact that Garth and Mikey had to step away from Daisy and Lily to protect you three." He motions to Ryke, me, and Connor.

And I suddenly realize what this interrogation has been about all along.

"*No*," Ryke snaps.

"*Yes*," our dad says, "you're all getting bodyguards. Maybe then they'll protect *you* from going to jail." Fine with me.

"That's a great idea," Rose says, raising her chin, her palms flat on her knees. "It was imbalanced to place bodyguards with all the girls and not the guys to begin with."

"You're getting one too," Greg tells his daughter.

Rose's eyes bore holes in his forehead. "No. I don't need one. I've proven that."

"Like you said, hun," Connor tells her, "it's an evening of power." He's happy about this—I see it in his deep blue eyes. He's wanted Rose to have a bodyguard since we became immersed in the media.

Ryke is pissed. "I don't want a guy following me."

"Why?" Greg asks.

Ryke runs a hand through his thick brown hair, an anxious tell. "Because," he says with a low breath, unable to let out his explanation. *Come on, Ryke.* Maybe he's censoring himself so he's not disrespectful or he's just having trouble explaining at all.

"That's not going to cut it."

"I'm twenty-five years old," Ryke proclaims, "*no one* in this fucking room can control the things that I choose to do with my life . . ." His voice dies off quickly, most likely remembering Hale Co. and what he's striving toward now, even if it's the last thing he really wants.

I'm trying to understand why he's firmly against a bodyguard, and I honestly can't figure it out.

"You don't have a job," Greg starts listing off facts. "After you were thrown in jail, every athletic endorsement deal you had for rock climbing disappeared. You are financially dependent on your trust fund that *your father* controls."

Ryke's face hardens. "Then he takes away my trust fund."

I shake my head at my brother. Losing his financial security over a bodyguard—it's not worth it.

"And what about my daughter?" Greg plays that card like he has the ability to remove Daisy from Ryke's life. It's fucked up.

"Dad," Daisy says with wide eyes, sitting next to Lily.

Ryke tenses considerably. And in a controlled voice, he says, "I don't want a fucking bodyguard speeding after me on a motorcycle, accompanying me to every rock face I climb." His chest rises strongly and he points at the ground. "I don't want a fucking bodyguard shoving me away from Daisy. And I don't want one trying to restrain *me* from protecting *my* little brother." He feels threatened by someone who doesn't even exist yet.

"Let's compromise," Greg says. "You'll have a bodyguard when you're in public with my daughters. Fair enough?"

Ryke struggles to accept this.

I place my hand on his shoulder and whisper to him, "It's a good offer."

Ryke takes a deep breath, and after a long second, he nods tensely in agreement.

"We need to have a talk about your future," Greg says to Ryke. I've heard those words too many times, from him and from Jonathan. It's weird having them directed at someone else. "I need you to do something for me involving Fizzle, but if you keep telling me that you're unwilling to help, then maybe you don't love my daughter like you say you do."

Ryke lets out a weak laugh, his eyes reddening. "I love your daughter like the sun, and I could say and do a thousand things, and you'd never accept me."

"You haven't even done one thing," Greg says with a raise of his brows. "I'm asking for *one*. This is easy. You'll hear me out after everyone goes to bed, okay?"

Daisy starts, "Dad, don't—"

"Dais, it's fine," Ryke says, squashing an argument easily. I wouldn't want to cause a rift between Lily and her father, and I know Ryke feels the same. He nods to Greg again. "I'll hear you out."

My dad has one-fourth of his drink left. He's fixated on it—or maybe I am. He's almost going to finish it off, and I can't keep speculating. On impulse, I step forward and steal the glass from him.

He cocks his head at me like *really, son?*

I sniff the liquid, just smelling lime, but I see carbonation bubbles. Gin and tonic?

And then Jonathan Hale, with his graying sideburns, narrows his deadly eyes and gives me a single dark look: *drink it, son. If you don't fucking trust me.*

I go cold, put the rim of the glass to my lips—

"Lo!" Ryke yells, his hand clamping on my shoulder, about to tear the glass from me.

It's too late. The liquid slides down, and my taste buds catch all the ingredients. Ryke rips the drink from my hands.

"Are you fucking kidding me?!" he yells at our dad. Not at me. Thinking he just broke his sobriety and mine too.

"It's just carbonated water and lime," I tell Ryke the truth, a pang of guilt hitting me. My dad wouldn't sneak around. If he was drinking again, he'd flaunt it. I shouldn't have questioned him in the first place.

Ryke isn't convinced. He takes a swig of the drink, and after he tastes the water, his muscles start to relax.

Our dad sighs at Ryke, "I understand why you don't trust me, son, but you should at least trust your brother. He wouldn't lie to you."

"My track record isn't good," I say under my breath and then rub my neck.

The silence stretches in the room—like I reminded everyone how many times I've fucked up. It's not like I can showcase my triumphs. They're hidden behind every mistake.

A redheaded girl abruptly climbs the stairs into the yacht's living room, adding to the strain. She pinches the stem of a wine-glass, her glossy hair draped across her shoulder in curls, wearing a silk green dress that's practically lingerie.

I tug at the collar of my shirt, my stomach tossing.

She's twenty-six.

And my father's date.

Seeing her sours my body, especially as she struts over to my dad and presses her lips against his. I turn my head the same time that Ryke does.

I spent my entire life watching women of all ages parade in and out of my house. Never once did he invite them for an extra night. He attended every party stag. No matter if I was five or fifteen or twenty. He was single in public. At night, he did what he wanted.

I never asked why he refused to marry again or to even date. But now that he's chosen to do it with a girl practically Ryke's age—it only makes me sick.

I try to breathe, and my ribs ache. I need air.

Without a word, I just head through the sliding glass doors, the moon illuminating the deck. I bypass the hot tub on the way to the railing.

I just . . .

I look up at the sky, full of stars, a glowing moon. And I inhale the sticky air, pain shooting through my lungs as they expand. I wince and rest my forearms on the railing, bent over like a force bears on my shoulders. Gravity is tugging me toward the ocean. Bringing me down.

I hear the glass door open and shut, but I don't turn to see which sorry person has decided to spend extra time with me.

"Do you remember the Cayman Islands trip?" Lily asks, staring at the water in reverence.

My heart pounds, an added beat, happy it's her. Here. With me. "When we were seven?" I think hard, trying to wash away the blurry haze of our childhood.

She nods. "Our dads had a business trip for the week, and they brought us on this yacht."

It starts coming back. We were carted around to most of their meetings instead of being kept in daycare. Just us two and a ton of older cigar-smoking men. "We built a fort in the bow with couch cushions," I recall. I smile at the image of her thin build and big eyes. She was quiet and shy, and when the stewards came around to ask us if we'd like any drinks, she'd whisper her order in my ear.

I also can't remember a night where we didn't sleep in the same bed. Innocent sleepovers. At first they all were, and somewhere along the way, we changed. I fell in love with her.

She smiles at a memory. "You used to tell me that if I didn't hold on to the railing, I'd fall right off the boat. Like an automatic spring would pop up underneath my feet and catapult me overboard."

I nod a couple times. "I didn't want you to get too close." I was scared of my best friend drowning. I feared that possibility over my own death as a kid. And then a bigger memory triggers. "You realize we were husband and wife back then."

She squints at me, trying to picture this.

I gape, teasingly. "You can't remember our first wedding, love?" I touch my heart. "I'm wounded." It was right before the Cayman Islands trip. We were just playing pretend, but after we went through the "ceremony" in our backyard, I called Lily my wife on the boat. My dad even fed into it, telling me to "go get my wife for dinner" when Lily was taking too long in the shower.

In our twenties, I never thought we'd be here again. With these feelings more intense than the first ones. With love more powerful. A bad day can overturn into a better one. And all we have to do is be with each other.

Unable to hide her own smile, she says, "We were husband and wife."

"We were." I wrap my arm around her waist, bringing her closer. And I kiss her nose.

She's glowing.

And the pressure on my chest—I realize that it's gone. Just like that.

I felt my son move tonight. It's a thought that puts every irritation aside. For the longest time, I thought maybe he hadn't really been alive. Maybe he was going to be swept from us.

I recognize now what's important to me. Him. Her. All three of us. "Lil . . ." I stare down at her green eyes that glimmer in the moonlight. "I'm remarrying you."

Her lips part. "What?" We haven't brought marriage up since before I first relapsed, over a year ago.

I turn to her and cup her cheeks in my hands. "Someday we're going to have another wedding, and it's going to blow our seven-year-old one out of the fucking water."

Her smile rises, but it's filled with heartache, and one of her tears falls on my hand. "Lo," she whispers, "it's okay if it never happens, as long as we're together . . . it's enough."

I screwed it up for us when I relapsed. She believed in something, and then I crushed it. "Seven-year-old Lily loved being married to me," I tell her with a weak smile. "I gave you a million piggyback rides."

"You said that's what married couples do," she notes, her eyes right on mine.

My hands fall to her hips. "Someday I'm going to make it right again," I say softly. "Promises from me don't mean much." I know this. "So I'm going to give you something better." I shift her behind me, and then I easily lift her onto my back.

I can feel her smiling as she wraps her legs around my waist, her arms around my neck. I hold her securely beneath her knees, and I walk toward the bow. "Fly away with me, Lily Calloway?"

She whispers, "Only if we make believe that we never, ever have to grow up."

"There's a problem with that, love," I say, carrying her on my back across the deck.

"What's that?" she asks, and I picture her adorable crinkled brows.

I'm smiling more than I have all night. "Our make-believe always turns out real."

From our pretend wedding to our pretend relationship—in the end, it's all become reality. And I would love to never, ever grow up with Lily Calloway. In one universe, we'll be young forever.

Twenty-two

Lily Calloway

stare hard at Lo's back. It's bare and naked and teasing me. Normally I'd be compelled to jump on him. Koala-bear-style. Now April and back in Philly, my belly has grown much bigger since Daisy's birthday, so large that it's a hindrance for all future piggyback rides.

He concentrates on the wall, running a paint roller across the surface. He only removed his shirt when he realized he had on his Cobalt Diamonds tee, a gift from Connor. And like my sister, Connor takes complete offense if you don't take good care of his gifts. He wouldn't appreciate a splatter of blue paint across his company's logo.

My space on the wall looks pathetic in comparison to his section. In defense, all I'm working with is a small paintbrush, and it doesn't help that I've been taking breaks. The rocking chair calls out to me. Not only is it the only piece of furniture in the room, it also relaxes all of my achy muscles.

Sitting on the floorboards, I languidly move my brush against the wall, not caring much about being neat or perfect. My eyes have landed on a new beauty.

Lo's butt.

It's beautiful.

Better than his bare, muscular shoulders. Then again, his butt isn't naked right now.

"You staring at my ass, Lil?"

I jump in surprise, paint catching my wrist. *Shit.*

He looks over his shoulder, a smile in his eyes.

"You have a nice ass," I tell him.

His grin descends to his lips, and then his gaze flits to the wide-open door. Across from our nursery there's another one.

Rose and Connor had all of their furniture imported from some boutique in Paris. They changed their mind about Hale Co. products at the last minute, and I think it has to do with Connor and Jonathan's prolonged fight.

Rose offered to ship some items for us, but we want to support Hale Co., so all of our things should be arriving sometime this month.

I spot the baby pink walls and the twinkling chandelier dangling from the ceiling. A room fit for a princess. Even the walls have artistic floral designs, hand-painted. Our nursery is bare except for the Hale Co. rocking chair and some muted blue paint.

I've never had a problem with my simple tastes, but I worry our kid might.

Maybe he should have a room fit for a prince.

Lo passes me to the door, shutting it quietly.

"Maybe we should hire someone to decorate?" I suggest. Rose has given me three business cards from various interior designers. She's not so subtle with her hints.

"Our nursery will look beautiful, Lil." He comes closer, placing his hands on my shoulders. "I mean, it may not have a chandelier." His lips lift.

I smile too.

"But it's going to be perfect," he adds. "And if Rose has a boy, you can bet she'll be jealous of all this." He motions to the half-painted blue walls. My sister is still pretending that fate is working in her favor and that she'll have a girl.

No one knows though. She won't check.

"She has to have a backup plan if she has a boy," I say. "Like some sort of on-call decorators. Rose is always prepared."

He shakes his head. "I don't think she does." He pauses. "Can you imagine Rose holding a baby?"

"No," I say honestly. It's such a weird image. She even holds dolls at a distance, as if they'll grow lifelike and start crying and spitting up on her. Rose is anti-babies, so the thought of her toting around a beautiful tiny one with her features . . . it's just strange. "She must be really scared," I realize. Rose keeps a lot inside, so it's not like she struts around with her fears on her chest. They crop up in the actions she takes, the paths she walks.

"She'll do fine," Lo says with more assurance. "She may be an ice queen, but she drops her whole schedule if you need her, Lil, even when you don't ask her to. That's love, you know?"

Selflessness. Something that Lo and I are trying to grow into. "You just complimented my sister," I point out.

His fingers slide up my neck, tangling in my short hair. "I know, it feels *so* wrong." He strokes the washed strands, not greasy.

Yesterday, my hair reached my armpits. I wasn't a fan. So I grabbed a pair of kitchen scissors and whacked it back to its usual length, resting against my shoulders. Magazines have already gone crazy over my new "botched" haircut. I don't know what they're talking about. I think it looks better.

I stare up at Lo while he towers above me. My eyes flit to his lips. *Kiss me.* The place between my legs pulses for a hardness that he possesses. His hand massages my head in a sensual way. A breathy noise escapes my mouth, and I ache to stand up and press my pelvis against him. But I know my belly will hit his body before my lower half does.

I don't want to have sex in our kid's nursery, but I do want to have sex with Loren Hale.

I realize I'm gripping his legs, forcing him right here, beside me. He tugs my hair a little, and another sound breaches. I slowly stand, my heart speeding up a hill. I watch his eyes trail my body with a heady gaze. His arousal only heats all the needy places inside me.

We had sex about two hours ago, before we began painting.

"I'm insatiable." I say the words that I've always known.

"You're perfect," he breathes, tucking a piece of hair behind my ear. "And after we finish this wall, I'll finish inside you."

Oh my God. I clench my thighs together. "You know I only have fourteen more weeks left . . ." My shoulders curve forward in regret for bringing up my due date like the sex-pocalypse. But it does feel like that. With the birth, I can't do it for six weeks.

"Are you nervous about abstaining?" he asks me seriously.

"A little," I admit. I've just been so monstrous about sex lately. I can't imagine not having it for twenty-four hours. Six weeks seems like forever. "But Poppy said I'm not going to want sex, so I've been less scared." She said that passing a baby through my vagina will make me not so horny, but I worry that I'll be an exception to this. "I'm sure I'll be so stressed out about Maximoff that I won't care about sex." I frown. That seems false though.

The more stress I have, the more sex I crave. I fuck to "placate" my worries, putting me in a subdued, content state.

I don't meet Lo's eyes. I know they're filled with overbearing concern. I just focus on his abs and outline the small ridges with my fingers.

His hands drop to my hips, holding tight. I ache to be closer, but I settle with splaying my palms on his bare chest. "If anything," he tells me, "I'm going to be the horny one. And you'll have to deny me over and *over* for six goddamn weeks."

I smile weakly. "Payback?"

He nods. "Oh yeah. For every *no* I ever had to tell your pretty little face." He pinches my cheeks, and I slap his hand away.

"*Your* pretty little face is going to be hearing lots of *no's* then."

"I'm counting on it." He leans in, closing the gap between us. His lips touch mine, kissing me softly and then deeply, pulling me awake. He cups the back of my head as I taste his minty breath.

I only break apart when my phone buzzes on the floorboards. Lo returns to the wall, dipping his roller in paint while I check my text, plopping back on the ground.

> The espresso machine broke. The force is not with us today. Want me to buy a new one or have someone come fix it? —Maya

I make an executive decision. *Have someone look at it first.* I press send. I've found out that one of our morning shift employees at Superheroes & Scones is a little aloof, like me, so it may just be an operator error.

I notice that I've missed other texts, some I've purposefully kept unopened all week. But I click into them now.

> Is there anything I can do to change this? —Ryke

> This fucking sucks. —Ryke

I've taken the immature silent treatment route this past week, but I haven't grown the courage to tell him that I've been aroused by his presence and that I feel gross by it.

While the same things happened with Connor, it only occurred twice and stopped there. Every time I see Ryke, I just feel weird.

Lo told his brother to give me some space, so he hasn't bombarded me in person like he usually would. He's just been texting me, being pushy from a distance. *Soon*, I think. I'll face him. But not this soon.

Lo's phone chirps like a bird.

"What's that?" Lo asks, his rolling stopping against the wall. I ditch my phone for his, one with internet and app capabilities.

"Uhh . . ." *My Twitter notifications on your phone.* ". . . a bird?" I'm a horrible liar. Well, that's not true. I did lie to my entire family for three years. I am horrible at lying to *Lo.*

"Lil," he says in warning.

"It's not Tumblr!" I greedily check Twitter and realize that someone has finally discovered my official account. Whoa. My third post about Raisy has been retweeted over a thousand times. "Raisy is alive!" I cheer, bouncing up to my feet.

Lo gives me a weird look and then snatches the phone out of my hand.

I don't care. I'm twirling. I did it. We succeeded! "No more three-way rumors," I singsong. "Everyone loves Raisy."

"I'm deleting your account," Lo says, his voice hollow.

I stop mid-twirl. I realize that I sang out loud and *actually* spun in a circle. My skin roasts. "What? Lo, it's working—"

"Did you read the replies?" His cheekbones are sharpening.

"No . . . I . . . celebrated too soon?"

He nods tensely and hands me the phone back. "Delete it, Lil."

I scroll through some of the replies, and my excitement is shot down like a pigeon in the sky. And yes, I deserve to be a pigeon, not a majestic eagle or a sprightly blue jay.

@littlehex99: @lilycallowayX23 you're for sure banging Ryke and trying to cover it up. I bet Daisy is still with that model guy, Julian. Isn't she??

No.

@Sherlock2Baby: @lilycallowayX23 I called this from the start!! You LOVE Ryke!!! You can't fool us, Lily!!

I'm not trying to.

@lotusflowwers: @lilycallowayX23 you're such a fucking slut. I hope you die from banging two guys at once.

I cringe. That's not nice.

"There has to be some good stuff here," I tell Lo.

"Lil, please, just delete the account. It's not worth the stress."

I don't want to give up yet. "Let me take a picture of you," I say. "I'll tweet it and ignore all the other comments."

He hesitates for a couple seconds. "Only if you don't respond to the negative tweets."

I nod vigorously, and my chest expands with more excitement.

He holds the paint roller, and instead of giving me a signature bitter half-smile, Lo produces a heartfelt, really attractive smile with dimples attached. I have to cross my ankles to keep from throbbing so much down below. I snap a quick pic and then upload it without a caption.

Words can be twisted more than pictures. Though the photo-shopped pictures of me on the yacht between two hot dogs was pretty bad.

Lo returns to painting, and I sit back down with his phone, logging into *Celebrity Crush*, just a quick perusal of all the headlines.

Ryke Meadows' Epic Fight in Mexico Caught on Tape!

The videos went viral. Lo says that whenever Ryke goes out now, people jeer at him—thinking he's easily provoked. Everyone wants to see a Fight Part Two. For him to feed their entertainment.

"Is Ryke okay?" I ask Lo. I know how overwhelming the paparazzi and general public can be. But if anyone can take it, it's definitely Ryke Meadows.

Lo briefly glances at me. "Why don't you ask him?" His tone is only a little edged.

Worry infiltrates my defenses. "I'm not attracted to your—"

"I know you aren't, Lil. You don't have to keep reminding me."

It's not porn. It's okay. That's what I need to tell myself.

I check another headline. *Ryke Defends Lily Calloway's Honor at Her Little Sister's Birthday.*

I hate that one. Because although it's the truth, it seems so wrong on the outside.

VIDEO: Loren Hale & Connor Cobalt Kiss in Mexico!

I perk up. Should I? My finger hovers over the link to the article.

"Lily," Lo warns.

"Lo," I say back.

"You have that look."

I blink. "The unsatisfied look?"

"No, the one that says you're about to do something bad."

I shake my head. "Nope. No. Not going to . . ." I lick my dry lips. But it's *so* tempting. I haven't even read fans' comments about the kiss because I've been avoiding the video clips for so long. Lo suddenly steals my phone . . . or rather *his* phone.

"How'd you get over here so fast?" I ask. My mouth falls and my eyes widen. "Your superpower kicked in."

His forehead wrinkles as he stares at the phone screen in concentration. And then his eyes flit to mine. "When you imagine me kissing Connor, how long is it?" he asks.

"Thirty seconds," I say, feeling my cheeks heat, which shows my lie too easily. "Okay, it's actually more like a minute . . . and there may be some tongue involved."

Lo groans. "Lil."

"I have an overactive imagination. It's not my fault. It's my dirty brain's fault."

He sighs, presses his phone's screen, and then turns it to me. Oh my God. He hit "play". I am watching the video. I am watching him . . .

I squint. "This is blurry."

"We were in a dark nightclub. They're all blurry."

It's not exactly brief, but it's not especially long either. Connor and Lo's lips lock, and then I have to squint to make out the rest. I can barely see their faces, but I do spot a pair of hands on Lo's neck. Connor obviously guided him so it was more than just kissing a wall, but it's too quick to really obsess over. And it's all grainy.

My shoulders drop. But it's okay, I think. Maybe it's even better than okay.

"Did I destroy your fantasy?"

I nod. "It's ruined."

"Good," he says, squatting down in front of me. My nerves light up just staring into those entrancing amber eyes. "How's this reality?"

I smile wide. "Much, much better," I realize.

Twenty-three

Lily Calloway

"Hale Co. is a multibillion-dollar empire," Daniel Perth repeats for the second time as we ride the glass elevator to the seventy-fifth floor. "If you think you're being brought in here for shits and giggles, think again."

He sounds so much like Lo's dad that I honestly wonder if Jonathan Hale hires people with his personality or if his employees just pick up the lingo after a while. When Daisy and I arrived in the lobby five minutes ago, Daniel introduced himself as one of the fourteen board members. He's in his late-thirties, has a prominent nose, fluffy brown hair, and a very expensive suit. And he is not about the bullshit.

He's told us that three times already.

"You're both about to meet the rest of the board. Handshakes and lunch. Easy."

Tomorrow they're meeting with Ryke and Lo. They wanted to split us up in pairs so they'd have a better indication of how we act on our own. So far, so good.

I nervously wipe my sweaty palms on my khaki pants, my baby bump visible underneath my silk top. Daisy towers beside me in high-waisted navy shorts and a white blouse, sans bra. She had her yellow cast cut off in March, so her wrist is decorated in gold bangles.

She's all stylish like she's ready to walk the runway, and I feel matronly—ready to sink into a couch and take a luxurious nap. But I'm here on a mission: ensure Loren and Ryke are *not* chosen as the new CEO. They've both spent years dodging this life, and there's no reason they have to fall back into it now.

I can tell Daisy is going to be tough competition, but I have to do better than her too. She just turned nineteen, and she's already worked most of her life. The corporate world is not calling her. Nope. I won't let it. Big sister priorities intact, I am ready to impress.

Although . . . I have never impressed anyone. My M.O. is to stand by the wall and blend into the paint.

This'll be a challenge.

Daniel fixes his tie. "We have the final say-so in which one of you becomes the CEO, and we're not going to pass the title over lightly. Whoever we choose will be the face of the company." His eyes fall to me. "And it's going to take a *lot* of convincing if you want to be that person."

A sex addict as the face of a baby company.

I can see why this may be a little problematic, but I have to put my best foot forward.

"She's going to do great," Daisy says with a bright smile. She slings her arm around my shoulders.

Daniel's eyes finally migrate to her, and they intensify in a different way. My sisterly guard rises about a hundred feet. *No. No. No.*

"You're charming," he says like he's filing the note in the "positives" category. Jonathan said the men thought as much about Daisy.

The ends of her blonde hair are dyed a muted orange, like the sunset, and she styled her locks so they cover the scar on her cheek. "You're up-front," she tells him.

"Honey," he says, "all fourteen of us aren't going to beat around any bush. Jonathan likes it that way." His gaze descends down her long, long legs. "If you were ten years older, you'd be perfect."

"Story of my life," Daisy mutters under her breath.

I wish I was taller. Even though I stand between them, they can easily have a conversation over my head. She's wearing high heels. He's past six-feet. I'm only five-five and a little bit extra. Ryke would *not* appreciate Daniel's lingering gaze, and now my friend instincts take over.

I cough into my hand, disrupting his staring.

"Yes?" he asks me.

"I'd like it if you stopped ogling my sister."

"She and *you* better get used to it," Daniel says. "You're both going to be 'ogled' from here on out." He even uses air quotes, and his eyes drift to my belly. "And don't be surprised if some of the women fawn over you. You're not only our target audience, but you're carrying Jonathan's grandson. They're all excited."

I flinch in shock that these women would be *excited* to meet me. "That's a strong adjective," I say softly.

"It's a correct one," he tells me. "Almost everyone loves Jonathan, and if we could repair his image, we all would. But it's too late for that."

The elevator suddenly pings. We're here. The seventy-fifth floor.

When the doors slide open, we see four women, the rest men, holding champagne flutes, servers wandering around. They all turn and stare right at us. Their expressions are severe, no-nonsense, poised and confident. They size us up immediately.

Daniel watches our stunned reactions and says, "Welcome to Hale Co."

Lunch begins, and I almost instantaneously lose my sister in this meet and greet. The high tables are lined with small sandwiches and tapas. I pinch the stem of a wineglass filled with chilled water and linger by a table in the corner, away from the limelight.

It's safe here. I chew slowly, using food as an excuse not to talk too much. I just nod a lot. All four women have flocked me, and they ask me about baby things, like which Hale Co. product I like the best. Easy stuff, but I suspect they're mentally jotting notes about my "personable" skills.

"I like the rocking chairs," I say between bites of cucumber sandwich. The women stare at me like a mouse has spoken. I take a large gulp of water. I secretly want to raise my hand and say, *introvert in the building!* But that's not going to help me.

They want someone like Daisy.

The men seriously love her. She already learned the art of schmoozing from her modeling career. Seven middle-aged men surround my little sister across the spacious conference room with floor-length windows overlooking Philadelphia.

"If we have a press conference, how would you handle personal questions?" the oldest woman asks me, redirecting my attention. She wears a conservative blue dress, has short blonde hair and an intimidating scowl. Irene, she said her name was.

"I'd answer them to the best of my ability," I say, tucking a piece of my hair behind my ear.

"Don't do that," Rachel tells me, a five-foot brunette woman. "The press will think you're uncomfortable."

I am uncomfortable.

"She is uncomfortable," Irene points out.

Shit. "It's just pregnancy stuff. I'm not one-hundred-percent." I almost want to touch my belly and thank Maximoff for the escape.

Irene doesn't buy it. "So if I asked you how Loren is, what would you tell me?"

"He's great," I say, my cheeks heating.

"Do you always turn this red?" Rachel asks.

I nod, eating slowly. After a swallow, everyone still looks at me for an answer. "It's uh, a thing." Oh my God. I need someone to bail me out of this. I search the room, and I stop myself, realizing I'm looking for Lo.

"A thing?" another woman says. I can't remember her name.

"Did you really graduate from Princeton?" Rachel questions.

I nod.

"Her GPA was appalling," Irene mentions, "which is why no one should be that impressed."

Jeez. Anger pumps out of my chest. I spent *years* busting my butt for that diploma. Sure, I had a lot of help, but I still worked for it. "I earned that degree," I say. "I passed all of my classes and studied for every exam. I may not have been the smartest person in the room, but at least I tried my best and succeeded."

Irene stares at me for a long moment, and I am about to shrink underneath her penetrating gray stare, but then her lips curve into a smile. "We can work with that."

I did kind of sound like Rose a little bit right there, sticking up for myself. I internally pat myself on the back. *Good job, Lily.*

Rachel asks me another question, but I'm distracted by the men's laughter. Daisy gesticulates with her hands like she's telling a hilarious story, and they're all eating it up. One even places his palm on her shoulder. It falls to her back.

And then lower, sliding down to the spot above her ass.

No. *No.*

"Excuse me," I mutter, on a new mission. Protect my little sister. I don't hear anything that Irene, Rachel, or the other two women say. I march over to Daisy, my pulse racing. It doesn't help that Maximoff decides *now* of all times to kick me in the ribs.

Great. Just great.

Daisy slyly tries to step out of the handsy guy's space, but he shifts with her. She bobs her head at him and the others like she's enthralled with the conversation. I notice that the handsy one has horn-rimmed glasses. After I binge-watched *Heroes*, I trust no one who wears those particular glasses. Paranoid. Yes.

But I've been an absent sister for most of my life. I plan on beating Rose and Poppy for the best older sister award, so I scoot closer to Daisy's side and try to wedge my body between her and Horn-Rimmed.

His hand falls off her back. Success.

I inwardly give myself a second pat.

And then every single man stares down at me like I appeared out of thin air. Not only that, I see their minds churning. It's like their eyeballs are imprinted with *she's a sex addict*. I'm a unique specimen, I suppose, but it only heightens the awkward silence.

I have no idea how to alter it, no plan on what to say after I interrupted their conversation. I thought I could coyly sneak in, be invisible, swat Horn-Rimmed's hand away, and sneak out.

I fucked up.

But Daisy is so good at integrating introverts that she wraps an arm around my shoulders and says, "I was telling them about the time we tested out Hale Co. bicycles as kids."

I vaguely remember this, but it's lost in a pool of other foggy memories.

"I was six," she quickly paints the picture for me, "and I decided to ride the bike without using the handlebars. I crashed into Jonathan's Range Rover next door."

Daniel, with his fluffy brown hair, speaks up. "So you've moved on to crashing motorcycles?"

All the guys laugh lightly, like flirty laughter, some even *nervous*. Like a gorgeous, confident girl automatically intimidates them. This is bizarre.

Daisy shrugs. "I like going fast."

Horn-Rimmed zeroes in on me. "What about you, Lily? Are you more cautious in your approach?"

My approach to life? All the eyes pin to my body, and my neck grows hot. And then Maximoff kicks me again, this time in the *bladder*. So hard that I have no opportunity to stop myself. The water I downed at the other table suddenly leaks.

My world is in slow motion.

Everyone waits for me to finish my sentence while a wet spot sprouts on my khaki slacks. Oh my God.

I am mortified. This ranks up there . . . high, *high* up there.

They can't see. They can't see. I pray that my face hasn't turned tomato-red yet.

"She's more analytical than me," Daisy says. I catch her gaze, and she looks at me like *are you okay?* No. Nope. Daisy smiles at all of them, trying to remove the attention from me.

"You're the impulsive sister?" Horn-Rimmed asks Daisy, eyeing her long, long legs like Daniel did.

"Very," Daisy says, "and I'm so impulsive that I have to whisk Lily away from all of you. Sorry. We just need a quick break." She hooks her arm with mine, and we head toward the ladies' room. I'm practically sprinting.

"What's wrong?" she whispers.

I shake my head. I can't say just yet. My body is petrified, and goose bumps run down my arms the longer I play the moment in my head, on rerun. My face flames by the minute.

When we disappear inside the bathroom, Daisy shutting the door, I inhale a deep breath. "I peed," I let it out like that.

Daisy stares at my pants and wears a pained smile. "Uh-oh."

I haven't even grown the bravery to look, but I do now. The spot is very wet in the front. I check myself in the mirror. And the back.

They all saw me pee myself. "I just screwed my chances."

"They all know you're pregnant." Daisy breezes down the bathroom, peeking in all the stalls to make sure they're empty before she returns to me. "If I peed my pants, it would've been weird."

Yeah. Okay. I can blame this on my baby. It's his fault. Oh God, that sounds awful too.

Daisy takes out her phone and puts it on speaker. She's the problem solver in this instance. Doesn't matter that I'm older. Our roles usually reverse given the circumstance. I've bailed her out of situations, and she's bailed me out of plenty more.

I've always felt guilty that she's had to act like the older sister toward me. But, I think, maybe I've been wrong all this time.

One of us doesn't have to be more responsible than the other just because of age. We're both vulnerable. We're both strong. We're both problem solvers.

I think, maybe, that's what being sisters is all about. Picking each other up when the other trips. Putting on our sisterly super-hero capes when the other needs us. We're both human in the end.

"Hey," Daisy says into the receiver. "Are you around the Hale Co. offices by chance?"

I expect Rose's icy voice to cut in, not this one: "I'm about to ride over to Ralph Stover, but I can pass through if you need me." Ryke Meadows. She called the one person that I am on a hiatus with.

My eyes widen in horror at Daisy, and I wave my hands to shut this down, and I mouth, *No!* Daisy gives me a look like *this is the only option.* But Lo . . . is working. Connor is working. Rose is working.

Everyone is working on Tuesday. Except Ryke.

"Dais? Is everything okay?" he asks. "I can pick you up if you want to leave early."

"No," she says quickly. "It's not that. Can you just grab some of Lily's clothes—"

"No, no, no," I cut in, my voice high-pitched. "It's fine. He has to go meet Ralph Stover. I wouldn't want to take him away from his friend . . ." I trail off at Daisy's smile.

Ryke answers me on the line. "Ralph Stover is a fucking state park." Rock climbing, I realize. He was going rock climbing. "What do you need, Lily?" I hear a door creak open from his end, and I wonder if he's already in my bedroom.

I think I'm a new shade of red called Fire Engine Embarrassment. I open my mouth to mumble out the articles of clothing, but I just eat air.

"A new pair of pants," Daisy tells him easily. "And panties."

I'd like to disintegrate now.

"What the fuck happened?" Concern infiltrates his rough voice.

"Ipeedmyself," I say so quickly.

"You pissed your pants?" Ryke asks with questioning, the sound of a drawer sliding open.

I make a noise of distress and rest my forehead on the sink counter, all hunched over. Daisy rubs my back.

"Hey." Ryke tries to soften his voice. "It's okay. I'll be there in a second, Lily."

Daisy holds the phone near her mouth. "Can you speed?"

"Sure," he says without hesitation. "I always break this fucking law for you, sweetheart." It is so cute that I almost swoon instead of roast, but this humiliation is just too strong today.

My invisibility powers have let me down once again.

Twenty-four

Lily Calloway

In the span of five minutes, Irene has checked on us once, and we told her that someone is stopping by to bring me a change of clothes. She actually turned her scowl into a pity smile for me. That's how bad this is.

"He's coming up the elevator," Daisy says, checking her texts.

I crack the bathroom door and peek at the fourteen board members, who all take the extra time to chat with each other.

"No one has bailed on us yet," Daisy whispers to me. She peeks through the top portion of the crack while I crouch below her. She's right. They're still eating, drinking, and smiling, which is good.

The elevator dings, and all of the board members quiet, rotating to face the sliding metal doors. Ryke emerges, wearing a leather bike jacket, zipped to the collar, and a black backpack with buckles across the chest. A green water bottle dangles off the lower strap with a carabiner.

No one approaches him. They're the ones stunned in silence now, not expecting him to be here today.

He's essentially crashing this lunch party, and he acts like he couldn't give a flying shit. He looks around the place and spots the bathroom where we hide. Then he begins his trek this way without introducing himself or even shaking a single hand.

Though he decides to snatch a couple mini-sandwiches on the way here, eating them in one bite.

"Is he self-sabotaging?" I whisper to Daisy. The board members murmur, gossiping about him, and Ryke ignores all of it.

"I don't think so." Daisy backs away from the door as he nears, and I do the same.

Ryke slips inside and shuts the door behind him.

I cover my face with my hands, refusing to meet his brooding gaze for multiple reasons. The first being: I just peed myself. And he can see the stains.

"So they said you're having lunch and they bring in bite-sized fucking sandwiches?" he curses. I hear him unzip his backpack on the sink counter, grateful he's not advertising my soiled pants yet.

"You'll have to eat before you come here tomorrow," Daisy tells him. I peer through my fingers and watch her hop up on the sink.

"It's a multibillion-dollar company; they could've ordered subs."

Daisy wears a devious smile. "Ladies don't put foot-longs in their mouths."

Oh my God. I am alone with Ryke and Daisy. *Flirty* Raisy. I need help. SOS. Someone save me. I drop my hands and reach for my phone in my pocket.

His eyebrows rise at her, his backpack right there. *Accio, my clothes!* They do not magically land in my hands. Harry Potter fail. I'm truly not a wizard.

"Calloway," Ryke says, "you've never been a lady, and it has nothing to do with taking twelve inches in your mouth."

Oh shit.

"Say that again." She smiles so big.

"No!" I interject with frantic eyes. They both look at me, and I use one hand to shield my gaze. "I don't want to know how many inches his . . . thing is." He cannot be twelve inches. That's just too big.

"I'm not twelve fucking inches," he tells me. Thank God. "Lily, you can look at me?"

"I can't," I say. I am trying to keep my "perverted thoughts" under the surface. I cannot be aroused. Nope. I will not let my body feel embarrassment, guilt, shame, and pleasure all at once. It's the most toxic, gross mixture.

I sense Ryke nearing, and I scuttle backward, my shoulders hitting a stall door.

"*Lily.* It's just me." There's pain in his voice.

I swallow a lump and slowly drop my hand. He is holding my pants out to me, really nicely. Daisy watches from the sink, and she gives me a thumbs-up. Something tells me that she'd planned for us to make up right now—and maybe that's why she called him out of everyone.

How can I say this out loud without seeming strange and weird?

"Maybe if you talk about it, we can clear the fucking air," Ryke says with hard brows. He's not even sure what he did. I've just been dodging him. "Here, take this." He pushes the pants to me, and I hold on to my clean clothes like a life vest.

And then I say, "I'm a pervert."

His face falls. "You're not a fucking pervert."

"You always say—"

"I'm an asshole," he suddenly tells me, licking his lips. "I say exactly what's on my mind, and sometimes it doesn't come across how I intend it to. Do you think perverted things? Yes. But so do I. It doesn't make either of us perverts." He takes a tense breath. "I don't want you to believe that you're one because of things I've said. It'd . . . honestly, it would break my heart."

Maybe his comments have affected me over the years. "I shouldn't have taken them so personally . . ."

He shakes his head a couple times. "No. I shouldn't have fucking said them in the first place." He lets out a deeper sigh, frustrated with himself.

I don't want him to feel bad. It's not even the source of why I've been dodging him. "You don't understand," I whisper. How can I say this? My face scrunches in a wince. And I stare at his feet, the shameful heat swirling around me. "I really am gross. I mean . . . I've been aroused so much lately that almost anything turns me on, even things that never did before."

The silence deadens the bathroom.

"Like what things?" Ryke asks, and I can almost hear the gears clicking in his brain.

I can't look at them.

"Us?" Ryke asks. "Or just me?" *Both.*

"I'm sorry," I say. My instincts scream *retreat, retreat, retreat!* So I dart into the stall and shut it closed, my heart thumping against my rib cage.

"Lily—"

"You don't need to say anything." I take this time to change into my clean clothes, unfolding the black pants and finding a pair of purple cotton panties.

I don't think too much about the fact that Ryke picked them out from my drawer.

"So this hasn't been about the three-way rumors then?" Ryke calls out.

"No." I've already accepted those rumors for what they are. The old me that would obsess and be affected by them has been buried away. I've been avoiding him because of something worse.

He keeps talking to me. "Look, I know you feel bad about this, but you shouldn't."

I frown, not expecting this reaction. After changing, I zip up my pants and step out of the stall, bundling my dirty clothes together. I need to see his face.

The minute I do, I only see compassion.

Daisy even looks empathetic. "We could've toned it down. I didn't know . . ."

I shake my head fiercely. "No, that was the last thing I wanted you to do. You're a new couple. You deserve to bask in it, and I didn't want to take that from you. Especially since Lo and I aren't discreet." It would've been hypocritical to tell them to stop when Lo and I are almost always touching. I stare between them. "Why aren't you disgusted by me?" I feel it. It's like every pore needs to be scrubbed clean.

"Because it's not disgusting," Ryke says forcefully. "It's fucking normal. People can get off by anything, even inanimate objects."

"But I know you . . ." I just don't understand how they can look at me and not see a freak? And why is that all I see when I stare in the mirror?

"I have a confession to make," Daisy pipes in, raising her hand as she sits on the sink. "When I was younger, I totally had a crush on Lo."

I end up smiling, and Ryke is staring at her like *what the fuck?*

"Really?" I say.

She nods. "I thought he was really hot."

"How young?" Ryke asks.

"Twelve, thirteen, somewhere around there. He was my first crush."

A cool breeze washes over my hot anxiety as I begin to realize that I may not be so different from everyone else. It doesn't extinguish all the bad parts, but it makes me feel a bit better.

Ryke stares at her with this hard, dark gaze. "My little brother was your first fucking crush."

"If only you knew me back then," she says, swinging her legs.

He shakes his head. "I'm glad I didn't know you back then. I would've been twenty." And then he glances at me. "We're okay now?"

I let out a deep breath. "I think so." I doubt I'll feel *good* about being aroused by their make-out sessions, but at least I know that it's not the biggest regression on my part. I just have to believe that it's okay. What Lo always says. And try to squash my arousal. I'm just happy that my hormones may go back to their usual level after I give birth.

At least, I hope they do.

"Good. I fucking missed you." He did? "Maybe you should pee your pants more often." He almost smiles. There is the Ryke Meadows I know . . . and yes, I love him too.

I squint, trying to narrow my eyes. "Not funny." And then I trash my dirty clothes and head to the door, possessing way more confidence than I had. I'm not sure where it came from. Probably both my sister and Lo's brother. It's strange how other people can boost you to a higher, better place than you were before.

Ryke clips his backpack to his chest again. "Alright, I'm fucking out of here."

I don't want to mention how he's made a very surly first impression with the board. It's best that he stays oblivious to it so I can beat him.

Daisy hops off the sink counter and says, "Can I ask for another favor before you leave? Don't freak out though."

His stares down at her, questioningly. "What is it?" I have no idea where she's going with this.

Though she seems nervous, fiddling with her fingers. "Can you . . . kiss me in front of everyone on your way out?" Oh, good plan! The men will realize that she's *clearly* with Ryke, and they may stop being so handsy.

"Why?" Ryke asks tensely. He's smart enough to guess, so the muscles in his shoulders already bind.

"I want everyone to know that we're together," she says with a forced smile.

Ryke sees through it. "Which one of those fucking guys is all over you?" *All of them.*

"None," she says. "A couple are just touchy-feely."

"Oh yeah?" Ryke is boiling. "Where'd they fucking touch you?"

"You said you wouldn't freak out," she says.

"I never made that fucking promise," he retorts. "There are so many reasons why I don't want you here, and this is becoming the worst one. Not to mention you're starting to hide your scar—"

"Just never mind," she cuts him off. "I'm sorry I asked for your help."

Is this the beginning of a Raisy fight? I will not let this happen. I interject, physically standing between them by the shut door. "I saw the men," I tell Ryke, pulling his attention on me. "And they really weren't that bad, but I do think it'd be a good idea if they were reminded that you two love each other."

Ryke's jaw muscles tick. "Maybe I should just stay for the rest of the lunch."

"*No*," Daisy says. "You have to trust me."

After a couple seconds, he nods. "Okay."

I exhale. Thank God.

He sets a hand on her head. "This is fucking killing me." He hates seeing her in this world. After this afternoon, I do too. There is something about Daisy that feels too contained and unnatural in a corporate setting. It's not the real her. She can't stand on tables and make speeches. She can't do cartwheels along the carpet.

She can't scream at the top of her lungs.

Or run naked down the hall with no one restraining her as she bolts away as fast as she can.

"It's better this way," she breathes.

"In what world, Calloway?" he asks. "Because in mine, you're free."

I step forward first and clasp the knob, waiting for them. Then Daisy nods to me like, *I'm ready*. And when I open the door, we all enter the conference room.

"They're back," Daniel exclaims, raising his glass to me. Everyone isn't staring at me with shame or pity. They just smile, talk, and wave me over to one of the high tables, acting mature about the whole ordeal. They are adults. I'm the one trying to fit in.

While I head over to Rachel and Irene, I watch Ryke and Daisy stop in the middle of the room. Their body language says that he's telling her goodbye before he leaves. And his hand is lost in her hair, after briefly eye-fucking, he kisses her with tongue.

I look away before my body responds, and I plant my gaze on the gaggle of men by a high table. Some shrink back, though the majority of the ten men stand tall. The moment that Ryke breaks from Daisy and begins walking to the elevator, he shoots the men one of the most territorial glowers. Now more than a couple guys step backward.

Message received.

"I'll give him this," Irene says, sidling next to me as Ryke disappears into the elevator, "he knows how to make an entrance and an exit." She sips her champagne. "Just like his father."

I have no idea who is going to win this, I realize.

If they warm to Ryke's personality as it is, then we're all screwed. The future CEO of Hale Co. could be any one of us. If I learned anything today, it's that Ryke and Daisy's relationship will not survive if one of them takes this position.

It has to be me.

Twenty-five

Loren Hale

How'd it go?" Lily asks me.

She chose after we had sex and took (separate) showers to bring up my meeting with the Hale Co. board members a few hours ago.

"They're already engraving my name on the door," I say, flashing a dry smile while I towel dry my hair.

Her lips downturn, not exactly excited about that possibility. "You don't really want it, do you?" She steps into cotton shorts and pulls on a baggy T-shirt to sleep in.

"It's my destiny," I say dramatically, touching my chest.

"I'm serious, Lo," she whispers, her eyes on the ground for a second.

It's easier to joke about it. I tie my drawstring pants and remember how all the board members treated me this afternoon. I went in with the same irritated expression I always wear, and they weren't put off by me. They listened to everything I had to say. Never dismissed my comments. Always seemed interested. It was strange. By the end, I realized that my father must've told them to treat me well. Something I never thought he'd do.

It's made me uneasy all night. I didn't earn this respect. It was just handed to me. My dad has always taught me to work hard for what I have, and for him to pass this over to me—it goes against too many years of screaming matches and lectures.

I tug her to my bare chest. "I'm grateful for this opportunity." It's as rehearsed as it sounds, but somewhere beneath the fear of *this* life I was meant to live, I am grateful.

I have the girl and the kid, the money and the house. Friends and a family.

None of that has to change by taking over Hale Co.—not unless I turn into my father. Being around him always magnetizes our similarities. I have no idea if corporate life will push me toward booze, something Connor and Ryke fear. Hell, something *everyone* has most likely written in stone.

I just worry that in twenty-four years, my son will be sitting where I am, thinking about all the mistakes that *I* made. How *I* fucked up his life, the same way that I look at my father.

I only hope that I'm not walking down a path that leads there.

"You did that well?" Lily says, her brows cinching in this adorable way.

"Honestly . . ." I wrap my arms around her waist. "I have no fucking idea." At first, I thought Ryke bombed the meeting since he told *two* guys to "fuck off" when they brought up Daisy. But the women warmed to him, a sign that they liked his protectiveness and took it as a positive attribute.

Even though we're "working together" right now, I wish Ryke did worse. Then I'd have an indication of who's the front-runner.

"At least you didn't pee your pants," Lily whispers, her cheeks reddening.

My hands rise to her warm face, her embarrassment and anxiety seeping into me. Christ. "No one even mentioned it today, love." I wish I could just remove every uncomfortable emotion from her body.

"Really?" Her lips rise. So do her shoulders.

That was easy. I smile. "Really—"

Our bedroom door flies open. No knock. "Emergency meeting," Rose declares, wearing a black robe, her hair in a pony. She acts like we invited her for a nightcap, aimed for the velvet purple couch against the wall. "Why is it so dark in here?" She takes a seat and cringes at the dim chandelier above our bed, as though it's not doing its job.

I ignore her last statement and check the clock. Midnight. "You're calling a meeting during the witching hour. Trying to harness your black magic, Rose?"

She narrows her yellow-green eyes at me. "*I* didn't call this emergency meeting." I frown, watching her shift uncomfortably on the couch, smashing a pillow behind her back. Having a pregnant belly hasn't made her look any less evil.

"So then who called it?"

Lily steps out of my grasp, wearing a guilty smile.

"Lil . . ." I draw out. *What's going on?*

"While you were at Hale Co., I was doing some research." She shuffles over to our end table. "I have notes . . ."

I'm still confused.

"Connor is bringing the accused," Rose says aloud.

And then Connor knocks on the wooden frame, standing in the doorway with his orange, slender tabby cat curled in his arms. "Has the meeting started?" he asks. Great. Everyone knows what the hell is going on but me.

I focus on Sadie, his cat. "This is about the cat?" I question, sitting on the edge of the bed.

"Yes," Lily says with a nod, scooting next to me with a handful of notes scribbled on various pink Post-its.

Connor glances at the chandelier. "Why is it so dark in here?" And then he flicks the light switch, brightening the room so much that I squint. Jesus Christ.

"Better," Rose tells him.

Lily watches Sadie intensely, and she scuttles back onto the bed, picking her legs off the floor. I get her paranoia since Sadie has hissed at her multiple times.

Connor sits next to his wife, and then she stretches out, resting her legs on the couch like it's a chaise, and he places a hand on her calves. She looks ten thousand times more comfortable. And I'm ten thousand times more aware that this isn't going to be a short discussion.

Rose has her phone in hand, scrolling through her own notes. "Before we discuss Sadie, we need to talk about the cliques in this house."

What the hell is she talking about? I tilt my head at Connor for answers.

He scratches behind Sadie's ears, and I can't shake how submissive a normally hostile cat is in his care. "We called both of you to see how Hale Co. went, and no one answered."

Lily raises her hand like she's in class. "I rarely answer my phone."

"Yeah," I say with a deeper frown. "We barely talk on the phone with each other." I motion between my body and Lily, who is now sitting behind me. She holds on to my waist and peeks from behind my bicep, seriously avoiding this damn cat.

"It just feels like we've been left out of important discussions," Rose says without blowing a fuse. I bet they both prepared and talked out this entire conversation before bringing up the subject. "Like the other day, *Ryke* mentioned how Lily's been having a hard time with her addiction. Where was I for this talk?"

I open my mouth to respond, but she already has an answer.

"I'll tell you where." She leans forward. "*Downstairs.*"

Jesus. This is not the first time she's complained about room arrangements. She's the one who chose the master on the main floor. The biggest room with the biggest bathroom with the biggest goddamn closet. Ryke didn't care. Daisy didn't care. Lily didn't care. I cared on principle, but I let it slide after I saw the amount of pressed shirts Connor owns.

Now she's worried about being "isolated" from the rest of us who room on the second floor. I ask, "You really think it's an issue of proximity?" Maybe she's bitching because Lily and Daisy are getting closer, and it scares her—being on the outs. Turning into Poppy Calloway, who'd rather be with her husband and child than spend time with her sisters.

Rose doesn't want that. She's made it *vitally* clear.

She raises her hand to silence me. "If it's not proximity, then it means you both favor Ryke and Daisy over us, and I'm giving you both the benefit of the doubt."

I look to Connor like *come on*. He can't agree with her.

"I don't believe you're playing favorites, but it's frustrating, even for me, to receive information later than I like."

I scan the room with my arms outstretched. "I don't see Ryke and Daisy *anywhere* for this conversation."

Rose sits straighter. "That's because we're on the second floor."

Lily pipes in, "Do you want to switch rooms with us?"

"No," Rose says.

Connor adds, "That solves nothing."

I recognize now that we're what bridges Ryke, Daisy, Connor, and Rose together. I feel Lily kneel behind me, her lips close to my ears. She whispers really quickly, "We're the popular ones." The surprise in her voice almost makes me smile uncontrollably.

I can't ever remember being this in demand.

"This is *not* amusing," Rose says, crossing her arms in a huff. But she can't really do the action with her baby bump, and she growls in frustration.

Connor rubs her ankles, and she calms down some.

I kind of feel bad. I mean, we're not intentionally trying to shut anyone out of our lives. When we were at the height of our addictions, we did it purposefully, all the time. Now we're actually trying to be inclusive. "You two usually just insert yourselves," I tell them.

Rose folds her hands on her stomach. "It's harder when you can go run to other people with your issues."

"And just to remind you," Connor says in his fluid tone, "Rose and I are certified geniuses. We can solve problems faster than the average human brain. If you're smart, you would take advantage of that."

"I don't take advantage of people until the third date," I banter.

His lips lift in a grin. "We've already kissed. I think we're past that point." The kiss in Mexico—it's been blowing up on social media, and it's causing more speculation for Connor and me than I thought it would.

"Are you okay . . . ?" I trail off because I suddenly realize I'm asking Connor Cobalt if he's doing alright. The self-confident expression he has is priceless.

"Of course I am," he tells me.

I am glad, but I wonder if there will be a day where he'll show me more of his cards. I wonder if I'll always just be the "liability" in his game of chess.

"We're going to move into one of the guest rooms," Rose suddenly blurts out, returning the conversation to its focal point.

Lily's jaw drops comically.

Rose has been body snatched.

I ask, "You're going to give up your giant ass walk-in closet?"

"I'll still keep some of my clothes in that closet, but all of my essentials will be going in our permanent room on the second floor."

Connor nods in agreement.

Wow. Rose loves Lily enough to sacrifice wardrobe space and a bathroom twice the size of the one she'll now be using. It's a huge statement, and Lily is stunned to silence behind me. And then she crawls off the bed and risks an attack from Sadie to hug her sister.

"What are you doing?" Rose says with wide eyes like Lily is about to burn her collection of heels.

"This is how I show my love," Lily says with a squeeze.

Rose replies back with a stiff pat, and they both whisper something to each other that sounds like *I love you*.

Then Sadie hisses at the girls.

Lily shrieks and darts back onto the bed, the mattress bouncing beneath me.

"Easy, love," I tell her, cautiously watching as she crawls behind me. At first my concern peaks since she's really fucking pregnant, but then she climbs onto my back in fright. And I shouldn't be smiling at her fear . . . but Lily is pretty precious when she uses me as a safety net.

"Sadie hates hugs," Rose says. "A woman after my own heart." She pats her lap, and Sadie curls on top of Rose's baby bump and purrs.

"Look at that, bitches congregate together," I say, regretting it the moment it escapes.

Connor arches his eyebrow at me, a small defensive warning, one that Rose misses because she gives me a death glare of ginormous proportions. I deserve that one.

"Lily," Rose says. "I'm giving the floor to you since Loren abuses it."

"Burn," I say dryly.

Lily clears her throat and peeks behind my arm, reading off her notes. "After surfing the internet, it has come to my attention that cats and newborns do not get along." That fact isn't that surprising.

Rose stiffens more, and she protectively holds on to Sadie. Connor studies his wife with more intensity than before—it's all really not making a lot of sense to me. I get that Rose has grown affectionate toward Sadie—well, as affectionate as Rose can be with anything.

But she had to have known about this cat and baby stuff. She probably did a ton of research about it.

Lily continues when no one interjects, "There've been instances where cats smother babies in their cribs. And they even suck the baby's breath."

"What?" I snap, turning to peer at the notes Lily took.

"I saw video clips," Lily whispers. "They like to smell the baby's milk and suck it out of their mouths." I'm not okay with this. I feel my face start to sharpen.

"I speak on behalf of the accused," Rose chimes in. "And these allegations are *all* urban legends."

I gape at her. "You're seriously going to allow *that* cat around your baby? Lily has . . ." I count her Post-its. "Seven notes—"

"Eight!" Lily says, waving around another pink Post-it. "I was sitting on one." Her skin splotches with red patches.

I hug her to my side. "*Eight* notes. That's evidence enough." I wait for Connor to jump in and speak up for Rose and his pet, but he stays quiet like a judge.

I have a suspicion he's going to make the final verdict anyway.

"We'll keep Sadie out of the nursery," Rose says. "And I'll acclimate her to the newborns before they arrive."

"How?" I question.

She types something on her cell phone and then holds it out to the tabby cat. The sounds of a crying infant blare through the speakers. Sadie arches her spine and *swats* the damn phone out of Rose's hand, hissing at it.

Lily clings tighter to me, and my mouth falls, imagining that as my son and not a phone. "*No way,*" I force.

Rose tries to calm Sadie with a pat on the head. "I know. Those are horrific noises."

Connor suddenly rises and snatches Sadie by the torso. "She can't stay in this house with little children, Rose. She's a jealous cat, and if she senses a change in our affections, she'll take it out on them."

"I'm not abandoning Sadie because she's territorial." Rose stands to her feet and defiantly plants her hands on her hips.

"I'm not asking you to abandon anyone," Connor says. "We'll give Sadie to Frederick for a few years, and then she can come back and stay with us."

This sounds like a good plan to me. "Would your therapist take her?"

Connor nods. "He's single and could use the companionship."

Rose doesn't break Connor's gaze. "This is why I don't like children, Richard. We're already sacrificing things that we love, and the baby isn't even born yet. In fifteen years, I don't want to look back and see how much I lost . . ." *It's a little late for that.* She must be thinking this because she stops herself short and inhales a strained, panicked breath.

My fears don't align with Rose's. Maybe because I've never been ambitious or had larger than life aspirations. I can't see things that my kid may take from me because there is nothing for Maximoff to take.

Connor lets Sadie down, and she sprints out the doorway. I watch him clasp Rose's hand in his. "You will not lose anything that you can't gain," he says. "You make sacrifices every day for your sisters. You just made one today, darling." He's talking about giving up the bedroom. "And in the end, those sacrifices are worth the love you'll receive."

"Says the man who used to scorn love," she retorts.

His mouth curves in a grin. "And I never wanted a child because of love, not until I fell in love with you."

What? I cut in, "Why the hell would you want a kid then?"

Rose sighs like she's expelling her fears. "Because he's completely egotistical and likes the idea of procreating for *power*."

Connor's grin overtakes his face. He kisses her forehead and adds, "We're already one-eighth Cobalt empire, darling. Seven more to go."

She punctures him with her stare. "That is yet to be determined. Don't finish the book before it's written, Richard."

Loud noises suddenly emanate from across the hallway. I frown. "What was that?" We all go quiet, listening harder.

Muffled screaming . . . and shouting.

Lily springs off the mattress. "They're fighting," she says in alarm, rushing out into the hallway. Rose is quick behind, more curious than scared like my girlfriend.

Lily is way too invested in Ryke and Daisy's relationship, and I'm partly praying they stay together just to dodge the emotional fallout that'll happen from Lily.

Connor and I follow the girls by *walking* instead of hysterically sprinting and bouncing down the hallway. By the time we reach Ryke and Daisy's room, Rose and Lily already have their ears pressed against the wooden door.

"They're nosy as hell," I mutter, and both the girls shush me. It's not like we can't hear them just by standing here.

"Stop being so pushy about it!" Daisy yells.

Her raised voice actually cuts me up in ways that I can't process. I've never heard her shout like that. I grit my teeth, a weird part of me wanting to throttle my own brother. The larger part trusts him fully, and I rely on that to keep me grounded here.

Connor casually leans his shoulder against the wall. "We knew this was going to happen," he reminds me.

Still, it feels worse than I imagined.

"It's a simple *fucking* fact, Dais," Ryke retorts. "You don't want to go, so you don't fucking go. Done."

"Great theory," she says heatedly. "So if I don't want to go get my bike checked tomorrow, it's fine. I don't have to fucking go."

"Your bike is fucked up. It *has* to get fixed."

"Theory disproven then."

Ryke growls in agitation.

Lily's eyes are as wide as saucers, and I see her reach out for the doorknob like she's going to intervene. I swiftly jog over to her and clasp her wrist.

"Lo," she whispers like *we have to do something*.

"All couples fight," I remind her.

She can't respond because Ryke's voice grows louder. "That's not what this is about! And you fucking know it!" I've been on the receiving end of Ryke's aggressive "tough love" behavior, and it's not always fun. Daisy's hard to communicate with though, so I have no clue who's in the right or the wrong here.

"That sounds bad," Lily breathes, and with my hand on her wrist, I feel her pulse racing. Her sex addiction has harmed Daisy's life in significant, irreversible ways, and Lily is holding on to this one good thing that Daisy has.

While I love my brother, Daisy can exist without him and still function and find happiness. They're not us—too codependent—and I thank God, Fate, whatever powers that be, for that.

"Shhh," Rose says, listening again.

We all quiet to the sound of a violent banging, from a body into a piece of furniture. I freeze and hear the proceeding sounds: a high-pitched cry from Daisy. "Ahhhhh! Ryke, *Ryke*!"

Shit. I internally cringe at *her* sex noises.

And then a deep grunt filters through the door. Both Lily and Rose back up from the wood like it electrocuted them.

I give Lily a look like *does that really sound bad?* To me, yeah, it's not what I'd want to fall asleep to, but it's better than yelling.

Lily is beaming, and she pumps two fists in the air and does a short victory circle in the middle of the hall. When she realizes that she's doing this *for real* and not in her head, she flushes bright. "Oh . . ."

I tug on her baggy tee and pull her into my chest, holding her tightly. Her green eyes are big and round and gaze up at me with longing and light.

There's something about Lily that makes all the terrible parts of me seem irrelevant. That makes a bad day momentary and a good one infinite.

It's love like this that's worth living for.

Twenty-six

Lily Calloway

ily! We're about to start!" Rose's voice sounds down the first-floor hallway.

"Two minutes!" I shout back, focusing on the piles of clean clothes. The laundry room might be as big as Rose's *old* walk-in closet, but I still have to separate my sisters' shirts and panties. Rose, Daisy, and I usually throw in our clothes together and let the guys fend for themselves.

I've never done my laundry with Lo, even when we were fake dating and sharing an apartment. It's not that it was too intimate. It's that we were both too lazy to harass the other person for their hamper and any other dirty clothes lying around.

I am one-hundred-percent certain that Connor does his own laundry, and he'll even wash Lo's on occasion. I assume that Ryke does his own too, but I've never seen him even *pass* this room, let alone venture inside.

I sit on the cold linoleum floor and fold panties, something I didn't know had to be done. When I returned Rose's undies to her all crumpled next to her neatly folded blouses, she gave me a serious stink eye. How was I supposed to know you fold underwear? Don't they naturally unwrinkle when you put them on?

Rose was not buying my argument. So here I am, taking my

time to separate our pajamas and panties and (unenthusiastically) folding them.

I set aside Daisy's "day of the week" cotton underwear and focus on the large pile. I apply the reach-in-and-grab method, never knowing what'll come next.

When I pull out dark cotton fabric, I expect a pair of Daisy's PJ shorts to reveal themselves. Instead, I hold a pair of boxer briefs.

Male underwear.

Dark green.

I know Lo's underwear, and that is not a Loren Hale color.

I drop them on instinct. They're either Connor's or Ryke's, but only one of them is rude enough to sneak his clothes into the girl piles.

Ryke.

I just touched Ryke's underwear! The same fabric that has also touched his penis. Does that mean by process of deduction that I just . . .

Grossgrossgross. I back away from the mound of clothes like it has turned into a tiny bomb ready to explode at my feet. *Do not imagine the underwear on him.* I'd rather be skeeved out than aroused, even if Ryke tells me it's okay to feel the latter. I may be able to look him in the eyes now, but it still feels a little wrong being turned on by anyone but Lo.

"Lily!" Rose calls my name again.

"Okay! Okay! I'm done!" Not really, but I'm glad for the excuse to leave his underwear behind. Where it should be. Far *far* away from me.

When I enter the spacious living room, I realize that I've been tricked. Not everyone is here yet. And the person I looked forward to seeing the most (Loren Hale) is blatantly absent. Connor stands by the window in black slacks and a white button-down, texting quietly, while Ryke lounges on the nearby couch, his hands all chalky from a morning climb.

"Where's Lo?" I ask Rose, who's sitting on the Queen Anne chair, as though waiting for her royal subjects to arrive. She's in a gorgeous black Calloway Couture dress, one of her prettier maternity designs, so she does appear regal.

"I don't keep tabs on Loren," Rose says.

"He's in the bathroom," Ryke tells me, his bare feet on a pillow. Rose looks like she wants to save the plush yellow pillow from his calloused soles.

"And Daisy?" I frown, not seeing my little sister anywhere either.

"Blow drying her hair," he replies. My brows scrunch. When does Daisy ever blow dry her hair? She's a *let-it-air-dry* kinda person.

I'm about to ask, but the six plastic babies on the heavy cedar coffee table distract me. When Rose announced that we'd all have to take baby CPR class, I almost had a mini panic attack. I could just see the headline: *Lily Calloway fails baby CPR. Another reason she shouldn't be a mom.*

Of course, Rose came up with an alternative: a "private" course, taught by her and Connor since they've both earned their certificates last week. I'm less nervous of tripping up in front of them.

"How is twenty-three so far?" Ryke asks me, making conversation as we wait for the others. I lean my butt on the love seat armrest, adjacent to his couch. I try really hard not to think about his underwear or the junk that goes in them.

"Huh?" My eyes flicker to his package like a nervous tic.

If he noticed, he brushes it off. "*Twenty-three*. How's it been?"

I'll be twenty-four in three months, after I have Maximoff, so it's not such a random question.

All the websites online say that twenty-three is the worst year in your twenties. Twelve months of identity crisis and "what the fuck am I doing with my life" realizations.

In the past year I've hit some major road bumps, including

forgetting my birth control. But I love this year the most. I have conquered immeasurable fears. Public places don't scare me as much. The articles and headlines don't make me want to touch myself. The world feels smaller and more manageable. And the best part, I can be *me* and not feel so ashamed by it. My crazy (controlled) sex life and all.

How has twenty-three been? "Better," I tell Ryke. "How was it for you?"

He rubs at the chalk on his palm. "It fucking sucked." He doesn't elaborate. I wonder if it's because he couldn't be with Daisy back then or because he was on bad terms with his brother. Probably both.

"Did you finish folding?" Rose cuts in. "I need my black shorts for tomorrow."

My cheeks heat at this. *Laundry* has now cursed me into a new shade of red. My life has taken a sad turn. Rose's glare intensifies my swelter.

"What about that is sexual?" she chastises me like I've offended her ability to talk to me without causing me to flush.

"Uhh . . ." I trail off. I can't exactly admit that I touched Ryke's boxer briefs. Can I? It's his fault they were in our pile to begin with.

"What did she say?" Lo's voice stirs me awake, and I pop up from the armrest, happy to see him but not so happy to be in this conversation still. His black crew neck outlines his fit, lean body, but it's his styled light brown hair, cut shorter on the sides, that attracts me like a panda bear discovering bamboo for the first time.

I think I'm drooling.

His eyes flit from my head to my stomach to my toes, assessing that I am all in one bright, tomato-red piece. "Lil?"

"Lo," I reply back.

His brows rise and then he grinds his teeth, his jaw twitching. *God*, I love that, and my body responds, my toes curling a bit. I smile and inwardly cheer with pom-poms and high fives. Nothing is better than being turned on by Loren Hale.

"Rose asked if Lily was finished folding," Ryke rats me out.

I gawk and point an accusatory finger at him. "It's your fault! You're sneaking *your* underwear into *our* laundry pile. Ha!"

Ryke rolls his eyes. "This is about my underwear?"

"So you're not denying it." *Double ha!*

"I'm not fucking denying it," he admits. "Do you have an underwear fetish now?" His tone is serious.

"No . . ." I say, roasting further.

Lo stands behind me and presses his hands playfully to my ears. "Don't say the word *fetish*, it turns Connor on."

I smile, and Connor wears a billion-dollar grin. "Words are my favorite sex toy," he says and then walks over to his wife.

I take a deep breath, not feeling so much like the abnormal sex-crazed monster now.

Ryke nods to me. "What's the deal, Lily?" He's trying to understand more parts of my addiction, especially since I opened up to him at Hale Co., so it's only right that I clarify.

"I touched your underwear." I scrunch my nose. That's good enough of an explanation, right?

It clicks for him. "It's a piece of cloth, not my fucking cock."

Please stop talking about your cock, Ryke. I spin around, wanting to leave before my body turns into Brutus, the ultimate betrayer. I turn right into Lo's hard chest. Perfect. I love it here.

Lo rests his hands on my shoulders, hugging me closer to him. *Even better.*

"What'd I do wrong?" Ryke asks, concern in his voice.

"Maybe don't mention your cock in front of my girlfriend," Lo says dryly.

I can practically feel him grimace. "Got it."

Connor chimes in, "Are you sure, Ryke? Those were really complex instructions. I can always transcribe them for you."

I peek from my Loren Hale cocoon to spot Ryke flipping off Connor. I let out another breath, glad to have overcome this little hurdle. I could've given Ryke another week-long silent treatment instead of sticking it out.

"What . . . did you do to your hair?" Rose suddenly asks, seeing Daisy first, and everyone quiets.

Twenty-seven

Lily Calloway

"Stop looking at me, *please*," Daisy announces to the entire room. All the couches are pushed aside, and we stand on the cream rug in a circle. Her hair has taken the spotlight for the past ten minutes. I'm kinda grateful to have a distraction. I hold my plastic baby, carefully attempting to emulate Rose's baby-cradling form. Sweat gathers under my boobs, which is a whole new feeling for me. I've never had big enough breasts for boob sweat.

"It's hard not to," Lo tells her, his doll cradled on his arm. "It's just so bright. I'm almost blinded."

I elbow him in the side to stop. Normally he'd mock wince, but his focus is on Daisy. She groans and covers her eyes with one hand. I notice how she holds her doll by the wrist, the plastic torso dangling.

"I know, I know. It's really bad," Daisy says.

Ryke tucks his doll underneath his armpit. Literally, he just shoved the baby's face in there. Only Rose seems to be paying attention to Ryke's placement, her eyes slowly narrowing to pinpoints. He's busy messing Daisy's hair with a playful hand. She exhales a breath.

Her medium-length locks are dyed *yellow*. Like a highlighter.

I'm with Lo on this one, it's bright. Over the past few months, Daisy has changed her hair to every color under the sun, some highlights, some a full dye job, some pretty, others ugly. All the while, she took the change with enthusiasm and excitement. This is the first time I've seen her visibly upset over the hue.

"What color were you trying to dye it?" Connor asks, his doll cradled a little differently than Rose's—the head more supported. I hone in on this detail and shift my doll to a better position. I glance at Ryke.

He's still suffocating his baby.

"Blonde," Daisy admits.

"You wanted to return to blonde?" Rose asks with a frown, not mentioning how Daisy may damage her hair if she keeps dyeing it so much.

Ryke's hand has dropped to the small of Daisy's back, more caringly, but his face has hardened to that familiar stone.

"Yeah, I don't know." Daisy grips her doll, dressed in a pink onesie, more securely underneath the arms. "Please, let's do this CPR class."

"Can we not call it a class?" I ask, my arms trembling a little with nerves. "I just graduated, and classes and I aren't the best of friends." I have bombed more college courses than the average person, but maybe I can blame Princeton for being unnaturally hard.

"CPR training then," Connor amends.

"Ryke has already smothered his kid," Lo jokes, nodding to his brother across our circle.

Ryke just realizes that he has his doll in a blue onesie tucked in his pit. He holds it in one hand by the waist like a football. "Why do we have to fucking do this again?" Ryke asks, motioning between himself and Daisy. "You all probably won't let us babysit your kid anyway."

"If you plan on holding him like *that* I'm not going to," Lo tells his brother.

Ryke adjusts the doll again, and I end up smiling at the way he's cradling the baby like Lo. They're both being as gentle as they can be, taking it more seriously. I thought Lo was going to throw jabs at Rose the whole time, but he's being considerate and looks kinda sexy with a baby in his arms.

"I just can't see any of you leaving your kid with me," Ryke suddenly admits.

Connor stares right at Ryke, and they meet each other's eyes. "You'd be surprised about what I'd let you do," Connor tells him.

Rose doesn't even disagree. I try to wipe the mental image of Ryke handling the doll with less care. Now that he pays more attention, it seems like he'd be okay with Maximoff.

Ryke looks to Lo like *you don't want me near your baby, right?*

"It's your choice, man," Lo says. "You don't want to be a part of my kid's life. That's fine." The edge in his voice doesn't match his words.

Ryke scowls. "You know I do."

"Then that's why you're here."

Daisy bounces on her feet, hugging the doll to her chest. "I'd love to babysit whenever you need me." She looks to Rose. "You'd let me watch your girl, right?" Her lopsided smile makes the room glow. Her hair helps.

Daisy might as well have kissed Rose's heels. Our older sister is beaming, so happy that someone else is playing into the idea that she's having a girl. Personally, I'd love for Rose to have a daughter. Just to see her happy. I think all of us want that. Well, except Lo. He wants her to have a boy in spite.

I expect Rose to flower Daisy with compliments and *yes, of course, you can watch her* words. Instead, she says, "If you pass."

Lo lets out a short laugh. "Are you going to make everyone who wants to touch your baby fill out a hundred-page questionnaire?"

"Maybe." She fixes her hair to one side of her shoulder while

Connor studies Rose with more concern, sidling closer to her. He whispers in her ear, and she nods to him. The bad thing about nerd stars: they're so high up that it's hard to hear or see unless you exist in space with them.

I'm not smart enough to even breach the earth's atmosphere, so I just try to watch from down below.

"I actually have something for you, Rose . . ." Lo says, detaching from my side. This can't be good. He sets his boy doll on the table and heads to the hall closet.

"If it doesn't come in a jewelry box, you can keep it," Rose snaps.

"I'm not keeping this." Lo rummages around for a couple seconds before returning with a flat box wrapped in green, pink, and blue paper. I wear a confused expression, not involved in this plan. Lo must've bought that on his way home from work or something.

Rose zeroes in on the colors. "I told everyone no baby gifts." She didn't want a baby shower. I think it would've overwhelmed her anyway, all the baby things and people staring at her stomach. I'm having one closer to my due date, but it's not a big event or anything. Just family.

"Which is why I decided to get you one," Lo says, topping it off with a half-smile. He walks over and shoves the box at her.

She stares at him blankly. "I hate you."

"The feeling is mutual," he tells her. "Just open it before you start hexing me."

She huffs and tears the paper gently while Lo returns to my side. I'm more nervous.

I stand on my toes and whisper to him, "Why didn't you tell me about this?"

He shrugs. "I don't know. It didn't seem like something that important."

But I can see that it matters to him.

"You can rip the paper," Lo tells her.

Rose shoots him a look and continues neatly opening the box. When she lifts the lid and brushes the tissue paper aside, her face softens and her lips part.

I frown further. "What is it?"

Rose holds up a bundle of pastel green onesies and shows off the top one: orange tabby cats printed all over. It's so cute and—

"Unisex," Lo mentions. "Just in case you have a boy." He doesn't add that the cats are just like Sadie, who Connor has already given to Frederick, his therapist, to take care of for a while. Rose was visibly upset the entire day that Sadie left, her eyes reddened like she'd been crying.

"I don't know what to say," Rose murmurs, her eyes traversing along the fabric.

"*Thanks, Lo, you're so sweet*," he tells her. "*I could hug you but I haven't oiled my rusted joints this morning.*"

She glares and delicately sets the onesies back in the box. "And now I hate you again."

Lo mockingly touches his heart. "I'll cherish that hate forever."

I clear my throat, making sure that none of the bickering goes too far. Lo drops his gaze on me and then brushes his hand against my hip before retrieving his doll. The embrace sends shock waves down my spine, and he stands very, very close to me.

"We should start," Connor says, checking his watch.

Rose places a hand on her lower back, like it hurts, but she stays upright with the rest of us. Connor watches her more cautiously but never draws attention to her.

"So what's the scenario?" Lo asks Connor. "The baby is choking on a button or a penny?"

My eyes widen in horror. "What?"

Lo strokes my head. "It's pretend, love."

"I thought we established that pretend things with us become real?" Have we just jinxed ourselves without realizing?

"No scenarios," Rose pipes in. "It's bad luck."

Connor looks affronted by the mention of *luck*, but he doesn't rile Rose, most likely because she's in some sort of pain. "You can do this sitting down, darling."

She nods and settles in the Queen Anne, pushed by the wall. The doll rests snuggly on her lap.

Connor has his eyes on her for an extended moment before he turns to us. "First, you want to check the baby's consciousness."

This sounds hard. "How do we do that?" My doll is certainly unconscious, definitely not alive.

"You tap the baby gently." Connor demonstrates by tapping the baby's shoulder and the bottom of her foot. "Magdala. Magdala. Can you hear me?"

Rose scoffs from her chair. "I got rid of my middle name because I hated it, not so we can name our child Magdala."

"Rose Calloway Cobalt," Connor says her full name, ditching Magdala and replacing it with Calloway. No hyphenation. She's been Cobalt since she married Connor. "Like Lo said, this is pretend. I can name our pretend daughter whatever I want."

She rolls her eyes dramatically and waves him on. "Please, continue. I hope our pretend daughter pukes on your shoulder."

Connor grins, and before he opens his mouth to respond, I redirect the conversation. "Back to the training," I announce. This is important to me. I really do want to know the information before Maximoff arrives. "We tap the baby and call out its name. Then what?"

"If the baby is unresponsive, you call 911. And then you place him or her on a hard flat surface." He motions to the coffee table in the middle of the circle. "And you start CPR." Connor takes us through the steps: thirty chest compressions with our fingers, opening the airway, and administering rescue breaths. I file all the information into the *important—don't ever forget* folder in my head.

My heart beats loudly in my chest. Okay, I can do this. I internally nod, boosting some of my self-confidence. I can't be declared a bad mom until I do something wrong. So *Celebrity Crush* and their polls can suck it.

I blow out a breath, and then I lightly tap Bert's foot. "Bert? Bert?" I say. "Can you hear me?"

"Bert?" Lo laughs at my name choice.

My brows pinch. "What's your baby's name?" Bert is awesome. He's already a winner. I can feel it.

Lo holds his doll to his ear, as though listening to him speak. He's teasing me, and I find myself hooking a finger through Lo's belt loop, holding Bert in the crook of my arm. "Knew it," Lo says with a nod, bringing his baby back down.

"What's his name?" I already feel myself smiling.

"Ernie," he says, and my heart swells. And then he taps his baby's arm. "Ernie, buddy? Can you hear me?"

The doorbell rings, and I jump in fright. "Who is it?" I ask.

Everyone shakes their heads like they didn't invite someone over today.

Connor sets his doll on the table and disappears in the foyer to answer the door. The room is layered with tense silence. Since we're all here, the person outside is most likely a bearer of bad news. Why else would they stop by?

Twenty-eight

Lily Calloway

D o you need a hand with that?" I hear Connor say.

"No, I have it."

I recognize the second manly voice: Sam Stokes. And in a second, both guys emerge in the living room, Sam carrying a box with Fizzle's logo on the side. He's in a suit like he's been at work all Saturday afternoon.

"Hey," he greets, but his gaze lands on Ryke, heading over to him. "The shipment came in today, and we'll need to talk later about the unveiling." He sets the box at Ryke's feet and squats down to open it. I remember Ryke mentioning that my dad wanted his help, but he shrugged it off and said it wasn't going to pan out.

So his face is darkened with confusion.

I find myself patting my doll's butt in comfort, like Bert is alive. My cheeks heat, hoping no one noticed.

"He really wants to go through with this?" Ryke asks Sam. "It's a fucking bad idea."

"It's not," Sam says, trying to cut through the taped package by ripping at it. He struggles as he talks. "We did multiple focus groups, and more people were drawn to the product when you were the face of it."

"I was *dropped* by multiple fucking brands," Ryke reminds

him. "My image isn't good, and I shouldn't be representing any kind of drink." Huh. My dad is creating a new drink?

Sam stops fighting with the box and looks up at Ryke. "You're masculine, athletic, and you never quit, which is what we're branding. If you don't want to help, all you have to do is say so. Don't waste my time."

"You don't have to do this," Daisy chimes in. "Not for me."

Sam catches sight of Daisy, and his eyes grow big at her hair. "That's a . . . new color."

"Neon I'm-Going-to-Blind-You Yellow," Lo adds. "What's terrifying is that some girl is probably going to copy her."

I don't elbow Lo again. Daisy is solely concentrated on Ryke, and I can read his expression pretty well. He wants to smooth things out with our parents, and she can't stop him from doing it. He reaches into his back pocket and pulls out a Swiss army knife. Then he bends down and cuts open the box for Sam.

Lo and I inch closer, too curious to stand back, and Ryke grabs one of the slim plastic bottles, translucent blue liquid inside. I understand the moment I read the silver label: *Ziff*. And below that is the flavor: *Blue Squall*.

It's a sports drink, the kind that can rival PepsiCo's Gatorade and Coca-Cola's Powerade. It's the one arena Fizzle has failed at multiple times, and I suppose he's hoping they can launch a new string of sports drinks with Ryke as the face.

"Ziff?" Ryke says with furrowed brows.

"It's Fizz backward, with two f's."

"I got that," Ryke says and then uncaps the bottle. I'm guessing it's blueberry flavored by the midnight color. We all watch Ryke put the bottle to his lips and take a swig. He instantly puts his bicep to his mouth, his face contorting in disgust.

Oh no.

Lo lets out a laugh. "Swallow it," he says in jest, reaching into the box to grab a bottle for himself. I blush at those words.

Connor even collects a bottle. "It must be bad if Ryke can't keep it down."

"I've tried it. It's decent," Sam says.

Ryke finally swallows the liquid and takes a breath like he was drowning. "What the fuck is this shit?" He stares at the label and starts reading the ingredients. "It tastes like deer bile and piss."

Connor arches a brow. "He's tasted piss before."

"And deer bile," Lo chimes in with a grimace.

"Fucking A, *you two* try it."

I'm glad I haven't been included in this. I'm not going near anything that tastes like pee. No thank you.

Daisy rocks on her heels. "I'll try it." Of course my gutsy sister would. Ryke passes her his bottle, and she sips Ziff about the same time that Lo and Connor drink theirs.

Daisy spits it out almost instantly and rubs her tongue with her fingers. "Ugh, that's bad."

Connor and Lo are able to keep their drinks down, but I can tell Lo needs a chaser, his forehead wrinkling in distress. I'm about to retrieve him a water, but Rose stands up and nods to me like she'll do it. She's already eyeing the bit of Blue Squall on the rug that Daisy spewed.

"Sorry, Rose," Daisy calls after her. "I can clean it . . ."

"It's fine," Rose says, already disappearing in the kitchen.

"I thought you said she swallows," Lo tells his brother. Oh my God. This time, I punch him in the chest, away from his ribs. He looks remorseful and more unsettled, probably because he realizes it was about *Daisy*.

Ryke runs a hand through his hair and glances hesitantly at Daisy, who has wide, large eyes. This is a *clear* indication that they discuss sex, and us, when we're not with them. This means I no longer should feel guilty when me and my sisters do it too. I nod at this resolution.

Sam mumbles, "I'm going to pretend I never heard any of that." He rises to his feet and nods to Connor. "It's not that bad."

"Ziff," Connor recites, "it's not that bad. Drink it." I crinkle my nose. Yeah, that's not going to sell anything.

Sam sighs in frustration and crosses his arms. "My hands are tied here. Even if it doesn't taste that great to you, it has ranked well among our other flavors on board. Greg wants to launch with Blue Squall soon."

We're all quiet for a moment. And then Lo says, "You remember Mountain Berry Fizz?" He just brought up an apocalyptic moment in Fizzle's history. I remember MBF very, very well.

"Don't," Sam says, raising his palm at Lo to shut it down.

"What's Mountain Berry Fizz?" Ryke asks.

I add, "The worst Fizzle flavor to ever be created. The aftertaste was like window cleaner."

"Or bleach," Lo says.

I nod quickly. "You couldn't predict the awfulness after the sip settled in." I realize I'm hugging on to Lo when Sam's eyes flit all around me in a judgy or curious way, but I don't care much. "It was pulled off the market after three months."

Light bulb moment for Ryke. "Which is why I've never heard of it." He stares at the bottle of Ziff. "How the fuck am I supposed to be the face of a product that I can't even drink?"

Sam checks his phone and then says, "You're going to have to drink it at the unveiling, *without* cringing. We've set up an event, open to the public, where you'll drink Ziff and then climb."

Ryke spreads his arms out. "Why the fuck are you just now telling me this?"

"Greg thought you'd agree to the terms, no matter what. If you want to earn his respect, you just need to suck it up and do it."

Ryke says, "I have to drink *water* before I climb. About a fucking liter."

"We'll talk about the event later." Sam shrugs it off and points to the box. "I'm leaving this with you so you can get used to the drink. I'll let you all get back to . . ." His eyes ping to the baby dolls in our hands. ". . . whatever you were doing."

No one even bothers telling him it's CPR training. As he departs, I whisper to Lo, "Does it really taste like deer bile?" That seems more abnormal and off-putting than bleach.

"No," Lo whispers back. "It's more like an iron, metal flavor. It's not refreshing."

My mouth falls a little. I picture blood, which tastes a bit like metal. This is a power drink for vampires. Mountain Berry Fizz 2.0 all over again. My heart goes out to Ryke. It feels like he's being set up to fail.

This is the hardest part about having friends, watching another life unfold in a messier way than it should. And not being able to help. I have no magic spells or tools to fix this. No one ever says, *let awkward Lily Calloway come to the rescue!*

I come, a lot. But it's never satisfied anyone but me.

And maybe Lo.

If my superpower is sex, then . . . I've abused it. I suppose I might've been a quiet, lurky villain this whole time.

"Lil?" Lo breathes, his lips brushing my ear. Everyone has gone back to their dolls. "What's wrong?"

"Is my superpower sex?" I ask him.

His face sharpens. "No."

"Are you sure?" My eyes burn, emotions stirring.

He hugs me to his chest. My belly bump hits him first, making it harder to be so close. After a long moment, he whispers, "Sex is your kryptonite."

Oh. "It makes me weak," I realize.

"And it makes you human, Lil." He kisses my cheek and then the outside of my lips and then . . . my body pulls toward him as his tongue slides against mine. I ache to be even closer, but I chant over and over, *this has to be enough*.

It is.

I won't let my weakness get the better of me. Or play with my mind. It's a daily battle that I'm beating today.

Twenty-nine

Loren Hale

> Current standings: Ryke
> Meadows (cursed out three men last
> meeting) needs to act more professional
> in a work setting. 6 out of 14 love you.
> Congratulations, son. —Dad

I read the group text with everyone else while Connor's limo sits in gridlocked traffic. We're all riding to New York for a Cobalt Diamonds dinner party.

"Was that sarcasm?" Lily whispers to me, pointing to the part about Ryke.

"Most definitely." The next text suddenly comes in. He's splitting them into four messages, I realize.

> Lily Calloway (only spoke to two
> women last meeting and hid by a
> plant) needs to be more personable.
> Too shy. 7 out of 14 love you. Sorry,
> Lily. —Dad

I want to sigh in relief, but anxiety knots my stomach. I have no clue how I came across to the board. We each had three encounters with all fourteen of them so far, and I can't tell who's making progress.

All I know is that Lily is due in a little over a month. Saddling this shit on top of a baby—it's starting to wear on me. And I'm paranoid that everyone is waiting for me to slip up and drink, watching me constantly. A nervous heat gathers on my neck, and I rub the back of it.

Maybe it's my own conscience that plagues me the most.

"Can someone please send me these texts?" Rose says with less fire in her voice. It's the first thing I've heard her say the entire limo ride. She's been glaring out the window, probably cursing every automobile for causing us to be late.

"I can," Daisy says, tapping her screen. I hear Rose's phone chime and so does Connor's, who sits next to her.

"Hey, look I'm beating Ryke," Lily says with a small smile.

"By one fucking person. Don't get so excited." He grabs a water bottle out of the ice bucket and passes it to Daisy.

My leg jostles while I wait for the next text to come in. I watch Lil tug at her plain purple dress; the fabric doesn't suction to her stomach like Rose's black one, but she's still uncomfortable from carrying more weight.

I pull her closer to my side, letting her lean against me, and she kicks off her heels and curls up on the stretched leather seat.

All of our phones ping at the same time.

Loren Hale (appeared interested in Hale Co. proceedings but looked exceptionally surly when asked about rehab) needs to work on communication. 10 out of 14 love you. Well done, son. —Dad

"That wasn't sarcastic," Lily says softly, worry flickering in her eyes.

It's good though. I can almost breathe again. "It's what I want, Lil." Maybe my voice sounds unsure because she pouts in this adorable way, her bottom lip pushed out a little farther.

And then her breath shallows.

Christ. I must be eyeing her mouth too much. She squirms, readjusting, and I touch her arm, her skin hot with arousal. *She'll be fine.* Her crazy sex drive isn't as high as it was in the second trimester, but she's still a sex addict.

"So much for working together," Ryke says under his breath next to me. But if the girls aren't chosen, the outcome is what I wanted. In the end, only one of us could win this position. Working together just meant they'd lose out.

"It's how it should be," I remind all of them.

Ryke shakes his head repeatedly. "You can't . . ." He trails off and his jaw hardens.

Irritation festers in my core, and I grit my teeth. "I can't handle it?"

He stays quiet, basically admitting that's what he was going to say.

"Yeah? Maybe I can't, Ryke." My leg bounces more. "But maybe I *can*. I should at least be given the chance to try." I want to be better. God, more than anything. I want to be like him.

"It hasn't even been a whole year since your last relapse," Ryke tells me in a controlled voice, trying not to curse me out. "I'm just *concerned*, as your sober coach but mostly as your fucking brother."

Lily hooks her arm around my waist, my muscles tensing like crazy. "Whatever . . ." I drop it there, especially as our phones ping again.

I check the text.

Daisy Calloway (sociable and well-spoken, very engaging) needs to stop fidgeting during group conversations. 12 out of 14 love you. Great work, Daisy. —Dad

My stomach falls, and the small fight I had with Ryke now seems insignificant.

Ryke drops his phone in his lap and runs his hands over his face. "Fucking fuck . . ." He mumbles out more curses, and I notice that Daisy isn't even paying attention to the texts.

"Are you okay, Rose?" she asks her sister.

Rose is pinching the bridge of her nose like she's in pain, and Connor is rubbing her shoulders and whispering in her ear. Neither of them says a word.

I tell Daisy, "She's probably about to cry because she knows *your* life is about to end." It's dramatic, especially for me, but maybe it'll knock some sense into this girl.

"You all have things you love to do," Daisy says. She braids her hair that's now platinum blonde, which pretty much resembles an alien to me. "I'm not giving up anything like you are."

"That's bullshit," I say. "I'm not giving up a goddamn thing by being the CEO of Hale Co. I'll still own Halway Comics." I'll just have twice the responsibility.

She's nineteen, started modeling at fourteen. This girl has worked more in her lifetime than I fucking have—that's the truth here.

Ryke adds, "You are giving something up, sweetheart. You're sacrificing the thing you *could've* loved. One day you're going to find it. Hale Co. isn't your burden, and I'm going to be fucking sick if you take it."

Daisy sips her water, mulling this over. We're older than her.

And I think she's feeling it in this moment. She slouches, her green eyes flicker between us and then she lands on Ryke. "Who would you rather see be the CEO, me or Lo?"

"Neither," he says immediately.

"That's not a choice."

He does look sick now. Like he's going to puke or something. And I watch his face twist in pain as he contemplates each scenario. I pull at the collar of my white button-down, the suit jacket warm on top.

"Daisy, if it's between you and me, he wants *me* to take it," I interject. He needs to back me up, to have faith in me and to give Daisy a bigger reason to step away.

"I didn't fucking say that," he retorts.

Goddammit, Ryke. I grind my teeth, my hand shaking, and he catches the irrepressible jitter. *I'm not going to drink.* The words scratch my throat, itching to come out like I could scream every syllable. But it just stays an urge, a thought, and I wear the sentence on my face instead.

"Rose?" Lily says, worry spiking her voice. My head whips toward Rose, who has her eyes closed, color lost in her cheeks.

"I'm fine," she says in a stilted voice. But she's almost hunched over, and Connor's hand tightens on her shoulder. "They're false contractions."

Jesus Christ. "You're having contractions right now?" This entire time?

"They're *false*," she emphasizes, growling out the word, and her eyes snap open, just to shoot me the evilest glare. She blows out a long breath. "I have three more weeks until my due date. It's too soon."

Now I notice how Connor's examining her movements, his gaze traveling across her body.

"Motherfuck . . ." She grips the edge of the leather seat and glances at the window. "We should be there by now."

"You're in pain and you're *still* worried about being late to a dinner party?" I ask like she's insane. She is. One-hundred-percent insanity. I'm watching it.

"We're still stuck in traffic," Lily says to Rose, passing over my comment to keep her sister calm. "Do you need some water?"

Rose shakes her head a couple times. I really can't tell if this is false labor or not. None of us have any prior experience as second-time fathers or mothers.

I watch Connor shrug off his suit jacket, maybe from the June heat. I lean over and try to speak through the limo privacy screen at the driver. "Gilligan, can you turn the air-conditioning up?" I ask. "It's boiling back here." Almost instantly, a gust of cool air blows out of the vents.

"Rose," Connor says, impassive like usual, "put your legs on the seat for me."

She's pretty much doubled over now, clutching her knees that have broken apart. Shit. "It's too early . . ." Her voice breaks in pain.

Connor doesn't wait for Rose to comply. He seizes her legs and spins her so she's lying along the stretched limo seat adjacent to where we sit. My pulse races. This is not happening.

"Her water didn't break," I point out. *This is not happening right now.*

Daisy scoots behind Rose, propping her head in her lap, and she rubs Rose's sweaty hair off her forehead. "It's probably false labor," Daisy says.

Lily is wide-eyed and slack-jawed, unmoving from her spot beside me. It's more nerve-wracking when Connor says nothing, when he hides his emotions, leaving us to guess.

He rests one of Rose's feet on his thigh, so she has room to open her legs. And then he covers her waist and lower half with his suit jacket, maybe so he can remove her underwear.

Ryke and I inspect the traffic out the window at the same time.

The accident up ahead must not be cleared yet because we're still barely inching forward.

"Connor," Rose cries in pain—her face full of it. I've never seen her like this.

The floodgate to Connor's emotions finally cracks, and I catch a glimpse of concern in his blue eyes. He reaches out, holds her hand tightly in his, and then glances between her legs. He keeps one palm on her bent knee. "I need someone to call 911," he says to us.

Rose doesn't even complain or put up a fight about it, which means she's hurting badly right now.

"I got it," Ryke declares, dialing the number in his cell. While he starts speaking to the operator, I talk to Connor.

"Her water didn't break," I mention again. "That has to mean this is—"

Rose screams—a horrific, bloodcurdling scream. Connor's grip tightens on her, as though he's holding her life in his hands. The terrifying thought: he just might be.

Lily is shaking, and I hug her closer to my chest, wrapping my arms around her body, and placing my hands flat on her belly.

"I want . . . an epidural," Rose demands, hot tears rolling down her cheeks.

Connor rubs her knee and squeezes her hand. "We both know it's too late for that. You probably broke your water in the shower this morning . . ." He checks his watch. "Around six, and you didn't realize it."

It hits me. She's been in labor for fourteen hours already. Thinking each tiny pain wasn't the real thing, not until right now.

Rose sits up more, leaning against Daisy's chest, and she clutches her legs. "Connor . . ." The fear in her voice rings through the limo, chills biting my neck.

He cups her face, his thumb brushing away her tears. "I won't

let anything happen to you or our child. You're going to be fine."
I can tell that he's partly convincing himself.

He's the smartest person I've ever met, but intelligence has its
limits.

Rose starts shaking her head at Connor, and his fingers firmly
hold her in place so she stops.

"Rose," he says softly, "your body is ready to have this baby.
And if you just let go, your mind will catch up, darling."

"I'm scared," she cries, wetting his hand with her tears.

Connor's eyes grow red as he stifles more emotion. "I'm not
leaving you." The limo is quiet, Ryke already off the phone. Rose's
forehead wrinkles as another contraction begins. She shuts her eyes,
and Connor glances between her legs before looking back at his wife.

And he asks her, "When you were fourteen, what was the first
thing I ever said to you?"

It looks like she wants to scream again, but the noise dies in her
throat as she concentrates on Connor's words. "Are you . . . quiz-
zing me?"

"Yes," he admits. I almost want to ask how much she's dilated,
but then I don't want to imagine it at all. I'm guessing Connor can
tell though, even if he's not a doctor. He's smart enough.

She chokes back a cry and lets out a trained breath. Rose opens
her eyes as she answers, "You said that I was your greatest competition."

"And now," he whispers, "you're my greatest ally." With one
hand on her knee, he says, "I need you to push."

This is actually happening.

In the back of Connor's limo.

Rose is having a baby.

I rub my lips while Rose pushes and curses, her language as
foul as Ryke's. She's threatened to kill all of us in the span of a
minute and declared her hate of pretty much everything.

Daisy pulls Rose's damp hair out of her face. "You're doing great, Rose," she cheers her on.

I make sure to keep my mouth shut, more worried about what's going to happen if the ambulance doesn't show up when the baby does. Or if the baby isn't breathing. Or if there are other complications with Rose. There are just too many things that could go wrong.

"Give me your shirt," Connor says to me, his voice urgent. I take off my suit jacket and unbutton my dress shirt. I pass it to him and then glance down at Lily.

She's stunned in silence still, and maybe if she wasn't pregnant too, she'd be less freaked out and more encouraging. I think the majority of us are terrified.

"One more push," Connor tells her, his hands disappeared beneath his suit jacket across her lap.

Rose looks exhausted, her eyelids heavy. "Connor . . . it's too much . . ."

"Rose, *Rose*, keep your eyes open." He checks her body before he says, "You're mentally capable of anything, even this."

Rose holds in a breath, and then Lily abruptly unfreezes from her state. She stretches her arm to clasp Rose's hand, shaking and sweaty, and the minute Rose meets her sister's gaze, it's over for both of them. They start crying profusely, and Rose nods repeatedly, gearing up to push one last time.

Ryke turns his head, not able to watch this. My hand shakes, and I ball it into a fist. I can barely keep my eyes trained on Connor and Rose either. It's hard seeing two put-together people face a situation that seems too damn big for them—with consequences that could cripple everyone. And there's nothing we can do to help.

Rose screams like someone is stabbing her in the chest.

Shrill. Pained screams.

My ears blister, and Ryke rests his hands on his head. I'm about to rub my eyes, to cover them, to tug at my collar. Something to distract my mind.

But then, the wail of a high-pitched baby follows Rose's cries.

I can't see the child yet. Instinctively, I look for Connor's reaction. And it takes me a moment to realize that real tears well in his eyes.

I've never seen him cry.

Not even close to it, and there's no mask concealing his emotions right now. It fills me with something pure and raw. It's even hard to breathe.

Rose collapses against Daisy, but her eyes stay like nervous pinpoints on her husband. "Is he okay?" she asks tiredly, her chin trembling.

She thinks that she's having a boy. Maybe it's what she believed this whole time, but in this moment, I can see that she'd be fine with it. She extends her arms to take him from Connor.

And then Connor lifts up the small baby, hands and legs tiny but moving and alive. The cries have softened some. "*She's* perfect, as far as I can tell." She.

Rose got her girl.

Connor rests the baby on Rose's chest, and she makes a high-pitched noise, not a cry but something that sounds content to be close to her mom. He kisses his wife's forehead. "Tell me if you're feeling off," he says softly.

Rose nods once, too fatigued to repeat the motion.

"You need to keep her on your chest, so her temperature can match yours until the ambulance arrives." He tucks my button-down around their baby, to make sure she stays warm.

"Hi," Rose whispers softly to the baby. "You're a little gremlin, aren't you?" Rose smiles as more tears spill. "*My* little gremlin." As she touches her hand, the baby's small fingers close around Rose's pinky. Christ.

I wipe my eyes, and I can hear sirens in the distance coming closer to us. I reach out and pat Connor on the shoulder. I have no words. He breaks his gaze from Rose and his child to meet mine, and he whispers to me, "This is the best and most terrifying day of my life." He inhales a strained breath, his eyelashes wet with tears.

"You want to know the crazy thing?" I say back to him. "I could tell."

Connor laughs into a weak smile, still overcome with things he's never felt before. He blinks, and those tears fall.

I don't think any of us imagined human life to be this powerful. I always pictured it as a bad thing—bringing a kid into a world of pain, misery, heartache. What's the goddamn point?

And I can't answer it in words. The point is in every feeling that ripples through my veins and grips my bones. It's something that shrinks the universe to a single place and slows time to a millisecond. It's too deep to articulate.

Ryke stares out the window. "The ambulance just parked in the emergency lane."

Everything is going to turn out okay. I remember back in February, on the yacht, I stood on the deck with Connor one night. The conversation we shared crashes against me.

I told him, "I know you think you're perfect, and that you'll raise the perfect kid and have the perfect fucking life. But is there any part of you—even the tiniest part—that is scared shitless?" Before he opened his mouth, I cut him off, "And don't bullshit me, Connor. *Please*."

Connor licked his lips in thought before he said, "I'm not scared."

It's not what I wanted to hear. I choked on a laugh, about to turn around and leave him.

But he caught my shoulder and kept me there.

"I'm not finished yet either." He carried a deep, tranquil serenity that just eased me in an instant. Then he added, "I'm not scared because I've accepted the future that you fear."

"English," I snapped.

"I'm not perfect." He shook his head at my growing smile. "Don't tell Rose or Ryke I said it."

"Deal." I nodded. I only told Lily.

"I don't believe my children will be perfect, Lo." He continued, "I understand that circumstances will change them, mold them. My own unforeseeable mistakes might even hurt them. And they may not be perfect, but they will be steadfast." He paused. "And yours will too."

Steadfast. A word that I would never describe myself as. Dependable. Loyal. A constant in a world of unstable variables.

It's something I'd die for my own child to be.

This birth should've scared me more for when Maximoff comes, but I'm no longer saddled with these fears. I want this imperfect, perfect kid. Flaws and all.

Because he's a life I'm meant to give. Because he's a part of Lily. And because he's my son.

Thirty

Lily Calloway

In the dead of night, I'm wide-awake, my back pressed against Lo, while his arms wrap snuggly around me. I stay utterly still, careful not to rouse him from his sleep. My thoughts won't stop replaying what happened in the limo a week ago.

I've been cautious during showers, jumping in and out so I recognize when my water breaks. I don't think I can handle having a baby anywhere but a hospital. I'm not prepared for the unexpected, and I think, maybe, that's what being a mom is. Being able to handle all the unexpected things in life.

My arms prick with cold. I'm not ready for this. Rose having her baby first has amplified all of my fears. And I can't push a pause button. I can't hit rewind to gain more time.

I am stuck on this course with only one end.

Cries filter through our closed door, from the nursery down the hall. It's the second time tonight. I hear Lo shift behind me, and I snap my eyes shut. He can't know I'm awake. He'll worry. Then I'll worry that he's worrying. It's just too much worry for two people.

"Lil . . . how long have you been up?"

I don't move.

"You're holding your breath, love."

"Oh . . ." I murmur.

I open my eyes. I've been bested, but I'd rather lose to Loren Hale than anyone else. The hall light flickers, and I see shadows through the crack underneath the door and hear the patter of feet.

Lo's hands find mine in the darkness, and he laces our fingers together in a strong grip. I fixate on the lamp light under the door, and my ears attune to the baby cries that alternate between soft and incessant. In a few weeks, that will be Maximoff. And what if I can't calm him? What if he cries and cries with no end?

What if he hates me? And then I turn out to be the terrible mother that everyone believes me to be.

"Lil," Lo whispers, "you're shaking." He props his body on the pillow and rubs my arm. "You're cold . . ."

I lie on my back, and he stares down at me. Pulled away from the door, I cover my eyes with my hands. I don't want to see the concerned wrinkles in his forehead or the pain in his amber irises at watching me tear up.

With a breath, I say, "I don't want to be a bad mom."

He tugs my hand down from my cheek. "It's okay to be scared."

I sniff loudly, and I try to drown in his eyes, the confidence that's flourished inside of them. "I wish I could feel more prepared . . . ready."

"Will that make you feel better?" he asks.

I rub my nose with the back of my hand. "Yeah. I think so."

He sits up and swings his legs off the bed at this. The mattress undulates from his absence as he stands. I frown and watch him saunter across the room, stopping at my side of the bed. He crouches so we're face-to-face.

"Lily Calloway," he says my full name like it's the prettiest thing he's ever heard, "there is no way to prepare for a limo baby." He smiles at this, and I almost turn into my pillow with an agonized groan. Reality is too cold.

He places a hand on my shoulder so I stay facing him. "But you can believe in yourself."

"I did . . . I used to," I tell him. Before Rose gave birth, I thought for sure I was ready. Now, it's harder to convince myself.

"We're going to change that." He rises and then extends his hand to me.

I frown and slowly sit up. "Where are we going?" My eyes flit to the clock. 2 a.m.

"We're taking a trip."

I wipe my splotchy cheeks. "To Hogwarts?" I ask hopefully.

He smiles more fully, something clear in the darkness of our room. "We're trying to banish your fears. Hogwarts has Death Eaters and Dementors."

"Yeah, but that was when Harry was in school," I whisper since it's nighttime. "I'd like to think it's become a pretty happy place since then."

"Me too." He wags his fingers, wanting me to take his hand still. "We'll go to Hogwarts another night." He doesn't remind me that we're not wizards or that we're not magical. It almost causes more tears to brim.

"Promise?" I reach for his hand, and he helps me to my feet. With my large baby bump, I feel heavier and rounder than ever before.

"Promise." He kisses the top of my nose, and he leads me out into the hall. The crying from the nursery has stopped, but the door is cracked open. We walk down there, and I peek inside.

In navy pajama pants, Connor cradles the small baby in a pale pink onesie, feeding her a bottle. Even though she was a little early, the doctors said she was perfectly healthy at seven pounds, two ounces. They checked out Rose at the hospital too, and she passed all the tests like an honor student would. Her body didn't fail her. But mine has betrayed me plenty of times before.

And I worry about all the headlines too. Even the normal news stations, not just the tabloids, ran the story about Rose giving birth in a limo and Connor delivering the baby. A week later and the media hasn't died down.

It's scary to think a good majority of the world will be watching and waiting for news about the birth of Maximoff. Sometimes I wonder if they're all hoping I'll make a giant mistake afterward, just so it'll be a nice story, some good entertainment.

For once, I'd like no complications, no speed bumps. Something peaceful. Something happy.

Maybe it's just a dream.

I watch Connor, never seeing him so smitten with another human being, except maybe Rose. But he gives his daughter a different kind of look, one that says *I'll do anything and everything for you*. I remember at the hospital when they asked Rose the name of the baby, and she didn't even hesitate. It'd taken her so long to pick a name, but in that moment, she went with her heart.

Jane.

Chosen from her favorite Charlotte Brontë novel.

Lo gently and quietly pulls me into the princess nursery. I'm not sure what he's planning, but my heart has taken a front row seat and decided to spasm and race.

"Lo," I whisper-hiss.

Connor already turns around, not surprised by our presence. I wonder if he could hear us breathing or our feet against the floorboards.

Jane's striking blue eyes focus on my forehead while she sucks from her bottle. I'm not scared to hold her. Rose hasn't been possessive of Jane, partly from being so exhausted. She's let all of us cradle her daughter at some point this past week.

Lo guides me to the plush cream rocking chair, and he sidles next to Connor, whispering. I try to read their lips, but all I can recognize is my name, not helpful.

When they spin back around, Connor sets his sights on me and nears. My attention falls to baby Jane, who looks content in her father's arms.

"She's so cute," I whisper to him.

"Why don't you give her the rest of the bottle?"

"Wha . . ." My pulse speeds again, and Lo raises his brows at me. This was his big idea? I'm now way more panicked.

"You won't hurt her," Connor says, suddenly about to rest Jane in my arms.

"No, wait," I say quickly. He stops midway to listen to my alarm. "What if I drop her? Or I choke her? What if she cries? Rose won't like it."

Connor's lips lift in a smile, amused. This isn't amusing. This is some scary stuff. "You won't drop her. You won't choke her. And if she cries, just rock her. I'm right here, Lily."

"And Rose?"

"Loves you," Connor finishes. "And she would be *more* than happy to ease your fears about doing this with Maximoff. You'll be great." Before I can protest, Jane is in my arms.

She's so tiny. Her little fingers wiggling and waggling as she sucks on the bottle. She barely makes a peep as Connor steps back from me.

It's not as terrifying as I thought. I breathe out, expelling some nerves.

I tilt the bottle and let Jane drink the contents.

Rose and I discussed breastfeeding some time ago, and to no one's surprise, she was adamant about using formula. She's not a maternal, touchy-feely person, so it makes sense that she wouldn't find joy in breastfeeding like other women do. For other reasons, I'd prefer formula too, even if breastfeeding has health benefits.

But I worry about the ridicule and backlash if the public finds out. I can see the headlines: *Lily Calloway chooses formula over breastfeeding. She cares more about herself than her child.*

Rose told me I shouldn't be shamed for my choices—no woman

should. But the pressure is already there, no matter where or who it comes from.

Jane finishes off the bottle, and she squirms a little in my arms.

"Put her against your chest and gently pat her back," Connor instructs.

With a nervous pit building in my stomach, I listen to his directions and press Jane to my chest. I give her a couple pats and rub her back too. She burps a bit, and then she begins to relax. I blow out a tense breath. That wasn't so bad. I cradle her, watching Jane tiredly close her eyes. And I feel my lips rise in a smile. She drifts back to a temperate sleep.

A minute later, Connor collects his daughter from my arms and delicately places her back in her white crib.

We all drift into the lit hallway, careful not to make too much noise.

Lo kisses my cheek. "How do you feel?"

"Better." Though Jane could very well be one of those genius babies that are easy to handle.

"I'll see you both in the morning," Connor says before he departs to his bedroom down the hall. Lo brings me to our room, and his hand falls to the small of my back.

"About that Hogwarts trip," I start.

His hand freezes on the doorknob. "Lil . . ." His voice is more serious. "You know it's not—"

I almost pounce on him to cover his mouth with my palm. "Don't say it's not real." It's just as bad as saying fairies aren't real. One of them will die as a result. We have to keep the faith.

He patiently waits for me while my hand is pressed against his pink lips, but his amber eyes glimmer like I'm really beautiful in this moment.

"Hogwarts is real," I say. "You know, we can go to Universal Studios and visit Diagon Alley." Sometimes we even head over to the UK to visit the castle where the movies were filmed.

Realization crosses his face, and I drop my hand. "Right. Of course, love."

"Well," I continue on, "I want to wait for Maximoff. When he's a little older. Maybe three or four. We could take a trip together."

Lightness bursts in his eyes, something that lifts me ten feet in the air. I am soaring inside. "He can't be sorted until he's eleven," Lo reminds me.

"Okay." I nod, knowing that's the rules. I'm a proud Hufflepuff. Lo is a bitter Slytherin. And together I kind of wonder what our child will be.

"Then it's a plan," Lo says, and I glow at his words. Maybe we shouldn't be making them so far ahead. Anything could happen. The worst could strike us cold.

But I choose to see the better future.

The one I want.

And if it doesn't come to pass . . .

I'll deal with it then.

"It worked," Lo tells me, his eyes flitting over my features. He turns the knob of our door and walks backward into the dimly lit room.

"What?" I follow him like our bodies are connected, like a short rope is hooked from my waist to his. I will wander with Loren Hale through every moment, good and bad.

Very softly, he says, "You believe in yourself again."

Yes. I smile. I think I do.

Thirty-one

Loren Hale

L o," Lily cries out while I thrust inside of her from behind. On our sides, I have her leg pulled over my waist. She clenches the red sheets, her mouth open as she trembles into these blinding sensations.

My cock throbs. Badly. Dying for a release, to thrust *hard* and come inside of her. My whole body is coated in sweat. My nerves light on fire as I keep this deep rhythm. Jesus.

"Harder," she whimpers, her feet arching.

I can't go harder than this. Even if I want to just as much as her. She's thin, gangly, and carrying our child. I feel like if I'm any rougher than my pace now, I'd break her in two. The closer she is to her due date, the more I worry about inducing labor.

Block it out.

I just want to fuck my girlfriend. I push deeper, which causes her whole body to quake. And I hold this position, pulling her leg higher. My eyes almost roll back.

"Lo, Lo, Lo!" She reaches out for me, but since I'm behind her, she can only claw at the sheets. She moans into the mattress, and I let out a ragged noise.

I make the most of my climax, staying inside as she pulses around my cock. A couple minutes later, I pull out and kiss her on the lips.

She's smiling as she rolls onto her back, but her eyes are starting to flutter closed.

I prop an elbow on the pillow, staring down at her. "That good?" I say, drawing circles on her belly.

"Mmmhhmm."

I feign surprise. "She can't even talk." It's rare that morning sex will put Lily back to sleep, and I suspect it's because we went at it all night. We're making up for the six weeks when we can't do anything. I enjoy it as much as Lil.

Others in the house don't. Rose heard us from down the hall last night and actually texted me to "put my dick away" and check in with Lily's therapist.

She may be worried that I'm pushing Lily to a bad place, but I'm not. I can tell when she's compulsive, and I don't feed into that. I shut it down when it happens. I do understand Rose's concern though. She can't know what I do with Lily in bed, so she just speculates.

"Mmm . . ." Lily says again, her eyes closing entirely.

I smile, watching her enter a peaceful sleep. I sit up and grab my phone off the nightstand, checking my email quickly. I scan through them and stop on something Lil sent me from 5 p.m. yesterday, before we had sex.

The subject line: *Don't be mad! But you need to see this.*

My smile fades. I glance at her, her chest rising and falling, and lift the sheet and comforter up to her collarbones. She barely stirs.

Then I click in to see a picture of me and Lil from Hale Co.'s Fourth of July party. Lily is passing me her corn dog with a big goofy smile. It's one of the cutest pictures I've ever seen, and I look infatuated with her.

She pasted in a link to a *Celebrity Crush* article. I take the risk and click it too. The headline: *Lily Calloway Shares a Hotdog with Loren Hale on July 4th* by Wendy Collins.

I skim the article. Wendy talks about the rumors concerning

me, Ryke, Lily, and *my* child. Other than that, she just says it's ironic that Lily is passing me a corn dog.

I wish Lily wouldn't read this shit. I return to Lil's original email and see that she typed a message to me: *I thought it was a nice picture of us. Right?*

My emotions just seesawed in the span of two minutes. I'm back to smiling. "Yeah, Lil," I whisper, my gaze flitting to her as she sleeps.

I don't trust her fully. I can't. I end up going through my phone's history to see what she was up to yesterday evening. My stomach drops. Tons of *Celebrity Crush* articles, Twitter, Tumblr—shit. I scope out those. No porn. Just television fandom stuff. She also Google searched "when should I take a paternity test" since it's something we've mentioned to silence the rumors about Ryke. I don't want to think about it right now.

I almost shut off the phone, but it buzzes.

> Are you up? I need to talk to you. I'm in the kitchen. —Connor

Instead of texting back, I carefully climb out of bed and put on drawstring pants before I leave.

Thirty-two

Loren Hale

After walking down the hallway, I descend the stairs, skipping a couple steps at a time, and then I enter the large clean kitchen.

In khaki shorts and a navy collared shirt, Connor pours himself a cup of coffee, no dark circles under his eyes or any visible signs of exhaustion. It's already been four weeks since Jane was born and he's a pro. "Should I expect to be as well rested as you?" I ask him, heading to a cupboard.

He turns around while I search for cereal. "Your normal sleep cycle is ten hours," he reminds me. "Mine is six."

"Noted." All I see is Ryke's granola cereal on the shelf, so I take out the box. "What'd you need to talk about?" I open the fridge and grab the milk.

"I want you to hear this from me before it appears anywhere else."

I slow my actions, not frozen in place, but more cautious of this conversation. I wrack my brain for the subject matter, and I come up blank. "Yeah, okay," I say, pouring milk into my bowl. I put the cereal back and wait for him to speak.

But in this rare moment, he has trouble producing words.

I stop moving and just lean against the counter, eating my cereal unhurriedly. "I can handle whatever it is," I remind him. "Is it Lily?" The granola lumps in my throat. I drink some of the milk to wash it down.

"No," he says quickly. He stands opposite me, cupping his coffee, and his blue eyes flit up to mine. "It's about me."

I frown and set my spoon back in the bowl. "Are you getting shit at Cobalt Inc. for the Mexico stuff?"

"When I kissed you?" he says with the tilt of his head.

I flash a half-smile. "I could've kissed *you*, you know."

"But you didn't. I kissed you," he says easily. "And no, I'm not getting flak from anyone directly, and I couldn't care less about rumors."

"Really? The Connor Cobalt that I first met was all about his reputation."

"My reputation has superseded anything I envisioned back then. It'd take more than a dare in Mexico to hurt it . . ." He sips his coffee. "You don't need to worry how people perceive me. It's something I've micromanaged my whole life. I'm equipped to deal with it now."

"So what is it then?" I ask outright.

"It's . . ." He stops short and lets out a laugh. "I almost never explain this to anyone . . . most people wouldn't view me the way I'd want them to. They wouldn't really understand, so I keep it to myself."

He looks up at the ceiling as he collects his thoughts.

And he starts by saying, "I admire certain qualities in almost every person, but I don't think like everyone else. My ideas and beliefs would be considered strange, and I've lived by the notion that *I* understand me, even if everyone else sees someone lesser, someone . . . they need. But as long as I know who I am, nothing else matters."

I don't understand completely, and off my confusion, he keeps explaining.

"I manipulate people's emotions. I've been with different people because they needed someone to love them, and I needed something from them. Rose used to call me an 'immoral asshole'—I wouldn't disagree. I've never claimed to be moral." He stands straighter and adds, "If you look closely at the things I say, you'll see more of me."

I process all of his words, but I can't hone in on the details, the significant parts of what he just said. All I wonder is if he's manipulated me before. If he saw a guy that craved love, in almost any form, and he took advantage of that. We've been down this road before, and I can't even remember what I told myself to let it go, to accept it and move on.

"I don't know . . ." I say quietly, the bowl of cereal cold in my hand.

I can tell that he's struggling to discuss this with me. Maybe he fears that I'll take it the wrong way and hate him for it. I'm trying to be as open-minded as he is with me.

He sets his coffee on the counter. "I'm never gender specific. I told you that I've been with different *people*."

It starts clicking. "You've kissed a guy before me," I mention. I've never brought it up. I didn't want to make anything awkward, and I was waiting for this moment—for him to just tell me parts of his past. I try not to pry into people's lives. In fact, it means more when they're willing to share on their own.

He nods. "Do you remember during the reality show, we were all asked if we've been with a man?"

"Yeah, I remember that interview."

"I answered it differently than you and Ryke. I said that many people want to be with me."

I didn't think much of it. I just thought it was Connor being conceited, but I'm recognizing that it's a lot more than that. "Are you bisexual?" I ask.

"I believe in attraction between people. To me, heterosexuality, homosexuality, bisexuality—they're just terms and constructs that people have built over the years." He meets my eyes. "Like boxes that we have to fit in. I don't fit into a box, Lo. I don't want to fit in one."

It's not as surprising as I thought it'd be. Maybe because I've never classified Connor as anything before. "Have you been attracted to a guy?"

He shrugs like it's not a big deal. I guess it isn't. "Many kinds of people interest me," he says. "But I've never been more attracted to someone than I have Rose. And that won't ever change."

"Does she know?"

His lips curve in a grin. "Of course. She's known my stance on this since I was sixteen."

I'd say those two have the strangest relationship, but I'm codependent with my sex addict girlfriend. "So are you worried something's going to get out to the media?" He started this whole conversation off with that fear.

"Like I said, I've done things in the past . . . and not everything may stay under the rug. I just wanted you to know where I'm coming from before the media starts twisting things."

I want to ask if he's had sex with a guy. It's . . . weird to think about.

He must read my expression because he says, "I've fucked men. Not always because I liked them."

It's a lot to take in, but he's not much different than the guy I've always known. It's something he proclaimed moments ago: *If you look closely at the things I say, you'll see more of me.* He's been saying all of these things for years, and subliminally, I've been accepting him as he is. Even if I couldn't see all of him.

"For what it's worth," I tell Connor, "it's kind of extraordinary you can transcend sexual orientations. You're like an amoeba."

"Amoebas are asexual," he says. "I'm more like a god."

I put my bowl on the counter and slow clap.

He grabs his coffee and raises it to me with a smile.

I nod to him. "Have you ever lied before and just said you were gay or straight?"

"All the time," he says without missing a beat. "Lily even asked me once if I was gay, and instead of getting into it, I assured her that I liked women. I knew that Lily was Rose's sister, and I needed Lily to want me to be with Rose."

Because Rose loves her sisters and she'd value Lily's opinion. "That's fucked up, love."

"Immoral," Connor says, pointing to his chest.

Footsteps sound on the stairs, and Connor and I instantly go quiet. I return to my bowl of cereal, and he refills his coffee. Ryke breaches the doorway with a hardened, unshaven jaw and unkempt hair.

"Don't fucking stop talking on my account," he says, his voice gruff like he just woke up.

I crane my neck to see the oven clock behind Connor. "It's already noon."

"It's Saturday," Ryke refutes, opening the cupboard. He doesn't work, and he rock climbs on random days, so I have no idea when he's going to wake up at the crack of dawn or sleep in. I bet Connor can predict him though. "And you're eating breakfast, so why harp on me?"

"Someone didn't get laid last night," I say.

He shoots me a dark look while he grabs his box of granola cereal. "It's a little hard getting a girl off when you have a baby wailing every five fucking minutes."

Connor pipes in, "Every five minutes? Do you exaggerate about your climbing times too?"

Ryke flips him off, but Connor still passes him a bowl for his cereal, and Ryke accepts it.

When Ryke glowers with sunken eyes, he appears more serious. "Look, Daisy already has sleep problems. She doesn't need a baby adding to that. I can have a bad fucking night's sleep fine, but hers pile up."

When he pours his cereal, only a couple pieces of granola hit the bowl, and the grainy dust plumes like flour. He's reached the bottom of the box.

He slowly turns to glare at me and my breakfast, which was the last of his cereal apparently.

"It tastes like cardboard," I tell him. "Honestly, I don't know how you can eat this regularly."

"Then why the fuck are you eating it, man?" he growls in distress.

"Because it's the only cereal left in the house, and I was hungry," I defend. "Buy some Cheerios or Frosted Flakes like a normal person."

"There's too much sugar in—you know what, fucking eat it. If you have the shits, that's fucking karma for you."

I practically finished the cereal before he walked into the kitchen, but I've eaten it before fine. It doesn't contain that much fiber.

Ryke retrieves the orange juice from the fridge instead. "Daisy and I are moving into the basement tonight."

I'm surprised it's taken him four weeks to reach this decision.

"You can take the master on this floor," Connor says. "It's vacant."

Ryke shakes his head. "Rose still uses the closet space, and Daisy doesn't want to take that from her."

"Just have a baby," I banter, setting my bowl in the sink. "Then you can justify getting shit sleep." I catch sight of a *Celebrity Crush* magazine by the coffee pot, something I'm sure Lily bought. I pick it up to trash it.

Ryke retorts, "That's not going to happen any time soon."

My brows rise, realizing he didn't discount it entirely. "You want kids?"

"*Not any time soon,*" he emphasizes this point. "I haven't even been with her for a year yet, anything can happen." I watch his features darken, and he knocks the empty cereal box over, just frustrated. Hale Co. is putting strain on his relationship. I can tell he's dreading the "anything can happen" future.

I head to the pantry to toss the magazine, but before I do, I catch one of the smaller headlines on the cover: *[POLL] Who makes the better mother: Lily Calloway or Rose Cobalt?*

Great. Like Lily hasn't been comparing herself more to Rose as the weeks go by. It's not healthy. Rose has faults, but they're much different than Lily's, and any way you look at it—Lily somehow always falls short in comparison. At least in terms of motherhood.

Which is just shit.

Has anyone heard the crap that comes out of Rose's mouth about kids? Not really. The reality show didn't show most of it, and the interviews that we do (from Samantha's persistence to keep us relevant) are usually censored. Meaning the Calloway's publicists will tell the journalists *not* to ask Rose about kids. Because Rose has no filter and will probably call them monsters to the entire goddamn world.

She even calls Jane a little gremlin from time to time. Oddly, it does sound affectionate in an "ice queen slowly thawing" kind of way, but I don't think the general public would pick up on that.

I open the article just to see the results of the poll and torture myself. Maybe Lily is rubbing off on me.

Who makes the better mother?

Lily: 46%

Rose: 54%

My blood goes from a boil to a simmer. It's not a landslide like I thought. I check above the poll, and realize they labeled the girls with their pros and cons. I scan Lily's first.

Con: sex addict, in a three-way relationship (rumored), boyfriend is an alcoholic

Pro: successful business, sweet, loves her long-term boyfriend (and her rumored second bf)

My teeth ache, and I realize I'm clenching them too hard. I go through Rose's list.

Con: sex tapes

Pro: successful boutique, married, Type-A personality

How the hell is Type-A personality even on here? Rose will be great at keeping track of her kid's schedule; I'll give her that. I'm pissed at myself for even entertaining this article. I chuck it in the trash and return to Connor and Ryke about the same time that Rose struts into the kitchen.

"Baby in the room," she says, cradling her newborn with one arm and holding an empty bottle with the other. Her hair is damp like she just took a shower and didn't have time to blow it dry.

"When you have eight children, are you going to announce each of their entrances too?" I banter.

Rose gives me a long glare as she makes her way to the refrigerator to grab another bottle.

"I'm just trying to prepare myself," I say.

"You won't have to prepare for eight kids. It's not happening," she retorts. Connor opens his mouth, and she raises the hand with the bottle to silence him.

"That would be more effective if you actually covered my mouth, darling."

"Don't make me hurt you," she snaps, and Jane lets out a noise close to a giggle. Rose is smiling from ear to ear, a smile that I've pretty much never seen from her.

"Ugh, stop," I say, shielding my eyes. "It's creepy."

"I love my daughter," she says adamantly. Jane does bring out something in Rose, a lighter side of her that's hard to spot sometimes. But she's still the same, so I wait for it. "She may mutter inarticulately, vomit on me, and look clueless until a certain stage of her life, but she's my unintelligible thing."

I bow. "I'm sorry, your highness."

Rose rolls her eyes, but there's a smile in them.

"I'll swap you," Connor tells his wife. "Baby for bags."

Her eyes pierce him, even if she's not on the offensive. "What bags?"

I just now notice the Chanel and Dior shopping bags beside Connor's feet. Of course he went to the stores this morning. Rose's demeanor shifts, her back no longer arched, and I worry she might chuck the baby in Connor's arms.

Jane lets out another squeal of delight, kicking her legs that are clothed in a green onesie. Orange tabby cats printed along the arms. And we all smile. She's ridiculously cute, even if she's spawned from Rose's womb.

"Looks like she's already inherited Rose's love of fancy things," I say.

"She's a baby," Rose tells me. Instead of hatred, the word "baby" is filled with mild disdain. "She doesn't know what we're even talking about."

I feign surprise. "So you're admitting that you don't have a genius child?" I turn to Ryke. "Did hell freeze over this morning?"

Before Ryke even reacts, Rose speaks. "I'm admitting that my child isn't superhuman." Rose hands Jane off to Connor and then goes for the shopping bags.

"With Rose and my genes, she's still very likely a genius," Connor adds.

Yeah. I know.

Rose unwraps her bags at the bar, the first item: a black silk blouse, one that Rose delicately folds into its original paper after examining it.

I nudge Ryke. "What's Daisy doing this weekend?" I genuinely care about other people's everyday lives—it's bizarre. Something I never saw four years ago, addicted and selfish.

Ryke just casually shrugs. "I don't know." He takes a swig of his orange juice from the carton. Rose is too busy fawning over her gifts to notice my brother's bad habits.

"What do you mean?" I ask him. "You're dating her."

"We like our fucking space."

Rose straightens at the sound of the f-bomb, and I punch Ryke's arm with force. He winces, since that spot is tender for him now.

"I forgot," he tells Rose, not even bothering to rub his bicep.

"I don't care if she swears when she's older," Rose tells him. "I just don't want her first word to be *fuck*."

"My sentiments align with Rose's," Connor adds, his daughter falling asleep in his arms as he rocks her.

We have a system in place: punch Ryke every time he curses in front of the baby. It's fun for all of us but him, and so far, it's not really working that well. His arm was bruised the entire first week Jane was home, and he *still* has trouble training himself to keep it clean.

"I'm trying my best," he says.

Rose nods. "I appreciate it." She returns to her clothes, and I backtrack to my initial conversation with Ryke.

"You like your space?" My brows furrow. "I don't get it. Are you taking a break or something?"

"What?" Lily's voice echoes from the doorway, and she enters the kitchen with eyes like saucers. It doesn't help that she wears her Wampa cap, dinosaur slippers, black cotton pajamas, and a fur coat. "You're on—on a . . ." Her green eyes somehow grow wider. ". . . a *break*?" Shit.

"For fuck's sake—"

I punch his arm, and he lets out an exasperated sound. It's the system in place. I can't help that. "Sorry, bro."

He sighs. "We're just not keeping tabs on each other. We're still together. We're still fu—*screwing*." He turns to me and points. "Do not effing punch me."

I clap. "You managed to avoid an f-bomb. Barely."

"Progress," Connor chimes in with a smile. Ryke even looks surprised by the compliment, not even a backhanded one. Maybe he can tell Ryke's seriously frustrated today.

Lily walks farther into the kitchen. "Are you sure, Ryke?"

"Yeah, Lil," he tells her sincerely. "We're not like you and Lo, okay? We like to give each other room to breathe."

"We breathe," Lily defends our relationship. My brows rise. Let's not kid ourselves. We struggle with our codependency on a daily basis.

"What in the world are you wearing?" Rose asks her sister. Lily waddles her way to the fridge. I want to wrap my arms around her and pull her close to my chest. I hesitate because A) we just had sex, and I'd rather not tease her too much and B) that codependency, room-to-breathe thing.

"It's cold in here," Lily explains.

Everyone looks to Ryke, the person who constantly lowers the thermostat. He glowers. "It's summer. It gets hot."

Lily shuts the refrigerator door, empty-handed, and snatches a banana from the countertop. "I also have an announcement."

Everyone quiets, and I go rigid. Whatever it is, she hasn't told me. Her eyes flit to mine briefly before they focus on her sister. "I'm going to remain inside the house until I have the baby. I can't risk having a limo-delivery. The only times I'll leave are for doctor appointments."

Fine with me. Knowing she'll be at home actually eases my worries. Someone will always be here with her.

"So that's the real reason you're dressed like the abominable snowman in July," Ryke says, like it's not his fault for keeping the house cold if she doesn't meet the light of day.

Lily shoots him a middle finger and begins unpeeling her banana. I grin. God, I love this girl.

"Hey, guys." Daisy slips into the kitchen with a yawn. "What's everyone doing today?" Her hair is still platinum blonde, but she wears it in a braid. She hangs around by the stove, putting distance between herself and Ryke.

"Taking care of a baby," Rose says easily.

"I have her, darling," Connor replies. "You can spend the day with your sisters."

Rose speaks in French with Connor at this, and Lily eats her banana slowly, watching them talk in the foreign language with no real clue what they're saying. Then she focuses on Ryke and Daisy, and I see the fear flash in Lil's eyes. No one wants their relationship to work more than her.

"Can you two just hug it out?" I tell my brother and Lily's little sister.

Daisy breaks into a charismatic smile, and she faces her boyfriend. "Do you want to hug me?" she asks playfully.

"No," he deadpans. He better be sarcastic, and I hate that I can't tell.

Daisy only smiles more, and she stretches her arms out on the counter. "Do you want to . . ." And she mouths, *fuck me?*

Oh shit.

"Every fucking minute, Calloway."

I punch his arm, and he turns around and decks my bicep with the same force. "Jesus Christ," I curse. And he double taps me again for those words. Shit.

"It hurts, doesn't it?" he tells me.

"Yeah, yeah, whatever." I wave him off. It's better than a swear jar. Money isn't a big enough penalty.

Lily is still entranced by Ryke and Daisy. After a couple seconds, I catch her attention, and her gaze falls on mine. I motion between us with my hand, and then I make a crude gesture with my mouth and my tongue. I watch her freeze, the banana midair while her face flushes in a deep shade of red.

Her eyes dance around the room, checking to see if anyone is watching us. They aren't.

And then she points to her chest and mouths, *me?*

I nod. *Yes, Lil. You.* Two more seconds later, I close the space between us, and I have her wrapped in my arms. These are the kind of embraces I live for.

Thirty-three

Lily Calloway

Still no photos of Jane Cobalt.

The headline on today's *Celebrity Crush* article has Rose full of glee. Since Jane was born, she's been on a mission to keep her daughter away from paparazzi. Yesterday, Rose stepped outside the gated neighborhood with Jane, taking her to the Calloway Couture boutique, and cameramen swarmed her.

I know this, not from firsthand account, but from watching entertainment news. In the video, it looked like Rose was walking through a concert festival of photographers, just to reach the front doors of her store. I hadn't seen her so protective and mad in a long time. If she wasn't holding Jane to her chest—the baby shrouded by a blanket—she would've definitely nut-kicked a guy.

Her bodyguard held them back, and I could even detect Rose's appreciation for Vic. She won't utter the words, but our parents were right about the extra security. The bodyguards are a helpful force.

Rose paints my toenails on her bed while Daisy makes faces at Jane at the foot of the mattress. The baby sputters happy noises at her aunt.

"Does it annoy you," I ask Rose and gesture to Jane, "that you can't talk to her yet?"

She dips the brush into the purple lilac polish. "It's aggravating at times. Life would be easier if they just came out of the womb with proper verbal skills. It's one of the many reasons babies are intolerable . . ." She pauses, and her eyes flit to her baby. "But Jane is different. She makes up for the blubbering in other ways."

Daisy clasps one of Jane's little hands. "Like what?"

Rose stays quiet for a moment and pensively watches her daughter, those big blue eyes and soft cheeks. "She just gets me." Her glare turns on me first. "And I know it sounds ridiculous, but it's what I feel, so it can't be wrong." She might as well go ahead and flip her hair over her shoulder to cap it off. Rose twists the polish, sets it aside, and scoots closer to the foot of the bed where her daughter lies.

She scoops Jane in her arms, still a little stiff, but Jane snuggles into her mom's chest anyway. Not offended by Rose's cold nature.

Rose touches her daughter's head full of thinly combed brown hair. "Don't tell Connor," she says to both of us, "but I was nervous she would like him more than me."

"I was too," I tell her.

Her yellow-green eyes pierce me, and Daisy laughs lightly, pooling her platinum hair to the top of her head.

"What?" I ask. "I thought we were being honest." This was sharing time, right?

"In all *honesty*, Jane likes us equally," Rose explains. "She's already perfect. Not choosing favorites." Rose plants a small kiss on the top of Jane's head and sets her back down on the light blue comforter. "You're going to be amazing, aren't you?" she asks her.

Jane smiles big, and it reflects off Rose's eyes, softening her icy exterior by a hundred degrees.

When Rose speaks to Jane, she uses her normal voice, so does Connor, no baby talk.

"I can't wait until you're old enough to choose your own

clothes," Rose tells Jane, "and your own hair styles, and your own words. And I get to see what kind of girl you grow up to be."

It almost brings tears. Rose doesn't want her daughter to be just like her. She wants her to be herself, a unique individual, to have an identity all her own.

My phone vibrates in my hand. I check the text.

You. Me. Bedroom. —Lo

My pulse begins to race as I text him back.
Now? I press send.

Unless you'd like to wait until later. —Lo

No way.

Now is good.

I take a practiced breath before I climb off the bed, my back aching from carrying so much weight. My stomach is so heavy that I feel like I'm going to explode at any moment. But I just think about those six weeks without sex, and I decide that I want to get as much Loren Hale time as I can.

"Where are you going?" Rose asks.

"Lo wants me."

"In bed," Daisy finishes with a goofy smile.

I roast another shade of red, but I don't deny it. "We're making up for the six weeks of abstinence." I pause and ask, "How is it going for you?" Partly, I wonder if it's really hard, but I recognize her struggle will be different than mine. Jane was born on June 10th, and it's already July 13th, so if Rose really wanted to, she could have sex now. Four weeks in. But the doctors recommended six, and Rose usually follows the rules.

"Connor thinks he can have his way with me the *exact* day I'm physically able to have sex again, and it's infuriating. Maybe I don't want to have sex on that day. *Maybe* he isn't going to win this time."

Daisy and I exchange smiles at how worked up Rose is becoming over her husband.

Daisy adds, "Maybe you don't want to be tied up too."

"Yeah," I agree. "Maybe you'd rather be spanked."

Rose gives me a look.

"I was being serious, not mean like Lo," I defend myself. I feel bad about throwing Lo under the bus, but I'll make up for it in the bedroom. I internally nod at this plan.

Daisy raises her fist in the air. "Girl power."

Rose exhales a breath and then her eyes suddenly light up, as if a devilish idea has sprouted in her brain. "What if I don't have sex during *your* six weeks of abstinence too? It'll be a solidarity pact." Rose loves those, but I can tell this is mostly about beating her husband in one of their mind games.

"That's an extra month for you," I remind her. It sounds crazy and tough, but my sister isn't a sex addict. She was a virgin until she was twenty-three, proudly.

Rose pulls back her shoulders in confidence. "I'm married to the man. I can have sex with him every day for the rest of my life. An extra month won't kill us."

I try not to contemplate Connor's sexual needs. I'm not sure if he'll be upset by waiting, or if he'll consider this an even bigger challenge and try to win Rose over.

"I'll join too," Daisy says with a smile.

My mouth falls. Whaa . . .

Rose claps her hands. "Perfect. I'll call Poppy, and we can all abstain in honor of Lily abstaining."

I whip my head around, wide-eyed. "You all don't have to do this." I point to Daisy, who twists her thumb ring in a fidgety manner. "You *seriously* shouldn't be doing this." *Ryke is going to kill me.*

Daisy's lips just pull higher. "You think Ryke will blow a fuse?" She gasps, and her eyes grow big. "The danger."

I snatch a throw pillow and toss it at her. She laughs while Rose protectively lifts Jane to her chest, avoiding a pillow assault on her baby.

"In all seriousness," Daisy says, "it's a big deal for you, and I want to be supportive too."

My throat closes up for a second. All of my sisters are willing to share in my struggle, and maybe they'll even show me that it's not as bad as I think it may be. I'm happy to be so close to them now.

I have to thank Rose for that. She never gave up on me. Every time I pushed her away, she just kept walking right back into my life, refusing to let me be ostracized. Now here I am, living in a house with my two sisters. Happy.

I'm happy.

"No more crying," Rose tells me. "That should be our second pact. We can make that one a blood oath."

"No," Daisy and I say in unison.

Rose glares. "I always sterilize the knife."

I smile and wipe my eyes that have misted with tears. My phone buzzes with another text.

Lil. Where are you? —Lo

When I glance up, I catch Rose typing on her own cell. She has a smug and possibly smitten look on her face. "Connor is not winning this."

I edge toward the door with a stupid grin. It's good to know that even with a baby, the nerd stars still align the exact same way.

. . .

take five steps into the hallway before a dull ache pounds against my back. My limbs freeze as worry and confusion run through me. My phone impatiently buzzes once more.

> Lily Calloway. Don't make me come get you. —Lo

He rarely sexts me, and this infrequent moment is being ruined by pain. I am not so far away from him. The door is right in sight. I can just brush it off.

As soon as I walk forward, a sharp pain grips my abdomen. *Shit.* This can't be happening. What did Rose call them? False contractions? Yeah, they're fake. Pretend contractions. My water hasn't even broken yet.

Wait . . .

Rose is not reliable.

She had a baby in a limo because of the same mindset. I quicken my pace to my bedroom and swing the door open. Lo lounges on the bed with an open comic book, his phone right beside him as he waits for me. When his gaze rises to mine, concern crushes his sharp features. "What's wrong? Lily?"

He jumps to his feet before I can even utter a word.

"I think . . . I'm having contractions. I don't know though." I wince as the pain throbs from my back to my stomach. Like powerful, mutant cramps. Oh my God, these cramps have superpowers. How in the hell am I going to defeat them?

Lo acts swiftly. He grabs his cell phone, bypasses me to push the door open wider and calls down the hall, "Rose!"

"Don't," I start, shoving his arm. "She's going to freak out." I can't even believe she was his first choice of comrade for this situation. Surely Ryke or Connor ranked higher on his list. But maybe he was thinking about my allegiance, and who I'd be most comfortable with.

He touches my shoulder in comfort, but he can't reply to me, not when he's on the phone. "Hi, this is Loren Hale," he says into the receiver. "Can I speak to Dr. Dhar?"

Rose emerges from her bedroom quickly. She's alone, so I assume Daisy stayed with Jane.

"What's wrong?" She scrutinizes our lingering presence in the doorway.

I hold my belly, my head dizzying a bit. "I don't know." It's the truth. I have no clue if this is real or fake or something in between. That confusion and darkness frighten me the most.

"I'll grab your bag," Rose says, rushing into my bedroom. *What bag?* is my first thought. Then I remember: *oh yeah, my hospital bag.* The overnight one that Rose basically packed for me *months* ago. The perks of having an organized, slightly neurotic sister.

I bury my head in Lo's chest while he continues to talk to the doctor. He rubs my back, and I grip his belt loops for support. *Thank you, belt loops, for always being there for me.*

I hear Rose from the depths of my room. "Connor and I are going to drop Jane off at Poppy's! Daisy will fetch Ryke, and we'll meet you at the hospital!"

No. I can't be giving birth today.

Can I? I look up at Lo with squinted eyes.

And he nods in confirmation like he can read my mind. I know I wear all of my thoughts on my face for him to pick apart and see.

He's not scared. Not as much as me. And the confidence that he's built up for weeks and weeks blows straight through me. I try to hold on to it as tightly as I can, even if it's just air breezing between my fingers. I try to breathe every little bit of it in. But the terrified bits of me are very, very strong.

I'm about to have a baby.

Oh God.

Thirty-four

Loren Hale

Lily's water broke while she was clinging to me. I got her to stop apologizing after we both took quick showers, and by that point, I could tell her pain overpowered her embarrassment—which for Lil means she's really hurting.

We made it to the hospital without an emergency labor, and now that we're in the delivery room, I'm positive I've glared at an entire staff of nurses on accident. Rose confirms it by saying I have a "bitchy" face. I just hate feeling helpless, having to watch Lil curve her arm around her eyes and shake in pain. It fucking sucks.

And it reminds me of the earlier days of her recovery, back when I had to constantly tell her *no* and grasp her hands so she stopped being compulsive. Where sex impaired her ability to be a normal, functioning person in society.

It's a time that I don't ever want to return to.

Six hours and an epidural later, Lily finally eases. Like she's ready to float away. I comb my fingers through her hair, preferring her drugged up than in agony.

I could tell that she wanted the meds, but the nurses gave her a hard time about it. Saying things about how recovering addicts should try the all-natural birth. It took all three of us—Rose, Ryke, and me—to try and quiet the nurses and convince Lily to listen to what *she* wanted. She's terrified. Of doing something wrong. Of hurting our son by a choice she makes. People shouldn't make her feel guilty for wanting an easier birth.

On the hospital bed, she smiles dazedly up at me. I sit on the mattress close to her and can't restrain my own smile at her cute expression. "Feeling better?"

She relaxes into her pillow like she's sinking into a cloud. "I love the hot-tempered triad."

I have no idea what she's talking about. "The what?"

The door blows open, and my father enters the luxury birthing suite, sipping a coffee. He's been in and out all day, just walking around the hospital like a lost soul. His dark eyes flit between me and Lil. "See, I thought one day this would happen. I told Greg that you'd knock her up around seventeen."

My face sharpens.

Greg actually interjects before I can, "Lily was a smart girl to wait."

Lily looks like she's floating even higher from the compliment. I've heard her dad praise her on multiple accounts, when he's not immersed in his work.

Our fathers aren't the only two people here. Lil wanted her sisters present during the long "waiting" process, and even though Poppy and Sam are watching Maria and Jane, everyone else came. Even Lily's mom, who peers out between a crack in the closed blinds. The room, filled with plush chairs and couches, is big enough for our families. They'll all leave once Lily's about to deliver.

My dad laughs into his coffee. "Technically, they had an accident—"

"Can you not?" I cut him off, especially as Lily descends from her cloud. Her lips frowning. I liked it better when she was flattered for making smart choices.

"Hey," he says, "I'm goddamn *happy* right now." This is my dad, happy. And I do see it, beneath his dark eyes and his severe face. "I'm getting a grandson." The pride in his voice takes me aback for a second.

He pats Lily's feet that are beneath a blanket. "How are you holding up?"

She nods. "Good."

Greg chimes in with a smile, "That's what I like to hear."

I watch my dad walk farther into the suite toward his friend.

"Updates?" Samantha asks the room as she hawk-eyes the streets below. They've been jammed with camera crews for the past two hours, hoping to snap a photo of any of us leaving the building. I'd like to say they're not important, but Lily perks up in interest.

"I have one," Daisy says. She's sprawled out on the white couch, her feet on Ryke's lap. She reads an online article from her phone. "According to an inside source, Lily Calloway is in labor and has been admitted to the hospital. We'll have more information in the coming hours."

"The main thing is to keep Maximoff away from the paparazzi," Greg tells Lily and me. "No child needs that stress."

Lily blows out a breath, and I squeeze her hand. Having a kid is anxiety enough. I brush her hair back and whisper, "We've got this."

She nods a couple times like she's trying to believe it too.

My dad sidles next to Samantha to peek out of the blinds with her. "I'm going to call more security for when we leave. This is ridiculous." He points at the window. "That chubby one is eating a goddamn Happy Meal while he waits."

On a shorter couch, Connor wraps his arm around Rose and says, "The cameramen are allowed to eat, as all human beings are."

My dad gives him a surly look and snaps, "Whose side are you on?"

"The logical side," Connor says easily. "You're probably not familiar with it, but it's the side that wins ten times out of ten."

My dad's eyes flash hot, and it's pretty apparent that his beef with my best friend is still ongoing. This isn't the time for that shit.

"Hey, this isn't the fucking time," Ryke cuts in. I nod to my older brother in thanks.

I'm almost regretting making the birth of my son a family event, but I can tell Lily appreciates everyone's company. Even if it's stressing *me* out.

My dad grips his coffee a little tighter, but his voice has less edge. "I'm just making conversation." He sips his drink, and Samantha finally pries herself off the window.

Her gaze surprisingly lands on Lily and me. "Are you two really set on his name?" she asks, sitting stiffly in a chair next to Greg. "There's still time to change your minds."

Lily shakes her head repeatedly, and before I accidentally say something nasty to her mom, Rose begins to defend our choices.

"Leave them alone," Rose says. "You shouldn't be adding to Lily's stress. This is a calm, *zen* environment." She inhales a deep breath to demonstrate how zen-fucking-like it is in here. Only her collarbones protrude like she has trouble exhaling.

"You were saying?" I tease Rose.

Her yellow-green eyes narrow to pinpoints at me.

It's *tense* in here, though it could be a hundred times worse. It feels like how it should be, probably. The unease from unexpected outcomes.

Ryke rests an arm along the back of the couch and holds his girlfriend's ankles with the other hand. "Maximoff is a good fucking name. It's strong."

My dad butts in, "It's strong until a kid calls him Maxi Pad."

"Says the man who named me Loren," I retort.

My dad faces me and counters, "It's about rising *above* your name. I'm not complaining about Maximoff. I think it'll be a testament to his character how he reacts to it."

I don't want his name to be a fucking test.

But I'm not letting our parents talk us out of something we chose together. Something we truly love. I hate that they have to taint it with their opinions anyway. But there's a place inside of me that's grateful for having people who care. For better or for worse, that's what family is for, right?

Lily's grip tightens on my hand, and she lets out a staggered breath before sinking back into the pillows. A couple nurses push through the doors and check her vitals. "I think she's about ready." One of the nurses leaves to retrieve the doctor. "We should clear out the room, a two-person limit during delivery."

I step off the bed.

"Don't go!" Lily clasps my one hand with two of hers.

I edge closer to her. "I wasn't going to, love." I kiss her nose lightly, and she exhales a large breath. Everyone stands to exit the suite.

Greg buttons his suit jacket and nods to Lily. "We'll see you afterward. You'll do great."

"Thanks, Dad." Lily looks high off the encouragement, or maybe it's the drugs. Either way, I'm realizing this is turning out to be a good memory, for both of us.

Samantha even acknowledges Lily with a smile, no words. But right now, I think it's better that way. The room is dwindling in seconds. My dad toasts us with his *coffee* like he has some giant glass of bourbon in his hand and then leaves with Lily's parents.

Ryke squeezes my shoulder, and Daisy gives her sister a side-hug.

"Hey," Ryke says, and I meet his brown eyes, more flecked with hazel than usual. "I'm here for you." He's the first person I'd go to if I ever felt overwhelmed. By now, he knows that.

I nod. It's all I can do, emotions starting to constrict my lungs. Somehow, though, I choke out, "Thanks."

He pats my shoulder before heading through the door with his girlfriend.

Connor slips his phone in his black slacks and nears the edge of the bed. Nurses begin to mill around the room. The doctor isn't here yet, but reality is still hitting me full force. "Don't blink," he says in a smooth voice. "It'll happen faster than you realize." He winks at me before he departs with a confident stride.

Don't blink.

My stomach is in knots.

"Rose?" Lily whips her head around the room, trying to find her older sister. Her eyes start to well with tears, thinking Rose left without saying anything.

I'm about to go find her, but she suddenly appears, walking out of the bathroom. "I'm right here, stop crying." She fixes her glossy hair with her fingers. "I didn't want to use the public toilets."

I wipe Lily's cheeks with my thumb.

Rose gives her a look. "We made a pact, no tears."

"That sounds like something a demon would say," I tell her.

She sets her hands on her hips, and Lily cuts her off, "Daisy and I rejected that pact. You were vetoed."

I laugh, no fucking way. That almost never happens.

Rose purses her lips. "Thank you for the reminder. You may cry then." She's fooling herself if she thinks she's not going to shed a tear when she sees Lily holding her son. Even if Rose isn't the softest person when it comes to her sisters, she can still turn into a puddle.

Lily lets out a long breath. "Can you give me a quick tip?"

"Don't be scared."

"In case something happens to me," Lily says—I shoot her the sharpest look. She holds her hands in defense and adds, "I just would like a hug."

I tell Lily, "Nothing is going to happen to you." I can't entertain the idea without losing oxygen, my eyes burning. Two nurses and a doctor stand in the room. We're in a hospital. Nothing is going to go wrong.

"IknowIknow," she says quickly. She lets go of my hand and spreads her arms out at Rose.

Her older sister looks like she was just asked to climb a ladder and clean the drain pipes. But she leans down and gives a stiff couple of pats to Lily's shoulder. "I love you," Rose whispers before she steps away. When she stands up, she brushes her fingers below one eye.

I tilt my head at her.

She points at me. "Shut up."

"I didn't say anything."

She raises her chin and marches right out the door.

Besides the hospital staff, we're alone. I keep my hand on her head, watching her eyes nervously flit around the room. "Are you in any pain?" I ask.

"No," she whispers. "I can't feel anything down below." She scratches her arm, and I swiftly take her hand in mine, lacing our fingers.

"Lily Calloway," I murmur, and she finally looks up at me. *I love you.* I don't even have to say the words before her eyes well with tears. I breathe deeply, my muscles wound tight. Years and years with Lily, my best friend, rush through my veins.

It's a connection that spawned early on, from chasing her around a golf course and hiding underneath pillows on a yacht. From escaping to a bedroom and playing pretend behind a bar. From shutting out the world until it was just us.

I open my mouth to say more, but it's hard to put everything to words.

A tear drips down her cheek. "I know."

I kiss her on the lips, one that nearly pulls her to my body, but I break it before she shifts out of place too much. My mind is spinning as the doctor says something to Lil, and then the nurses flock her sides. I focus on Lily, holding her hand as I stand by her side.

About two hours pass with Lily pushing, her cheeks splotched red from fatigue.

"One more," the doctor instructs.

Lily's brows scrunch as she tries again, not giving up. Time seems immeasurable. Too fast. Too slow. "Good job, Lil," I tell her as she finishes another push.

Dr. Dhar says, "Last one."

Lily collapses back in exhaustion and stares up at me like *she just said that, didn't she?* Fear floods her eyes, and I kiss her head, and my lips brush her ear. "You're almost done, love. Everything's fine."

"Okay," she says in a shaky voice. Her hand tightens around mine. She closes her eyes to try to push again. She pants, out of breath, after that one.

The female doctor focuses on the monitors. "The baby's heart rate is a little low."

I turn back to Lily, and her eyes flutter like they're about to close. "Lil?" I cup her face; she's in a cold sweat. "Lily?"

The second nurse runs to the nearest machine, and she places an oxygen mask over Lily's nose and mouth.

I comb back her hair. "Hey, Lil, look at me, love." My eyes are on fire, and for a split second, the fear of losing her takes me for a ride. I can't . . .

It's a pain that tears right through me. It stretches. I swallow a rock. *Look at me. Please.* And as she takes a few deep breaths of oxygen, her eyes meet mine again, and she gives me a nod.

Okay.

"Lily, one last push," Dr. Dhar coaches. "I know you're tired, but we all want this baby out."

Lily looks like she's about to cry. I hover over her and tilt her chin so she meets my gaze again. "This is easier than every battle you've been through." I wipe the tears off her cheeks.

"One more time?" she asks like a question, even though she's trying to boost her spirits.

"Yeah, Lil. One more."

She inhales and shuts her eyes tight as she pushes. I clench my teeth, my jaw hurting the longer this goes on. *Please let this be it.*

And then, the next sound just floors me.

A cry.

Dr. Dhar has the baby in her hands.

I'm not the kind of guy anyone wants to see give life. Nasty, harsh, spiteful—a bastard. But I'm employing my brother's motto for this one: *I don't give a shit.*

I don't give a shit.

Maybe some people don't deserve second chances. But I'm worthy of this moment and this girl and this life I live and the one I created.

No one can tell me otherwise. Because the minute they place our baby on Lily's chest is the minute that I *feel* a piece of me that I'd been keeping submerged. She's already in tears, joy erupting through her features, and I feel all of it course inside me. I'd been unwilling to let myself experience this. I'd been filling the hollow places with pain, and I'm done.

I'm done with that torture.

One nurse dries the baby off and keeps a warm towel on him. The other removes Lily's oxygen mask. "Lo," she chokes into a laugh, her chin trembling as tears cascade. I realize my cheeks are wet.

I lean closer to her, feeling lighter than I ever have before.

He's tiny; his eyes are pinched like the light is too harsh for him. But he squirms a bit and lets out a couple high-pitched noises, not cries exactly. Just saying he's here.

After about fifteen minutes, the world feels calmer, people start slowing down. He's swaddled in a blanket and content. "Will you hold him?" Lily asks me like she's wondering if I won't.

I don't hesitate. I lift him gently in my arms. God, I can't get over how small he is.

"What do you think?" she asks.

I realize I haven't said a single word. And I break into a smile, my eyes glassy. "He looks powerful."

Even through her exhaustion, she beams like she's risen a million feet. "Like a superhero?"

I nod a couple times and brush my finger over his soft cheek. He responds with a mumble of acceptance. I never thought I could love someone the way that I love Lily, but my world has just expanded, plus one.

I whisper softly, "Definitely like a superhero."

Thirty-five

Lily Calloway

For the past week, we've been camping out in Maximoff's superhero-themed nursery on the long blue couch. I may be biased, but the city painted on the wall, the *X-Men* blanket, and Thor's hammer mobile beats Jane's pink princess room any day.

This afternoon, we've been watching FX's *X-Men* marathon on our bed with Maximoff between us, and he's been sleeping well past his usual nap time. "Is he alive?" I whisper to Lo. We both sort of hover over him, watching him sleep more than we've been watching the films.

Paranoid, yes. We've been reading too many pamphlets about sudden infant death syndrome, which can be caused by what feels like *anything*. The baby can't sleep on his tummy. He can't be wrapped too tightly in a blanket. One wrong move and *bam!* Baby down.

I have this dark, horrific image of waking up and finding Maximoff blue and . . . yeah.

I've already made Connor give me refresher tips for baby CPR.

"I'm sure he's alive, Lil," Lo whispers, but his brows knot with as much uncertainty as mine.

"How do we know he's breathing?" I ask.

Lo stays quiet for a moment, then he says, "Maybe one of us should poke him or something."

I nod wildly. "Good idea. You do it." Our baby barely stirs, so peaceful, and he rarely ever cries either. Jane has more fits than him . . . maybe that's why I'm more nervous about his quiet nature. I can't tell if it means something's wrong or if he's just a really good baby.

Lo leans closer on his side and taps Maximoff's little foot in his blue onesie, a lightning bolt on the chest. My heart stops beating for a couple of seconds and only starts again when he kicks his little legs. I exhale a breath of relief. He's alive. All is well.

And then he wails loudly.

Oh no. "He woke up." I cringe at his shrieks and sit up at the same time as Lo.

Lo gives me a look. "I thought that was the point." He scoops Maximoff in his arms and pats his bottom as he rocks him. Our son hushes in seconds, his slate-gray eyes closing in a sleep, his little lips parted as he breathes. Lo wags his brows at me. "He loves me."

I can't help but smile, and I kiss Lo quickly on the lips. I want to say: *you're easily lovable, Loren Hale*. But sadly, that's not true for most people he meets. I fell in love with Lo like a little girl opening her heart to magic. It always seemed surreal until the moment it became true.

Lo checks the clock on the end table. "We should probably feed him." He climbs off the bed and looks down at me. "*Lil*."

"What?" I try to restrain my smile, biting my gums. It doesn't work too well.

"You can't look at me like that every time I hold him. It's driving me insane, and I can't do anything about it for six weeks." He says I have this "adorable happy glow" that makes him want to straddle me. But I have no sexual urges for maybe the first time ever. I'm sore down below, and the thought of something hard sounds too painful to consider. And thankfully my hormones are even back in check.

I spring off the bed. "I can't help it. It's the most beautiful thing I've ever witnessed."

"Like Magneto saving mutantkind without destroying mankind, I know. You've told me."

I point a finger at him. "That is a damn good metaphor, and I came up with it all on my own."

Lo shields our baby's ears playfully. "No cursing, Lily Martha Calloway."

I crinkle my nose. "I don't like my full name."

"Don't worry," he says with that teasing look, "I'm going to make you a Hale soon."

I want to revel in that fact, but my smile fades. I've reminded him so many times that it's okay if it doesn't happen. He has a lot on his plate, and orchestrating a wedding is too much. I wouldn't want to cause him more stress. Plus, I fear our parents taking over and turning it into their day again. It's best to just set weddings aside. Contemplate it in five years' time when things settle and Maximoff is older.

Neither of us ever suggests eloping. The idea feels like another deceit or lie that we've concocted.

"It's going to happen," Lo says, his gaze slowly narrowing. He still rocks our son in his arms.

"I know, I know." I try to drop the subject. "What color eyes do you think he'll have?" The doctors said that a baby's eye color changes in their first year, so we're not one-hundred-percent sure on the hue.

While he answers, I lead Lo out the door, and I can feel his body tensing behind me. But he follows me into the hallway regardless.

"Your green ones," he says. I spin around and peek at our son.

His eyelids open as he stretches his arms, and he *giggles* when he stares at my eyebrows. Oh my God. He has the cutest dimpled cheeks and little nose. At six pounds, two ounces, he came out a bit small but heart-stoppingly adorable. It sounds cheesy, but it's my baby. I feel like the cheese-factor rises once you reproduce.

"You melt every time you see him," Lo tells me. "Here, so you can drool a little longer."

I gape as he hands Maximoff off to me. "That's so mean, Loren."

"I'm only stating the truth, Lily Martha."

I squint at him, hoping to penetrate him with my glare. Instead he laughs, his smile overtaking his face. I give up. "I think he'll have green eyes too," I relent.

Ryke has already professed that they'll probably be amber like Lo's. But that was before Maximoff was even born.

With the baby now in my care, we descend the staircase together. As soon as we breach the stainless-steel kitchen, I hear noises. I strain my ears.

It sounds like . . . muffled arguing. I can't be sure. Living with Ryke and Daisy, I've overheard their distant sex noises and sometimes they sound like full-on fighting. Bodies slamming against things. Stifled yells (of ecstasy). Things of that nature.

I whip my head around the barren kitchen, expecting to find a couple, maybe even humping on the counter. *Not* that I want to catch anyone in the act. Porn. It would be like real porn in my face.

Plus, I'm holding a baby. Someone I feel vitally protective over. Maximoff is allowed to watch porn *never.* Not even when he's a teenager. Or in college. Nope. No. No. I'm putting my foot down on that one.

The noises suddenly stop.

"Lo," I say as he scans the room, nothing but sparkly clean granite countertops, leather barstools, and dim lights. "I think we have ghosts in this house."

His brows shoot up. "Ghosts that fuck?"

I adjust my baby in a one-handed cradle and then punch Lo's arm. It's only fair. F-bombs have been banned in the presence of baby ears.

He rolls his eyes. Something knocks in the pantry, like a can clattering to the floor. I jump, thankfully clutching Maximoff tighter and *not* dropping him. *Dear God, don't let me drop my baby.* I cannot ever be that startled.

Lo stretches his arm out, keeping both me and our baby away from the pantry. "It's probably just mice."

My eyes grow big. "Large, mutant mice."

The pantry door slowly creaks open like something from a horror film. When I see a shirtless Ryke, my nerves plummet to nothingness.

"Or it's just my horny older brother," Lo says with a bitter smile.

"We weren't screwing," is the first thing Ryke says. His gym shorts are slightly askew, and he lifts them higher on his waist, his hair so disheveled that I can tell a girl ran her fingers through it. His lips are pink and raw like he's been in one serious make out session.

I break into a huge grin. This image does not turn me on in any way, shape, or form. I love my hormones again.

"I'm sorry," Lo says dryly as he goes to warm up formula. "Did we interrupt you?"

I strap Maximoff in his navy blue bouncer. I chose what I'm most comfortable with in terms of breastfeeding, listening to Rose's advice. It's my choice. And plus, it gives Lo the chance to feed and bond with his son too.

"No," Ryke growls back, his eyes focusing on me, dark and accusatory. Oh jeez. "Because *someone* made a pact about not having sex for *six fucking weeks*."

Lo looks too worn-out to even contemplate punching him. I am too. I'm beginning to wonder if everyone's a lost cause for cursing.

"Were you fighting?" I suddenly fear, worry popping in my head. I do *not* want to be the cause of a Raisy breakup. Nononono. Raisy until the end. The end being death.

"We weren't fighting." That comes from Daisy, who finally slips out of the pantry behind Ryke, her neck dotted red like he kissed her for a long, long time.

Even *that* thought doesn't make me aroused. Ha! Take that. I'm not sure who I'm "taking that" to, but in this moment, I feel invincible.

Daisy fixes the strap of her bra and hops on the barstool, swiveling around to face me in the middle of the kitchen. She wears a crooked, mischievous smile. So they *were* having sex?

"I'm officially confused," I announce.

"Nothing below her bra or her underwear, thank you for that," Ryke deadpans. No sex. Definitely no sex.

"It's not her fault, for the fifteenth time," Daisy says to him. "I want to do the pact, so stop nagging Lily."

"Yeah, stop nagging me," I add and *almost* stick out my tongue. I restrain myself. I'm a mom now. I have to show a level of maturity. I cross my ankles, my feet warm in dinosaur slippers. Those haven't lost their cool factor since I was seventeen.

Lo would agree.

"Let me fucking complain in peace," Ryke growls, running a hand through his tousled hair.

Lo sits on the floor beside the bouncer, bottle in hand as he feeds Maximoff.

Daisy gives Ryke a roguish smile, something Lo can't see on the ground in between the counters. "You know, you can still masturbate." I'm slightly terrified at the idea that "masturbate" may be my son's first word.

"Yeah, Ryke," Lo eggs on. "You can still jerk one out like the rest of us." Obviously, Lo doesn't share the same concern. Maybe it's because I'm a sex addict. Right? *Right?*

I let it go with a breath. I'm surprised Lo is fueling this conversation at all. A year ago he would have gagged at the mention of Daisy talking about sex or his brother or any combination of the two. How things change.

Ryke nears us and leans on the bar counter beside Daisy. "Not if she cracks first."

That's a dirty game. So he was trying to kiss on my little sister and make her beg for sex. It's low. Also devious. Definitely a solid plan in my book—The Lily Calloway Sexy Times Book that is. It's only in my head, but it's very resourceful.

Daisy tries hard not to smile. "I don't come easily." Ooh, that was super dirty too.

"Calloway, you've only ever come with *me*. I think I know how to get you off."

"By chocolate cupcakes," she says with a lopsided grin. Is that a sexual innuendo?

"Sure, sweetheart. Chocolate fucking cupcakes and a nine-inch—"

I plug my ears with my fingers. I did not hear his size! Food. He was still talking about food. I only drop my hands when his lips stop moving.

"You two are so adorable," Lo says dryly. "Please return to the pantry."

Ryke shoots Lo his middle finger, and I'm close enough to punch him in the arm. He doesn't even sway from the force.

"What was that for?" he complains. "I didn't even say the f-word."

"You did it with your finger," I refute, pointing accusingly at his chest. *Everyone* saw it, not just me. "You can't teach my week-old son that."

"He can't even learn the ABCs yet, Lily. He doesn't know what this means." He goes and makes the rude gestures with *both* of his hands now. He's a horrible influence.

"You just want to be the cool uncle, admit it," I combat.

"You're just scared that Moffy is going to like me more than Connor, admit *that*."

I cross my arms over my chest. "Will not." Though I can't deny that he's given Maximoff a cool nickname, one that I wish I'd thought of first.

"Uh-oh." Daisy goes rigid, her phone in her hand. She slowly hops off the barstool and sidles next to her boyfriend. Instead of showing me the screen first, she flashes it to him.

He takes the cell from her, and I watch his jaw harden to stone.

Thirty-six

Lily Calloway

W hat is it?" My heart palpitates. Bad news? The media? It can't be a three-way rumor involving Ryke. I had a paternity test a week ago, per our publicist's advice after lots of pushing. And the results were already announced: Loren Hale is Maximoff's father.

Ryke glances hesitantly at his brother before he says, "*Celebrity Crush* posted a photo of Daisy and me leaving the grocery store."

My shoulders slacken. *It's not about me.* A very selfish thought, I realize. "That's good, right?" The more they're shown together, in public, means that people will accept them as a real couple.

Lo rises with Maximoff in his arms. We have this chart for feedings and diaper changes. All very organized. All very Rose Calloway-esque. She helped me chart out daily activities and how much the babies should be drinking. Basically, leveling out all my anxiety into a list. Now I kind of understand her obsession with them. It was like therapy. List-therapy. It's a thing.

"What's wrong with the photo?" Lo asks skeptically.

Daisy shifts on her feet and tugs at the hem of her white tee. "We . . . you know how you guys put us in charge of shopping for the house this week?"

This isn't about me . . . is it?

"Spit it out," Lo snaps. Maximoff detaches from his bottle and begins to wail. Lo's body tightens even more. "I'm sorry, little guy." He bounces him a bit, and then he quiets, returning to his bottle.

"Here." Ryke holds the cell phone up to Lo. I crane over his shoulder to read it. The headline: *Ryke Meadows and Daisy Calloway shopping for baby Cobalt and baby Hale!* There's an additional zoomed image of the grocery cart, some of the labels visible in the white plastic bags. Diapers. Cereal. Lightning Bolt!. And baby formula.

I don't understand. It's not that bad.

I skim down and read the article by Wendy Collins.

Inside sources close to the Calloway family tell us that not one but both *Calloway sisters went for the formula option to feed their babies. The sources say, "Lily and Rose would rather have assistants and their grandmother look after their babies. They don't want the responsibility. It's a big reason why they chose formula. Rose and Lily aren't prepared for motherhood, and they know it."*

I stop reading there. None of us even have nannies. It's too hard to trust someone with something so precious when we've been burned before. We all thought it was safer to raise our children without them.

"That's complete trash," Lo declares. "Who's this so-called *inside source* anyway? Samantha Calloway?"

Daisy and I exchange a look, trying to gauge whether our mom could even do that. No . . . my mom isn't that self-serving. "What would she get out of it?" Daisy asks.

"Right here . . ." Lo points at the phone. "*Especially from the grandmother.* Who do you think that is? Connor's mom is dead. And my mom is five hundred miles away, not caring about *me* or *any* of this shit." His harsh tone is like acid, scorching my ears.

It's been so long since he's even mentioned his mom. Years, probably. Emily Moore might as well be a figment, a ghost. I haven't even met her, but when I do think about her, my stomach starts to roil. It's not a pleasant feeling, and I imagine, for Lo, the sensations are a million times more harrowing.

But maybe he's buried it so deep down that he doesn't feel anything anymore. Shut it out and said goodbye. I know when he met her, he closed the door on that part of his life for good.

"If we know anything," Ryke says, handing Daisy back her cell, "it's that Connor probably has a million fucking lawyers on this. They basically called his wife a bad mom."

"Yeah, but they always call *me* a bad mom," I say. "So the one time they blatantly call Rose a bad mom, everyone is going to throw a tantrum?" My heart sinks.

Ryke extends his arms. "I didn't say it was right. I'm just saying prepare yourself for that double-edged sword, Calloway. It fucking hurts." He rocks back like someone is going to punch his arm, but I don't care about swear words anymore. It seems unimportant.

I appreciate Ryke's warning, I do. It's nice being back to these conversations without feeling weird around him, but it's days like these where I wish none of us were in the spotlight at all. It's where I wonder how life will be like for Maximoff, famous since birth.

We all lived our adolescence out of the public eye. They're going to be raised right in it.

Thirty-seven

Lily Calloway

Rose's version of camping is unlike anything I have ever known. She hired a person to put up a fancy tent in the backyard with a fuzzy rug laid out over the grass, complete with plush pillows and a small table for sliders and macaroni and cheese—takeout from a five-star restaurant. Lamps are staked in the ground, and Rose has sprayed something that might be magical. Not one mosquito or bug has ventured into our territory.

It's the perfect setting for our girls' campout, and I already love it. Being pampered in the outdoors is much better than swatting flies. However, Ryke called it "fake camping" and "over the top" but he shut up when he saw Daisy's face. She smiled like Rose re-created a scene out of *Hook* for her.

Good thing too, since this is all for Daisy tonight.

She wants to try and sleep away from Ryke, battle her insomnia out here with us. I'm only two weeks post-pregnancy, so I try to take it easy and lounge on the soft pillows. Rose and I have our baby monitors by our side, and all the guys are indoors with Jane and Moffy. I can go one night without hovering.

I think.

I situate my flower crown with a row of purple lilies. I feel like a fairy princess. The crowns were Daisy's contributions to the girls' night. I realize that I only brought myself. Which is not really a contribution at all, but oh well.

I wash a bite of mac and cheese down with Fizz Life. "So you're not going to do anything?" I ask Rose, trying to ingest this bit of information. I'm still stuck on the fact that she has surrendered to the journalists over the baby formula comments.

I should be grateful that there's no double-edged sword like Ryke mentioned, but I just don't understand. My sister usually goes on the offensive.

"What am I supposed to do?" Rose asks me. Her blood-red flower crown filled with roses makes her look even fiercer. "Kick and scream and cry?" She rolls her eyes. "I have to choose my battles, and honestly, this is a trivial one. If they want to believe that I have a flock of assistants raising my child, then so be it."

My brows furrow. "Is this like the sex tapes then?" I know she chose to let the lawsuit go to use the publicity to their advantage, but with more and more tapes being revealed, it doesn't ever seem worth it.

She shoots me a withering glare, and I shrink back. Whoa. I feel the icy burn, and it's not so pleasant.

"I don't want to talk about the sex tapes," she says, a hint of pain behind her words.

Oh. I didn't realize how much they'd been affecting her. She puts on a good front.

"Let's talk about something else then," Daisy suggests, crossing her legs. She braids a fringe pillow, her bowl of mac and cheese already empty. "I read a tabloid yesterday that said you looked thin."

"That's the magic of black peplum dresses," Rose says in a wistful voice. "I still need to lose about fifteen pounds before I go back to my original size, but I'm sure my love handles are here to stay." She glares at the house behind Daisy. "Connor is obsessed with them."

I instantly smile. It ticks Rose off that Connor adores her curvy hips and butt. But secretly she loves him for it. Yep. After years, I'm beginning to understand these flirty fights a bit better.

I tug at my red Marvel onesie that's snug around my abdomen. I'm only twenty pounds heavier right now, if that. And my belly is still pooched, but I figure once I have sex again, I'll burn some calories. "Are you working out?" I ask Rose. My eyes widen at the idea of Rose running miles down the street.

"Just from videos in the *privacy* of my bedroom." Meaning she does not allow anyone to watch her. Message received. "And I'm doing this for me, not for Connor." She eats some popcorn from a bowl between us. "How much have you gained?" Her question is directed to Daisy.

"Since when?" she asks.

"Since your lowest weight," Rose asks, curiosity in her eyes. Ever since Daisy quit modeling, she hasn't been as hesitant to eat the foods she likes.

"Fifteen pounds," Daisy says, tucking her platinum blonde hair behind her ear.

"You look beautiful," Rose tells her in the nicest voice she has.

I nod in agreement. She's healthier than I've seen her in a long time.

"Thanks." Daisy smiles. "I definitely don't feel as bony. Ryke says that I have more muscle in my legs again."

Ryke is a good one. In a lot of ways, he brought Daisy back from a really dark place. I wish that we could've been there for her, but Rose and I were dealing with our pregnancies. And my addiction. I had no idea . . .

"Don't cry," Daisy says sweetly, scooching closer and wrapping her arm around my shoulder.

"I'm just happy," I whisper to her, rubbing my eyes with the back of my hand.

Rose's phone suddenly glows bright blue and dings, not a texting sound.

"What's that?" I ask.

"I have alerts for whenever there's an article about Jane."

I gape. This changes *everything*. "I cannot be faulted for checking the media now." If Rose is doing it, it has to be sane. Lo may disagree with that logic, but it seems sound to me.

Rose ignores my statement, her eyes skimming the article, and I watch them slowly narrow.

Oh no. "What?" I ask, fear invading my voice.

"Those little shits posted the photos." She shakes her head in disbelief and passes Daisy her cell phone. I think I already know where this is going.

Yesterday, Rose and I brought our babies on a walk down the neighborhood street. Since it's gated, we thought it was safe to use strollers without any blankets covering the top. About five minutes in, the prankster teenagers sprung out of their passing Range Rover, snapping photos of Jane and Maximoff.

A part of me thought *maybe* they were just joking and wouldn't sell them to the press. Not so. I peek over Daisy's shoulder. I am staring right at a picture of both Jane and Moffy in their strollers, small, tiny babies who were wide-awake and began wailing after the sudden commotion.

Sure, the pics are a little blurry, but that obviously doesn't matter to the media.

The caption: *First baby photos of Jane Cobalt and Maximoff Hale! So adorable!*

I smile. "Look, they called them adorable."

Rose glowers at me again. Zero for two today. "They're babies. No one will call a baby an ugly gremlin."

"You will," I refute. Then I pause. "Wait . . . are you calling our babies ugly gremlins?"

"Of course not," she says quickly, her cheeks flushing. "They're adorable gremlins." She's hurting my head. "My point is . . ." Thank you, I need the point. "That these assholes are profiting off of our children. It's wrong."

Daisy theatrically hops to her feet and raises her fist in the air. "So let's retaliate." The soft yellow daisies on her flower crown match the glow of the crescent moon.

Rose and I stare up at her. "What?" we say together. I whip my head back to my older sister, surprised she sided with me.

I ask Rose, "You weren't about to end your speech with retaliation?"

"No, I was going to suggest cursing them out for the next hour and burning the articles." Of course there is fire involved. She turns her attention to Daisy. "What were you saying?"

Daisy is the Peter Pan of our group, I realize. She has her hands planted on her hips like she is a clever, youthful creature, up to no good. "You remember back when they shot paintballs at the house?"

That feels like forever ago, but also just like yesterday. They terrified Daisy, an innocent bystander with PTSD, insomnia, and a boatload of other issues. Being here in this house, all together, has unified us and hopefully helped her some.

"You all said that I could choose whether to do nothing or to retaliate," she reminds us. I thought she was afraid of speaking up, so she just let it go. "Well, I'm making my choice now."

Rose is full-blown smiling.

I am too.

"I choose to do something. Let's get those fuckers back." She wears a shrewd grin. "And I have the perfect thing in mind."

The darkness is our friend.

I repeat the mantra over and over as we tiptoe through the manicured yard. Rose and I saw the teenagers sprint into this stone mansion after they snapped the baby pics. So we can at least inflict damage to one of them.

"Here," Daisy whispers, handing me a roll of toilet paper. Sneaking into the house to raid our pantry for extra rolls was easy. All the guys were down in the basement, so our covert mission is already going as planned. We even waited until midnight, hoping everyone in the house would be in bed.

I gingerly accept the toilet paper while we crouch behind a bush. We're all in our pajamas: Daisy in green knit shorts and a gray crop top, Rose in a black satin pajama set. Me in my onesie (hood on my head for extra stealth). And we crouch behind a prickly bush.

"The lights are off inside and out," I whisper. Perfect. I've toilet papered plenty of houses with Lo. On boring nights, we used to grab a few rolls and drive to some jock's home. It was harmless fun.

"Mission a go," Daisy says with an *okay* sign.

I'm about to race out from behind the bush, but I remember that I gave birth two weeks ago, and I can't move that quickly. Walking here, I was a tortoise, step-by-step slow.

Daisy darts off to the largest oak tree, a wild grin on her face. I carefully scurry toward a half-grown magnolia tree with Rose. Like riding a bike, I position the paper the correct way before throwing it up and over a limb. A giddy, rebellious energy bursts in my belly. Just like old times. Except now my comrades are my sisters. One of whom is trying and failing at tossing the roll onto a tree limb.

Rose gives me a glare when she catches me staring. Her eyes flit between the dark windows of the house and my perfectly arched stream of toilet paper. I've already covered the left side by the time she huffs in defeat.

"How'd you do that?" she finally asks.

"Watch the pro," I reply, gathering my paper and completing the same arch.

I expect Rose to fumble again, but she performs the angle perfectly. My teaching skills are on point. When I turn back at Daisy, she's already finished the oak tree and runs with the toilet paper, covering all of the front bushes like she's decorating them with streamers.

I now know which sister has done this before. Though it's no surprise we're taking Rose's TP-ing virginity. Acts of juvenile rebellion and Rose Calloway don't mix often.

Rose splits from me, now adept enough to take a new section of the yard. Within a few minutes, we've successfully covered the trees and bushes in toilet paper. We still have about three rolls left, and Rose is working on the front porch railings, muttering curse words under her breath.

Then a bedroom light flickers on. Oh shit. I walk hurriedly to Daisy, who scatters toilet paper on the grass. "Daisy," I whisper-hiss.

She must hear the panic in my voice because she looks straight up at the house instead of at me. "Uh-oh," she says, dropping her roll immediately. She runs to my side and a second hall light flicks on. Shit. Shit. Shit. "To the bush, to the bush." In another life, my little sister would make a great criminal.

I point at our lingering, oblivious sister, who is in a pissed-off rant, taking her anger out on the front porch steps. "Rose—"

"I'll get her," Daisy whispers. "Go, go, go."

With this encouragement, I power walk to the prickly bush near the magnolia tree. Rose is still blinded by fury, not even noticing the lights.

Daisy clasps Rose's arm. "Let's go."

"One more," Rose insists. "I need this."

Daisy turns to me and mouths, *Go!*

I realize I've frozen in the middle of the lawn. I defrost at the same time the floodlights illuminate the front yard. Oh shit.

This shakes Rose out of her trance, and she finally unglues

from the porch, skipping steps to head down to the grass. I walk faster to the bush, adrenaline keeping all the aches and pains to a dull roar.

By the time I crouch and hide, Rose and Daisy are squished beside me. We all go completely silent, the only noise comes from my heavy breathing. Rose shoots me a look to *shut up*. I can't stop breathing! What does she want from me? I'm already in an uncomfortable position, unwilling to shift and lessen the strain on my quads.

The front door swings open. "I know you're out there!" a woman yells. "If you don't show yourselves, I'm going to call the cops to come chase you." That doesn't sound fun.

Daisy is trying hard not to laugh. Of course she'd like the idea of that scenario. She can sprint and flee and climb trees.

I can waddle. I'm as fast as a penguin. It's the sad, sad truth.

"Where are you hiding?! Behind the bush? Come out right now!"

No. She has to be bluffing. Right?

The three of us share a look, undecided on our next route of action. If we reveal ourselves, she could call the cops anyway. Once she learns the famous heiresses from that trashy reality show toilet papered her yard, she'll take revenge. They all do.

There's only one solution.

I pull out my cell.

Thirty-eight

Loren Hale

In the basement gym, I sit on the edge of the weight bench, not even going for another rep. I steal a glance at the baby monitor, paranoid that my son needs me and I'm two floors below.

"He's fine," Connor says, taking off his gloves.

"Did you develop magical powers in the last five minutes, love?" I ask, knowing it will irritate him.

He doesn't even blink. "Process of deduction," he tells me. "If you can't hear him crying, it means he's still sleeping. There's no magic involved in that."

Ryke drops down from the pull-up bar and picks up his water bottle. "Move," he tells me. "I need the bench."

I check my watch. "Aren't you going a little hard there, bro? It's past midnight." He's already lifted thirty minutes ago, and he usually prefers a core workout in the gym since his arms are pushed to the max when climbing.

"Just move." His jaw muscles tick.

And then it clicks, and I break out into a grin. "Is this you working off your sexual frustration?"

He runs a hand through his damp hair. "I don't know why you're fucking smiling at me. You aren't getting laid for four more weeks either."

"What can I say, I like when people share in my misery."

He throws his dirty towel at my face. I catch it in the air just as Connor switches the television channel.

"What about you?" I ask Connor. "You angry Rose is doing this pact?"

"Angry, no," Connor tells me. "She says it's her way of being supportive of Lily, but she's doing it to one-up me." He combs his fingers through his hair, fixing the wavy strands. "She forgets that I can wait without a problem, even if I don't enjoy it. If this win makes her feel better, then I'll give it to her."

He's lucky Rose isn't here. She'd kill him for that last line. I don't think she likes being handed a "win." I shake my head at him as I switch the weight bench with Ryke. "Rose would gouge out your eyeballs for that."

He grins. "I know." He sets his gloves aside. "I'm going to make up for the lost time in one night. She's not going to like me by the end of it."

Ryke mutters, "I don't even want to know what that fucking means."

I point at Connor. "Kinky. Hardcore."

Connor leans against the treadmill with a larger grin. "You forgot infallible genius."

I open my mouth to play into his arrogance like I usually do, but my cell rings on the floor. I quickly pick it up, already seeing the caller ID: LILY.

Ryke shoots to his feet, and Connor is by my side in seconds. My brother won't admit it aloud, but half the reason he's working out until exhaustion is because Daisy's sleeping outside. Without him. The first time in a while. He's worried about her.

I put the phone to my ear.

"Lo," Lily whispers, so softly that I can barely hear. "Lo, are you there?" Her voice edges on alarm.

My muscles constrict. "Why are you whispering?" Maybe

there's a bobcat outside or some kind of animal. I scratch the back of my neck and take a deep breath, forcing myself not to jump to conclusions.

"We're on a mission . . ." She trails off. "We need backup. STAT. Over and out."

What. The. Fuck.

I hear Rose's voice. "Not *out*," she hisses. "You didn't even give him our location."

"Lo, you still there?"

"Yeah—"

Ryke tries to grab the phone, to put it on speaker. I shove him back and press the button, just in time for Lily's reply.

"We need a getaway ride. We're at the neighbor's house. The big stone one. You can't miss it. There's . . . um . . ."

"Toilet paper," Daisy finishes in a whisper.

"Okay. Bye," Lily says and hangs up.

Ryke sets his hands on his head. "You've got to be fucking kidding me. All of them?"

I walk past my brother to grab the baby monitor. "She was whispering. They must be hiding behind a tree or a bush." I hand the monitor to Ryke. "You stay here."

"No *fucking* way," he curses, his muscles just as tight as mine. "If they get caught—"

"They're not getting caught," Connor says calmly, trying to ease the tension in the room. But if these people press charges, the girls could be booked for vandalism.

"*You* fucking stay here then," Ryke retorts.

"I'm not staying back," Connor says firmly. "Rose will be the first one arrested—"

"You *just* fucking said they weren't going to get caught."

Yeah, Connor was trying to convince Ryke to stay behind with our kids. None of us wants to wait here.

"We'll bring the babies," I say.

Ryke's face darkens. "No, I'll fucking meet you two—"

"Hey!" I shout at him. He is *pacing*. "She's fine. It's not Paris."

Ryke is physically shaking.

"It's *not* Paris," I repeat, my eyes burning. I taste that night. The screaming. The paranoia. The uncertainty. The riot flares up in my mind. We just have to forget about it. Not imagine anything like it happening again. I place my hand on his shoulder. "Come help me get Maximoff into the car seat."

Stiffly, he nods, his nose flaring as he tries to expel his emotions

Connor is already headed upstairs. It takes us five minutes to situate Jane and Moffy into Rose's Escalade, and that's at our quickest pace. The babies only stir when we buckle them in, falling back asleep when Connor pulls out of the driveway.

"By the time we fucking get there, they'll either be caught or on their way home," Ryke complains from the passenger side.

"Can you shut up?" I snap. "You're going to wake the babies." I sit beside Moffy's car seat.

Ryke pinches his eyes. I get it. The last time Daisy came into contact with these guys, they scared her pretty badly.

Lily can't even run. She just had our kid, so I'm worried she's in pain or really anxious.

I don't even blame them for hitting up the house tonight. I've had to convince myself more than once not to do anything in retribution. I'm honestly just surprised they snapped before Ryke, Connor, or me.

It takes one minute before we spot the house. Toilet paper drapes from nearly every tree limb, even the mailbox and bushes, hidden beneath layers. If I wasn't worried, I think I might be proud.

"Fucking A." Ryke's voice freezes me over. I have to strain my neck to see past his headrest. The girls aren't hiding anymore.

In the center lawn, illuminated by floodlights, stand Rose, Daisy, and Lily in their pajamas, each holding their flower crowns like they're ski masks or something. A middle-aged woman in a white bathrobe jabs her finger in Rose's volatile face, a volcano about to erupt.

I just hope they haven't called the cops yet.

Connor parks the car, and he jumps out quickly with Ryke. I open my door, shoving it wide so I can have a clear view and hear the fight. But I hang back with the babies.

"You're a grown *adult*," the mother says coldly. "Act like it."

"It's toilet paper. We didn't set your lawn on fire," Rose combats. "And you're so lucky I didn't. I was *this* close." She pinches her fingers together.

"Are you making a threat against me?" the mother sneers. Her husband walks down the porch steps with his cell phone to his ear. Jesus Christ.

"I used the past tense," Rose snaps. "So *no*, I wasn't threatening you."

"We're really sorry," Daisy pipes in.

"No, we aren't," Rose retorts. "Do you even know what your child has been doing to us?"

The mother looks disinterested in that story. It pisses me off, and I realize my hands are vibrating. *Goddammit.* I don't want to drink. Even if somewhere deep, I do.

Ryke and Connor make the short trek up the lawn. I'd join, but the babies—and Lily looks fine. She wavers beside her sisters with beady eyes like a deer caught in headlights. I can tell she'd like to run away from this argument.

I shake my hands out and cup them to my mouth. "Lily!" I try to shout in a whisper.

She whips around and relaxes at the sight of me.

"You *both* just had babies," the mother suddenly snarls. *No.* Lily freezes cold, and Rose's eyes flash murderously. Of course these people know about our kids. It's everywhere.

"Don't you dare," Rose starts.

"You shouldn't be here, vandalizing our property," the woman continues. "It's irresponsible. If you cared at all about your newborns, you'd be at home with them."

Rose steps forward, fire in her gaze. "Who are you to say that to us—"

Connor wraps his arms around Rose's waist, pulling her a safe distance away from the woman.

"Richard!" Rose screams, tears pricking her eyes.

"It's okay, Rose," Connor says in a soothing voice.

I shake out my hand for the second time and lick my lips. "Lily Calloway!" I call.

She spins around again like I startled her. This time she slowly retreats from the fight, aiming for me.

"It's not okay," Rose snaps. "Her son has been harassing us, but she wants to file a report about toilet paper." She sets her glassy, heated gaze on the woman. "*Toilet. Paper.*"

The husband interjects, "If that's what you want to tell the police . . ." He still has the phone to his ear, avoiding Connor, who stands a good five or six inches taller than him.

I want to yell something. My throat aches to intervene—but from past experience, I know I'd just make the whole thing worse. I stay glued to the curb. I recognize what keeps me here more than anything. My eyes flicker into the dark backseat, where Maximoff sleeps, his lips parted as he breathes.

I whisper, "Thanks, little guy." *You're saving me from myself tonight.*

"It won't happen again," Connor says, using his fake damage-control voice. "We're sorry for waking you. If you could not press charges, we'd be extremely grateful."

Rose is fuming. But this is what has to happen. They're *not* going to jail over this. It's dumb. Ryke is whispering to Daisy a few feet away from the woman. And Daisy suddenly spins out of his arms and says to them, "I'll clean it up tomorrow. Just let my sisters off the hook for this."

"That's ridiculous," Rose tells Daisy. "They should clean it up for be—"

Connor covers Rose's mouth with his hand and whispers in her ear.

"Are they here? Are they okay? Lo . . ." Lily practically catapults over me to peer inside the car. I grab her tightly by the hips.

"They're fine, Lil." I hold her face between my two hands. And her big, round green eyes meet mine.

Fear spikes her voice. "I worried about him this whole time. I didn't forget—"

"You don't have to convince me, love," I breathe. "You're a good mom." She's not fucking negligent. "That woman can go to hell. She doesn't know you or me or your sisters."

Lily lets out a deep breath.

"Okay?" I ask her.

She nods and peeks past my bicep. After a short moment, she says, "He's so cute."

I roll my eyes, but my shoulders drop. Glad she's not scratching her arms, biting her nails, or crossing her ankles. I'd like a drink though.

Great.

"What's that?" Lily breathes.

I follow her gaze to a second floor lit window. Two teenagers are peeking out of the blinds. They must see us because one drops his pants and sticks his bare ass against the glass.

I grit my teeth. Classic.

"Do you remember when you peed on the side of Todd Border's house?" Lily says with the tilt of her head in remembrance. Her words strangely ease the tension in my muscles.

I wrap my arm around her. "He was a dick," I say. "And I

drank way too much rum that night. I had to piss somewhere." We were fifteen.

It's weird. Revisiting bad memories doesn't have the same impact on me that it did a year ago. I can touch them without splintering.

As I gauge Lily's mental state, I realize the same can be said for her. While Connor tries to calm down the parents, I pull Lily even closer to me. She rests her cheek on my chest. "Hey, little criminal," I murmur.

"So much for my getaway car, huh?"

"Sorry about that." I tug at the red sleeve of her Marvel PJs. "You should've worn black, you know."

She smiles. "All my favorite superheroes were supposed to protect me tonight, but I suppose I forgot the best one."

"If you say a DC character like Green Lantern, we're no longer boyfriend-girlfriend," I tease.

She lifts her chin up at me. "I forgot *you*."

I try hard not to laugh. "That . . . is the most rom-com thing you've ever fucking said to me. Take it back."

She gapes. "I will not." She hugs me tighter. I love being this close to her.

I kiss her temple, and that's about when the man's voice escalates. "Fine, fine. If someone cleans this up, then we won't press charges." He begins to head back into the house, but his wife lingers.

"You're all exactly what they say." She motions to Ryke and Daisy. "The jackass and the daredevil." She points an accusatory finger at Lily and me. "The alcoholic and the sex addict." Lily stiffens against my body. And the woman just keeps going, facing Connor. "The smartass." When she turns to Rose, I think she won't say anything. She's using the labels from *Princesses of Philly*, and the producers called Rose a *virgin*. It doesn't apply anymore.

The whole world knows it doesn't.

"And you," the woman briefly pauses, "the porn star."

Lily's jaw unhinges and mine tightens. That's something *I* wouldn't even say to Rose, under any circumstance.

Rose has enough. She lunges this time, and Connor lifts her up in his arms, restraining her easily. "We're leaving," he says loudly, shutting down the fight before it reignites.

"Fuck you," Rose adds, practically spitting at her. Connor tries hard not to smile while he gives Rose a commanding look.

Daisy starts marching toward the woman.

"Now's not the fucking time to be a hero, Calloway," Ryke says, grabbing Daisy around the waist.

I stare down at Lily. "You're not moving out of my arms, Lil."

"See, I told you you're better than Wolverine and Spider-Man and"—she scrutinizes all the characters on her PJs—"Captain America."

I shake my head at her, but the corners of my lips have already curved upward.

Ryke lifts Daisy *on* his shoulders, like she weighs nothing. His upper-body strength is insane. Her legs dangle against his chest, and she stops fighting with him. In fact she inhales like she can breathe better up high. It's times like this where I see how well my brother knows Daisy.

He looks over at me, and he scans my body, as though assessing how I'm doing.

I'm not shaking anymore. Thanks to Lily.

He motions with his head down the street. And I know he's going to return to the house with Daisy on his shoulders, just like that.

I nod to him, and he heads toward our house.

"Walk, darling," Connor says to Rose, rotating her so she's in line with the car and not the stone mansion.

From the "safety" of her lawn, the woman keeps antagonizing Rose, "I'm sure she'd prefer you to *force* her to the car." Her husband is calling her to come inside.

Connor speaks fast in French, and he ends up carrying Rose in his arms.

"Put me down, Richard," she snaps.

"I'll put you down if you can tell me the first twenty digits of pi," he says casually, only about ten feet from the Escalade.

"Three-point-one-four-I-fucking-hate-you," she practically screams. I'm surprised she hasn't bitten him yet.

"Incorrect."

Rose huffs, "Why can't you be angry? They called me a—"

"I'm *livid*," he says, letting some of his emotion deepen that word. "You just can't see it, and I'm not showing it in front of these people so you can go to jail."

I speak up. "Sounds smart to me."

Rose lets out a growl. "Don't compliment him."

"Well, I'm definitely not going to compliment you," I retort. Connor sets Rose on her feet beside the passenger door.

When Rose notices the babies in the car, she swats Connor's arm. "You *woke* up our daughter? Are you insane?"

"I assure you, my sanity is more intact than yours tonight." Then they both start talking in French again, shutting us out of their conversation. Whatever. I'm used to it.

The front door to the house slams closed, cementing the fact that the girls got off the hook tonight. But Lily and I stare up at that damn window again, and the two teenagers are still there, snickering.

I flip them off.

Lily notices it and copies the gesture. With both hands. From Lil, in a Marvel onesie with a flower crown hooked around her wrist, it's hardly threatening. But it's goddamn adorable.

I feel like we're seventeen again.

The best seventeen. When every time I stared at Lily Calloway, I wanted to drop to my knees.

But I can't ignore the chill in the air. The eerie presence of what may come after tonight. Whatever it is—I just hope we all can handle it.

Thirty-nine

Loren Hale

Almost three weeks into Lily's celibacy period, I'm feeling the effects. I step into the shower, expecting to do nothing else but wash. Then subconsciously, I mentally file through an image of Lily last night. She grinded against me, digging her pelvis into mine on impulse, but she rolled over and controlled her urges on her own.

Still, I remember how she scooted her ass into my cock. And I just wanted to slip right inside her.

Christ. Standing naked underneath the shower water, my dick throbs, screaming to be rubbed out. I haven't masturbated yet. I thought it was only fair since Lil's not allowed (ever). I didn't realize it would be this difficult. Going from fucking multiple times a day to nothing at all.

I feel like I'm walking a mile in Lily's shoes.

I lean my shoulder blades against the tiled shower wall and shut my eyes. My brain has warred against me. All I see is Lily lying naked, with her legs spread open, begging for me, clutching the sheets like she may touch herself if I don't hurry.

And when she stares at my hard cock, her pussy starts to soak. She cries and pleads.

I rest my head back, my hair wet. The longer strands stick to my forehead.

I'm torturing myself. She'd want me to jerk off. She'd feel guilty otherwise, but I'm going to feel like an ass if I do it. I just hate that she can't touch herself, but I can. Beads of water drip off my eyelashes as I think.

Screw this. She's in the nursery right now. She won't even know.

I grip my shaft, and the touch instantly pulls me out of my confliction. My lips part, and I stare up at the ceiling. I stroke my length, every nerve amplifying the sensations. I continue the movement, harder and determined.

I imagine Lily.

She has the "I have to come right now" expression, an urgency that always makes me push deeper. I ram between her legs, and her fingers dig into my back like she might fall.

"Lo!" she cries.

What gets me off most are her reactions, not our positions. She writhes beneath me, delicate and ravenous. She wants to be filled so deep that she can't see straight, and it's written all over her face.

In the shower, my strokes quicken, and I let out a gruff noise. God I want to fuck her. I want to feel how wet she becomes just by looking at me. To thrust until she clenches around me. It drives me over.

"Christ," I groan. Here in the now, I release so rapidly that I let out a staggered breath. My hand keeps moving, milking the orgasm for all its worth. I lean my head back against the wall again, taking a moment to come down.

After I clean myself and shut the water off, I turn for my towel that hangs on the glass. I freeze, noticing a shadow by the crack of the bathroom door.

I had closed that door . . .

Lily.

Please, no.

The bottom of my stomach falls.

The worst thing that could happen: turning on Lily Calloway while she's supposed to be celibate.

Forty

Lily Calloway

He didn't see me. He didn't see me.

I'm a Peeping Tom. A loser who spied on her boyfriend jerking one off in the shower. A red-like rash has spread from my forehead to my toes, and I scamper into our bedroom, away from the shower, the bathroom, him . . .

The spot between my legs keeps clenching for his hardness.

That hardness that I just saw. I want it. In me. Now.

I didn't even mean to look. After I put Maximoff in his crib for a nap, I had a funny thought about panda bears or maybe superpowers. I can't even remember what it was, but I planned to share it with Lo. And as I cracked the bathroom door, I witnessed something very hot. Maybe too hot. My body is overheating in a bunch of bad-good ways.

I could have stopped looking after the first minute but . . .

It's just been so long since I've seen Lo masturbate. Hell, it's been so long since I've seen *anything* remotely that sexual.

OhmyGod. Was that porn? Did I just watch a Loren Hale live porno?

Oh no.

"Lily," Lo calls, and I take the opportunity to dart into our closet. It's not as big as the master, but it's a walk-in. I act like I'm searching for something important. Anyway, I really do need to. Rose said she didn't believe that Lo and I used handcuffs, and I told her that I'd find them for proof. We also wanted to compare which guy buys the better ones. I think it's Lo. She thinks it's Connor.

It's yet to be proven.

"Lily?" Lo opens the closet.

"Huh?" My heart is exploding out of my chest. *I can't look at you.* I focus on the long rows of black, red, and gray graphic tees that he wears. He's concerned about me. My coping mechanisms have always been sex. And babies are stressful. Even if Moffy is a good baby—it can be a lot. The lack of sleep mixed with the temptations at night, especially as the soreness wears off.

Without sex, I turn into a paranoid person who browses the internet for trashy gossip sites and craves touch like an itch I can't quite scratch. It's all a mess.

I'm a mess.

But I've been doing my best. No sex. No penetration. No self-love.

It's the longest I've been abstinent in years.

The moisture on my panties is not helping things. But I won't take back what I saw . . . unless it really is porn. Then I kinda feel guilty. My elbows are burning.

"Please don't play dumb with me," Lo says. "Lily." He grabs my arm and twists me around. His amber eyes rush over mine, reading where my head is at.

He has a towel wrapped low around his waist, and my eyes travel along his wet, glistening chest. The ridges in his abs, the cut of his biceps. I am picturing a fully naked body. His hand on his erection, rubbing and stroking and pleasing himself. It's so hot that I think my brain will fry.

"*Lil,*" he says sternly, pinching my chin and lifting my gaze back to his eyes.

"*Lo*," I reply in the same voice.

He licks his lips. Those pink lips . . . *Kiss me.* "Did you see me jerk off?" he asks.

"Yes." I don't deny it. I know I can't.

He curses under his breath and rubs a hand on the back of his neck. His hair is damp, the sides shorter and the long top strands pushed back. He is drop-dead gorgeous. I'm a goner. "Lily, focus," he says, his large hand holding my jaw. "Can you erase that image from your mind? Please?"

My lips press closed. No. I can't. *Never.*

He drops his hand and steps even closer. My breath hitches. Oh my God. Slowly, he fishes *my* button through my jean shorts. I watch in captivation. Once he loosens them, he lowers the zipper and reaches his hand down the front of my shorts.

I hold on to his arm. *Yes. Please.*

He cups my panties, feeling how soaked I am. I press my head to his firm chest and let out a whimper. *Please. More.*

This is torture. Sheer torture. "Harder," I whisper. It's my own fault. I was the Peeping Tom who couldn't walk away.

He stays still. "How long were you standing there?" he asks, practically reading my mind.

"I don't know."

"Lily."

"Like three minutes."

"I was only doing it for three minutes."

"Oh. Maybe shorter then." Lies.

"Sure."

He makes a move to retract his hand, and I cling to his wrist, forcing him still. Before he can say something about it, I blubber out, "It wasn't porn, right? Like live porn?"

I glance up and see the concern flash in his amber irises. I'm not sure if it's from the fact that I've taken his arm hostage or my confession.

"It wasn't porn, love. I'm your fiancé."

Relief lifts my shoulders to a natural state.

"Can I have my hand back?" he asks.

Oh. Yeah . . . I release my grip, and he pulls his hand away from the spot that craves him. My fingernails dig into my palms, resisting the desire to replace his touch with my own. Surrounded by T-shirts, hangers, and boxes of miscellaneous things, I should just go back . . . to something.

"I'm ugly," Lo suddenly tells me.

"What?" I frown, staring up at him like that's the most impossible thing of all things.

He rests his hands on my shoulders, a great deal of space between our bodies. "Just know how ugly I am, and maybe you'll be turned off."

That's a strong maybe. "You're ugly," I say, trying to buy into his words. "So ugly."

"Grotesque and *smelly*. Oh, God, you don't even want to inhale around me, I smell so bad." He wafts his hand in front of his face with a mock cringe.

I bite my lip, suppressing a smile. He smells really good actually. Like soap and citrus. "You stink," I say.

"You are incredibly repulsed by me."

"I'm repulsed by you," I say, nodding my head, playing into it. Yeah. Sure. Repulsed.

"You can't stand to look at me." What? "And it even *pains* you to touch me." *No.* I don't like this game anymore. He must see the hurt on my face because his features shatter. "Lil . . ."

I shake my head and tears begin to sting my eyes. "I love you, Lo," I say. "I don't want to feel bad for being turned on by you, and I don't want you to have to work me up into hating you for it." This feels like another fight when it shouldn't be. We have about three weeks, and then we can fuck like rabbits again.

I rub my eyes and inhale a deep breath. "Let's just forget about it, okay? I'll be fine."

I go to pass him and leave the closet, but he sidesteps and blocks me. That didn't work. "Please don't end a conversation with *I'll be fine*," he says, frustration in his voice. "I don't want you to *just* be fine. You know that."

My throat begins to swell closed. I don't know what I feel anymore.

"Come here." He motions to me, and I walk into his outstretched arms, sinking into his bare chest and warm embrace. I sniff a little bit, and when he draws back, his lips suddenly meet mine. He catches me completely off guard. Lately, he's been stingy on the groping and kissing.

He doesn't hold back.

His tongue tangles with mine, his hand cupping the back of my head with firm force. A pressure that I've missed. I melt beneath his weight, intoxicated by another person. Skin-to-skin. A pleasured noise scratches my vocal cords, and I reciprocate the kiss with extra intensity, probably too much.

My arms glue to him, my body bucking forward into his. *Please* . . .

He pulls away almost instantly. *No.* "Relax, love. Take a breath." He strokes my hair kindly, and I hide my face in his chest, my body trembling against him.

"Are we going to do anything?" I wonder, hopefully. I am pulsing. Clenching. So very ready.

"I'm going to rub you some," he admits. "But my cock isn't coming out."

I focus on the positives. *He's going to rub me.* My heart starts to hammer in excitement. Wait . . . "You're rubbing my clit, right? Not my boobs or something else?" I have to be clear, even if my red rash returns with embarrassment. I'd rather not be disappointed.

His lips rise. "Your clit, yes." The words from his voice light me up in a whole new way. My legs want to buckle. I do end up dropping, and he catches my waist and begins to lay me gently on the carpet of our closet. My head rests on a pile of clean socks.

"Wait . . ." I stop him again, just as his hand moves to my belly. "We can't." I wince. "My sisters made that pact for me; I can't break it." But I worry about not having this release at all. Lo knows how much it'll plague my mind and body. It's going to be painful. For hours. Nothing. And . . . and . . .

"Shh, love, don't cry," he breathes, wiping beneath my eyes. "This isn't sex. And if it concerns you that much, just tell your sisters they can start having sex, or that dry humping is game."

Okay. Okay. He's right.

He sets his hands on either side of me, positioned right over my small frame. "You ready now?" His voice is all playfulness.

I nod fiercely, my gaze dropping to his towel.

"That stays on, Lil," he reminds me.

"IknowIknow," I say quickly, slurring my words.

My shorts are already unbuttoned and unzipped. He keeps his body weight off me, even though I *need* it. I want it. I'm too greedy. And he likes to tease.

His hand lowers down my shorts again. I'm about to watch, but he kisses me deeply, slowly, making me lose concentration of his other languid, hot movements.

That is, until I feel his fingers brush against my wet panties. I break the kiss and whine, straight up. My legs quiver. "Please . . ."

His lips touch my ear as he whispers, "You're soaked for me."

I nod rapidly. *Yes. Yes.* "I need you," I whimper. I arch my back, hoping that my pelvis connects with his. Something harder. Deeper. His body is snug between my legs.

"Shh, Lil," he breathes.

I'm afraid he's going to sit up, away from me, so I cling to his body, latching myself on to him.

He rests his forearm on the ground, less distance between us, and he combs my hair back, his lips a breath from mine. *Kiss me.* He does. Oh. He does *so much.* The earnestness in his lips heats my core, a kiss like he's supplying me oxygen to live one more day on this Earth. *Thank you, Loren Hale.*

I'm fueled with love and lust.

He rocks his body forward, *grinding* against me. Holy shit. I cry, "Lo, *Lo.*" And his fingers begin to rub the outside of my panties. Oh my God.

I need his fingers. Not the cotton. Skin-to-skin. I whimper even more. Desperate and horny.

"I've got you," he murmurs, then he kisses my neck, sucking on the tender place. Between my thighs, his finger hooks in the cloth, and he finds the small, throbbing bud. As soon as he touches the sensitive skin, I jerk and buck up. He presses his body harder against me, keeping me still, and adding more pressure.

God. Yes.

He whispers, in a deep, edged voice, "I'm inside of you." His fingers quicken. "Slamming into you." *Yes.* "Filling you." His pace quickens, building me so high that my eyes flutter closed. My head lulls. *Please.* I hold on to his wrist and place my hand on top of his, feeling the way he's moving his fingers against the spot. Feeling how small I am compared to him.

"Deeper," I plead.

He only rubs my clit. And he says, "I'm so deep inside of you, love, that there's no more room to go any farther."

I cry into his shoulder, my body reaching a high. Nerves electrify, my pulse speeding to new levels, and I constrict multiple times. I stop breathing and float up to the clouds. From here on out, every touch on my sensitive flesh has me twisting and spasming. Lo presses on my clit, the intensity numbing me. Then he removes his hand and collects me in his arms, bringing me on his lap.

My breathing is like an out-of-shape whale. I can feel his hardness beneath his towel. "Again?" I question with a pant, longing in my eyes. I know the answer though. I shake my head at myself.

"No more, Lil." He carefully raises my shorts. I didn't even notice them fall to my thighs. He buttons and zips them back. *No more.* I'm trying to be satisfied with this. I am.

"Are you going to . . ." I stare at his crotch. ". . . touch yourself again?"

"Don't think about it," he tells me. Maybe it's better that I don't know what he does. I want to offer my services, but his jaw sharpens in this no-nonsense Loren Hale look. Something that shrivels people. It only steals my breath.

I try not to think about blow jobs or hand jobs or any kind of job. I clear my throat. "Do you know where the handcuffs are?"

His eyes narrow.

"They're not for me," I say quickly, realizing this was bad timing. "I have to show Rose."

His expression does not soften. "Why?"

"Long story."

He shakes his head and lets out a breath. He lifts me up to my feet just as he stands. And then he squats back down by his rack of Vans. He reaches for a box and pops it open. The silver cuffs are simple, but they have this black leather that makes them softer. We don't use them often. Maybe like once every few months.

I prefer my hands to be touching him.

"Alrighty, thank you." I reach out to take them.

"Kiss first," he says.

I grin and glance down at his cock.

"Not there, love. On my lips."

Damn. I look back up, and he's smiling. For a second, I wonder if I can postpone the kiss, just to see him smile longer.

He can't read my mind.

Because he kisses me first.

I realize, though, that I like this just as much.

Forty-one

Loren Hale

I never thought I'd see the day where Lily and Rose combine their birthdays into one party. For as long as I can remember, Rose *insisted* that it'd never happen. You know those people that milk their "special" day until it's dry? Making others wait on them and do favors, as if they've suddenly been born into royalty?

Times that by a million and you have Rose Calloway.

August 5th is my least favorite day on Earth.

The fact that I get to be happy for Lily's birthday four days before heading over to hell doesn't help. So today, August 3rd—exactly two days after Lil turned twenty-four and exactly two days before Rose turns twenty-six—just might live in infamy.

"So, Rose," I say, gripping a can of Fizz and leaning back into the suede couch, "when you imagined your twenty-sixth birthday, I know this is what you had in mind." I wear a half-smile.

After a five-course meal, we've all retired to the parlor for cake and presents. Her parents' Philadelphia mansion has been decorated in a combination of lilies and roses. A small party. Just family. Our parents sit in the dining room, visible through the archway. They drink champagne and fawn over the babies. It's a mundane, normal event. Like Samantha Calloway threw one of her usual dinner parties. Nothing special.

I motion to the parlor space. "Perfection, right?"

Rose gives me a withering glare. "Stop talking, Loren." She had some kind of getaway trip planned months ago, but logistically with her baby, she decided it was better to stay in Philly. I know a part of her must have cracked when she handed her birthday plans to her mom.

Lily plops down on the couch beside me, barely causing a wave. "This is the fanciest birthday I've had since I was eleven," she comments, scanning the room with big eyes.

Rose clutches a wineglass, Connor's arm across the love seat behind her head. "That's because you never wanted a birthday party," Rose says. "Mother would've thrown you one in a heartbeat."

"And invited all of her friends," Daisy adds, ambling over from the dining room with a plate of chocolate cake. Since the couch is full with Sam and Poppy, Lily and me—and the love seat and chair are taken—she can either sit on the floor or on my brother.

As she lowers her ass to the expensive rug, Ryke grips the hem of her skirt and pulls her onto his lap. Smooth. Daisy eases against him, sharing the cream suede chair.

Poppy counters, "Any of us would have thrown you a party too. You didn't have to go to Mom for one." Sam is French braiding his wife's hair. It's distracting, to be honest, especially because Poppy is next to me.

I'm biting my tongue to keep from making a remark. But I must be doing a shit job since Sam speaks up. "When you have a daughter, you'll learn how to do things you never really thought about before."

When I have a daughter? My brows rise. It implies that one day I'll have another kid. One day I'll go through all of this again. One day, I'll love another person with my entire soul.

It seems improbable.

"Whatever, Sammy," I say dryly, not wanting to start more shit with him. He's being nice. I'm an ass. I just want to leave it at that.

My gaze accidentally travels across the room, landing on their daughter. Now seven, she entertains herself at the breakfast table, sketching pictures of ball gowns. Maria literally wants to be Rose. I fear for the world.

Lily redirects the conversation back to the topic, thankfully. "I'm not complaining about all my other birthdays. I never wanted a big party. All I wanted was . . ." Her eyes widen and her cheeks splotch red. I hug her closer, trying not to smile at her embarrassment. But she's cute, even when she's a tomato.

Ryke has an arm draped over Daisy's shoulder. "Yeah, we all know where that's fucking going." He nods to Lily. "And for what it's worth, Calloway, birthday sex is the best."

Lily groans. "Don't remind me." She stuffs her face in a beaded maroon pillow. She's still on her post-pregnancy celibacy. Exactly three weeks left now.

"Can we please talk about this abstinence pact?" Sam asks as he ties off his wife's hair. She passes him his champagne and then leans into his chest.

"Yes, please," Connor agrees, sipping red wine like Rose. I'm more aware of the alcohol today than usual, and my eyes keep flitting to Ryke as a reminder that he's sober too. Lil's not drinking either, but it's different.

My father always made it seem more masculine to grip a fucking whiskey. To drink at parties. If I didn't, I was a pussy. I'm still trying to rewire my brain and not feel less than Connor and Sam. I'm consuming soda. But so is my brother.

"Wait," Ryke says, confused. He points at Poppy. "You're doing this too?"

I laugh at that realization. Goddamn. This is a big deal for the Calloway sisters then.

"Six weeks isn't that long," Poppy declares, her wooden bracelets clinking together as she reaches for her gin and tonic.

Behind her, Sam chugs his entire champagne, not agreeing.

"This is rich," I say under my breath. Lily hears me and smacks my chest. I mock wince, and her eyes drop to my lips. I'm about to kiss her, when Poppy leans forward, just to make eye contact with Lil.

"Before you know it, Lily, it'll be over."

Lily is rigid as hell, the spotlight on her. And now it's about sex. I whisper in her ear, "Relax, love." I feel her blow out a breath, her chest collapsing.

"Dry humping shouldn't be allowed," Rose snaps with an icy tone. Her glare is set on me. Like I violated some contract written in blood. "It should be all or nothing. Be strong."

"You take pacts to a whole new psychotic level," I retort. "Rules are meant to be broken, Magdala."

"You're a child," she shoots back.

"Weak."

"Children," Connor interrupts now, staring between us both. "Can we return to the issue, or move on from it, whichever will stop this first?"

Daisy raises her fork in the air. "I approve of dry humping."

"Done," I add, definitely siding with whoever sides with me. Even if it's Lily's little sister, someone I've never wanted to imagine dry humping anything living or inanimate.

Daisy makes a chopping motion with her arm. "Case closed."

I watch Lily hug that uncomfortable beaded pillow, which is meant for decoration. I steal it from her and toss it on the floor. She looks at me like I stole her vibrator. And I'm intimate with that look. I've seen it every time I trashed her toys.

I pull her onto my lap, and her expression morphs into content. Though I watch her catch glimpses of our parents, and her anxiety flares. My father has Maximoff in his arms, taking the most interest in him. Greg Calloway is a close second, sitting nearby.

I think they just connect more to the boy.

Maybe that's why Samantha only pays attention to Jane. I

haven't seen her hold Moffy or anything like that. But I have to believe it's his gender and not because he's Lil's baby. Even if it's an option, it's just too terrible to entertain.

Rose and Connor speak quietly in French, but Rose keeps nervously glancing at Ryke.

"I'm not fucking listening to you," Ryke growls back. "Stop staring at me."

Rose lets out an irritated breath and switches to what sounds like German. Although she speaks far slower and her accent isn't as polished or fluid as Connor's.

Lily leans into my arm. "Can Ryke speak German?"

I shake my head. "I have no clue." The only languages I'm certain that he speaks are Spanish, Italian, and French. I ask all the time what else he knows, but he shuts down. *It's not important*, he says. *Why does it fucking matter?*

I wonder when he'll realize that there's no reason. That it'll never matter. It'll never be important. He should just tell me because we're family.

But he didn't grow up with that sense of inclusion. The Calloway sisters did.

I did because I had Lily.

He had no one.

I get that now.

Lily pokes me in the arm. "My mom gave me these." She hands me a small stack of business cards. I flip through them. I zone in on the profession. *Nanny. Nanny. Daycare specialist. Nanny. Nanny. Childcare assistant.* My stomach rolls over.

I've already told Samantha that we're not hiring nannies. "Rose," I say, licking my lip. "Did you get these?" I stretch and pass her the business cards.

Her shoulders stiffen as she inspects them. "No."

Lily swallows hard. "I'm doing an okay job, right?" Her voice cracks at the end.

Poppy reaches out and places a hand on Lily's knee. "You're doing amazing. Don't worry about what anyone else says." Her voice carries warmth, and I see Lily's fear pop in her expression. She's worried that she doesn't sound like that. It's easier thinking you're a warm person next to Rose Calloway, but stand next to Poppy and anyone appears rough around the edges.

I rub Lily's back, making small circles. "Don't even think about your mom," I tell Lil. "Just remember the fantastic belated birthday sex you'll be getting in a few weeks."

She simultaneously blushes and inhales with more eagerness. I wrap my arms tighter around her waist, and she holds on to them.

My father laughs loudly at something, and it distracts all of us for a second. Connor takes a larger swig of his wine. He'll need a refill soon. "Has the board made a decision yet?" he asks.

We have no more news than the previous standings, but we've been to another function. I can't tell what the board is thinking. They're as poker-faced as Connor sometimes.

I drink my soda, craving something sharper. "The board doesn't need to make a decision," I say. "It's my title. So you can all self-sabotage any day now." The edge in my voice hurts my ears. I hate it. "By the end of the month, you can call me Mr. Hale, CEO. We'll even have a party." I feign excitement with a small gasp. "Ryke can bring the tacos, and Connor, here, will supply the Glenfiddich. Won't you, love?"

The entire room deadens.

The tension and silence is so thick that it's hard to breathe.

I don't know why I said that. To be an asshole. Maybe it's something deeper. But everyone catches the hidden meaning behind my words.

The first time I ever relapsed was by drinking a bottle of Glenfiddich.

Connor's bottle.

I wait for Connor to banter back and ease the tension. Like he always does. But he stares off at the rug, not even looking in my direction.

"Come on, it was a joke," I say dryly, my ribs binding around my lungs.

Connor suddenly rises to his feet, *visibly* upset. And he's trying hard to hide it, avoiding everyone's gazes. "You'll have to excuse me for a second," he says softly, sidestepping past the armrest.

"Connor," I say before he leaves. I feel sick. Like I might puke. "It was a *joke*." I think if I emphasize this, he'll forgive me.

He doesn't turn back.

Not once.

I watch him walk out the parlor door, vanishing from sight.

Forty-two

Loren Hale

I glance at the doorway for the fifth time. I really thought I'd never be able to upset Connor. That no matter what I'd say, what I'd do, he'd always be my friend. I rub my lips, not able to even stomach the idea of losing him over a fucking comment I made.

Lily slides off my lap. She cups her hands around my ear. "Just go," she whispers, encouraging me to talk to him. Should I though?

I've never had a real guy friend until Connor. Pathetic, sure. But I didn't grow up with *bros* or teammates and sports. I had Lily. And the friends I have now, I can count on my hand. Hurting them means something different to me.

This pushes me over. I rise from the couch.

I stop on my way out just to look at Rose. I don't want to make things worse. She gives me a single nod in confirmation, like I'm doing the right thing here.

Okay . . .

In five seconds flat, I'm out the door. He's not on the patio. Or in the kitchen. And he didn't head to the bathroom. I pass the library, the last room. I want to check there before I head upstairs. The wooden door creaks as I open it; then I silently curse myself for not looking here sooner.

It's a goddamn library. Of course he'd be here.

Bookshelves line every wall, top and bottom floors, sliding ladders accompany them. No windows. This room has always been for show. I can't remember a time when I'd seen anyone in here. Except maybe hide-and-go-seek when we were little. Lily always tried to wedge behind a bookshelf. It freaked me out when I got older, thinking it'd fall on her or something.

It's weird now, seeing a person in this room. Someone actually perusing the shelves and removing a dusted hardback from its permanent position.

Connor's back is turned to me, but I'm sure he heard me shut the door.

I step forward, thinking he'll spin around.

He doesn't.

He blows off the dust and flips through the crisp pages.

A lump lodges in my throat, and I clear it with a cough. What the hell is wrong with me?

"Rose is looking for you," I lie. My breath cages as I wait for him to speak. It's in this moment that I know how much I value our friendship. And how it's not invulnerable like I hoped.

"If she were looking for me, she'd be here instead of you." He shelves the book and chooses another. I open my mouth to respond, but he cuts me off. "I'm not in the mood to talk with you, Lo."

I can't hold back. "It was a joke, Connor," I snap, on the defensive. "I didn't mean it like you think I did." Did I, though? I can't exactly tell. Something black is crawling out of me. Slowly. Eking like tar.

He returns the hardback and rotates to face me, stuffing his hands in his pockets. I'm overly aware of how fragile I am in his presence. And I fucking hate it right now. He lets nothing cross his face. Nothing that makes me feel stronger and better.

I just feel like a fucking idiot. *No.* Screw this. "You can't get upset over one fucking *joke*," I sneer, pain in my voice. I wish it wasn't there. So goddamn apparent. Part of me wants to forget about this. And just move on. The other part knows I brought it up for a reason.

"It's not a joke to me," he says flatly.

I let out a weak laugh. "Right."

Connor looks incensed for once, his chest rising and falling heavily. His blue eyes narrowing at me.

"Am I poking the robot?" I ask him with a bitter, painful smile. "Do you feel something, huh?" I extend my arms. "I'm your fucking liability. You should've known this day was going to come." And everything just explodes in my body. Words my father said. Why would Connor keep me around? To manipulate me? All so he could get closer to Rose? I have no clue, and it's ripping through me. To think that I could've—

"I carried you in my arms," he suddenly says, his eyes bloodshot. "That day you relapsed was the worst night of my life." He points at the ground. "It's *not* a joke to me."

I have no memory of it—I blacked out. I choke out another laugh, only this one hurts a million times worse. "Great. I'm glad we have that worked out." I have nothing else to say. Honestly, I'd like to down Maker's Mark.

"Lo . . ." He attaches nothing else to my name. I can't read his mind, so I turn around, expecting him to leave it at that. But as I head to the door, he runs after me.

Connor catches my arm and spins me around. "Lo, wait." I've never seen his eyes this red before.

"I get it," I tell him. He carried me while I was passed out, and he was freaked.

His hand drops off me, and he shakes his head. "No, you don't."

A weight builds on my chest. And I have to ask. I can't just guess anymore. "Am I a liability to you?" I clench my teeth hard, suppressing everything that threatens to overflow.

"Yes," he says truthfully.

I nod a couple times, letting this fact sink in. "Have you manipulated me?"

He twists his watch on his wrist, his gaze falling to the ground in thought before flitting back to me. "I can tell what people need, and I—"

"Stop," I choke out. I don't want to hear him explain. That he pretended to be my friend. He used me. "All you have to say is yes or no."

"It's not that simple," he tells me, a tremor in his usually brick-walled voice.

"It is!" I shout at him. I point at my chest. "You either fucking played me or you didn't!"

"I love you," he refutes, his gaze daggered on me.

It takes me aback. Because Connor has admitted to only loving himself. To then loving Rose. No one else. But I know this isn't sexual or romantic. It's the kind of love that I have for my brother. The kind that Rose has for her sisters.

He grimaces like the fact is hard for him to accept. "Lo, I don't . . . love many people. But there is *no* manipulation in what I feel for you. The truth is, I gave you what I thought you needed, affection and praise, but I had no motives for it. I didn't use you for anything."

I open my mouth to speak, but he raises his hand quickly.

"Wait, let me finish." His Adam's apple bobs. "You're my liability *because* I love you. The night you relapsed, I thought you were going to die." He pauses. ". . . and that fact nearly crippled me. I couldn't even *drive*, Lo." He shakes his head like he doesn't want to imagine that night. "I care about you, what happens to you, and it's a weakness any way I look at it. Like your father once asked, what do I get out of it? I told him the truth. I get your friendship. That's all I want."

I process his words. I didn't think he cared about me like that.

In the back of my mind, I really believed that he endured my personality because of my status and my connection to the Calloways. I've tried to be okay with it.

Even after years, it seemed like I gave him more of myself than he ever gave me. He's seen me at some brutal lows, and I've never seen him flinch. Except maybe right now. It's like he took off some of his armor for me, just to say that he loves me.

It's honesty that I needed. I feel like I can breathe more easily, knowing from Connor, not from Rose, that our friendship is real.

I meet his eyes. "Most people can't stand me, you know."

He laughs into a million-dollar grin. "And most people can't take all of me. I've realized that the people who can are the ones I love deeply."

"Is this all of you?" I ask him.

He nods. "Yes. Mostly."

"Mostly?"

"I can't always express myself the way that you want to see . . ." He trails off.

Anger, I realize. He won't let me see his. Not to the degree that it can reach. "Okay," I say. "Okay." I exhale a strained breath and then freeze as a thought hits me cold. "You mentioned my dad . . . does he know?" I frown, my brows pinching.

"I've been fighting with Jonathan because he thinks I'm toying with your emotions. He found out that I'd slept with a guy before. Years ago, no one you would know. Just a friend of a friend . . ." Connor trails off, loosening his tie.

I'm sure my dad thinks Connor is coming onto me or something stupid. It's not like that. But after the video in Mexico where we kissed . . . "Shit." I pinch the bridge of my nose.

"He's just protecting you," Connor says. "And his way of doing that is by telling me to put a considerable amount of distance between us. With the threat of *or else*. I'm not frightened by his open-ended warning, just annoyed that it exists at all."

My hand falls to my side. "I'll talk to my dad—"

"*No*," Connor forces the word.

"My dad loves me," I retort. "I can help."

"You'll make it worse," he says. "If you go to your father and tell him to stop threatening me, he's going to think that I manipulated you to say it. Think about this, Lo. I could have brought you into this library, told you that I care so deeply for you, just so you can turn around and get him to do what I want. That's not what this has been about today. Just forget it and let me handle it."

I blow out a strained breath, my last one. "Okay." I'm basically throwing up my hands, but I know he's right. I can't do anything to help him fix this mess. "Is our friendship really worth it to you?" I ask. It seems like there are not a lot of positives in it for him.

He doesn't even hesitate. "Yes." He adds, "I've never met a problem that I can't solve. Your worry is better placed on Lily."

I nod. He's right about that too. "Can you promise me one thing?"

"What?" he asks.

"Next time, tell me if one of my jokes sucks ass." I smile. "Like really blows."

His lips pull in another grin. "Always, darling."

Forty-three

Lily Calloway

While Lo talks to Connor, I stay seated in the parlor, nodding every time my sisters start a new topic, but my mind has transported to bad places. I daydream about birthday sex that I won't be having. I picture icing, body parts, hard things, and *intense* dry humping.

Oh wait, dry humping is allowed. I perk up at the thought. I wonder if Lo will consider it.

A baby cries, slicing through my trance. And guilt seeps into my veins like liquid ice. Becoming a mom hasn't changed my personality or made me less compulsive. I still have a filthy mind. And now I despise these thoughts more.

I'm sitting here, in the company of my sisters and their significant others, thinking about cock and cake frosting. To top it off, my baby is in sight. I'm about to stand when I notice my mom rocking Jane in her arms and shushing her. Moffy sits idly in his bouncer between Jonathan and my dad. He giggles as my father makes a goofy face at him.

Jane is clearly the one wailing, and Rose is already on her feet, strutting across the parlor and through the archway before anyone says a word.

I try to unroast from my red flush of shame. It's the worst shade.

"You okay, Lily?" Ryke asks with a dark frown. Daisy has fallen asleep on his lap, which should make me happier, in a sense. That night in the tent she admitted to only sleeping a couple hours total. I'm staring at a good thing, my little sister getting some shut-eye, but I'm feeling something different. "Lily?" Ryke asks again, his voice quiet.

Poppy and Sam now focus on me too.

I clear my throat. "Mmhmm." I can't even form actual words. I went from being handed business cards for nannies to being plagued with sexual thoughts. I should be concerned about Moffy. And I hate when sex overtakes that. It's not right. It's gross.

Ryke presses a hand over Daisy's ear, really gently so she doesn't wake up or hear him speak. "Try again."

He's very pushy. This is known. "Nannies aren't bad, right?" I ask, the business cards between my fingers. "I mean, we all had them. And normal people have them too. For working moms and dads . . ."

The heat of Ryke's gaze shrinks me into the couch. I seek comfort in other places. Like Poppy.

"We had a nanny once, when Maria was little," Poppy says. "But you shouldn't hire one just because you feel obligated to do it." She tenderly collects the business cards out of my hand. "How about I hold on to these for you?"

It's like a bunch of bees just stung my esophagus, swelling it closed. I nod unsurely.

Ryke sets the plate of half-eaten chocolate cake on the coffee table so it doesn't fall off Daisy's thigh. "Look, if you ever feel overwhelmed, you have Daisy and me. We're always around."

Overwhelmed? Pressure compounds on my chest. I'm not a selfish monster. I care about Moffy more than sex. I do. I *do*.

"*Lily*," Ryke says my name again, so forcefully that Daisy's eyes snap open in fright. "Fuck."

I'm scratching my arm, I realize. I retract my hand, jailing it between my knees. What is wrong with me? I watch Daisy sit up straighter on Ryke, her skin pale. She looks like she's going to puke. The guilt creeps even further inside of me.

I think I just inadvertently caused my sister a minor panic attack.

Ryke adjusts her in his arms, concern washing over his features.

"I'm okay," she says in a deep inhale, able to breathe fully.

Ryke hardly relaxes.

"I'm sorry," I apologize.

Daisy shakes her head at me like *no, don't be*. It's my fault though. Everything. My sex addiction going public did *this* to her. The fear. The ridicule. I can't ever forgive myself for that.

Anxieties continue to pile on me. I need to shut my thoughts down, but my head is all messed up. I wish it would go back to normal. I peek over my shoulder, hoping Lo will appear. I can't rely on him, no matter how much I want to.

Poppy scoots on the couch and swings her arm around my shoulder. I feel so much worse. She should be comforting Daisy. Not me. But Poppy gives me a sisterly squeeze. "When I had Maria, I felt panicked a lot. Thinking I was doing something wrong. It's normal."

My brain is not normal. If she could see inside of it, she'd realize how disgusting it is. I keep nodding and rubbing my eyes, trying to take the attention off me. I don't want to admit the source of my anxiety: sex over a baby. But sitting here, agreeing with them that my panic is a normal motherly emotion, makes me feel like a lying liar.

"I just need some air," I mumble and push off the couch. I pause and lock eyes with my little sister before I leave. "I'm really sorry . . . for everything."

"It's not your fault," she says softly, exhausted tears welling in her eyes. "I wish you would accept that. It'd make me feel better."

Humans are cursed, I think. These are emotions too complex to overcome. Maybe it'll take a lifetime to finally let go.

I just nod. It's all I can do. On my way outside, I pass the dining room and retrieve Maximoff.

"We can watch Max," my dad says, staring fondly at my baby, who has a little grin on his face. My dad even reaches out and tickles Moffy's foot. His garbled happy noise melts my heart. I glance at my mom, who feeds Jane a bottle, Rose sitting next to her.

"It's okay," I say quickly. "He hasn't been outside all day." I don't know if I still look upset, but I sense the worry from all corners of the room, cloaking me like a hot blanket. It's almost suffocating.

I want them to believe that I'm strong enough to be a good mom.

Some days, I think I am. Other days, I have to convince myself all over again. But I'm going to get there, and I won't give up.

I buckle Maximoff into his carrier and then pass through the side door into the back patio. The weather lingers in the awkward stage between summer and fall, unsure of what it wants to be. I place the carrier on an iron chair and sit on the adjacent one, folding my legs beneath my butt.

"You know I love you, right?" I ask him, fitting his little blue hat snug over his dark brown hair that's grown in. He grabs on to my finger with both hands. And my melted heart starts to swell. "More than anything in the whole world . . . right up there with Loren Hale." The warm air billows, and he lets out a tiny baby squeal, kicking his legs. I smile and sniff, rubbing my runny nose.

The glass door slides open, and I crane my neck to see who followed me outside.

"Hey." Lo's voice almost ignites another wave of tears.

"Hey," I whisper, blinking repeatedly to restrain the waterworks. "I'm just getting some air."

"Yeah, Ryke told me that you were out here." Lo drags a chair near me, the iron legs scraping the cement. He sets it beside me and then touches Moffy's cheek with the gentle rub of his finger. Our baby is glowing at the affection.

"He loves you," I say.

"He loves you too, Lil." His amber eyes narrow on me. Confused. Concerned. All of the above. "Are you going to make me ask?"

I exhale a heavy breath. "I don't want to be thinking about . . . *you know what* when I should be thinking about him. It's not right." I run a shaky hand through my thin locks, not greasy. I did wash my hair this morning. I remember to do that more now.

He frowns. "That's it?"

My mouth falls. "That's bad enough, Lo."

His forehead creases, and his expression carries so many words: *no, not even close.* "Normal people think about sex and other things besides their children. It's okay."

"Then why does it feel gross?" I tickle Maximoff's chest, and he smiles so wide that he drools a little bit on his chin. What a goober. God, I love him. I wipe the spittle up with the edge of his blanket.

Lo turns to me, trying to hide his smile. "It feels wrong because you've conditioned yourself to think that even the thought of sex is bad. It's not. It's just your way of keeping yourself grounded. I've thought about screwing you plenty of times since we had Moffy. It's all normal."

My shoulders loosen. "I just don't want to choose sex over him."

"You won't," Lo assures me. "If you're worried about it, I know you won't. And thinking about it isn't the same as making a choice between him and sex. Okay?"

"Yeah, okay."

It's his turn to let out a heavy breath now. "We have therapy in a couple days. Can I bring this up? Maybe we can talk through it again."

I nod. "I'd like that."

He leans forward and kisses me lightly on the lips, warming all the cold in my veins. When he breaks away, his hand drops to my neck, his thumb brushing my skin. "You were thinking about birthday sex, weren't you?" His smile dimples his cheeks.

"Belated," I remind him.

"Belated birthday sex. Tell me all about it."

I love how he makes me feel normal. How my brain isn't some vast deep filthy wasteland to him. In his eyes, I'm some kind of perfect.

Forty-four

Loren Hale

Lily is tangled and twisted in our red sheets and champagne comforter, even more when she rolls over onto her back.

"You practicing to be a taco?" I ask her, kneeling on the bed. I fed Moffy this morning and let Lil sleep in. She's been getting shit sleep lately, too restless from the lack of sex.

"Maybe . . ." she mutters, peeking from the edge of the comforter. "Do I look like a good taco?"

"I'd eat you," I say with a nod.

Her cheeks redden. Shit.

"Two more days, Lil." I tap her foot in encouragement and clasp her ankle, yanking her closer to me. The comforter and sheets come with her.

"It seems like an *eternity*," she whines.

I scan her body quickly, noticing how the blankets rise and fall with her ragged breathing. I peel the heavy comforter off, just leaving her wrapped in the red sheet. "You remember when we were teenagers?" I ask, spreading her legs apart with a firm hand.

Her mouth slowly falls as she hones in on my movements.

I sink my weight onto her, and my lips brush against her earlobe. "When we were alone in my living room, pretending . . ." I kiss the base of her neck, using my tongue. Her body trembles beneath me.

We always "practiced" together. Not going all the way but far enough. We'd put on a show for passing staff in the house, just in case they reported back to my father. I always pushed her limits. I know this.

"I would have you against the wall," I breathe, my gaze traveling along her collarbones, peeking from a black V-neck shirt. My shirt that she wore to bed. "And I would brush my fingers through your short hair." I run my hand up the soft flesh of her neck. She's small beneath me, thin and delicate, even if she's likely to jump on me and grind.

"Lo," she chokes, her voice hoarse. I can remember the past fully now. To say the words, to bring it up and relive some moments—it doesn't hurt anymore.

I think we've both accepted it for what it is. Our fucked-up beginning. But it's our beginning. And no one can take that away from us. "Do you remember what I would do next, love?"

She's fixated on my lips. "You'd press yourself against me." Her neck flushes. "I could feel your erection, did you know that?" Her eyes flit up to mine, eager for my answer.

"I knew you made me hard, yeah," I say with a smile.

She hits my arm. "Not that."

"Yeah, Lil, I was a dick," I remind her. "I wanted you to feel my cock." I drink in her features: round face and big green eyes.

"You hoped I would ride it, huh?"

"Every day." It also doesn't hurt admitting these things to her anymore. I can see the lightness in her expression too. We have each other now. That will never change.

"Guess what?" she says.

"What?"

"I want to ride it now and every single day." She lifts her head like she's ready for a kiss. "Promise you'll let me?" Christ—I could fuck her right now. Impatient, she inches downward, wiggling beneath me so that she's in line with my cock. Abandoning the kiss.

I have to control every muscle in my body to keep from taking her. After a moment of concentration, I let out a dramatic sigh and grip her waist, pulling her higher. "Unfortunately, I can't make that promise with you, Lily Calloway."

She squints at me, waiting for my punch line. I take my time and then press my pelvis against her heat. Her breathing staggers, and she drops her hand as my cock digs into her.

"You see," I say, continuing where I left off. "There are going to be days where *I* want to ride you."

"Oh . . ." She licks her lips, and I start rocking against her. *Goddamn.* My cock screams to be inside of her. To toss away the sheet. To remove my drawstring pants and her underwear. I ignore my dick and focus on her reactions.

Her toes curl. Her hips buck. Aching for pressure.

I lift one of her legs higher, thrusting deeper. Fabric separating us. She hooks her other leg around my waist and moves with me, grinding against my erection. *Jesus.* My mouth opens as a heavy breath leaves me.

Moans breach her lips. One that escalates the longer I move. High-pitched. Desperate. Like I'm her ice in the desert. It's like when we were teenagers. Only it's not.

I have her this time.

I'm not just hers.

She's mine.

I kiss her deeply, sucking on her bottom lip until it swells.

"Lo, *please*," she begs, her hands trembling. She wants to touch herself, to meet her peak.

"Okay, okay, shhh," I coax, smoothing her hair off her forehead.

I reach down, beneath the sheet and her panties, and start rubbing her with my thrusts. Her eyes flutter at the new sensation, and she takes a shallow breath. Her lips part, and I expect more moans. But she manages actual words.

"It's really going to be like when we were younger," she says in a dazed smile. *I* wait for the punch line this time. ". . . with you coming in your pants."

I raise my brows, trying hard not to smile. "Who said I was coming in my pants?" I grab her chin in one hand and stare down at her beautiful mouth that starts to form a perfect "O."

I kiss her cheek, her jaw, her lips, quickening the speed of my fingers on her soft flesh. "But you first, love."

Her eyes say, *yes*. A million times over.

descend the staircase, showered and about to head out for lunch with Ryke and Connor. The girls are spending the Saturday with Jane and Moffy, giving us free time.

"We all have two more fucking days until we get laid," Ryke says as he leans against the foyer wall, waiting for me to finish tying my black Vans, "so why do you look so happy?"

"My girlfriend likes blow jobs," I tell him with a shrug.

Ryke gives me a glare. "Why don't you write a fucking book?" he says. "You could call it: *Perks of Dating a Female Sex Addict*."

"Or you could write one," I shoot back, rising to my feet. *"Perks of Having the Hots for a Sixteen-Year-Old Supermodel and Having to Wait until She Turns Eighteen, Only to be Cockblocked by Your Bastard Half-Brother."* I flash a bitter smile.

"That title needs some work," Connor says, clipping on his Rolex watch. "And that's if we all agree Ryke can write a full-length novel."

"Dude, I was a fucking journalism major."

"And look how far that got you."

"Let's just go," I cut in. "I'm starving and our bodyguards are probably bitching us out in their Escalades." They have to follow us anywhere in public, including the local Mexican restaurant downtown.

Ryke turns the doorknob, and I step out onto the brick porch with my brother.

The minute my foot hits the welcome mat, liquid suddenly cascades in violent sheets, dousing Ryke and me. It's slow motion. And I shut my eyes as the warm liquid tries to sear them. The smell is overpowering, sharp, and too familiar.

"*What the fuck!*" Ryke yells, horrified.

It's not water.

We're drenched in something worse. After the gushing stops, a bucket tumbles a second later. I marbleize in realization. Fully processing what just happened.

We were just showered in alcohol.

By inhaling, I can tell that it's bourbon.

I slowly open my eyes. I'm shaking, too stunned to do anything. I'm swept up in years and years of bad deeds and terrible nights. I look to Ryke, and his hair is wet, his gray shirt plastered to his chest. He's breathing unevenly, filled with fury. "This is so fucked up."

And then he meets my eyes. His features burst with too many emotions. Panic for me. Rage at the teenagers.

The smell is killing me. On instinct, I lick my lips. It's bourbon, for sure.

"Lo, don't fucking taste it," Ryke says quickly, grabbing my arm like he can stop me. He can't.

"We're soaked in booze," I state like he can't see it. "It's too fucking late." It doesn't mean I broke my sobriety. Not again. I have to believe this. No matter how much my brain wants to say I fucking lost a battle today. I didn't. *I didn't.*

My face twists with my stomach. God. Dammit. I squat for a second, collecting my breath.

"Hey," Ryke forces, bending down to me. He clasps my shoulder. "You're okay."

"No matter how much you say it, it doesn't make it any fucking truer," I retort in an agitated voice. I'm pissed. At the situation. Not at him. I grimace. "Just . . ." I'm trying not to lose it.

"Take off your clothes," Connor says from the doorway, with an inexpressive voice.

It almost makes me laugh, but my features only morph into hurt. "How forward of you, love."

"He's right," Ryke actually agrees with Connor. My brother lifts me up so I'm standing straighter. He starts removing my sopping shirt since my joints are locked tight. When I unfreeze a bit, I pull my crew neck over my head. Ryke tugs off his own shirt and tosses the wet fabric on the brick with mine.

I instinctively run a hand through my hair. I pause at the smell. At how much it's seeping into my skin. *Christ.*

Ryke is saying something. My mind is on a hundred paths, speeding. I stare off at the road, expecting to find an audience. No one is there. Not these stupid, bored teenagers that've turned malicious. This is low. The girls TP-ed one of their houses. And in return, they decided to shove me a thousand steps back in my recovery.

Ryke is right. It's fucked up.

It's really, *really* fucked up.

"Lo!" Ryke shouts, lightly slapping the side of my face to get me to concentrate.

I inhale a deep, strained breath that burns my muscles. "Don't worry about me," I say. "I'm not going to pass out and die."

"You're shaking," Ryke says.

"I'm *pissed*," I sneer, putting some distance between us. "Just like you are."

He nods, but the concern never leaves him.

I turn to Connor, who wears a similar expression as my brother now. "I'm not the Wicked Witch, okay?" I snap at him. "I'm not about to melt onto the floor." My body binds the longer I stand here. Anger doesn't accurately describe the feeling coursing through my veins.

I wasn't ready for this type of retaliation. But it doesn't mean that I can't handle it. I'd give anything not to be the weak one right now. For them to look at me like I can take this. *I can take it.* I know I can.

"You should go shower," Ryke advises.

"In a second," I say.

"Lo."

He's not going to let up. Fine. "You need to take one too," I say with an edged voice. "You reek."

"I'm right behind you."

I pass Connor into the house, kicking off my shoes. And then I run up the stairs, two at a time, while Ryke disappears to the basement. As soon as I slip into my bedroom, Lily pops up from the comforter where she'd been napping.

"Lo?"

"I'm fine," I say quickly, aiming right for the bathroom. I disappear inside and start removing the rest of my wet clothes. I'm not surprised when Lily follows me, my black V-neck tee covering her thighs. "I have to take a shower." I sound more detached than usual.

She clutches on to the door frame as she watches me strip. "What happened?" Her nose crinkles. "Is that . . . ?"

"Bourbon," I say under my breath.

She catches the word. "What?" Her voice spikes.

After stepping out of my boxer briefs, I enter the glass shower. "The teenagers used the water bucket trick. I'm just going to wash off and then head to lunch." I don't wait for her to respond. I switch on the faucet, the hot water pouring down on me. My muscles tense, and I rest a hand on the tiled wall, trying to relax before I grab the soap.

The juvenile pranks, I understand. The malicious intent, I get even more. That's me. All of those teenagers are *me*. And I should call the cops like my father would, but how can I? It's a waste. I'll make it worse with their parents, enrage them more, and ruin their lives before they've even started. This feels like my final test. To be a better person than I was.

I keep waiting for my self-preservation to kick in. To say: *fuck you all*. To tap into the selfish, dark parts of my soul.

But I give a shit. I think about that young guy I held the night of the paintball shooting. I think about my son and Lily. Her sisters. And I can't find an answer that solves everything—the happy ending that I've been fighting for.

It's there. I know it's there. Just one last shadowed road. One more bout of pain. I can take it.

"Lo?" Lily peeks through a crack in the glass door. "Can I come in?"

I give her a stiff nod, and she slips into the shower, still half-clothed. The water rains on her small frame, suctioning the black tee to her body. I watch her snatch a washcloth and a bar of soap. I'm caught in a tornado of memories. Of Lily trying to drag me into the shower while I was hungover.

My lips begin to rise. Back then, I could wash myself fine, but I liked how Lily tried to help me. Her being that close meant more to me than she ever knew. She was my best friend—*is* my best friend.

After she lathers the washcloth, she gently begins scrubbing my abs. And then her eyes flit up to mine for the first time. She pauses. "What's so funny?" My smile is full-blown. From cheek to cheek.

"I've always loved you, you know," I breathe.

I can't stop staring at her. She's been through every piece of my life with me. And it's overwhelming and incomprehensible. The universe that I want to be in is the one where Lily walks through that shower door. Every time.

She opens her mouth to speak, but emotions pummel her first. She wipes her eyes, which is silly and adorable since beads of water roll down her cheeks from the showerhead. "I have something in my eye," she mumbles.

"Sure," I whisper. Then I draw her closer, kiss right outside her lips, and just hold her for a second. It's like embracing the happiest parts of yourself. I can't quite explain what it feels like—but I'm certain it's somewhere near heaven.

Forty-five

Lily Calloway

After the shower, Lo changes into clean clothes, and I take the opportunity to scoop his bourbon-soaked jeans and toss them into a trash bag. I want to eliminate any temptations, and I worry the pungent smell of alcohol will trigger his cravings.

I clip the baby monitor to the band of my leggings and check that it's working properly (a constant habit) as I head downstairs. Daisy and Rose are huddled around the kitchen stove, *whispering*.

I step on the metal foot of the trash can. "What are you two gossiping about?" I take an extra long minute to shove my bag in the overflowing trash, smashing boxes of empty cereal.

Rose straightens up, her hands perched on her hips. "Retaliation number two."

Daisy twists her hemp bracelet, a Ziff bottle under her arm. "They can't get away with what they did."

An uneasy feeling settles in my stomach like a hollow pit. "Retaliation number one ended badly," I remind them. "I'm not sure if we should do it again." And I love a good stealth mission.

"I agree with Lily." The commanding voice originates from the hallway, Connor's loafers clapping on the hardwood as he emerges in the kitchen.

Connor Cobalt just agreed with me.

This is a monumental occasion. I almost start cheering, but Rose's yellow-green eyes have penetrated Connor's incoming six-foot-four body.

"You don't have a vote here," Rose dismisses him easily. "Girls only."

He steps nearer. "Are you asking for special privileges because of your gender?" It's a question that causes Rose to cringe. Her husband faces her, only a few feet apart.

"So what do you want us to do?" Rose combats. "Nothing? Wait for them to attack again? Next thing you know, they're going to throw dildos in Lily's face!"

"That's already happened before," I mumble.

"Not from your own neighbors." She makes a good point. No sex toy projectiles have landed my way while around the house. "This is supposed to be a safe place for everyone. It's why we're living together. I'm not torturing myself with Ryke's constant mess and Loren's presence for nothing."

Daisy spins the cap on her Ziff bottle. She claims the flavor is better the longer you suffer through the iron-like taste, but deep down, I know she's drinking it to be a supportive girlfriend. The Ziff rock climbing event is soon, and Ryke will officially become the face of the sports drink.

"Can we call the cops? Or file a report?" Daisy wonders.

"Not without evidence," Connor explains. "And as soon as one of us makes a claim, it'll be on the front page of every tabloid." This is a big reason why I hesitate to run to the police. I ping-pong between protecting Moffy at home—from the teenagers—and then protecting him from the rabid media, which'll explode with the new headline. They always swarm after a good story.

The neighborhood teenagers seem harmless compared to the psychological damage that the media can cause. I don't want my son to be five years old, afraid to go outside and be berated with cameras . . . like I was when we first entered the public eye.

The doorbell rings, and I jump. "OhmyGod," I slur. "What if it's them?" Maybe they've come to apologize? Yeah, okay, fat chance.

Rose's heels clap as she marches to the door.

"Rose," I call out, eyes wide. "It could be a trick." Like another bucket or worse.

Daisy hops off the stool, but she hesitates and lingers back. My fearless sister is frightened right now. I clasp her hand and watch Connor take a few lengthy strides, his legs much longer than Rose, and before his wife can protest, he's in the foyer and opening the door.

Very softly, Daisy whispers, "I don't want to be afraid anymore."

Chills prick my arms. "You won't be . . . one day." I nod resolutely at this idea. "It'll just take time." From someone who's battled pieces of her mind, I know this fight. We can wish for it all to be better, but it's bigger than us. It feels out of our control, but somewhere deep down, it's in reach.

I want to express this to my little sister, but the new voice in the foyer extinguishes my thoughts.

"I should really have my own key. Three of my four daughters live here." My mom—she shows up unannounced all the time, but never to see me. I usually hide out in my room or the nursery. Maybe that's my fault too. I should be more sociable.

"I'll have one made for you," Connor says as he returns to the kitchen. Rose looks ready to claw out his eyes. Then again, Connor could be lying to our mom. Trying to win her over.

In two quick seconds, Samantha Calloway appears: her strand of pearls choked against her neck, her brown hair pulled into a strict bun. She places her white designer purse on the bar counter.

"To what do we owe this pleasure?" Rose asks unenthusiastically.

"Don't be so hostile, Rose," our mother refutes. "I just wanted to stop by and say hello. It's Saturday."

"So it is," Rose grumbles.

Our mom spots Daisy, and her demeanor lightens as if she's found a purpose for visiting. "Oh, honey, I thought you were planning on dying it back to honey blonde." She approaches Daisy and inspects the platinum blonde strands between pinched fingers. "I'll make an appointment for you at the salon—"

"No, it's okay," Daisy cuts her off quickly. "I'm not sure what color I want yet. But the next time I dye it will be the official color." She shrugs. "No more changes for a while."

Our mom purses her lips, as though concocting ways to convince Daisy of the honey blonde color. I squeeze my little sister's hand, supportive of her decisions. Whatever they are, as long as she makes them herself. I'm standing very close to my mom now.

My chest tightens as I prepare for the inevitable cold shoulder. Very little eye contact. Even less conversation. It's her go-to with me for the past few years.

"Where's Jane?" our mom asks, avoiding my nearby presence. "I'd like to see my granddaughter before I leave." Her silver bracelets clank together as she fingers her pearls.

The exclusion of my son rings in my ears like a blow horn. It's been plaguing me for some time. I can handle the silent treatment directed at me. But I envision a future where Maximoff is ostracized by his own grandmother. I'd rather him be surrounded by love than know that kind of pain.

My words overflow, too strong to contain. "I have to talk to you." She startles like I yelled in her ear. My voice is almost a whisper. "In private."

Her shoulders constrict, her collarbones jutting out, but she nods anyway. Not shutting me down. It's a start, I think. I make a point to do this on my own, leading my mom into the bright sun-room without glancing back at my sisters.

I shut the oak door behind her, the hollow parts of my stomach twisting in real knots. The last time I shared my mom's company, alone, was years ago. I believed that I wasn't vocal or strong enough to confront her, but I have a reason to try now.

She stands, uncomfortable and rigid, beside the floral couch.

"You can sit down if you want," I instruct.

She chooses to stay upright. "Are you planning a date for your wedding?" It's a safe topic. One that I've trained myself not to contemplate for long.

I lick my chapped lips. "No . . ." *Just tell her how you feel.* It's not as easy as it seems.

She crosses her arms, scrutinizing all of the brass furnishings in the sunroom. "I think you should choose a date in the summer. May or June. It'll give me plenty of time to plan it." I follow her to the floor-length window; outside the leaves are dark green in the middle of August.

I swallow a lump. "I need to know something . . ."

She spins around, and her cold, daggered eyes zero in on mine. It's not like Rose. She carries an air that says: *you are not what I wanted you to be.* "Yes? Speak."

I muster the bits of courage inside of me to ask, "Why are you more interested in Jane than Maximoff? Is it because he's my son?" The question is as pained as it sounds.

Her stoic face hardly fissures. "I've never had a boy, Lily. I'm more comfortable with Jane." She pauses like there's more, and she touches her dangly pearl earring in thought. My heart beats rapidly, waiting for a slice of the guillotine. "You . . . and I, we've had our differences. I don't want to cause anymore unnecessary drama."

This is partly my fault. I've been avoiding her too, and now it's like we stand on two separate planes of existence. I miss the days where she would stick up for me if Rose was being too harsh. Where she'd cut in during family luncheons and ask me about college. I messed up. So badly.

"I'm sorry," I whisper. "I blame myself, every day, for what's happened. And I don't know what it'll take for you to forgive me." My eyes begin to sear with hot tears.

"Just time," she says softly.

I shake my head. "It's been years." I stare up at her with glassy eyes, and her impenetrable defenses start to fracture. She can't look at me anymore. Her gaze is on the shiny hardwood.

"I've forgiven you," she says quietly, "but I can't ever forget what your choices have done to this family. You almost collapsed your father's entire business. And it's taken a long time to reestablish the reputation we once had. It's just messy, Lily." She won't look up at me. *Look up.*

Tears spill down my cheeks. "Mom." It raises her eyes for a second. And I say, "I'm sick."

Her penciled eyebrows twitch, and her lips part at my words. I wait for her defensive nature to arise, but she's more affected by me than I thought she'd be. Staying silent.

"When . . . I was little," I begin, "I had sex because it made me feel like I was worth something. Because every time I was at home, I felt worthless." My chin trembles. "I'm not trying to blame you. I take responsibility for everything I've done, but there was a piece of me that craved something . . . more. And I was desperately trying to find it." I fiddle with my fingers. "Sex . . . made me feel better. Not whole. But better."

I've rehearsed this speech a thousand times in my head. I've imagined her reaction a million different ways. Some indifferent. Others warm and apologetic. Standing here now, I wonder which one I'll meet, which reality is mine.

Her eyes have reddened. "I don't understand . . ." Her voice cracks. "I'm sorry." I can't tell if she's apologizing for her confusion or more than that.

"You used to fawn over Poppy, Rose, and Daisy—"

"I thought you liked being with your father more," she says, skimming a finger beneath her eye, skillfully not smudging her mascara. "He loved taking you to Fizzle's offices, and Loren was your best friend . . . We gave you so much. It doesn't make sense to me. I'm sorry, Lily."

Water drips down my cheeks. Maybe our perceptions of our lives are too disjointed to ever fit together. Maybe we all think too differently to bridge at a common point. "Do you love me?" I ask.

She suddenly steps closer and hugs me. Like a motherly embrace that I've seen her share with Daisy all the time. The one where she wraps her arms around me, placing a hand on my back. Her lips are near my ear as she says, "I've always loved you, Lily. You're my daughter." She draws back and brushes my tears away, careful to not poke me with her manicured nails. "I'm sorry if I didn't show it in the way you wanted . . ."

It's a backhanded apology, but one I cherish very much. Partly because I know it may be all I ever receive. "Can you stop punishing me for my mistakes?" I ask her, the avalanche of silent tears starting up again. "Please?"

She's crying. Her hand falls, and she's no longer attempting to dam her waterworks. She nods tensely. "You were always so shy when you were little . . . I thought it was better to let you be."

"I just wanted to know that you cared."

"I do care about you," she says strongly, touching her chest. "I'm sorry . . . for things I may have said in the past. I was hurt . . ." She has this look in her eye that says: *I want things to be different.* I do too. For so long I've wanted that. But we've both just never confronted each other until now.

Years.

It took years for this moment to occur.

She strokes my short hair and asks, "What can we do to make this better?" Her arm is still around me. She sniffs loudly, something unladylike. But I've never seen my mother cry this much. I think all this time, we've just been viewing the same story through opposite lenses. My picture wasn't hers. And even now, we're not seeing exactly the same portrait, but at least it's in the right frame.

That has to be enough. "I need to know that you'll treat my son the way you treat Rose's daughter. No favoritism." That's what I want most of all. "Is that possible?"

I wait for her answer with more hope in my heart than I've ever had before.

Forty-six

Loren Hale

I press my ear against the oak door, shoving Rose in the shoulder as she tries to wedge past me. I rushed downstairs when Connor told me that Lily was having "the" talk with her mom.

Their voices have quieted, barely audible through the wood. "Fuck," Ryke curses as Rose elbows him in the ribs.

"Shhh, I can't hear the rest," Rose hisses.

"Children," Connor says from the hallway. He leans against the charcoal-gray-painted wall, watching the three of us fight for prime real estate against the door. "Patience is considered a virtue to some."

Daisy sits on the ground beside him, eating a cherry Popsicle as she watches us. "Just let Rose at the door, and she can translate for all of us."

"We already tried that," I remind Daisy. "She was terrible at it." Rose delivered cliff notes half the time. And the other half, she didn't even bother to relay the information.

Just as Rose opens her mouth to snap back, the door swings open. Samantha Calloway stands poised and rolls her eyes at the sight of us. It reminds me so much of Rose that I have to bite my tongue to swallow a retort. Comparing Rose to her mother, out loud, is a low blow that I'd like to avoid.

Anyway, I don't believe Rose is *exactly* like Samantha. For starters, she's more self-aware. I listened to what Samantha had to say to Lily, and honestly, it was ass-backward. Samantha should've apologized to Lil first. She should've admitted to treating her differently than her other daughters. But she just doesn't get it. I don't think she ever will.

There's one thing I never want to do—and it's be so blind to my kid's life because I can't see my own faults.

The room silences the longer Samantha lingers in the doorway. Despite seeming strict, her blush is tear-streaked and her eyes are red.

"Where are the babies?" Samantha asks, skirting past Rose's body. "I want to see them before I go."

Rose pulls away from the door. "They're in the nursery. You can follow me there." Rose cautiously glances back at Lily on her way out, but Lil is still hidden in the sunroom.

My pulse skips, and I force the door open wider. Lily sits on a wicker ottoman, her eyes swollen and her head hanging in exhaustion.

I slide between the door and Ryke's chest, trying to enter the room. Lil rubs her eyes by the time I kneel in front of her, collecting her hands in mine. I kiss her cheek and whisper, "You did good, Lil. I'm proud of you." She needed to confront her mom. The silence had been eating at her for years.

"She said she's going to treat him just like Jane." Lily sniffs before she cries heavily again. I stand and wrap my arms around her thin body, lifting her to her feet. She rests against my chest and stares up at me. "I never thought she'd try, but she said that she wants us to have a better relationship."

I nod a couple times. "That's good, Lil." I'm always going to be cautious of Samantha. I can't help it. My barriers will rise if Lil drops hers. And she should try to lower hers some. That's her mom at the end of the day.

"I know she doesn't understand me completely or what happened," Lily whispers, her hands tightening around me. "But she can have her truth, and I can have mine. It's better than a lifelong standstill." She must be thinking of Moffy.

She's willing to bury this fight for our son. Closing old wounds.

Our choices will affect him, and for the rest of our lives, we'll make decisions in his best interest, not ours. I thought it was going to be hard—being selfless. But when you love someone with the deepest parts of your soul, they become your biggest exception.

I know he's ours.

Forty-seven

Lily Calloway

My fiancé is the sexiest person on earth. Fact. It's a biased fact, but many people would agree with me if they had my view.

I brace the red sheet to my chest, my back against the headboard, and gawk as Lo walks buck naked to the bathroom. His ass. His muscular back. His lean, toned body. I am in my kinda heaven.

I'm sure he's grinning, aware that I'm filing this mental image in my spank bank for eternity. It will remain in a section called *naughty things*. Granted, that portion of my brain is jam-packed with Loren Hale.

He disappears behind the wall. All the pictures pop in an instant. "We should go again," I call out, scooting to the edge of the bed and bringing the heavy champagne-colored comforter with me. "We need to make up for lost time."

Today is *the* day.

We've already had sex once. The kind that slams backs into walls and causes the bed to aggressively shake. I'm ready for a round two. Possibly even a three or a four. If I can control myself. The insatiable beast has to remain locked away, and I'll need to stop when I have to stop.

He returns from the bathroom with a glass of water, taking small sips.

"I've overworked you?" I ask with a frown.

He gives me a look like *really? Because I'm drinking water?* His brow ticks upward a notch. "You think this is work for me?"

"You get all sweaty and out of breath so . . . yeah," I mutter. "It can be work for me too though." My words tumble out fast. "Lots of limber positions and . . . stuff." *Shut up, Lily.*

I twist in the sheet and comforter, tangling up and being suffocated by the fabric. After a quick decision, I roll onto my belly, untwisting a bit. Now I'm in the perfect position for my *favorite* position. I prop myself on my elbows and peek back at Lo.

He's watching me intently while he casually sips his water. Torture. Sheer torture.

"You just gonna stand there?" I ask.

"Maybe."

I squint. "Are you teasing me or do you need some help . . . ?" I flush. "You know . . ." I nod toward his cock, which doesn't look like it needs any aid. *Good job, Lil.* I internally give myself a pity-pat on the shoulder.

"It's me, love," he says, sauntering to the dresser. He finishes off his water and sets the glass down. "You don't have to be embarrassed to say what you mean."

He nears the bed and climbs on top, the mattress rocking with his weight. His hands travel up my hips, and he easily flips me onto my back again. His eyes dance across my flushed face.

"So say what you mean," Lo says in a soft voice, his warm breath tickling my flesh as his mouth descends toward my chest. He sucks gently on my nipple, teasing.

"Hmm . . ." My eyes flutter closed at the new sensation. I clutch the sheet underneath me. "Do you . . . want me to give you a hand job or a . . . a . . ." *think, Lily!* ". . . a blow job?" I open one eye and then both, smiling. Nailed it.

His tongue flicks the sensitive bud before he says, "No. But that's adorable of you to ask."

"Now your turn." I nudge his leg with my foot.

His lips lift in amusement. "Lily Calloway, would you like me to give you a hand job?" *Yes*. His palm brushes over the tender spot between my thighs. A gasp catches in my throat. "Or head?" *Double yes*. He kisses a trail from my breast to my belly button and down, down, *down*.

I almost moan as his mouth reaches *the best spot ever*. But he stops just before he relieves any ache. He raises his head once more, awaiting my answer. I'd love to say yes to both, but I would love both of us to get off even more.

"Or," I say with a shallow breath. "Option C." I go to turn over again, but he grips my hip bones firmly, keeping me flat on my back. That didn't work.

"Option D," he combats. That sounds good. All I hear is *Option Dick*. My mind, I tell you. No one should be allowed to enter. I absorb each little movement he makes. Still kneeling, he snatches a pillow and stuffs it underneath my bottom.

He begins to peel off the sheets and comforter, exposing my naked body. My heart drums with each passing second. I remember the days where I'd jump him right off the bat. Where I couldn't control myself. But I take pleasure in this moment, in his self-assuredness and ability to please me so entirely.

I can lie here and watch and wait. It builds me to a better place.

His hand skims the length of my leg before he lifts both of them higher. Then he bends my knees, tucking my leg underneath his arm, grasping the other. My heart misses a beat as his pelvis fits perfectly against my entrance.

Missionary. Anal sex. Together, this has become way more intimate.

Slowly, he fills me, every inch of his hardness ignites fireworks inside my body. The most electric, sweltering sensations that I want to bask under night and day. When I've taken all of him, he leans forward and kisses me deeply.

I struggle to reciprocate, heady and dazed. "Lo," I whimper against his lips.

"Relax, love," he coaxes. And then he thrusts. Deep and rhythmic. I grip his hard biceps and focus on keeping my legs raised so he can go further. I inhale sporadically, short breaths that sound like gasps. One minute in, and I stop exhaling, my head dizzying with this bliss.

Lo pauses mid-thrust. "Breathe."

I buck against him, trying to complete his cock's travel. Lo drops one of my legs and grips my hip instead, his fingers digging into my flesh. "*Breathe.*"

Okay. Okay. I take a deep breath, my head less light than before and my chest not as constricted. Satisfied, he continues his course. His gaze carries this hypnotic intensity that pulls me under, amber swirls filled with lust and passion and want.

Cravings that mirror mine.

My nerves sing in euphoria, and then his hand finds my wetness, his fingers filling me even more. I moan into this bed, not able to keep eye contact anymore. The world is spinning. His movements in sync. His fingers. His cock. They pound, pound, pound. His breathing as ragged as mine. His mouth that falls open in pleasure.

He is ice. So cold it burns.

My moans escalate, uncontrollable.

And then the worst sound in the entire world breaches our bedroom.

Crying.

Babies crying.

My heart catapults. "Stopstopstop," I slur together. My eyes flit to the baby monitor, the light blinking as the noises emit from the speakers. I frantically push him off, even though he's already backing away.

In a panic, I jump off the bed and throw on one of Lo's baggy crew neck shirts. The black fabric falls just above my knees.

"Lil, calm down. He's fine. He can cry for a bit and be okay," Lo consoles.

No. I made a promise to never choose sex over him. This is my first real test. And I'm going to pass. "I'm going to check on him," I say, tying my damp hair into a messy bun. "You can finish yourself off in the bathroom."

Surprise shrouds his face. "Did you just tell me to masturbate?"

Yeah, that happens *never*.

I don't have time to answer him. I'm already on my way to the door. He sprints after me before I open it, and his hand catches hold of the wood, blocking me in.

"Lo," I whine. I cringe at my voice.

"Take some breaths," he tells me. "I don't want you to panic every time this happens. Just relax, okay?"

Deep down, he must sense that this is more than just a baby crying. "I'm relaxed," I say in a stiff voice.

"You have nothing to prove, Lil."

A lump rises in my throat. "You don't have to masturbate," I tell him. "If you can wait for me, we can finish together later."

"Yeah?" he asks.

I nod.

"If I open this door, will you promise to walk to the nursery and not run?"

"Promise." I hold up my pinky, and instead of hooking his with mine, he kisses me on the lips. My heart thumps, and then he draws back, removing his hand from the doorframe.

I gingerly walk down the hallway, all the while feeling his hot gaze on my back. When I slip into the nursery, I pick up my pace and dart to Moffy's crib.

"Hey, shhh, it's okay," I whisper, lifting him in my arms. I check his diaper. Clean. And then I start the good ol' pat-and-rock technique, attempting to calm down a six-week-old baby. He's not supposed to be eating for another hour.

From the nursery across from Moffy's, Jane cries incessantly. I peek out into the hallway and crane my neck. Connor and Rose's bedroom door is still closed. We all agreed on not employing the "cry it out" parenting method since there are two newborns in the house. It's just way too loud.

If Jane keeps crying, Maximoff won't stop.

A second later, Lo exits our bedroom in a pair of black drawstring pants. I glance at his crotch. What happened?

"I couldn't wait." He kisses me on the cheek. "Sorry, love." And then he rubs Moffy's little head and tuft of dark brown hair. "You hate your cousin's crying, don't you, bud?"

And like magic, my sister's bedroom door blows open. Connor appears—holy shit. I don't have anything to shield my eyes with. My hands are occupied with a baby. "Lo," I call for help.

He easily reads my thoughts, based on my red flush and alarm. His palm covers my eyes, even if it's a little too late. I saw Connor's bare chest, glistening with sweat. And *more* than that. *His* drawstring pants are way more revealing than Lo's. Maybe because he's in the moment where there is much more to be revealed.

Oh my God. *Forget, Lily, forget.*

I'm trying.

"Excited to see me?" Lo banters.

"Always, darling," he replies lightly. "Sorry I took so long, Lily." Lo drops my hand about the same time that Connor disappears into Jane's nursery. A safe view.

I rock Moffy in my arms, but his blubbering doesn't cease. It's most likely because of Jane, but my nerves only heighten. Feeling helpless, I pat him a little more. Hoping he'll calm soon.

"Here." Lo collects our son from me, and the wails grow, more high-pitched and screechy. It's like daggers in my heart. "It's okay, little guy. You're safe with us."

Jane's screams soften. Maybe he had to change her diaper, or she wanted to be held. Connor leaves the nursery a minute later, even though Jane hasn't stopped completely. Lo and I are in the doorway, waiting for her to quiet so Maximoff can go to bed.

"She's still crying," I state the obvious.

Connor hesitates in the hall, his eyes flitting to his bedroom in concern. "I have to check on Rose for a second," he tells us quickly. "I'll be right back. I promise."

"Wait, what?" Lo snaps. "Look, Moffy won't stop unless Jane does. Can you please deal with your baby first?" I'm about to offer some help. Lo can rock Moffy and I'll take care of Jane, but Connor speaks fast and walks even quicker.

"In five seconds, I won't be alive long enough to deal with my baby." When he opens his door, I hear Rose curse him out.

My eyes widen. "Do you think she's like . . ." Tied up? I can't even utter the words. It's not an image I want in my head.

Lo cringes. "Let's not go there." Fine with me.

I kiss Moffy's head and rub his small back while Lo bounces him lightly. We wait for a couple minutes before both Rose and Connor emerge from their bedroom together. Rose, in a black silk robe, has reddened, flushed cheeks. She looks more pissed than aroused.

When she sees us, she points at Connor. "Blame him."

"What'd he do to you?" Lo asks in jest. "Steal your broomstick?"

She glares. "I'm not telling you." And then she stomps into the nursery with her husband. In an instant, Jane's cries start to die down.

"Thank God," Lo mutters. Maximoff's eyes start fluttering closed, his lips parted as he breathes.

I smile at him, running my finger over his smooth cheek. "Do you think they'll be friends?"

"Who?" His brows scrunch. "Janie and Moffy?"

I nod, trying not to smile too much at Jane's nickname, also coined by Ryke. Connor and Rose have made a point not to use it, but it's going to catch on. And I envision Maximoff growing up with his best friend Janie.

Even though he'll never have siblings, he'll have her. And I bet he'll look after her too. If he's anything like his dad, he'll want to keep Jane safe.

"As much as the idea of Rose's spawn terrifies me," Lo says in a quiet voice, setting Moffy back in his crib, "I would kind of love them being friends."

"Me too," I whisper. After leaving the nursery, we both tiptoe back to our room, and when Lo shuts the door, his attention turns to me.

His hands lower to my waist. "Finish what we started?"

It takes me a moment to realize that he's talking about sex. A light bursts in my brain, bright and beautiful. I'm not as evil as I thought I'd be.

Lo said as much.

"I love you," I tell him. He's my teammate. My sidekick. The person I want to tag in for every tough moment in my life. My very own Scott Summers.

Forty-eight

Lily Calloway

> tweet: Getting ready for Hale Co. charity event with my sisters #raiding-RoseCobaltcloset

I attach a photo of Daisy and me jumping on Rose's bed. I'm a bit blurry and flailing in the pic, but Daisy looks cool, her fists raised and platinum blonde hair sticking up mid-bounce.

"Try these on, Lily," Rose says, splaying a gray Calloway Couture dress beside a lilac one on the edge of the bed. Right as I climb off the light blue comforter, my phone chimes in quick succession, a bunch of Twitter notifications.

"Did you tweet?" Rose asks flatly. She tightens the strap to her silk robe. Like Daisy, I'm only in a bra and panties while we figure out what to wear. But I made sure we were fully clothed when we took the earlier pic.

"Maybe . . ." I hesitate. "The publicists never said *no*." I'll admit, the response, at first, wasn't what I wanted. *Celebrity Crush* ate up a story about how I was "trying too hard" to promote Raisy. But the fans seem to like all the interaction. Like photos of Lo and my sisters and status updates. Since *Princesses of Philly* ended, people are naturally curious about our daily lives.

I'd rather give them the real story than the media create something fake. And with social media, we have the chance to do that.

I even expressed this to my mom yesterday (in person) over coffee at Lucky's, and she agreed with me. Like really, *really* agreed.

"Mom said it was a good idea," I remind Rose.

She rolls her eyes. "Of course she does. She wants our family to be relevant for as long as possible."

"But this is something in our control," I express. "And we're a part of a *fandom*." There is nothing more exciting than that.

Rose stays quiet on the matter, straightening the fabric of the gray dress, but I can tell she's mulling over the idea of social media.

I check the Twitter replies and smile.

@ToriKPierce3: @lilycallowayX23 Lucky! I want to raid Rose's closet too!

@Pippa_Woo: @lilycallowayX23 ILY! OMG!

"Speaking of fans," Daisy says with a mischievous smile. She pulls out a manila package from her purse.

I frown while Rose's back arches in sisterly protection.

"Security goes through fan mail now," Rose retorts. She stopped opening the mail about the same time people were sending her black whips, ball gags, and amateur porn videos.

"It's not fan mail." Daisy jumps up on the bed theatrically and pumps the package in the air. "I was browsing through fan sites, and I stumbled on a merchandise store." She wags her brows, her grin so contagious that my lips curve upward.

I snatch the lilac dress before it wrinkles and watch her open the package.

Rose plants her hands on her hips, intrigue glimmering in her yellow-green eyes.

Daisy reveals a pair of boy short panties. She flashes me the butt. White letters say: *I LOVE LOREN HALE!* They even have a cute pink heart beside his name.

I wear a dopey grin. "For me?"

"Who else would they be for?" Rose snaps.

I try to shoot her a withering glare, but hers kills mine in an instant. Oh well. I'm too happy anyway.

Daisy tosses me the panties. "Will Lo like them?"

I nod repeatedly, already imagining his surprise when he sees his name on my ass. "I'm wearing these to the party."

Rose rolls her eyes again. "You're not having sex at the charity event."

"But I just like the idea of having him near my butt." I realize that came out kind of wrong. "Not like that," I add quickly and then frown. "Okay, kind of like that . . . I'm confused."

Rose sighs and ushers Daisy to keep opening the package. Rose likes presents, so maybe she's expecting a bedazzled fan shirt for herself.

Not too shy about changing in front of my sisters, I switch panties, and the new ones fit perfectly. Daisy bounces on the bed a little as she displays the next article of clothing. "I bought some too." She shows off *I LOVE RYKE MEADOWS!* panties, only with a sun instead of a heart.

"So cute," I say with a bigger smile. "You should wear them tonight too."

She nods. "Definitely."

"Please tell me there is not a matching Connor Cobalt one," Rose says with narrowed eyes. She is drilling holes into our littlest sister.

"These are *cute*," I remind Rose.

She raises her hand at my face, and then Daisy chucks a pair of black cotton panties at Rose. I sidle next to her as she inspects them.

Rose lets out an unamused laugh. "No."

They say: *I LOVE CONNOR COBALT!*

A lipstick kiss included.

"He'd love it," I tell Rose. I can see his million-dollar grin at the mere *thought* of this saying on Rose's ass.

"Exactly," she says. "I don't need to pad his ego."

Daisy laughs. "It doesn't say *Connor Cobalt is the smartest guy ever.* It just says that you love him."

I interject, "Exactly. Ha!"

"Ha nothing," Rose retorts, though the panties are still in her hands. And she still scrutinizes them more closely.

Daisy springs off the bed, landing on her feet. While she changes panties, she tells Rose, "You're not losing a game or anything. You're winning it."

I nod repeatedly. "Daisy is right. You're in a power position. You can tease him." I touch my chest. "Trust me, I know. I'm a sexpert." I never thought I'd be able to say that without blushing or feeling ashamed. I bite my gums to keep from smiling. I'm proud of myself, and it's a weird thing to be. I revel in this triumph. I'm nearing the last stretch of a long bumpy road, bruised from falling, but still running. It feels good.

"I'll never live it down if I wear these," Rose tells us, folding them neatly. She pauses, hesitates. And then begins unfolding. "Fuck it." She takes off her panties beneath her black robe.

Daisy and I hop together, cheering Rose on. "Put them on! Put them on!" we chant.

She hisses at us to be quiet, her eyes on the door like someone is going to walk in any minute. They aren't going to. It's locked—

The door swings open. I *thought* I locked it. Lo shuts it behind him, but thankfully Rose has already finished switching out her panties.

"Loren!" Rose shouts, about to claw his face to shreds.

He shields his eyes with his hand. "Jesus Christ. You're not even dressed yet?" He checks his watch. "The event starts in an hour." Daisy disappears into Rose's closet for an outfit, and I slip the lilac dress over my head.

"We were having wardrobe malfunctions," Rose lies.

Even with his eyes covered, he produces a signature half-smile that's drop-dead gorgeous. "That's not what Twitter said."

Rose glowers at me, one that should belong in the depths of hell.

I recoil, and my phone slips out of my hand, clattering to the floor. Rose follows Daisy to the closet, and I bend down to retrieve my cell.

The minute I stand back up, I spin around and lock eyes with Lo. He wears a full-on smile, no longer bitter or sarcastic. This one dimples his cheeks. I scan him from head to toe. His black tailored suit, black button-down, and red pocket square fits his personality. His longer hair on top is pushed back, the sides short in this stylish, cool way. Loren Hale is edgy. Always has been. And even if he has to please a board of fourteen people, he hasn't changed.

My whole body heats in a good-bad way. Especially as he slowly nears me, never breaking from my gaze. And then his hands fall to my waist. And then lower. To my ass. My heart thuds. Especially as his hands vanish beneath my dress.

Oh wait . . . he saw me bend down and . . .

He snaps the hem of my panties, and I almost crumble in his arms.

"Where'd you get these?" he asks, turning me around, so my ass faces him. He lifts up my dress. I'm caught already.

"They were supposed to be a surprise," I tell him as he checks out my butt, and he even squeezes. I can't—holy shit. "Lo . . ." My breath shallows.

He kisses my neck and then rotates me once more, my ass no longer his visual. My arousal has peaked a little bit. And he says, "Later tonight, I'm fucking you hard."

I nod with growing eyes. *Yes. Yes, please.*

He spanks me lightly. Oh my God. I fling my arms around his waist, holding on tight. This is nice.

"Do you need me to zip you?" he asks.

"Wha . . . ?" I frown.

"Your dress, Lil."

"Oh yeah. Sure."

Without moving me, he raises the zipper up to my shoulder blades. My sisters' chatter in the closet is muffled by the wall, and for the most part, a heavy silence falls in Rose's room.

I look up at him and realize he's no longer smiling from ear to ear. He seems far off in thought.

Under his breath, he says, "I came in here to talk to you about tonight."

"Oh . . ." It's one of the last Hale Co. events before the board picks a new CEO. During it, Moffy and Jane will be with the best babysitter in the world. Poppy even told me that was her official title, so I haven't worried too much about him.

Now the meaning behind this event hits me like a tidal wave. Lo and I haven't talked about the CEO position much. There's been this quiet understanding between Ryke, Daisy, Lo, and me that we're all trying to win the spot for each other.

Lo holds my face, his fingers now combing through my hair. "Lil . . ." His eyes bore into mine, so powerful that it steals my breath. "I need you to believe in me."

The bottom of my stomach drops. "I do . . . I always do."

He licks his lips. "Then *please*, trust me to take this job. No one thinks I can handle it, but I at least need you to."

I frown deeply. For me, it's always been more than his addiction. "I don't want you to work for Hale Co. if you don't want to."

"I'm telling you, *I want to*."

I don't know if I believe him. And that's what he's asking of me. That's the scary part.

His chest falls heavily as he reads my reaction. "Please, Lil."

He's asking me to self-sabotage. I see it in his eyes. I open my mouth but nothing comes out at first. I want to believe him. More than anything.

He draws me closer to his body. "I would be more hurt watching you in Hale Co. than I *ever* would by being there. I don't want to suffer through that. *Please*." The conviction and sincerity in his voice pushes me to one side and solidifies my choice.

I don't hesitate this time. "Okay," I agree, and my anxiety starts to lessen. I'd planned to schmooze tonight—or at least try and put my best foot forward, even if it's like swimming with sharks.

He exhales like I just lifted a hundred-pound weight off his chest. It makes me feel like I chose right this time. He hugs me and then kisses my temple. "Thank you."

I whisper, "Not that I was your biggest competition." I ranked near the bottom of the list. Daisy and Ryke are far worthier adversaries.

I can sense him smiling before I even look up. "You were a great opponent," he tells me. "I think Ryke was scared of you."

I perk up. "Really?"

He nods. "Oh yeah." He partially teases me, and I punch his arm lightly. He mock winces and rubs the spot.

"What do I do then?" I ask him. "Should I not go?"

"No, you have to go," he tells me. "Just be standoffish. Stay by a plant or something and eat."

"Like we usually do?" I ask with a smile.

He doesn't share it. "I have to talk with the board, so you'll be alone . . ."

Oh. Right. "Yeah, yeah," I say softly. "I can be aloof though." It's my natural state of being. "I'm rooting for you, just so you know."

He breaks into a laugh, his eyes welling with tears—like it's the first time he's heard those words. In this context, I realize that it most likely is.

My heart swells. Yep, I'm rooting for you, Loren Hale. *You got this.*

Forty-nine

Loren Hale

Hale Co. has thrown a massive fall charity event in support of a children's hospital downtown. By massive, everyone with deep pockets in Philly was invited, regardless if they're involved with Hale Co. or not.

It's simple. Serve drinks, good food, and have people share their stories of how Hale Co. reached out to them when they were in need. Afterward, people will open their checkbooks. I've been to so many of these that they feel more routine than any school function would.

I sip a glass of water while a speaker finishes her story, and then I head toward the crowds to find Daniel Perth, one of the board members. But I don't have to squeeze between bodies. The moment I step near, they break for me.

Seas of people create paths, just so that I can pass through. I've never been anything more than a nuisance. I expect glares to drill into me. But they just nod and smile. It's been like this all night. I feel different. Older. Stronger.

I carry more confidence in my gait, and I wonder if, all this time, I just needed to believe in myself. And then I'd receive this response. It overwhelms me in ways I can't explain.

But I just move forward.

A minute later, I find Daniel by the cheese and wine bar with three other board members. One female, two males.

Daniel raises his red wine in welcome. "Enjoying yourself?"

"The wine could be better," I banter with a half-smile.

He laughs at the joke and pats my shoulder. "I was just telling Irene about your idea for a designer clothes line for infants and toddlers."

Irene, a severe woman with a narrowed stare, tries to crush me beneath a harsh gaze. I return hers with a colder one, not at all intimidated by her or him or any one of the board members. They don't compare to my father. Not even close.

Her lips twitch into a smile as she asks, "Are you sure you can have Rose Calloway agree to this partnership?"

"We're not best friends," I say dryly, "but I know I can convince her."

"How so?" Irene looks doubtful as she eats a cracker.

"Because she's like my bratty older sister. Even though we can't stand each other at times, we still love one another, and she'd be willing to do this for me." I know she would. "Though, she'll need to be a partner in that division. Rose likes her titles, and she won't want to take orders from me." I'm always honest with the board.

I decided early on that I won't lie for anything anymore. It's not healthy. It's not worth the pain. And if I want to live my life as a better, more whole person, this is what I have to do. It's like I can breathe with every sentence. I'm no longer dreading my future.

For the first time, I yearn for tomorrow and cherish yesterday and live for today. It's peace that no one will take from me.

"You should talk to her and start pitching names for the clothing line," Daniel says as he finishes off his wine.

Irene nods. "It's a strong concept, and most women like Rose."

Another guy asks, "Are you prepared to work with her?" He

wears a bemused smile like he understands Rose's reputation for being a handful.

"I am. And if we don't kill each other, I'll call it a success."

They all laugh. I understand that they're used to someone like me. I pretty much share the same humor as my dad, so it doesn't fall on deaf ears. I've fit in more easily with them than I ever thought I would.

"Hey." My brother's voice sounds behind me. He sets a hand on my shoulder. "Can I talk to you for a second?"

"Yeah." I nod to Daniel. "I'll talk to you all later."

"Maybe the wine will grow on you by then," Daniel jokes.

"If only," I banter back, my brother's fingertips digging into my shoulder. I turn around quickly and head over to an empty high-top table by the wall.

He starts, "You're not drinking—"

"No," I retort. "It was just a joke." *One I can fucking handle.* My clutch on my glass tightens, especially as I scrutinize his wardrobe again.

He's wearing a business suit, something my dad loved seeing him in. Navy blue, tailored, wide tie. He even shaved this morning, an attempt to try harder and be something he's not.

"You look stupid," I tell him.

Ryke glares. "I heard you the first four fucking times."

I feel my jaw jut out as I clench my teeth. I hate that he's taking this route to win. He's cursed out too many of the board members to be a real option anyway. He can try to change his appearance, but he can't change a lot of things that make him who he is.

And honestly, I thank God for that.

"What did you want?" I ask.

He runs an anxious hand through his hair. I notice dark circles under his eyes, like he hasn't slept much. "Have you seen Dad's text?" I realize he's grasping his cell phone in a fist.

My brows knot in confusion, and I pull my cell from my pocket. I set it on silent for the event. With one click, I scroll through all the missed messages.

> New standings. Maybe this will put a fire under your asses tonight. —Dad

I skim all four texts, sent almost at the same time.

> Lily Calloway: the board thinks you're still too quiet. And since Maximoff's birth, you've become aloof and disinterested. 4 out of 14 board members approve. —Dad

I look over my shoulder. Lingering by the chocolate fountain, Lily snacks on cheese cubes with a toothpick. I'd feel guiltier by leaving her alone if she didn't have this silly grin on her face. She's absorbed in her new smart phone—social media, I'm pretty damn sure.

I'm happy that it's making her happy and not the inverse for once.

I try to let out a breath. She's out of the running. She won't go out of her way to try either. It's less pressure on me. It makes this easier.

I swallow hard and continue reading.

> Loren Hale: everyone is overall impressed (as they should be). They find you charming, likeable and tough. The few that had problems with me are still hesitant on committing to you. 11 out of 14 love you. —Dad

How do I even convince these last three to like me? I'm so much like my dad. I internally grimace as I contemplate different avenues. I try to block them out before I read on.

> Ryke Meadows: you've vastly improved. You're approachable and show willingness to change. The majority believe you'd be a strong leader for the company. 11 out of 14 love you. —Dad

My stomach sinks and cold bites my neck. I'd counted my brother out for the past month. I go rigid, not able to say anything. My eyes hit the screen again.

> Daisy Calloway: you've shown maturity and seem genuinely interested in the company. You're also beyond personable with great energy and enthusiasm. 13 of the 14 love you. Irene hesitates to have you as CEO. She thinks you're too wild and young. Find a way to please her, and the company is yours. Congratulations. —Dad

Now I understand why Ryke rushed over to me. A worse outcome than Ryke taking over the company would be Daisy. My brother's features are hard as rock.

"This can't fucking happen." He points at my phone.

I pocket my cell. "What you're feeling now is self-inflicted," I shoot back. "You can end this—"

"Fucking stop," he growls lowly.

I shake my head. "All you have to do is tell her. Just say it, bro. You'd rather the position go to *me* than her." He thinks he's subjecting me to hell, but he's not. It's not unbearable. This is where I was always supposed to be.

"I can't fucking choose *her* over you, or vice versa." Darkness sweeps over his face like a passing storm.

It's like this is a sin he refuses to commit. "It's *not* a sin," I tell him outright. "I'm not going to hate you for choosing a better life for the girl you love. I'm not that fucking guy." *Not anymore.*

He stays silent, his muscles constricted.

So I lick my lips and add, "Let's do this together. You and me, like we were supposed to do from the beginning. It'll be a fair fight. We're even right now. Just get Daisy the hell out of this." And then I'll find a way to win. There is no way that I'll let my brother live this kind of life. It's not even remotely something he'd want.

He's just too selfless to let me have it without a fight.

Ryke opens and closes his fists. Even when he's in deep contemplation, he looks aggressive. After a long moment, he says, "Fuck." He lets out a pained laugh. "She's not even a Hale."

"Neither are you."

His face contorts in a cringe. "Don't justify what you're doing, Lo."

I grit my teeth. "I'm just stating a goddamn fact. Another fact—she's beating our asses. So unless she self-sabotages, she's going to be handed the company. You and I both know that's a darker fucking world for her than it would be for us."

Ryke rests his hands on his head for a second and then drops them. He just shakes his head over and over.

"This isn't going to break me," I tell him. "But it'll ruin her. Do you want to live with that?"

He looks sick to his stomach. "No . . . but—"

"There is no *but*," I force, setting a hand on his shoulder so his gaze lifts to mine. "This is it."

A full minute of pure silence passes between us, the type that vacuums the air. And then he says, "I need you to come with me."

I frown. "Why?"

"If I'm going to convince Daisy to self-sabotage, we need to gang up on her."

Fifty

Loren Hale

I just barely wrap my head around this plan before Ryke adds something else.

"Don't expect me to fucking lie down and give this to you," he says quickly. "If you *really* fucking want this, Lo, you have to beat me for it."

He doesn't think I can. At the start of this, I would've agreed. Years ago, I wouldn't have even tried, knowing the end result would be the same.

Fuck that guy.

There is nothing that says I can't measure up to my older brother.

I may be a bastard, a failure, a natural-born loser, but I can win in the end. For once in my goddamn life, I'm going to do it.

Hey, guys . . ." Daisy says hesitantly. We've dragged her away from Irene to the lobby outside of the hotel's ballroom. It's quiet, except for the occasional server that passes through with empty trays of food.

Ryke and I have our arms crossed, towering over her. Even so, she stands straight, unflinching. "Let's try this again," Ryke tells her. "I don't fucking want you taking this position."

She sighs. "Ryke—"

"I've thought about it," he cuts her off, "and I've decided that I'd rather Lo become CEO than you. So you can stop fighting for this and start cheering on my brother."

Daisy laughs like he's joking, but our no-nonsense postures never change. Her laughter dies. "I don't want you to choose me over him."

My ribs constrict, and I expect this to pain Ryke enough to retract his statement.

Instead, he says, "Too fucking bad, Calloway. I chose you."

She hesitates, and so I interject. "Come on, Daisy. You're not a Hale. It's weird if you steal this position from me. It's *mine*."

Her shoulders drop and begin to curve inward. She meets my edged features still. Not scared off by them. "I worry about you and . . ." She can't finish that statement. But I get it.

My lips lift in an agitated smile. "You think this'll push me to drink?" It sucks that Lily's little sister sees me like a breakable doll. I have been put together too many times to let Hale Co. pull me under.

"We all do . . ." she replies, looking to Ryke for affirmation. *Stay fucking strong,* I glare at him.

He does well, not once shifting toward me or wavering with an unsure glance. He just focuses on his girlfriend. "Lo can handle it."

The foreign words ring in my ear. Even if it's constructed for Daisy, I like hearing that phrase from my brother.

"See," I add to her with the tilt of my head. "I haven't self-destructed yet."

"This is between Lo and me." Ryke layers it on, not letting up. "This isn't about you, Dais."

The guilt trip actually works this time. She can't meet our eyes anymore. She concentrates on the carpet like the ugly fucking gold pattern is suddenly more interesting than this conversation.

"Come here," Ryke breathes as he seizes her hand and tugs her to his chest. She hides her face in a hug, and he places a consoling hand on her head. "We're not trying to beat you down, Dais. We're just trying to make you understand."

"Okay," she suddenly murmurs.

Ryke and I exchange surprise. "Okay what?" I ask.

She takes a single step back with a heavy exhale. "Okay, I'll self-sabotage." Her green eyes flit to ours. "If that's what you both want . . ."

"It is," we say in unison.

She twists the bottom of her white blouse, untucked from her green skirt. "So next week, I can—"

"No, *tonight*," Ryke almost growls out the word. He's nervous about her winning before then. I am too, but he cares more deeply for Daisy. His concern is a higher wattage than mine.

"Tonight?" she repeats, her mouth dropping. "Ryke, this is a *charity* event."

I cut in, "I'm going to write a check, so it'll make up for whatever happens." I know that's not the right thing to say. Daisy looks petrified, her eyes widening at the thought of hurting people. She's not going to, but in her mind, maybe that's what she sees.

Ryke cups her face, and she stares only at him. "Dais, we're not asking you to humiliate yourself or anyone around you. Just throw out this fucking etiquette book your mother gave you, and do what you feel."

She blinks back tears. It's hard to watch, but I can't turn away either. "Maybe . . . next week," she hesitates.

"No." Ryke pulls her into his body with both hands on her cheeks. "Today, tomorrow—be wild, Calloway."

She inhales strongly. "What if that's not who I am?"

"Then be who you are, sweetheart," Ryke says passionately. "But don't change for them."

Daisy fingers his business suit, and I think she's going to comment on it. Maybe this fight is a sore one because she doesn't mention the change he's made for the company. Though, she stands on the tips of her toes to kiss his shaven jaw. He tenses, and then she lands on her feet. "Don't stop me," she tells us, and she actually smiles, her eyes twinkling deviously.

"I rarely do," Ryke reminds her.

She blows out a breath like she's embracing something inside of her that she's locked away these past months. And then she begins walking backward toward the ballroom door. Her grin grows as she plants a playful gaze on Ryke.

I have no idea what she's about to do, to be honest. I just hope it's enough to persuade the board that she's too reckless to be a CEO. That she's still young.

She pushes through the doors, and we're close behind. In the packed conference room, Daisy wags her brows at us, then spins toward the groups of boisterous people, no one on stage right now.

She does one cartwheel, and her skirt flies up to her waist. Revealing underwear that says . . . I roll my eyes. But the similar underwear reminds me of Lily.

Beside the chocolate fountain, Lil holds a stick with a banana. A smile overtakes me. It's an old trick of ours. Act like you're contemplating dipping a piece of food into the fountain when you're just killing time.

I peel my gaze off her and onto my brother. He's trying to suppress a rare smile of his own, completely infatuated with Daisy. She's on the fourth cartwheel and gathered more attention from people. When she does a handstand, people watch her. A few board members shake their head in disapproval.

I LOVE RYKE MEADOWS is upside down.

I catch a few people snapping photos with their camera phones. That was expected.

"Your name is on her ass," I state blankly.

"I'm so fucking in love with her," is all he says. And I believe every word.

When she drops her feet, she takes a small bow, and a couple guys clap. Probably for showing her ass. I shoot them a look, but that doesn't stop them from ogling Daisy. It irritates me, but that feeling vanishes the moment Daisy locks eyes with my brother.

The moment she *runs* straight out of the ballroom with the biggest, brightest smile. She's a ball of light that Ryke is going to catch up to. I can see it in his eyes.

And he's off behind her.

I head to the window that overlooks the street, and I feel a presence slide next to me. Chocolate banana in hand, Lily presses her nose close to the glass. "What are we looking at?"

"Your sister, my brother," I tell her.

I wait for them to exit onto the street. It's something Daisy would do. And maybe three minutes pass before a platinum-blonde girl sprints out of the hotel and into the parking lot. She removes her shirt and her skirt as she races forward. We're only on the third floor, so I make out her overpowering smile.

It's like watching someone break free.

And my brother—he runs after her. I know everyone thinks he chased Daisy to stop her. They were nodding in approval about it as he left, but he wasn't.

As soon as he falls in line with Daisy, he runs by her side.

"They're going to last," Lily says with a hopeful nod.

Yeah. They just might. I tear my attention off the window and onto her. She's pulled out her cell and concentrates on typing. "What're you doing, Lil?"

"Tweeting," she says and then flashes me the screen: I'm Crazy for Raisy.

I mock wince and shield my eyes. "Christ, Lil, you blinded me with Team Raisin."

"*Raisy,*" she corrects me with squinted eyes. She's so fucking adorable.

"*Raisin*." I drop my hand and draw her body to mine. "It's my favorite ship name. Let it be."

Her jaw unhinges. "Your favorite—" I cover her mouth.

"Not my top favorite." And my lips brush her ear. I can't stop smiling. Not anymore. "My absolutely, without a doubt, favorite . . ." I pause with a breath. ". . . is *ours*." Then I kiss her.

I kiss her like I need her soul tangled with mine.

She kisses back like it's happened already for years.

I almost forget about the last couple of steps I have to take with Hale Co. I almost forget about someday soon needing to beat my brother. But the unwritten future still lingers in the back of my mind.

Fifty-one

Lily Calloway

Y ou did what?" Lo gapes at Connor, and my eyes threaten to pop out of my head.

We're surrounded by bottles of Ziff, stacked in pyramids on tables. September gusts of wind threaten to knock them over, but many Fizzle employees stand guard. A terrifying one-hundred-fifty-foot-tall cliff towers behind us: all gray rock and green foliage. Ryke stands at the base with Daisy and my dad before the media and public appear to kick-start the Ziff event.

However, my attention remains strictly on Connor, who cradles Jane while she naps. It's not his daughter that's alarmed me either. It's the words he just uttered.

"Whaa . . ." I actually begin to say aloud.

"I know," Rose says, crossing her arms. "I already yelled at him for not bringing me along." She purses her lips like that's his greatest offense.

No. That's beside the point.

"Next time, I'll tag you in, darling." Connor uses his free hand to comb Rose's hair onto one shoulder, and then he kisses her bare neck lightly. It's a regal, effortless kiss that has Rose *almost* flushing.

"Good." She raises her chin.

My mouth is on the floor. Or rather, the earthy ground. Are Lo and I the sane, mature ones here? The world is really upside down.

"You're both officially insane," Lo beats me to that comment. "We agreed not to confront the teenagers or their parents."

Connor's brows pinch in this conceited fashion. "By history alone, I'm the most qualified to reason with their parents."

"We should've *talked* about it," Lo snaps. "This affects everyone, Connor."

Connor's jaw muscles tick, a single sign of his true emotions. "No offense, but I didn't feel the need to ask for your permission, or for Ryke's, when my wife and my daughter were shot with a water gun on our front porch."

"Fruit punch, not water," Rose corrects him. "And they owe me a new fucking dress." I didn't see it happen. Yesterday, Rose was alone with Jane, switching out the welcome mat to a fall-themed one. She had Jane in her arms when the teenagers sprayed her with fruit punch.

I kinda wish I saw Connor's reaction when he returned from work and learned about the ordeal. But maybe this was it. He was livid enough to storm over to the house and confront their parents.

"I said a water gun. I didn't say that it was filled with water," Connor retorts.

Rose whips her head to him. "One detail, Richard. You were wrong about one *small* detail."

"If that were true, I'd agree with you," he says smoothly, his lips beginning to rise. "But it's not, Rose." Normally I love a good flirt-fight, but the nerd stars need to cool it right now because we're still partially in the dark about the teenagers and parents.

Rose sighs heavily and glances at Jane in his arms. "I pray that your narcissism isn't seeping into our daughter."

"Narcissism can't *seep*. It's not tangible, and who are you praying to, darling?"

"Any god that will tell me why I procreated with you."

He grins fully, a blinding million-dollar one. "Because I love you just as you love me."

Rose presses her lips together, but she shifts closer to him. "That wasn't meant for you to prove that you're a god, Richard."

He laughs into a brighter smile and then kisses her forehead.

"Can we please get back to the real problem here?" Lo asks with a narrowed stare. "You talked to the Patricks, and you haven't even said how it went." All Connor mentioned was that he spoke to the Patricks, who live three houses down from ours. That was enough to put my mind in a tailspin.

Connor seems casual and calm, but his smile has vanished from sight. "If I knew I was trying to reason with a household full of morons, I would have dumbed down my opening speech."

It went badly then.

Lo glares at the sky like *why, God, why?* Our son wiggles in a navy-blue sling across Lo's chest, and he rocks him a little.

I have to catch myself from staring too hard. Lo holding Moffy in the sling has topped the cuteness charts. Even *Celebrity Crush* featured photos of them calling Lo "one of the hottest celebrity dads."

It's undeniable.

"I don't like paraphrasing, but the conversation was honestly too aggravating to repeat," Connor says, adjusting his daughter as she wakes from her nap. Just before Jane lets out a boisterous wail, Rose digs into her black Chanel diaper bag to retrieve a soft stuffed lion. The moment Jane's tiny arms cling to the animal, she quiets.

I think we're all glad Jane has grown attached to the toy.

"The cliff notes version." Lo waves Connor on.

"They repeated the same phrase at least five times. *It was a water gun, not a real gun.*" He pauses, and I can kinda tell that he's struggling to remain composed. "Their argument was that all teenagers like to have fun, and I should remember being their age and doing the same exact things myself. As a result, I should let this pass." Connor lets out a weak laugh, and he shakes his head. "But I was never a normal teenager. I didn't do the same exact things, and a deep part of me believes I *shouldn't* let it pass."

"But you're going to?" Lo says, as if Connor needs to stick to the original "wait it out" plan. The uneasiness makes me queasy. I just don't want this to escalate any further, but I also don't want to cause a media uproar.

"I'm not going to file a complaint," Connor says. "If a tabloid hears the story, their headline will make me seem juvenile and obtuse, and it'll help no one."

Lo nods a couple times, digesting this news. And then Sam and Poppy approach, the former dressed in khakis and a white-collared Fizzle shirt. They both have Ziff bottles in hand, and I notice their daughter staying back by the shady picnic tables with our mom.

I spot cameramen and regular people with crossbody purses and hats walking down the dirt path toward the roped-off area. Food vendors are set up underneath white tents, and the sweet smell of kettle corn fills the breezy air.

"You all ready?" Sam asks us. His gaze darts around our bodies, as though searching for—

"Where are your drinks?" Poppy asks with a frown. She shields the sun with her hand. Apparently Maria snapped her sunglasses on the ride here; a sign, Rose said, of their daughter being a bigger terror than hers.

"My hands are full," Lo lies. But he demonstrates by wrapping his arms underneath the navy-blue sling. Moffy smacks his lips together and then gurgles a noise like *ahh*.

My smile cannot be stopped.

Connor adds, "Same." He lifts Jane to illustrate his predicament. Her lips part in a half-sleep, cuddling with her stuffed lion and then tucking into her father's chest for warmth and security.

Rose scoffs. "You both are seriously using our children as scapegoats?"

Lo flashes her a half-smile. "You're only bitching because you *wish* you were holding Jane right now."

She crosses her arms but doesn't deny it. Ziff tastes *that* gross. Last week, Ryke goaded me into trying a sip, and afterward, I gargled mouthwash for a solid ten minutes to avoid gagging.

It's not to be sipped a second time. Nope.

Sam collects two bottles from the pyramid, and my eyes pop out again.

"We can't break the pyramid formation!" I suddenly shout. I even wave my arms frantically. I heat all over in embarrassment.

Sam doesn't miss a beat. He shoves the bottle in my hand. "There are plenty more to rebuild the pyramid."

The silver label crinkles against the plastic as I clutch the bottle. The Blue Squall flavor is more like *Blood* Squall. Maybe if I try imagining myself as a vampire, I'll have a more delightful experience.

Sam lowers his voice. "You don't have to drink much. You can even pretend to take sips. We just need pictures, and the public needs to see you too."

"Wow, Sammy," Lo says, "you're a modern-day crook." Lo touches his chest with a *free* hand. "I'm too honest to associate with people like you."

Connor arches a single brow, his grin growing. I'd stay to hear Sam's reply, but I have a feeling he'll stick with the eye roll.

"I'm going to check on Daisy and Ryke." I don't think I said the words loudly enough, but I dart away regardless. I plan to carry the Ziff around and act like it's delicious.

I near the cliff where Ryke stands. He's shirtless with low-slung gray shorts and a chalk bag around his waist. He also holds a *brunette* girl's hand.

My heart skips, and the sight takes me aback. I stop dead in my tracks.

Fifty-two

Lily Calloway

focus on the brunette girl.

She rocks on the balls of her feet, restless while she faces the State Park Ranger and my dad.

I blow out a breath.

It's just Daisy, I remind myself.

It's been years since her hair has been light brown, her natural color that matches mine, and so I'm still trying to grow used to it.

The color suits her though. Maybe because she's been smiling more often with the change, and while Ryke has stayed impartial about the whole hair-color process (to avoid influencing her decision), he let his thoughts slip to me yesterday.

His exact wording: "I was afraid she'd look too much like you, but she doesn't. I didn't realize how fucking attracted to her I'd be." Apparently Daisy met him at a quarry, took off her motorcycle helmet, and revealed the finished product. Then they had outdoor sex.

The idea is better than reality. I know firsthand.

As I near, I watch the State Park Ranger shake his head fiercely at Ryke, trying to push a harness and rope at him. Ryke raises his hands.

I reach hearing distance just as he says, "I've already signed a fucking waiver. If I die, it's not the park's responsibility."

"It's windy and still dangerous. If you're looking for a challenge, you can try for a second pitch. Not a lot of climbers do it on this rock face."

Ryke growls in frustration.

My dad steps in between them. "If Ryke says it's safe to climb, he should be able to climb. He understands the risk involved."

The Ranger asks, "Is he repelling down?"

"Yes." My father nods. "Two people are already at the top with gear for him."

The Ranger sighs, resigned from the fight. "Fine. I've said everything I can." With this, he walks off, and my dad pats Ryke's shoulder and mutters a *good luck.*

I realize I've frozen halfway there, and I anxiously shift my weight from one foot to the other. *No sex,* I chant over and over as the familiar urge attempts to sweep me. The Ranger's warnings seem logical. This is dangerous. It is windy. And what if he falls? Ryke said it himself.

He'll die.

While Ryke whispers with Daisy, he turns his head and catches sight of me. His usually hard features soften a fraction. And I read his eyes well enough: *I'll be okay. Don't worry about me, please.*

Ryke never wants anyone to agonize over his well-being, but he's so much a part of my life, of Lo's, that if he disappears, it'll be like severing a foot. Moving forward will be hard.

"Hi, Lily," my dad suddenly says next to me.

I almost flinch at his presence, and I'm even more surprised when he chooses to stay put. "Do you . . . want to watch the climb with Mom?" I ask.

He stuffs his hands in his pockets, dressed in an identical white-collared Fizzle shirt like Sam. "I'm good here."

I take a glance over my shoulder at Lo. With concerned wrinkles along his forehead, his eyes are trained solely on his older brother. Ryke kisses my little sister and then picks up his bottle of Ziff, about to chug it before he ascends.

The chatter escalates from reporters and more people, drowning out the buzzing wind.

"Lily . . ." My dad starts but then hesitates, and his lips close. He smiles nervously like he's unsure of what to say or how to say it.

A lump rises in my throat, and for a split second, I contemplate clearing it with Blue Squall.

But he speaks again before I venture down that road. "I was upset for a long time."

My bones lock, and my eyes widen in surprise. I can't say anything. He hasn't mentioned my sex addiction to me *ever*, and I have a feeling that's the direction he's going.

"I just couldn't find a reason why you'd do . . . that." He pauses, his eyes dropping to the grass. ". . . when I'd given you so much."

A violent breeze tangles my hair and waters my eyes. I'm going to blame the wind as my father finally admits to blaming me. The pain wells like a pit in my ribs. "I'm sorry," I barely croak.

He shakes his head, and his reddened eyes meet mine. "Don't be. I felt betrayed and hurt because I couldn't face the reality." He gives me a saddened smile, and I'm more aware of the gray strands that salt his brown hair. "I spent over half my life working for my daughters, to provide you with a better life than I had, and it's a very hard realization to admit that what I worked so hard for ended up doing the inverse of what I dreamed."

I shake my head. He blames himself. For my addiction. Tears threaten to fall, and I try desperately to suppress them.

He takes my hand in his and says, "You've been my shy little girl for so long, and I should've recognized that you weren't all there. As an adult, as a parent, and as your father, *I* am so sorry."

Hot liquid rolls down my cheeks. Why here? Why now? I ache

to ask these questions, but I see the answers in his watery gaze. And as he wipes my tears. No one can really pinpoint a reason why and when someone grows courage.

It happens over time, and my father has cemented this painful, raw reality—the one I have always been living in. And what's funnier, it's more peaceful with him here. It doesn't hurt as much.

"Thank you," I whisper, sniffing and blinking back more tears. I have to ask . . . "Would you want to . . . maybe come to therapy one day with me? If you don't want to, I completely understand—"

"I'd like that, Lily." And then he hugs me, my heart bursting. A moment passes, and he asks, "Now how do you like Ziff? Be honest."

Oh no. I rub my nose with my arm, very unladylike, but my father doesn't care. "Uh . . ." I wince like I can't exactly say my thoughts aloud.

"That bad?" he asks, his brows shooting up his forehead in worry. He steals my bottle and inspects the label. "The recipe did well with kids your age." I remember Sam saying as much about the multiple test groups.

"Maybe it's just me." I shrug.

He gives me a tight squeeze. "With Ryke as the face, it has a good chance to succeed. That's what I'm hoping." He never intended for Ryke to fail. All this time, he was hoping Ryke could help Fizzle, a company that my dad considers a fifth child. It's nice to know that he had good intentions, even if we all predict a Mountain Berry Fizz 2.0 with a short shelf life.

After another brief second, I focus on the cliff with my father. The tension is nearly gone, and he keeps his arm around my shoulders. The waterworks almost start up again.

In a matter of minutes, Ryke scales the rock with speed and precision. Twenty feet high. Then fifty. He's to the top faster than those bottled pyramids probably took to build. With a sweaty chest and slicked-back hair, he chugs another entire bottle of Ziff again.

The crowds roar with enthusiasm. It's a picture-perfect moment, a brilliant ad for a magazine or a commercial. Everyone claps and cheers. Even my father. With a prideful smile, his palms smack together.

He likes Ryke. He may not want him with Daisy, but it's hard not to admire Ryke's bravery. He defies the impossible every time he climbs.

I try to let out a breath, but it tightens the moment Ryke begins to put on a harness, preparing to repel to the base. Ryke once mentioned that the most dangerous part of rock climbing isn't the ascent but rather the descent. So my stomach flip-flops all over again.

And then he repels.

Down.

And down. And down.

When a big gust of wind blows through, the crowds seem to shush at the exact same moment. But it's nothing to Ryke. Within seconds, he safely touches the grass. Then he stumbles over his own feet and reaches out for the rock face as a support.

I don't understand what's wrong.

Daisy sprints over to him, and when Ryke raises his head, I notice the color lost in his skin.

I find myself walking quickly toward him with my father, and I sense Lo, Connor, Rose, Sam, and Poppy in tow.

If Lo didn't have Moffy, he'd most likely run over to his brother, but we all end up surrounding Ryke at the same time. He's hunched over with his hands braced on his thighs.

"Give me . . . a fucking . . . minute." He breathes heavily through his nose.

"You're really pale," Lo says, worry spreading across his face. "Was it that hard of a climb?"

Ryke shakes his head repeatedly. Then it hits me. He chugged two bottles of Ziff: disgusting, putrid, Blood Squall Ziff.

The nausea surfaces in his features and he gags.

"Alright, let's back up." My father waves all of us to move away from Ryke. "Give him some room—"

He pukes, an avalanche of blue liquid.

All over Rose's heels.

"Jesus Christ," Lo curses.

Rose is horrified, and she immediately shuts her eyes. "This is not happening. *This is not happening*." She inhales strongly, her collarbones protruding.

With his brows knotted in concern, Connor moves quickly, handing me Jane, who begins to cry like a banshee.

"Connor!" Rose calls, permanently fixed to the grass, refusing to budge, open her eyes, and see the mess on her feet.

In seconds, Connor lifts Rose in his arms, cradling her while she tries to exhale normally. More than just destroying a good pair of heels, Rose's OCD is kicking in. Connor's lips brush her ear while he speaks fluid French, carrying her toward the nearest bathroom.

I'm sure my eyes are still hanging out of the sockets. I watch Ryke stumble again, but Daisy holds him by the waist from behind, keeping him upright. And this time, he vomits off to the side.

"Ryke, why are you sick?!" a reporter yells. Camera flashes go off like fireworks.

I jostle Jane in my arms while she cries for her mom and dad.

Sam tenses and says to my father, "We should move him away from the video cameras."

"No, no." My dad rests a hand on Sam's shoulder. "His health comes first. Go find the medics. Get them over here as fast as possible."

Sam nods once before he leaves with Poppy.

"Jane, shh," I whisper. Where is her lion? Oh my God. She did not drop her lion in vomit. I search for a quick second but can't find it anywhere.

Lo sidles next to me, keeping an eye on his brother, who breathes shallowly. A Fizzle employee hands Ryke a water, and he takes small sips.

"What a weird day," Lo whispers.

"Yeah." I nod in agreement, Jane still wailing in my ear. *My dad apologized to me.* I can't say the words now, but I know I will later. It's a phrase I didn't ever expect to receive. Definitely not today of all days.

Even with babies in our arms and mayhem all around us, I have the sense that we're the pillars standing still.

The kind of people that others may be able to lean on.

Fifty-three

Loren Hale

Heavy rain beats against Connor's bedroom windows, the glass fogged from an afternoon storm. My shit mood pretty much resembles the weather. My throat is lined with sandpaper, and my fingers shake the longer I read the printed email in my hands.

I rub my mouth with my bicep. "Where'd you get this?" I ask, my voice hollow. I can't move off the edge of his bed.

Connor leans against the wall, having trouble masking his emotions. Distraught lines cross his forehead. "I have my sources," he says softly.

Tears sear my eyes, threatening to fall and soak the paper. A part of me wants to scream, to cry, to let it all combust—but it stays tight inside my chest. Eating me from the inside out.

Ryke sits on the wooden surface of Rose's vanity, his bare feet resting on her velvet-lined stool. Without raising my head, I can feel the heat of my brother's concern. "Lo . . ."

I crumple the paper in a fist and shut my eyes.

"Lo," Ryke repeats, his tone deep. "It doesn't fucking bother me. We should just ignore it like we always have."

My leg bounces. These days are the hardest. The ones that make me forget about all the months I've spent sober. The ones that could give a flying fuck about tomorrow or yesterday—the ones that only think of right *now*. And right now, I am in so much . . . pain.

"This isn't just about you," I tell him. I ball the news article, a prerelease emailed to Connor. The time stamp is dated for tomorrow morning.

In less than three hundred words, they discredit a legitimate paternity test. They point out how Maximoff has dark brown hair.

My father's hair.

Ryke's hair.

I have lighter brown, a color shared with my birth mom. The article stretches and twists the truth into a disgusting, ugly goddamn lie. Earlier, Connor said, "People believe what they want to believe, and no proof will change stubborn preconceptions."

His cynical view on humanity may be right, but this isn't about Ryke's feelings. It's not about my feelings. I've learned to bear false accusations. I can take this. The ache in my stomach is not for me. Or even for Lily.

All the agony that courses through my body, razor-sharp and unrelenting, belongs to a two-month-old in the room next door.

I pinch the bridge of my nose as emotions roil. "I don't want my son confronting shit like this *every damn day* . . ." My voice breaks, and I take a breath. I smooth out the article, my vision too blurry to read the words. But I fold the paper into threes this time. "It's bad enough that he has to live under a microscope. He shouldn't have to answer any questions about who his real father is."

With a rock in my throat, I rise from the bed, my thoughts already set in place. I can't tell Lily about this. I don't want to have to. I exhale deeply and face Connor. "I need a favor." My shoulders tighten. I rarely ask him for favors, and I know that Connor Cobalt attaches a million strings to a single one. He does something for you; you do something for him.

That's how it works.

"For you, darling, anything." He smiles genially, but I trace grief in his blue eyes. Or maybe that's just my own.

Ryke interjects, "You haven't even heard the fucking favor yet. Keep it in your pants, Cobalt."

"Just so you know, your jealousy keeps me warm at night," Connor says and then winks.

Ryke flips him off.

I can't even join our usual banter. I'm just trying to climb out of this quicksand. The moment Connor retrains his attention onto me, I prepare for a rejection. But he waits for me to speak at least.

"I need you to make up with my dad," I say.

Connor doesn't blink. He doesn't say much of anything either.

I continue, hoping to convince him without pleading like a little kid to a parent. "He can bury this," I explain, passing the folded paper to him. "But you have the sources."

Connor pockets the paper. "I don't think it will be that easy, Lo."

"Can you try?" My eyes burn. This is my only option. My best friend and my father. That's my last card. I have to play it. Even if these are just rumors, even if they're dismissed in a couple of weeks—this is a rumor that I *never* want Moffy to hear.

Not even once. I want him to grow up without a fragment of a doubt that I'm his father. There is a future for him that's painted without hardship and judgment.

I know that future is not his. No matter what I do, there will be cameras pointed at his face. People will ask questions. Over and over and over. Until his ears ring. There will be a day when he learns that his mom is a sex addict. And there will be a time when he's ridiculed for it.

But there is another future full of promise and certainty, even with the knowledge of our pasts. It's *this* future that I'm clawing to obtain. It's the one where he knows that he was conceived from love.

That no one and nothing can deprive him of that notion. Because nothing and no one brings doubt into his head.

I can't change other people's beliefs. But I can stop them from spreading their lies.

I just need help.

I'm not too prideful or too ashamed to ask for it.

After a long moment, Connor steps away from the wall. When his blue eyes flit to mine, he says, "I'll drive."

Fifty-four

Loren Hale

The ride to my dad's is short and void of bodyguards. We didn't take the time to call them, not when his house is gated. My thoughts race. Different paths. Different options. It's possible my dad could refuse to help, just on the basis that he'd have to work with Connor.

I reject that theory. My father can be vindictive, but when it comes to his family—when it comes to *me*—he'd do almost anything. I clutch this thought tightly as Connor slows the Escalade and rolls down his window.

"103190," I tell him the security code, and he types it into the pad. Soon after, the iron gate groans open.

He parks. The mansion just outside the car door.

Ryke hesitates in the passenger seat and then turns to me in the back. "This may not work. And it'll be okay if it doesn't. Moffy won't have a bad life. We'll all fucking protect him from the media."

He's trying to prepare me for the worst. But I'd rather look to a better future than agonize over the darkest one. I'm not going to sit here and torment myself.

I don't say anything. I just climb out of the car, the cool air filling my lungs. I lead Connor and Ryke to the front door, a lion metal knocker on the black wood. Fumbling with the key, I finally stick it in the lock and enter my father's mansion.

I wipe my clammy hand on my jeans and head down the hall. It's three o'clock on a Sunday. My dad could be anywhere, but I'm sure he's here.

I peek into every room desperately wanting to end the search as quickly as I can.

When I near the den in the back of the house, I hear his voice and no one else's. Like he's speaking on the phone.

"I know she spent the night at my house, Greg. I wasn't fucking blind back then." My blood runs cold. He's talking about Lily. I know he is.

I stop midway to the cracked door, the hallway dim, and as I listen, I skim the photos framed on the wall. Me, as a baby. Me, as a toddler. Me and Lily, as kids. Me and Lily, as preteens.

"You knew my parenting methods were more relaxed than Samantha's. I wasn't going to hover. If either of you had a problem with it, you should've kept her at your home." He pauses. "Oh, come on, Greg, stop blaming yourself. You're a good goddamn father." And then I hear the sound of ice cubes clinking against glass. "We all make mistakes."

That sound.

Ice against glass. It breaches my ears like hammered nails. Memories wash over me in a hazy blackness. Shadows filling parts of me. I can practically feel the crystal glass in my hand. And I can visualize the one in his. Not just lime and water.

It has to be.

I have to believe it is. He's sober. My dad *is* sober.

Ryke sets his hand on my shoulder. I can't move. Something cements my feet to this place. Maybe fear.

"We all knew they would end up together. Christ, it was Lily and Loren. How the fuck were we supposed to know she'd become a sex addict? The best goddamn fortune teller wouldn't have predicted that."

The edge in his voice is sharp, *too* sharp.

He's sober.

My teeth ache, and I realize that I can't hide behind this wall forever. My feet move before my mind does. I take a step forward, and Ryke's hand falls from my shoulder. When I slip into my father's den, I am washed deeper in memories.

The leather couch, the dark wooden cabinets, organized desk, computer hutch, flat-screen television—it's the home of a night I'll never forget.

I was fourteen, and I'd just fought with my father in that same hallway. When I returned to the den, Lily was waiting timidly on the couch, our sci-fi show paused on the TV. We'd always been more than just friends.

We were *best* friends.

She had all of me by then. I had most of her.

And I let Lily drown my pain with a kiss. And then something more. I lost my virginity here. Right *here*. In the torment of my fucked-up childhood.

For years, I avoided this den. Like it contained every calloused feeling from that night. I can walk through it now and not be pulled under. I believe this.

I have to believe it.

The minute I enter the den, I focus on my father, who gazes out the large window. Rain slides down the pane. His right hand cups a glass . . .

I freeze halfway to him. "Dad?"

He spins slowly, and it's not a mistake—what I see. Amber liquid floats in the crystal goblet. Scotch. The bottle is on his desk, next to a box of cigars and a stack of clipped papers. I force myself to raise my gaze onto his.

His eyes are narrowed, sharp and black. Far gone. The difference is easy to spot now that I've seen him sober.

"Greg," he says into his cell phone. "I'll have to call you back." He clicks his phone off and tosses it violently onto his desk. It falls and thuds on the carpet.

He swishes his drink, not even pretending that it's something else.

"Let me guess," I say sharply, "it's just water?"

"Macallan 1939," he replies. And then he takes a long sip, practically slapping me in the face. I rock back, but our cold eyes never separate. He tries giving me that look—the one where he says, *you're just a little fucking kid. Grow up.*

I am grown up.

I'm more of an adult than him.

"What the *fuck* is wrong with you?!" Ryke shouts, his face blood-red as he steps nearer. I shove him back before he storms ahead.

Connor even helps by grabbing Ryke's bicep and forcing him beside us. Before he yells and reignites old arguments, I just want simple answers.

"How long?" I ask our dad, a tremor in my voice. "How long have you been drinking behind our backs?"

He prolongs the answer with another swig of scotch. His smug smile irritates me the most. The way his lips curve. Like it's funny that he's drinking, and I'm not.

That's it for me. I just snap.

I run across the den before I can process my movements. And I struggle to pry the goblet from his iron grip. Somewhere in my head, I'm thinking: *if I can get it away from him, it ends this.* But it doesn't end like this. I know better than that.

"Loren!" he sneers and pushes my shoulder. With two palms, I shove him back even harder. He stumbles into the window and clutches a waist-tall vase for support.

I've never been physical with him, not like this. But I am screaming inside. Disappointment and hurt crush beneath everything. I take a couple steps toward him and try to remove the glass again, but he raises it above his head.

"Stop acting like a little shit!" he shouts. "Talk to me like a grown fucking man."

My throat is on fire. "Like you, Dad? Talk like you?! Are you a grown fucking man?" I point at his chest. "Is that what you are?" I swallow a brick. "How long? How fucking long have you been lying to me?!" My face twists with too much pain.

I get it.

I get relapsing. I am a master at it. I also understand pretending and lying. It eats at vital pieces of you, but it rips the people you love apart.

I am at the mercy of it.

I am on the other end. Shreds of a former self.

"Get a fucking grip, and we'll talk," my dad sneers.

"Fuck you!" That's Ryke. Seething behind me. "You're a sad, pathetic excuse for a father. And I *believed* you when you said you'd fucking try." He steals the bottle of scotch. "What is this?" The pain in his voice silences my father.

He goes eerily quiet.

"WHAT IS THIS?!" Ryke shouts again.

My dad flinches and shuts his eyes.

With raw lungs, each breath comes roughly for me. My head spins, but I ask my dad one more time. "How long?"

His eyelids open and his hollow gaze meets mine. "Since Daisy's birthday on the yacht."

Nausea builds. That was *months* ago. A lifetime ago.

Ryke laughs angrily, which morphs into a scream. He pitches the bottle at the wall, and it shatters, alcohol sliding down the paint. He destroys the nearest bookcase, knocking over paperbacks and tearing apart a shelf. His rage has always been in his fists.

Mine resides somewhere else.

"Congratulations," I say dryly. "You're a better liar than me." He raises his glass like he's toasting to my words.

"Stop," I tell him before he presses it to his lips, panic shooting into me. "Just stop, Dad. You can always try again. It's not over."

He shakes his head like I'm wrong. I've always been wrong. "It's over for me, son. I'm not going to pretend anymore." And then he finishes off his glass.

Ryke squats, breathing heavily, and then he kneels. He can't look at our dad. He knew—early on, I guess—that if our dad relapsed, he couldn't be convinced to try again.

It's harder the second time around. I know it. I've been there. "Please," I beg. "I know it doesn't seem like it now, but you can do this." I sound pathetic—that's what the worst part of me believes. I refuse to give into that part. This is right. What I'm saying is *right*.

"You don't understand," my dad tells me in a controlled voice. "I don't *want* to try again. So stop pleading like a little—"

"Okay," I cut him off, not waiting for the insult that I don't fucking deserve. I can't give up on him. Ryke wouldn't give up on me. But I'm not prepared to be a sober coach.

My dad sets down his empty drink, and he finds a new target across the room. His probing gaze lands on Connor. "Does Loren know what you've done in your past?" he asks him. "Or better yet . . . *who* you've done." His brow tics, and his features darken in distaste.

"This isn't about me, Jonathan," Connor replies with ease. "Deflecting the issue here won't help you."

He lets out a weak, shrill laugh. "*Nothing* will help me." He buttons his suit jacket with a shaking hand, one that almost matches mine. "In less than a year, I'll be gone." He turns to Ryke, broken picture frames lie by his knees.

My brother must feel the heat of our father's gaze because he raises his head.

"You can stop assaulting my things and celebrate," our dad says. "Your dear old *pathetic* father will be dead. Hooray."

My lips part in confusion. "What are you talking about?" He's not making sense.

"*That.*" He points to the glass on the desk. "Has killed me. Or *will* kill me." He flashes me a dark, agitated smile. "I received the news a couple weeks before the yacht trip. Liver disease. Cirrhosis. Nonreversible."

Before my legs buckle beneath me, I dazedly find the couch and sink onto the leather cushion. The weight of his words silences the room. I rub my lips as I process his declaration.

He's dying.

I choke on a pained laugh. He's really dying.

The only parent who has ever loved me. The one person who gave me a chance at life. He's going to be gone? Just like that.

I hear his voice. "Stop crying, Loren. Don't be a baby."

I go to wipe my eyes, my stomach roiling at his words.

"Fuck you," Ryke sneers. He rises to his feet. "You tell him you're dying, and then the next minute you say shit like that? Who the fuck are you?" Connor reaches Ryke's side and places a hand on his shoulder, partly, I think, to restrain him.

My dad scowls at the liquid dripping down the wall, I'm sure wishing it was all in his glass instead.

I clench my hand that trembles brutally. I can practically feel the alcohol sliding down my parched throat. The bitterness and power. All in one.

I breathe out. "If you have liver disease, you shouldn't be drinking." Hasn't he thought of this? My doctor educated me on the topic, even sat me down with a dietician to create a post-recovery health plan. But it doesn't take that formality to see the obvious.

"I'm dying anyway," he says with edge. "Might as well revel in life's few luxuries. Whisky and women."

Women. The word stands out to me. "Is that why you've been bringing dates to functions?" I ask. Why he's been choosing women half his age. Why he hasn't even attempted to hide this part of his life from me.

"I'm enjoying the company while I can," he admits.

I shake my head, heavy and weighted, but it's starting to clear. "There have to be other options."

"There's not." He shuts it down immediately.

"What about a liver transplant?" I ask, knowing this road exists.

He laughs. "I'm so far down the donor list you can barely see my name. There are some things money doesn't buy."

He's forgetting something. "I have your blood type. We'd be a match—"

"No."

That's all he says.

I grimace. "What do you mean, *no*?" I shoot to my feet, my veins pumping. "This could save your life, and you're just going to say no?"

He stares at me, square in the eye, no retreating. "You're not doing that for me." So this is pride? Compassion? I don't understand.

"You don't get to decide that," I snap. "If I want to be a donor, I'm being your donor."

"You want to try, have at it then," my dad combats. "Your liver is in tip-top shape, I'm sure."

"It's better," I argue. Like most alcoholics, I used to have fatty liver disease. But it goes away with the right diet and sobriety. I've been healthy for almost a year now. "They only need to remove a portion of it, right?" I turn to Connor for confirmation.

He nods once. "It's not an easy recovery, Lo. This is a major surgery."

I don't care. It's life and death, and I'm not going to stand by and watch my dad die. I can't do that, no matter how terrible he can be. He deserves a second chance. Everyone deserves another fucking chance. I'm going to give him one.

My dad opens his mouth to protest again, to tell me *no*. I'm sick of that word.

"I'm doing this," I say first. "You're always telling me how you saved my life." He wanted me when my own mom didn't. "I want to save yours."

He blinks a few times. It's not like he decides all of a sudden. He stands there and stares at me like it's a contest of who backs away first.

I don't move. I might have a year or two ago. Maybe even five months. Ryke would've been the one to rival Jonathan Hale. To stand up to him. To shut him down.

Now it's my turn.

I never flinch or give him the easy road because I love him. I love him, so I'm going to give him the hard road, the better one. Like Ryke always did with me.

"You look different," my dad says. Fear flashes in his eyes . . . the most human thing I've ever witnessed from him.

"I'm older," I remind him.

He shakes his head, just as Lily had done before. "It's not that, son," he says in a whisper.

I know. I feel different.

He sniffs loudly, controlling his emotions. Then a minute or two later, my dad finally shuffles to his desk. He crouches behind a drawer, and I hear bottles clink together. He emerges with four handles of whiskey. My alcoholic father, who has spent more days with liquor than without, tosses his whiskey in a nearby trash bin.

And he walks away from them. Heading toward me.

I let out a long breath. When I turn to look for Ryke, I think he'll be happy about our dad's choice. But he's not here. I spin around, casing the area. He's probably outside. Where he can breathe.

"I'll talk to Jonathan about our situation," Connor says, reminding me why we first showed up. "You should go find him." Ryke, he means.

I hesitate to leave Connor alone with my father, who already seems aggravated at the idea of conversing with him. I'd rather not push my dad toward the four bottles of booze he just rejected.

But I'm too concerned about Ryke to stay.

My decision is an easy one.

Fifty-five

Loren Hale

find Ryke in the driveway. The rain has stopped. Without Connor's car keys, he's left waiting by the Escalade. He sits on the edge of the pavement where the cement meets the grass. His knees are tucked to his chest, face buried in his hands.

My pulse quickens. "Hey," I say softly, approaching my older brother.

He runs his fingers through his hair but never looks up. His gaze transfixes on the ground.

"It's all worked out," I tell him.

He shakes his head a single time, and his fingers clench his thick brown hair.

I rub the back of my neck. "I know you don't like him . . . and you probably don't want me to be the donor. But I can't just let him die."

His eyes redden, and his jaw hardens. I'm saying the wrong things. *Christ.* What do I say? Ryke's not me. He doesn't think like me. He never has. It's why we've had too many fights. Why it took years to build our relationship. We're always on separate pages. Different chapters of the same story.

I waver uneasily, wondering if I should bend down to comfort him or stay upright, towering above his frame. I end up frozen in place. "Ryke . . ." I choke out his name.

His nose flares, and he lets out a heavy breath. His hands fall to his sides, and he finally raises his head. Tears surface that he couldn't bury. "He told us that he was dying," he says, voice trembling, "and the first thing I felt was *relief*."

I watch the tears roll down his cheeks.

"That's sick," he breathes. "Really fucking sick." He gestures to me. "You're the one who should be relieved. You're the one he's abused. You're the one who had to live with him." His throat bobs. "But you didn't even hesitate to help him, even when he didn't ask for it." More than vulnerable, Ryke stares right at me, his chin quaking and his features torn up.

I've personally seen him like this maybe twice before. When he learned his mom betrayed him, outing Lily's sex addiction to the public. And then in Utah. When we fought each other with our fists. Almost a whole year ago.

And then he says, "You always think you're the bad guy, Lo. But you're not." His head hangs. "You're fucking not." He buries his face in his bent knees again.

This time, my joints work, and I sit beside my brother. I wrap my arm around his tense shoulder that shudders with his body.

"I know him better than you," I defend. "That's why I want to help him."

Ryke stays quiet for a minute. "What if you can't, Lo?" he asks in a whisper. "What happens then?"

The bottom of my stomach nearly drops. I don't want to think about it.

"Because you know there's only one other option." Ryke stares at his calloused hands, chalk residue on his palm. "And I don't know if I can make the same choice as you."

I pinch my wet eyes and squeeze his shoulder like *it's okay*.

There's a good chance he shares the same blood type as me and my father. But I won't ask Ryke to be our dad's donor. That's too much. He's already done enough.

"It's okay," I say the words aloud.

"It won't be," Ryke refutes, choking on a sob. "You and I fucking know it won't be. Because in the back of your mind, every day when you have to fucking look at me, you'll be thinking the same thing."

"No," I tell him, shaking my head adamantly. *No, I won't.*

"You'll think I killed him," he finishes. He swallows hard again. "And here I thought my relationship with Daisy would ruin you and me."

"Stop," I snap, shaking him a bit. My fingers dig into his shoulder. And I feel his tears fall on my hand. "It's not going to happen, Ryke." *It's not going to happen.*

But somewhere in his mind, he's doubting everything. "Yeah . . . we'll see."

Fifty-six

Lily Calloway

For the tenth time Lo checks his cell phone, his mind far, *far* away from the comics that line his desk. I've accompanied him to the Halway Comics office above Superheroes & Scones. He asked me to.

I can tell that he yearns for the quick fix, even if it's the very thing destroying his dad.

Maximoff sleeps in his carrier on the couch, and I set down an old *New Mutants* comic and rise from the blue sofa, careful not to wake him.

"When did they say they'd call?" I ask Lo, resting my butt on his desk.

"Hm?" His brows knot as he stares at the indie comic. He's been on the same page for ten minutes. Lo is a slow reader but not *that* slow.

"The hospital," I clarify, nudging his arm with my finger. "When are they supposed to call?" He got tested this morning to see if he'd be eligible for the liver donation. The surgery frightens me, but I'd support Lo no matter what. His emotional distress would be harder to watch than any recovery from the transplant.

"Today or tomorrow." He pushes his rolling chair away from the desk and swivels to me. With one hand, he reaches out and clutches my hip. I smile as he guides me to his lap. I find myself straddling him.

A very good position, indeed.

He brushes my hair from my face, his fingers grazing my skin with lightness and care. "I know you're nervous about it, Lil," he breathes. "But it's all going to be okay."

The office door suddenly swings open, and about the same time I spin around, the wood shuts closed, the person out of sight.

"I'm sorry!" Maya calls through the other side. "I should have knocked . . ."

Lo laughs, a real humored one. Then he whispers to me, "She's carrying about ten plastic Thor hammers."

I smile at *that* image of my super geeky store manager. She's also proven her loyalty by not sharing any personal info with the press.

"It's okay!" I shout back to her.

Lo kisses my cheek before I climb off him. "You're not red," he states like a fact.

I look at my arms. No blushing elbows. No rash-like flush. I beam. "My superpowers are—"

"Kicking in?" he finishes for me, his hypnotic amber eyes right on mine. His lips pull upward.

"It's a lame superpower, isn't it?" I ask as I head to the door. The ability to avoid roasting from head to toe—it's not very grand or epic, but at least it's something. Right?

"Horrible," he banters. "You're better than that, love."

I smile. "Am I?"

He nods. "Most definitely."

With this nice confidence boost, I open the door. Maya lingers with a heap of plastic Thor hammers in arm. Her glasses fall to the bridge of her nose, and her straight black hair frizzes like lightning struck her. "I'm sorry, Lily," she apologizes again, her eyes permanently widened in terror.

"We weren't really doing anything," I tell her quickly. Heat gathers on my neck, a *red* heat. Damn. That lasted too short. "Do you need help?" I motion to the merchandise she juggles.

"This? No, no, I have it. It's just . . ." She leans in close and whispers, "There's a girl who keeps asking for Lo. She's been here the past two weeks, and she says she'll keep coming back for as long as it takes."

Jeez. I gently shut the door to Lo's office, not wanting to disturb him. He's in a weird place, and I don't think he should be handling super fans.

"Maybe she'll be satisfied with just me?"

Maya nods repeatedly.

I leave Moffy with Lo and descend the twisty staircase into the Superheroes & Scones break room. A few employees perk up by my sight. I haven't been present much since my son was born, and it's been easier to communicate by email and phone.

Entering the store will be like slipping into a version of outside, a smidgen less boisterous but still chaotic and loud. I like coming here after closing when everyone is gone. It's just red vinyl booths and racks of comics. But I take the risk now, and I push through the door.

The store is packed. Every booth is occupied by a group of people, some just drinking coffee, others reading too. And people actually peruse the shelves like they're interested in comics and not just spotting the Calloways.

It makes me smile.

Though the moment I scoot behind the counter, heads whip in my direction and the line outside the door suddenly rushes to the store window. People pull out their phones and snap photos. Inside the store, others do the same.

I shrink only a little. I'm used to the constant gazes now. Maya trails me, some plastic hammers swinging by their price tags and clanking together. "Where is she?" I ask.

But the moment the words escape, a girl springs up from the floor near a rack of *X-Men* comics. Her light brown hair in a messy braid, she slings an old jean backpack on her shoulder and walks slowly toward me. She fixes her large round glasses on her nose with shaky, nervous hands.

I thought she'd be excited, like the girls who shriek outside every time I glance their way. Instead, the color drains from her face.

With the checkout counter separating us, she's not too close. "Hi." I smile, but she doesn't return it. Oh . . . what if she hates me and only loves Lo? I didn't think this through.

"Is Loren around?" she asks. "I really want to see him." She pushes her glasses up again.

"He's working," I say with the scrunch of my nose. "It sucks. But I'm here." I smile again, but her frown deepens. I'm a shit alternative to Loren Hale's six-pack and sharp-as-ice cheekbones. Daisy is also better at small talk than me, but she's taught me some things during our Hale Co. competition. Compliments get you far. "I like your pin," I tell her.

"What?" she asks in a daze.

This is not going well. I point to the well-worn pin on the strap of her backpack. The blue words are half-scratched off but I can read the saying: *Mutant & Proud*. I add, "*X-Men: First Class* is one of my favorites too."

Her clutch tightens on the strap, and she adjusts the weight of her bag. "Is there any way I can see him? Tomorrow, maybe?"

I can't promise her a one-on-one meet and greet with Lo. He's dealing with so much that it's just not a good time to be shaking hands with strangers. But I want to give him the option. "I'll have him email you," I tell her. "That's as much as I can offer."

Her shoulders rise in shock. "Yes, *please*, thank you."

I find a notepad beside the register and slide it to her with a pen. "Write down your email address for me."

While she scribbles, the chimes on the door ding, and the noise level increases. Loud, obnoxious boys enter the store, a group of four stumbling through. One knocks into a cardboard cutout of Cyclops, which is just rude.

Maya groans in distress beside me. "They're awful."

I frown. "They've been here before?"

"Twice. And they always make a mess."

They can't be any older than seventeen. One of them clutches a brown paper bag. They're drunk. A guy with a black hoodie trips into a not-so-empty booth. A couple girls curse them out as they leave the table, and the guy slurs, "Bitches." He even flips them off.

My heart speeds as I text my bodyguard: *Superheroes & Scones needs your assistance, Garth.* He took a bathroom break ten minutes ago, mentioning that the Lucky's chili isn't sitting well with him. I warned him. I love Lucky's, but that chili is never to be eaten.

And then I text Lo: *There are some rude guys down here. How should I kick them out?*

When I press send, the girl hands me the note with her email. She seems like she's genuinely interested in comics, so I'm not surprised when she says, "I'm going to stick around if that's okay? I was in the middle of *Messiah Complex.*"

"Of course," I say with a smile. She slowly retreats back to the floor near the row of *X-Men* comics. I read the note before I pocket it: *willowbadaboom33@gmail.com*

My phone buzzes.

I'm coming down with Moffy and Ryke. —Lo

What? No. I quickly text back: *No, I have this . . . wait, what's Ryke doing there?*

I called him when you left. He was
in town. I'll see you in a second.
—Lo

Before I reply with a more forceful text or even process Ryke being here, the break room door swings open, and Ryke and Lo emerge. It's like the floodgates open, shrieking and screaming from outside. And the chatter escalates in the store. Almost everyone has their phones pointed at us, except the employees.

Moffy cries in Lo's arms like he's being attacked. My heart catapults, and I instinctively pry him from Lo and tuck him into my chest. Lo hardly even notices. His eyes are on the booth of rowdy, drunken guys.

"No fucking way," Ryke curses, his tone more shocked than angry.

"What?" I gape.

"Those are the guys," Lo tells me with gritted teeth, "the ones who've been pranking us."

Oh. *Oh.* Shit.

Fifty-seven

Loren Hale

Ryke and I squeeze into both ends of the red booth, blocking all four guys from a quick, easy exit. "Hey there," I say with the most agitated half-smile.

The teenager in the hoodie sits closest by the window, and he makes a show of swigging from the paper-bagged bottle. Ryke rests his forearms on the table, itching to trash it, but he forces himself to stay seated.

Most of the teenagers wear normal clothes: jeans and a nice shirt. I can't stereotype them as anything more than bored rich kids. Something I'm pretty familiar with.

Next to Ryke, a guy with jet-black hair speaks first, "Where's your prick friend?"

"Yeah," a redhead next to me asks, "is he going to show up and lecture us for an hour?"

"Let me guess." I point at the redhead. "Your last name is Patrick."

He crosses his arms and slouches. "So what?" *So Connor talked to your parents and only pissed everyone off.* This has to go better than that. But maybe it's a lost cause.

Regardless . . . I still plan on trying.

"I'm not going to lecture you," I begin, but the guy in the hoodie leans forward.

He sneers at me, "You *can't* kick us out. We have a right to be here like everyone else." He's the one I remember most, with tousled brown hair and a soft face. The one I grabbed when they shot paintballs at our house.

A guy with a buzz cut pipes in, "Yeah, it's our first amendment right to be here."

They're lucky Connor isn't at Superheroes & Scones. He'd tear into that statement, and he'd probably make them feel small.

Ryke rolls his eyes dramatically. "You all smell like cheap fucking vodka."

"Sorry," the hoodie guy says dryly. "We'll buy better stuff next time."

"That's not what I . . ." Ryke growls in frustration as two of them make crude gestures with their hands and tongue. He loses his patience, and his eyes flit to me, tagging me in.

"Come on, you all look no older than seventeen," I tell them. "Drinking underage is illegal, so you're not in a power position here." I nod to the guy in the hoodie. "What's your name?"

"Fuck you," he curses and then switches his V-shaped fingers into one middle finger, flipping me off.

Ryke and I exchange a look like this isn't going anywhere. What's worse, the booth is pressed against a window, and people keep snapping photos of us.

"How was that bourbon bath?" the jet-black-hair guy asks with a laugh. And then he high-fives his friend across the table.

Ryke's eyes flash hot. "You think it's funny?"

"Ryke," I interject and shake my head.

The hoodie guy mutters, "Pussy." It was directed at me. One hundred percent.

The redhead snickers. "Nice, Garrison."

"*Dude.*" Garrison gapes, his hood falling off his head. And when he catches me watching him, he practically spits at me. "What are you looking at?"

"You," I say, with just as much venom. And his guard lowers an inch, hurt flaring in his eyes. Instinct guides me to a new place. "Here's what's going to happen. You all have two options." Surprisingly, they quiet to listen to me. "You can stop the pranks and *never* come around our house again. If you're *that* bored, I wouldn't mind hiring some of you to work here. If you don't want a job, I get it. You can have a discount on comics, if that's your thing."

Ryke adds, "And I'd be willing to teach all of you to rock climb at the gym. But you can't drink."

"Sounds like so much fun," the redhead says with the roll of his eyes.

Garrison picks at the paper bag, his gaze far away on the table. "And the second option?" he asks.

"You vandalize our house again or harass our girls, and we'll press charges. The minute we even see your goddamn pinky toe on our lawn, I'm calling the cops. Take it from someone who's been in jail, you don't want to be there. Even for a couple hours."

Garrison lets out a short, irritated laugh. "When were you in jail?"

Without blinking I say, "I doused some asshole's door with pig's blood."

"No way," the redhead gapes.

Garrison sits up straighter. "Yeah? Where's that asshole now?"

I shake my head. "I don't know. That shit is long gone, man. You're going to leave prep school, and you're only going to take your mistakes with you." I eye the bottle of booze. "You can stay here if you hand that over and don't cause any commotion. Otherwise, you have to go."

"We'll go," the buzz-cut guy says and then nods to Garrison. "Let's buy that six-pack and head to the elementary school playground."

My stomach twists, but I can't force anyone to do anything. I know this. I stand up the minute the rest of them do, and they all gather to leave. As he passes me on his way out, Garrison gives me a long once-over, his lip either curling in distaste . . . or maybe something else.

And then he pushes the bottle in my hands. "Here, you won't be such a pussy if you drink."

"If that's what you think," I say without falter. And then I chuck the bottle in the nearby trash.

His bewildered face is priceless.

I turn my back on them, hearing the chimes to the door as they exit. I feel Ryke next to me. And to my brother, I ask, "Do you think that'll work?"

"I don't know."

"What do you know?" I ask.

He pats my shoulder. "That I'm really fucking proud of you."

It takes me aback for a moment, and I breeze through the previous conversation. I wasn't malicious or hateful or vindictive. I didn't treat those teenagers how my father would've treated me. I was just honest.

I let out a breath, and then I scan the store for Lily and our son, not spotting her behind the checkout counter. "Maya," I call out as I see her zipping down an aisle. "Where's Lily?"

"Break room. Garth is with her. Thank you for handling those guys!" She gestures to the now empty booth.

"If you have trouble again like that, text me."

She nods and then shouts a phrase in Korean. I've learned that it's actually supposed to be in English, a saying from *Battlestar Galactica*: "So say we all."

Just as I'm about to leave Superheroes & Scones, someone says, "Loren?"

Ryke goes rigid as a girl sneaks up behind him and slides closer to me. My face falls as I get a good look at her.

No.

It can't be . . . I shake my head in a daze. She's older, I guess around seventeen now. The first and only time I'd ever seen her, she was in middle school.

Jesus Christ. That was a long time ago.

"Hi," she says, nervously adjusting her backpack. She keeps licking her lips like she doesn't know what else to do.

Ryke butts in, "Do you want an autograph or a picture or something?" He's nice about it, but he's six-foot-three and intimidating to stare at. In fact, she tries to meet his eyes but can't.

She pushes her large glasses up her nose. "No . . . thanks."

Ryke turns to me like *what should we do?*

She's not being weird. There's no manual on how to go about these things, and I can't believe she had the courage to even find me. It must've taken weeks in order to get this close.

She takes a deep breath and looks straight at me. "I'm—"

"My sister," I finish. *My half-sister.* Like Ryke, only on the other side. "Willow, right?"

Her mouth drops. "You . . . remember me?"

"Yeah." I give her a weak smile. "The day I met my birth mother is one I really can't forget."

"Oh . . ."

Ryke is stunned to silence. His eyes flicker back and forth between us.

"Do you want to talk over coffee?" I ask. "Maybe in the break room?"

Without hesitation, Willow nods, and her eyes well with tears. Relieved. She's relieved. There was a chance I could've slammed a door in her face. Told her to hop on a bus back to Maine. I didn't.

I won't.

After truly knowing Ryke, I can't fathom shutting the door on a sibling. It's a bond that's different than a friendship. One that hurts more if it breaks, but when it's whole, it means everything.

Fifty-eight

Loren Hale

The break room clears out some when I take the bright blue couch with Willow, coffees in hand. I plan to talk to Lily later, but for now, Ryke whispers to her and ushers her upstairs to my office with Moffy and Garth.

Willow sets her ratted jean backpack on the ground, one of the pockets torn open from overuse. "I . . ." She trails off and cups the coffee with two hands.

Too many questions hit me at once, but we have to start somewhere. "How'd you find out about me?" I ask the most important one.

She tucks a piece of hair behind her ear. She's timid and a little shy, but I can't tell if that's her personality or just her reaction toward me. "My parents divorced about a year ago," she mumbles.

My brows knot. "I'm sorry." That wasn't the image I left behind in Maine. I pictured a perfect family: Emily Moore, her two daughters, and a class-act husband.

She shrugs like it hasn't affected her, but her gaze never meets mine. She pushes up her glasses. "Ellie had her sixth birthday about a month ago, and it was the first time my parents were together since the divorce." She pauses. "I heard them fighting in the kitchen about how my mom had a son, and she . . . abandoned you."

I scratch the back of my neck. "I had my father, so it was okay." My throat closes for a second, and I swallow before I ask, "Did you confront her about it?" I thought Emily had finally confessed, but Willow learned about me in the worst way. Overhearing the news.

She nods. "Yeah, right then. I asked her about it, and it took some screaming for her to really tell me the truth." She wipes below her eyes to hide her tears.

I turn my body more toward her. "I'm sorry you had to find out like that." I warned Emily when I met her—I told her to at least come clean with her daughters. It stung to learn about my brother the way I did, and I didn't want Willow to experience that kind of betrayal.

"I ran away," she blurts out with a sob.

My stomach sinks. "You what?"

She cries. "I just . . . I was so mad. I told my mom that I was going to find you, and she couldn't stop me. So . . . I hopped in my car and drove to Philadelphia."

I pinch my eyes as I realize what this means. "You've been here for an entire month? Does Emily know—"

"She knows," Willow says, sniffing. While she talks, I stand and search for a box of tissues. "She's waiting for me to run out of money. She doesn't have any vacation days left to leave work, so she can't come get me."

My chest tightens. Now that I have a kid, I can actually put myself in the place of a parent. I would be a wreck if Moffy ran away as a teenager. I'd hunt him down within the hour, but I also have the means to follow him all across the world.

I reach for tissues on top of the employee fridge, and I return to the couch. "How much money do you have left?" I ask, passing her the box.

She plucks one out. "I'm not going back."

"Willow," I force, *"how much money?"*

She bites her lip to keep from crying again. "Enough for a couple more nights at the motel."

She's staying at a motel? Jesus Christ. "I'll pay for a hotel tonight and tomorrow, and I can get you a plane ticket back to Maine."

"No, *no*," she says. "Please don't make me go back. I just met you, and . . ." She hiccups and removes her glasses, wiping the wet lenses with her striped blue and green shirt.

"Aren't you in high school?" I ask.

She stays quiet, and I take it as a *yes*. She's missing class by being here.

"Your mom is probably sick over this," I tell her.

"*Our* mom," she emphasizes, putting her glasses back on. She has my nose. And my hair color. The longer I scrutinize her features, the more I realize we look related. "And I don't care what she is."

I grimace. "Willow—"

"She *lied* to me." Willow points to her chest, the hurt tearing through her voice. "I don't want to be around her ever again."

Her anger is talking. I understand all of that. I thought I was going to cut ties with my dad too. The moment I found out he'd kept so much from me, I couldn't fathom ever seeing his face again. Time heals wounds that deep, and hers are too fresh.

"How about I call Emily and see where her head is at?" The minute I say the words, my muscles constrict. I never believed I would hear her voice again. Not for anything. I can't even believe I offered this.

After a brief second, Willow nods and lists off Emily's cell number. I type it into my phone and rise to my feet. "I'll be quick. Are you hungry?"

She shakes her head, but I silently question how much she's been eating just to save money. I motion to a young employee at a table.

"Can you get her a muffin from the front?"

He sets down his sandwich. "Sure thing."

I disappear into the employee bathroom, locking the door behind me. It's a single stall, so it's not like I'm taking away five toilets from the staff.

My hands shake, and I don't end up calling Emily first. I dial another number instead.

Fifty-nine

Loren Hale

Still in the employee bathroom, Lily's eyes widen the longer I rehash everything that's happened. She hangs on to my belt loops and stares up at me like I'm sharing the plot of a new Marvel movie.

"No way," she says when I finish.

"Yes way." I rest my elbow on the sink. "Now I have to call her mom—*my* mom." It's weird to say, especially since Emily doesn't really consider me her son.

I called Lily to the bathroom because I want to do this with her. I feel stronger when she's around. Maybe it's her expression, the way she stares at me like I can do anything without faltering.

"I want to do this fast," I tell her, the phone heavy in my hand. Ryke has Moffy in the break room, and while I love my brother, he's never been alone with my kid without Daisy present.

Lily peers at the phone. "Are you going to press the button?"

My finger hovers over the green call sign, and I hesitate to make this real. "You do it."

Like she's touching fire, she quickly taps the screen and scuttles closer to me. I put it on speaker so she can listen too.

The phone rings four times; I think she's not going to answer.

On the fifth one, it clicks. And my pulse races, my forehead beading with sweat.

"Hello?" she says.

"Hi . . ." I clear my sandpapered throat. "This is Loren Hale. Before you hang up, I need to seriously talk to you. Willow is here . . ." I blank on what else to say. I look to Lily, and she flashes me an encouraging smile.

"Is she okay?" Emily asks, her tone high-pitched with worry.

"She's angry and broke, but besides that, she's doing great." I can't restrain the edge in my voice, and I just pray she stays on the line with me.

Emily speaks frantically, "I just called her yesterday, and she said that she had enough money. I've been trying to convince her to come back. But I can't leave work, and I didn't want the police involved."

"You should've called me and said she was here," I retort. "I would've seen her the minute she drove out to Philly."

Emily goes quiet, her voice no louder than a whisper as she says, "That wasn't an option for me. I don't want the media to know about my attachment to the Hales."

I realize that she didn't want to call me. Never wanted to speak to me again. Not even for this. I cringe and grip the sink with white knuckles.

Lily wraps her arms around my waist, and her warmth eases the tension in my chest.

"I can fly you out this weekend," I tell her. "You should talk to Willow, face-to-face, and then maybe she'll return home with you."

"She's not going to want to come back," Emily whispers. "She just learned that her half-brother is famous."

I glare at the ceiling. "It's not about that." If she saw the pain in Willow's features, she'd understand that it's deeper. It's about struggling to face a person who's caused you agony. Hating that parts of your life were shadowed with uncertainty and doubt.

If this was about celebrity and fame, she wouldn't have cried about her mom.

"And if she doesn't come home, I'll be right."

"You won't," I snap back. "If she doesn't want to come home, it's because she still can't stomach living with you." I realize how harsh that sounds, so I add, "I'm sorry, but it's the truth."

"You don't even know her," Emily retorts defensively.

"You're right, but I've been in her situation before." I spent ninety days in rehab away from my father. When I returned, I began thinking about restarting a relationship with him. But I needed that space. What's different here—Willow is in *high school*. She's not a legal adult yet. "Let me fly you out," I try again. "You can talk to her and go from there."

After a long pause, she says, "I can only take off one day from work, if that."

"You'll be in and out of Philly within the day then," I tell her.

She contemplates this option for another second. "Okay. I'll text you my email." Then she hangs up on me.

I pocket my phone.

"Lo," Lily breathes, her fingers hooking on my belt loops again. "I want to apologize for her meanness to you, but I don't know how."

"You just did, love," I whisper, kissing her temple. I take a deeper breath and kiss the corner of her lips. It feels good having Lily this close. I press her small body up against my hard chest. Her rib cage rises and falls in a sporadic, aroused motion. I'm careful not to build her up too much, but I just really want to kiss her here . . .

My lips meet hers, connecting our bodies on another level entirely. My hand disappears in her hair, and my tongue slides against hers. She moans and trembles, and I restrain myself from pushing harder—lifting her around my waist. I can't right now.

My lips break from hers and then brush her ear. "Later."

She nods in acceptance, and I scan her body for signs that she can handle not going further. She's flushed, but she's not crossing her ankles.

"I'm okay," she tells me.

"Do I need to check?" I ask seriously, my eyes traveling to her zipper.

"I'm already wet, but not soaked." She nods again, this time adamantly. Though she reddens even more.

I smile. "I love you, Lil." I wrap my arm around her shoulder.

"I love you too, Loren Hale."

I feign surprise. "You love me? Holy shit."

She punches my arm playfully, and I hug her close as we leave the bathroom. The minute we exit, we both halt in place at the same time.

In front of the couch on the carpet, Ryke sits beside Maximoff who rattles a *comic book* like it's a damn maraca. While my brother plays with him, my son chews on the corner of *Young Avengers*. I notice Willow picking at a muffin on the couch, hugging the armrest.

"Close your eyes," Lily whisper-hisses and practically catapults her body at me to shield my sight from our son desecrating a comic book.

"It's too late, Lil. I've seen it."

But she climbs up my back, and I hold her by the legs. Her fingers barely cover my eyes. "You didn't see anything," she repeats like she can hypnotize me.

And then I *hear* the sound of paper tearing from the spine. "Ryke," I groan. "I blame you for this."

"He's not even crying right now. I'm doing a fantastic fucking job." The *fuck-and-punch* tactic to eliminate cursing barely lasted. Ryke just grew more pissy, and I hated punching him every two seconds. At first, it was fun. Then it just became exhausting.

But if Janie or Moffy's first word is "fuck"—he owes Connor and me, big time.

"You gave him a comic book, and he can't even read yet."

"He's starting early then," Ryke says. "Maybe you should've given me his diaper bag or something."

Lily drops her hand. "We're in a store with *tons* of toys on the walls. You could've taken a Green Goblin action figure."

I add, "Or Wolverine, Black Widow, Hulk, Spider-Man—"

"For fuck's sake, okay. I got it." He pries the defiled comic book out of Moffy's clutch and then lifts the baby in his arms. Moffy laughs, like a giggle. My lips rise. My brother's not too bad with my kid.

"You should babysit more often."

"Fucking hilarious," he curses, passing me Maximoff while Lily slides off my back, her feet thudding to the floor.

That's when I reroute my mind to the serious topic. Willow has already finished eating, and she straightens up as soon as I focus on her.

"Your mom is going to fly out this weekend to talk with you. Until then, you can either stay with us in a guest room or at a hotel. I'll pay for the expense, no problem."

"A hotel works," she says. "I don't want to . . . impose any more than I already have."

Moffy squirms and kicks out, and Lily thankfully takes him from me so I can concentrate. "If you change your mind, the invite is always open." Before she interjects, I ask, "How old are you, by the way?"

"Seventeen."

"That's what I thought." I think about this for a second. "You know, Daisy is pretty close to your age."

Ryke shoots me a look like *that better not be a slight at me*. It wasn't one.

I continue, "She'd probably love showing you around Philly. Is this your first time here?"

"Yeah, but . . ." Willow nervously rises to her feet since we're all standing. She holds the strap of her backpack like it's her life-line. "I'm not sure she'd like me. I mean, I don't like motorcycles and . . . other stuff like that." She avoids Ryke's gaze. We all have reputations that circulate in the media, and I'm guessing that's all she knows about us.

"Neither do I," Lily says. "They're terrifying."

"You haven't even ridden one," Ryke retorts.

"*Because* they're terrifying," Lily notes.

Willow's shoulders slacken. "Yeah, same. I've never been on one, and I'm scared too."

Lily brightens when Willow agrees with her, and she points a finger at Ryke. "Ha!" Moffy gurgles like he's trying to mimic that sound, but it's incoherent baby talk.

Ryke says to Willow, "Daisy won't care that you're not into bikes. She'd honestly do anything you want."

"I'll take off work some days this week too," I tell Willow. It's the one good thing about being the CEO of a company. I have the luxury to make my own hours. But even if I neglect Halway Comics some, I can't ditch Hale Co. meetings. I'm still competing for the title against my brother.

After the charity event, only three board members thought Daisy would be a good fit for the job. Irene has more sway and convinced everyone that Daisy was too young.

"Okay then," Willow says. ". . . where do we start?"

"How about lunch?" I ask.

Everyone voices their approval like they're starving, and I wait for Willow to say something. Her glasses mist with tears again.

"Thank you," she says beneath her breath.

Ryke has been a great big brother to me. And if I can pay it forward and do the same for her, I'll try my hardest. I may not be the best at anything, but I can be better than mediocre.

Sixty

Lily Calloway

Lo stays inside of me for an extended minute or two, and I didn't even have to ask. Sweat gleams on my skin as I lie beneath the weight of his toned body. Even as I come down from an epic climax, I ache for one more. Per the usual.

But I've learned to wait until tomorrow or the morning. Compulsive, needy Lily is put to rest, somewhere far, far away. In a dystopian land before this peaceful place.

I stare at Lo's beautiful pink lips. Mine still sting, and it's like I can feel him on me, even though we're a breath apart.

Kiss me. I realize that I actually said it aloud when his lips touch mine in a gentle, tender kiss. When he pulls out, he props his body next to mine and combs my damp hair off my forehead.

"October tenth," he says the date with a growing smile.

I've yet to fully believe that we're going to be married sometime soon. Less than a month away. "Are you sure you don't want to postpone?"

His smile vanishes instantly, and I regret even asking.

I sit up and clutch the red sheet to my chest. "It's just that the board members are choosing a CEO on October first, and . . ." I trail off at the sight of his sharp jawline.

"If you want to pick another date, that's fine, Lil, but I don't want your reasoning to be about my emotional stability. I've been ready to marry you since I was seven years old, in case you forgot." He flashes that half-smile that somehow draws me closer to him, not farther away.

I easily straddle his waist while he sits up and rests against the headboard. Without saying anything, I plant both of my palms on his defined abs, watching them rise and fall with his body. "I love October tenth," I whisper. We chose the date spontaneously, while cooking tacos for the house. It felt right. It still does, but doubt likes to creep in and destroy all good things.

He holds my face in a comforting hand. "That day isn't going to be tainted by anything, love. I know you can't believe that yet, but you're going to see it."

It seems like a dream. I kiss his sharp jaw quickly, and he kisses back even faster on the lips. I smile, my body heating all over again. I grind against him, and a deep noise escapes his throat.

He pulls back once and says, "Are *you* sure about lavender and cranberry?"

Those are the colors we chose for our fall wedding. I nod wildly, my eyes only on his lips. He tilts my chin up with two fingers, and I melt into his intense amber irises.

"Because I sent the maid of honor all the details, and she freaked when I changed the dinner menu yesterday."

Rose doesn't like messing with the set plan, but she's been really relaxed as far as offering her opinion. She just suggests certain things. Like lisianthus as the flowers, a deep purple bouquet. I didn't even know what that flower was, let alone how to pronounce it. She handed me a bundle of them a week ago, and I knew. It was perfect.

"No more changes," I tell him. "I like everything we picked." At first, we went formal with the reception menu: bite-sized entrees of lamb and scallops. Then we realized that we're only inviting family, and we'd rather eat what we like. So everyone will be served five-star chicken, shrimp, and fish tacos, margaritas, and taquitos.

It's like it was always meant to be this way, but it just took some time to reach this place.

Lo's smile returns. "So do I." He leans in to kiss me again, but his phone buzzes on the mattress. He frowns at the caller ID, lines creasing his forehead.

"Who is it?" I try to crane my neck and catch a peek.

"The hospital." Oh. They must have his test results back. It's only eight p.m., so it's not too late for them to call. Lo licks his lips and then presses the cell to his ear. "Hello?"

His reaction is like an incoming wave. I know it'll crash against me. I just wait and wait for it, wondering how strong the impact will be or if the tide will sweep us both. His lips downturn, and his chest stops falling as he holds his breath.

One of his hands stays on the small of my back, even as he says, "I understand. Thanks." He clicks off the phone.

"And?" I ask. But I read his eyes as they rise to me, the sadness behind them. "You can't donate."

"My liver isn't healthy enough. My dad was right." He rests his head back and lets out a pained laugh. "My dad is going to die, and there's nothing I can do." I hug him and he hugs me just as tightly. I wish I could donate. I would, but I had my blood type tested. I'm not even close to being a match.

"I have to text Ryke," Lo breathes.

"What are you going to say?" Clung together, I watch him use one hand to type a message.

It's sweet, and tears begin to build with each word that he texts his brother.

Just got the news. I can't donate. Please don't feel obligated to do it. I love you no matter what.

He presses send. "There," he whispers. "It's over." He holds me. "You and me and Maximoff, we're going to make new beginnings."

I add, "With no sad endings."

His smile lights up his face. I love that it returned one more time. "No sad endings, love. Those aren't meant for us."

Good. I'm ready for a happy one.

Sixty-one

Lily Calloway

Someone needs to spank him twenty-six times—*not* me," I clarify quickly. "I'm not touching Ryke's butt." September 19th marks his birthday. We're all on the back patio, grilling barbecue, while Ryke grumpily slouches in an iron chair next to me.

He's said four words all day. Two of them were "fuck" and the other two were "off." He's been sullen since Lo received the news from the hospital. A lot weighs on his mind.

"I'll do it," Lo offers. He threateningly waves a greasy spatula back and forth. "Turn around, bro."

Ryke shoots him the middle finger, unamused. Lo scowls at his brother and shakes his head. They're both frustrated for different reasons.

The sun disappeared for the night, and the cool evening air chills my cheeks. I adjust my white fuzzy Wampa cap on my head and then tug the flaps of a mini-Wampa cap over Maximoff's ears. Rose sewed the *Star Wars* one for Moffy, and his cuteness has now broken all cute scales. He sleeps on my thighs, all bundled in a red Marvel blanket.

Rose has Jane snuggled against her chest, beneath a black fur coat, asleep too. Beside the grill, Connor sips wine, and I sometimes catch him observing his wife and daughter with this reverent smile, treasuring this moment and them.

Daisy wags her brows. "I can spank Ryke later." In one swift sentence, she deflects the attention off of Ryke's moodiness. Since they've been together for a little under a year, the comment is not as awkward as it could be. She sits behind Ryke, on the table, running her fingers through his thick hair. He has one hand on her leg that drapes over his chest.

The only time he looks like he's semi-enjoying himself is when Daisy distracts him. I've seen her lean over, and he'll grip the back of her neck for an upside-down kiss. Five minutes ago, I even tweeted a picture of that kiss (with Daisy's approval) with the caption: *#Raisy is alive!*

I'm forever waiting for it to trend.

Connor wears a million-dollar grin as he says, "If there's not a bruise, you're not hitting him hard enough."

Lo feigns surprise. "You like bruises? Jesus Christ, love. I don't even know you anymore." And then he cocks his head at Rose. "What about you, Mrs. Cobalt? Did you know this?"

Rose's yellow-green eyes pierce him, throwing a thousand daggers his way, and then she whips her head to *me*. I stay strong against the fire of her gaze. "Tell Loren that I think his jokes are subpar and wouldn't make a clown laugh."

I recoil. No way am I stepping between their fight.

Lo spins to Connor and says, "Tell Rose her retorts make me feel sorry for her *and* that she has horrible taste in company names."

Connor sips his wine, staring between his best friend and his wife like they're his evening entertainment.

I just don't want it to escalate. That's always my number one priority.

"I have *great* taste," Rose refutes. If she wasn't holding Jane, I think she'd spring to her feet by now. "And if you hadn't noticed, you asked *me* to be a partner in a subdivision of Hale Co., and I can still reject you."

"We're not calling the clothing line Blossom Babies," Lo retorts. "It sounds like we're dressing Cabbage Patch Dolls."

They've been fighting over the name for the past week, and I'm still alarmed that they've agreed to work together at all.

"I'm not calling it Hale Co. Baby Clothes. *I'm* the designer."

"You don't even *like* babies," Lo says.

"Then why are you asking for my help, Loren?"

Because he needs Rose. And she actually wants to be a part of this project. For the past week, Rose has sketched infant and toddler clothes, overly excited at the prospect of having a clothing line in a department store again.

He stares at her blankly and then says, "We'll keep brainstorming."

Rose sits even straighter like she won a spelling bee. Even though I love Lo dearly and I'm on Team Loren Hale, I am also Team Calloway Sisters, so my smile still exists.

It takes a lot for Ryke and Lo to smile, but I check on Ryke to see if he's cheered up a bit.

Wishful thinking, I suppose.

On my left, Ryke stares off into space, his gaze haunted and lips downturned. It's his birthday, and he's plagued by too many thoughts. I lean close and whisper, "Ryke."

It takes him a second to register my voice. When he does, he slowly turns his head.

"Do you want to open presents?" I ask. Usually, he tells everyone to buy him climbing gear, but this year it's like he forgot it was his birthday. He never mentioned rock climbing or the equipment he needed.

Lo and Connor even had a cardboard cutout of Ryke from his Ziff promotional campaign. Our publicists blamed Ryke's pukefest on food poisoning, so the sports drink could live to see the light of day. We were going to play "pin the harness" on Ryke, but with his downcast mood, it seemed like a bad idea. I think Lo shoved the cutout in a closet.

"Maybe later," Ryke says morosely.

Lo's jaw tics. "Okay, I can't take it anymore." He passes Connor the spatula.

Then Lo faces his brother. Ryke stiffens in his chair, his brows hardening in confusion as he watches Lo. Lo . . . the guy who used to run away from bullies, who shouted insults until his throat burned, who always fell down in the end—he stands upright with magnetic confidence that pulls us all in.

"You're not dying today," Lo tells his brother, pointing adamantly at the ground. "We're all alive *right now*, Ryke. Maybe in a year, Dad won't be around, but it doesn't mean we'll stop moving. Out of everyone, *you* taught me that. Don't look back. Just go forward, run through quicksand. So pick up your feet, man. For one, it's your birthday. For another, no one likes to see you *this* pissy. It's depressing."

While Ryke mulls over these words, Lo searches for me, maybe for affirmation or just because. His amber eyes find mine in seconds. And his lips begin to rise.

We've been obliterated, and we've come together whole for the first time. Our lives are meteor showers on rewind. I don't think we even knew what we'd be once we pieced ourselves back.

Maybe we do belong in space with all the stable, constant stars. We're just the more destructive, more disastrous chaotic pieces, the comets that head toward earth.

After a long moment, Ryke slowly pushes to his feet. He's an inch taller than his brother. More brooding. But Lo is more severe.

Stone vs. Ice.

Hardness vs. Sharpness.

For a second, I wonder if they're about to fight. But then he reaches out and clasps Lo's hand. Ryke leans in for a bro-hug-pat.

And my shoulders lift like I'm soaring. They've been to hell and back for each other, and I know they'd both be willing to take a second trip if they had to.

Lo always poked fun at me for having three sisters, citing all the extra, added drama. He thought being an only child was easier—better. But I can tell that he wouldn't trade Ryke.

And now he has a sister of his own. Lo cares for Willow, and he doesn't hide this fact from anyone. He's been checking his phone all day for her texts, partly responsible for her while she's in Philadelphia. Tonight, Emily flew in and she's eating dinner with her daughter to discuss the future. Whether or not Willow will return to Maine is up to her.

While Ryke and Lo hug, the air is quiet and calm.

Peaceful almost.

And then Daisy suddenly tenses. "Did you hear that?" Her panicked, high-pitched voice pricks my spine.

Sixty-two

Lily Calloway

Daisy cautiously climbs off the table, her collarbones jutted out like she's holding her breath. And her wide green eyes zero in on the glass sliding door, our entrance to the house.

Ryke and Lo separate, and Ryke's face floods with concern. "Dais . . ." Is she hearing things? My face twists. No. My sister is *not* making things up in her mind. She's okay.

A violent crash sounds somewhere, like pots and pans or a bookshelf. Clattering to floorboards. I jump in my seat, almost startling Moffy, swaddled on my lap.

Partially, I'm happy that my sister did not make up the noise. It has to be nothing though. We're all safe here.

"Maybe it was a rat," I suggest, biting my nails. I drop my hand quickly.

"Don't even." Rose glares. Rats. She hates rats. Sadie used to take care of those for her, and now the cat is with Frederick.

"Shh," Connor says, raising his hand. Everyone silences again. The guys are closest to the back door, and their rigid postures put me on edge. If it was nothing, they'd throw out some jokes too.

I blow out a breath and protectively lift Moffy to my chest, Wampa cap securely on his little head. I pat mine. It's still there. All is well.

"HEY, FUCKERS!" A muffled shout rings from up high.

I flinch and gullibly follow the noise to the second-floor window. Two gargoyle horror masks with horns and pointed teeth stick their heads and arms out, their hands gloved. My heart somersaults and thrashes. *They're in Maximoff's nursery*, is my very first thought.

I have to get Moffy. I take a step toward Lo, and then a baby wails in my arms, reminding me that our son is already safe with me.

"Guess what?!" one calls out. "We're getting inside the Calloway sisters this September!" Then they snicker and perform pelvic thrusts against the window.

"They're in the house," Daisy says in a haunted whisper. Her whole body is frozen, and the terror in her wide-eyed gaze is palpable. My heart is on a nosedive. I'm torn between racing into the house and running scared.

Ryke, Connor, and Lo hesitate to leave us. I can see it as they stand between the door and our bodies, wavering uneasily between the two. Seconds pass as everyone assesses, but I see a black-clothed figure whisking through a hallway, breezing by a window. *They're just harmless teenagers*, I remind myself. It eases the fear in my gut.

I look back at Daisy, to maybe comfort her with this sentiment. That's not a good idea though. To my little sister, teenagers are not just harmless. They're worse than cruel.

I'll hold her hand then. I reach out to be the big sister, the better one that I've strived to be.

But Daisy doesn't notice my outstretched hand. Something bad happens. Her jeans begin to soak at the crotch, the dark spot blooming. Like she . . .

"I can't . . ." She chokes on a breath.

"Hey, *hey*." Ryke sprints over to her, scanning her quickly, head to toe. And he pulls her into his chest, setting a hand on her head. "I'm here, Dais." He holds her tightly, forcing her body into his so she can feel protected and safe. Even though she peed her pants, Ryke consoles Daisy the best that he can.

I begin to shake as hysteria strains the air. More and more windows open, and the cackling from the teenagers rattles my defenses. I'm not immune to the fear. It tries to cling to me, and it's freaking out Moffy, still crying in my arms. I rock him, and it's only been maybe a minute.

It feels like a lifetime of uncertainty.

"Lo?" I breathe.

In the pit of my ear, I hear Connor calling the cops. I smell our barbecue burning on the grill. And Rose keeps repeating, "I'm going to strangle them." Her clutch tightens on a shrieking Jane.

"Lily!" Lo shouts.

He's holding my cheeks between his warm hands. His body as close to mine as it can be without squishing our son.

I'm scared, I realize. I'm terrified right now. And it's not a fear for my well-being. It's for Moffy and Lo. "Don't go," I say first.

But he's already telling me, "Lock yourself in Rose's car and drive to your parents' house with your sisters."

"No." I shake my head fiercely. He left himself out. "Come with me."

"We have to make sure they don't escape, Lil," he says quickly. "This ends tonight."

Tears sting my eyes. "I'm not leaving you," I croak.

Lo whispers rapidly, "They're not going to kill me, love. They're just teenagers."

My chin quivers. "That's what I thought, but the more I think about it . . ."

"Lily," he forces my name so I understand. "They're *just like me.*"

I can't say that Lo would've never done this. If pushed to a breaking point, he might have. If drunk enough, he most likely would have too. "You're not like them anymore," I tell him.

"I was like them," he amends. "And I'm not scared of a single one. But you are."

"I'm not," I refute. "I was never scared of you."

"Lil." He smiles weakly. A decision has to be made soon. Before they destroy all of our things.

"If you won't come with me, can I come with you?" I ask, sidestepping every sexual innuendo in favor of fear. "Moffy has toys inside. I can distract him—"

"Okay," he agrees before I even finish. "But *only* because they're just teenagers. Otherwise, you'd be in a car right now, understand?"

I nod. He's not afraid that they'll do something to me and Moffy, he's saying. Or else he wouldn't even chance this. He clutches my wrist and begins to guide me behind him, shielding my body by keeping me very close to his back.

I glance once over my shoulder, and I notice Rose and Connor following, in a similar line, with Rose behind Connor to protect Jane. It's one of the few times I've seen her walk behind her husband and not beside him.

Ryke and Daisy are the only two that don't join us. He lifts my petrified sister in his arms, cradling her easily, and he carries her to the garage, where they can drive off in one of the cars. Lo wanted all the girls to flee, like in the horror movies, but reality is a bit different. It might seem stupid, but being by his side, not splitting up, feels right.

Lo grips me hard, maybe worried that I'll break away. But I want to stay pressed against him as we enter through the sliding door.

When we near, a gargoyle-masked teenager whizzes past with "spirit fingers" and darts upstairs. I almost startle backward, but Lo pulls me closer to his body.

This ends tonight.

I really, really hope so.

Sixty-three

Loren Hale

My son's distressed cries are nails in my eardrums. I can't stand it. The sound triggers my fight-or-flight response and elevates my pulse. I'm not running away. I want to run toward them. Wherever they're hiding.

After stepping into the house, I guide Lily to the living room. Jesus fucking Christ—they've cut up the couch with a knife, foam poking through the cushions.

"They're morons," Connor says, his voice tight.

"Morons with knives," Rose retorts, her brows pinching in anxiety. She taps her heel repeatedly on the floor.

Someone shouts "BOO!" at the top of the staircase.

Trying to be creepy, they cock their gargoyle heads, masked and empty-handed. Police should be here soon. Maybe in a couple minutes. We have no time to block every exit, but if I grab one, he'll rat out his friends.

"I have this," I tell them. I can barely meet Lily's gaze without all of my muscles coiling—a natural instinct to shield her. To ensure that *no one* touches her. Or my son. But I have to do this.

As I force myself away from her side, Lily scoots closer to her sister. Bouncing Moffy in her arms. For some reason, I expect Connor to distrust me, to step in. To take control of the situation.

But he gives me a single nod and then whispers to Rose in French. He zips Rose's fur coat, hiding their daughter beneath it.

I attempt to exhale the rock in my chest. It's nearly impossible. I head to the banister, the staircase tall and wide, and the teenager towers above me at the top. His red Vans match the ones I wear. I scrutinize his lanky frame, his gray jeans, black crew neck, and dark blue gargoyle mask.

With about twenty stairs separating us, the teenager slowly extends his arm and points at me. He thinks he can freak me out.

He can't. "It's not going to happen," I tell him flatly. I've never been frightened of horror movies. Never been terrified of the dark. I've always considered myself a bigger monster than every creature on Halloween.

In my life, I've only ever been in peril when I feel like I'm losing Lily. Mentally, physically, entirely. But these teenagers aren't going to hurt her or my son tonight.

I'm not even entertaining the idea.

It's just me and him right now.

He takes two steps down, bridging the gap between us. And then he tilts his head, slowly. The banging and clattering upstairs suddenly die down. Then I realize that his friends have gathered at the top of the staircase behind him. I count five bodies.

One pats their friend's shoulder and gestures to the hallway, antsy to leave. The friend waves him off and stays put.

"You want to know what I see?" I say, a bitter taste rising in my throat. I want to hate them, but I can't. I hate their choices. I hate that they've broken into my house and terrified everyone. But I can't hate them.

"What?" the closest one asks, his voice muffled behind the mask. I can't tell if he's Garrison, the one who's been the most vocal with me. He cranes his neck over his shoulder and whispers something to his friend, his fingers nervously curling into a fist.

I step nearer, my hand skimming the railing as I ascend the staircase. "I see five teenagers who are going to spend a lifetime regretting this night." As soon as I pick up my pace, they curse, and the guy sprints back up the stairs, joining his friends as they rush down the hallway.

I run after them.

"Go, go, go!!" they shout at each other, passing Jane and Moffy's nursery.

"Head for the back staircase!" another yells, banging into a picture frame on the wall. They have maybe five feet on me.

Before they reach the corner of the hall, the closest guy trips over his own two feet, his red shoes, a size too big. I have a minor flashback to the last time I chased these teenagers down the dimly lit street. He struggles to stand, but I grip his black shirt. As he flails out toward his friends, I yank him back to me, knotting his tee around my fist.

"LET ME GO!" he shouts with more alarm.

His friends hesitate by the corner of the hall. The police sirens are audible in the distance. The cops might even be parking in the driveway.

"I warned you," I grit. "I told you that we'd press charges this time."

"We need to go," one of the other guys says. "I'm not going to jail, man."

"Neither am I," another says.

The guy in my clutch thrashes. "DON'T LEAVE ME!" he screams. "YOU CAN'T LEAVE ME!" Fear trembles his voice, and his so-called friends disappear around the corner, sealing his fate.

He's shorter than me, thinner. I easily lift him by the waist and carry him toward the staircase, even as he fights against me. "It was a fucking joke!" He keeps repeating, *can't you take a joke?!*

My stomach turns, and I pause at the top of the staircase. I firmly grip his wrists behind his back. "That's funny," I say dryly. "Really funny. Destroying someone's shit. Hilarious stuff." And then I pull off his mask.

My mouth falls some.

The red hair is familiar, one of the guys I met at Superheroes & Scones. But he's not Garrison. His face is splotched red with anger, and I push him forward so he heads downstairs. When we veer into the living room, my pulse heightens a level.

I scan Lily, who leans her ass on the couch. Without her jacket, I notice her reddened arm, like she'd been scratching. Dammit, Lil. Nausea churns, but I focus on Moffy in his blue onesie. His glassy eyes seem to connect with mine, and he outstretches his arms, squirming like he'd prefer to be held by me right now. Lily tries to comfort him, refitting his mini Wampa cap that he smacks off his head. Like Jane, he's inconsolable.

"*You* little penis," Rose curses.

For some reason, I think she's insulting me. But her penetrating yellow-green eyes are planted on the redhead in my clutch.

"Where are your friends?" Rose almost shouts at him like he's under interrogation.

The redhead presses his thin lips shut.

Rose spins on her heels and begins marching to the back door. "We need to find his friends quickly." Since Connor has Jane, she must feel free to chase the rest of the teenagers. Problem is: she's in heels. And she's Rose. Anyone with two feet can outrun her, including her seven-year-old niece.

"Yeah, you do that," I tell Rose. "Fly in your magic bubble, Glinda."

"Shut. Up. Loren." She huffs as she gets ten feet from Connor. And then he catches up to her, and he hooks his arm around her waist.

"They're gone, darling." He tugs her to his body.

"Richard—"

"You can't run after them," Connor says. "But he'll rat out his friends."

The redhead lets out a pissed laugh. "Like *hell*, you prick."

Connor's lip tics, and he straightens up, his arm wrapped around his wife's shoulders while he holds Jane. She cries into his white button-down, soaking the shirt.

In a controlled voice, he says, "Burglary is a felony. In case the severity escapes you, I'll clarify. You will now have *severe* trouble obtaining a job and applying to colleges. That Ivy League you dreamed about is now scratching you off their lists. And inside your social circle, you better hope you have loyal friends. Because those that care about status will write you off just as quickly as everyone else. You're a social carp, a bottom feeder. You take the meager scraps that the more fortunate hand out to you."

Rose opens her mouth to pipe in, hopefully not to call him a penis again. I wait for her retort, but her lips close and her shoulders constrict. She cautiously looks to Connor.

I frown and inspect the redhead.

He's crying.

His eyes redden as tears streak his face. If I was more callous, I'd feel good right about now. I'd feel justified in his pain. He fucked with us for a while. He deserves this, right? But the pity that surfaces belongs to a guy who's been there. Who's hated everyone and everything. Who just wanted to go and drown.

I didn't want them to choose this. But I will *never* have another night like tonight. There will never be another shadow passing through our hallway. No amount of empathy will change my mind.

Connor's demeanor softens as he says to the redhead, "Or you can make a deal. Reduce your charges; try to turn this felony into a misdemeanor."

I see where Connor is headed with this one. "You'll just have to give up your friends."

He laughs weakly and then nods a few times in agreement.

Right then, the police burst through the front doors with handguns outstretched and bulletproof vests, shouting multiple things at once.

It's over.

I release my clutch on the guy, and he staggers forward with his hands in the air. I immediately lift a terrorized, wriggling baby out of Lily's gangly arms. He latches on to my chest, and I press a hand to his back, rubbing him as he settles down.

Lily hides her eyes behind her Wampa cap, like she's hiding from me.

"I'll talk to the police first," I barely hear Connor say. One of the officers is about to near me for questioning.

"Can I have a minute?" I ask him.

With two authoritative hands on his belt, he nods once and steps back.

"Lil?" I whisper, watching her cross her ankles with anxiety. She's not doing well. I put two fingers in her waistband and pull her to my chest.

She shuffles forward and sniffs loudly.

My ribs bind around my lungs. I lift the furry white cap higher on her head. Lil's green eyes well with tears—her delicate, round face as splotched as our son's.

"I disappeared there for a moment, didn't I?" I realize. She must've heard us banging into the walls. They could've been armed. Lily Calloway's imagination fucks with her on a daily basis, and I bet it constructed a pretty devastating end.

She wipes her nose with her arm.

If I provoked them longer, I think they would've tried to jump on me, shove me down the stairs. But they were more scared of me than I was of them. I didn't feed their hate with my own. I just let it rest.

"Don't do that again, okay?" Her chin quakes.

"Love," I breathe, my heart aching. I hug her closer, melding her small, wiry frame to my body. And my lips brush her ear. "You and me."

She chokes on a laugh. "Lily and Lo."

My chest swells. "We're going to make it in the end." I smile wide because I can see it now. God, I can see it.

It's closer than I ever realized.

After the police write down our statements, a few of them scour our house for any signs of the other four who escaped. I think they all ran down the street to their homes. And I have more than a gut feeling the cops will knock on their doors within the hour.

The redheaded guy, Nathan Patrick, ratted out every single friend that was here tonight. The names burn in my brain as I sweep glass off the kitchen floor, a couple flower vases shattered.

Dillon, Kyle, John, and Hunter.

"What was that guy in the hoodie's name?" Lily asks me at the bar counter, her laptop open in front of her. I briefly mentioned that the guy wasn't here tonight.

"Garrison." I brush the glass into a dustpan and instinctively check on Moffy by the fridge. He's quietly awake in his bouncer beside Jane, both entranced by dangling mobiles. Hers: a solar system of stars and planets. His: lightning bolts and stuffed superheroes like Wolverine.

I smile as he focuses on the red Spider-Man. Even though my kid has the cards stacked against him with addicts as parents, I think he's going to turn out all right.

"Do you think he planned to come tonight?" Lily asks me.

"No clue." I dump the glass in the black trash bag and check my cell for missed calls. None. I've called Ryke about five times, and he texted back: *I'll call you in a second.* It's been an hour. I pick a green wrapped present off the ground, the box smashed.

I open it and inspect the damage.

The wooden picture frame is bent, a fissure running along the glass. I carefully slip out the photo that I framed for my brother. One of the few we really have that's ours, not taken by paparazzi. From this summer, we're sitting on the edge of the pool outside. Daisy called our names, and we turned our heads the same time she snapped the photo.

Even caught off guard, we look happy. It's in our eyes, in our fleeting, rare smiles. We even look like brothers.

"Did you pick one out yet?" Rose's voice cuts into my thoughts. I put the picture in a drawer and chuck the rest of the broken present.

"I like the dark gray leather since the cream suede gets dirty," Lily says.

Rose hovers over her sister's shoulder, peering at the laptop screen. "It's ugly."

"It's a couch," I tell her. "It's not fine china."

"It still has to match," Rose retorts. "What's your second choice, Lily?"

Lily bites her nails and shifts on the stool. My muscles tense as I walk around the bar counter, and I notice she has her heel pressed up against her crotch. At least she's not in an ice-cold tub, crying. In our fucked-up world, she's doing pretty good tonight, all things considered.

I can tell that this is our forever. Lily won't ever be one hundred percent. I won't either. But these small bumps are easier than any brick walls we've faced.

"This one," Lily says and squints at the screen. ". . . the beige tufted sofa."

"Can we have it shipped tomorrow morning?" Rose asks and unsurprisingly slides the computer in front of herself, typing away as she discovers these details. We all wanted to piece back our house as much as possible for Daisy.

Rose has been pouring her energy into these preparations since Daisy hasn't returned her calls either.

Screw it.

I'm not waiting for another hour. I dial my brother's number for the sixth time and press it against my ear. On nearly the last ring, the line clicks.

"Hey, I'm fucking sorry. I've just been . . ." He takes a deep breath like he's expelling the night. "Are you okay? Is everyone—"

"We're all fine." The minute I say the words, Rose lets out a surprised gasp.

"You got ahold of them? Put it on speaker."

I shoot her a look. "No *please*?"

"Loren," she snaps.

I talk to Ryke in the receiver, "Queen Rose wants to be on speaker."

"That's fine," he says.

I drop the phone and press the speaker button. Connor even slips into the kitchen, leaning a shoulder on the door frame. "Where are they?" he asks us.

Ryke must hear the statement because he answers, "We're spending the night in a hotel downtown. We'll be back in the morning."

I nod at this. That's good. We'll have time to really fix this place up before Daisy returns.

"How is she?" Rose asks, her voice higher than normal. We all moved in together *for* Daisy, so that we'd offer her a better kind of security. It hits me all of a sudden.

We failed her. Our whole plan went to shit.

Story of my life.

You think you've figured it all out, the one gear in the cog that'll solve your problems. And it only makes a mess of everything.

Life is a big shitty bag of trial and error. And the error always seems to come at someone's expense.

"She's still fucking rattled," Ryke tells us. "I've calmed her down some . . . but I think she'll be better in the morning."

Lily practically whispers, "Is she going to move out?"

The weirdest feeling washes over me. It takes me a second to process it. Jesus. I don't want Daisy to move out. Not alone. Not even with my brother. I like having everyone here. One house. Together.

We're a family.

Ryke lowers his voice. "We've been talking about it, but we haven't made a decision yet."

"We can move," Rose suggests, guilt sagging her shoulders.

I shake my head at her like she's crazy. We've spent months putting up with the teenagers and now that it's ended, we're going to move? We'll be dealing with the same shit all over again. *No way.*

"Daisy doesn't want you to do that," Ryke explains.

Lily clears her throat and speaks louder. "We want you both here."

Rose nods. "I second that."

"I third it," Connor says, his lips rising.

"Me too," I add.

Ryke sounds overwhelmed as he says, "Thanks, guys. See you in the morning." And he hangs up. I forgot to wish him happy birthday, so I end up texting it.

I can understand what he's going through. Having to watch someone you love teeter on the brink of their anxieties and fears with no real way to fix it. We can only pick them up. Each Calloway girl fights a similar battle in different ways. As I pocket my phone, I catch Lily scratching her arms, and I know mine is headed toward that familiar edge.

Sixty-four

Lily Calloway

I can't sleep. I lie on my side, tangled in the sheet, and I listen to the creaks of the walls, hugging the baby monitor to my chest.

"Lil," Lo murmurs, his hands on my hips as he spoons me from behind.

"Huh?" An ache pulses between my legs. *Ignore, ignore, ignore*, I send these signals to my brain. Even if they're incomputable. They must go there.

"You're grinding against my dick, love."

Shit. I stiffen, not wanting to scuttle away from him. I like that he has a strong handhold on my hip bones and that his warm chest presses against my back. My bony butt has betrayed me. And maybe so has my nether region.

"I didn't mean to." Anxiety flushes my skin.

"It's okay." He props his elbow on the pillow and kisses my cheek. Oh God. I want those lips right on mine.

"Lo," I whine. I hate my needy voice. I turn my face into my pillow and moan in distress. I'd like to escape my mind tonight. And the best, easiest way to do that is sex. The problem is: I fear for Moffy's safety, and *why* do I have to be the weird girl who'd like to drown those worries with a climax?

Lo climbs over me, resting either of his knees on my sides, and he flips me on my back. I stare up at him, his sharp jawline that's visible in our dark bedroom.

Very softly, I say, "I'd like to be normal tonight."

His brows knot in concern. "You are normal, Lil."

I shake my head a little. "I want to fuck you."

"Funny, I want to fuck you," he retorts.

I laugh weakly into an even weaker smile.

"It's true," he says in a playful tone. "My best friend"—he pinches my cheeks—"has turned me on since I hit puberty. I love everything about her, and there's not *one day* that I go without thinking, *I'd like to fuck that girl*." He lowers his lips, those beautiful pink lips to mine, a breath away, and whispers, "So there."

I tremble beneath him. "Lo." *Fuck me.* I shut down my brain's naughty request and press the baby monitor to my ear, just in case I missed something.

Lo watches me tentatively. "He's okay, Lil." The seriousness floods back to his voice.

"I'm just making sure."

Before I even finish the words, Lo climbs off me and the bed. He flicks on the lights.

"What are you doing?" I ask, sitting up. He's wearing black boxer briefs and sweatpants. Normally he wouldn't have those, but he's trying not to dangle the goods in front of an addict. Still though, I stare at his butt and his bulge, depending on which way he turns to me.

Dirty habit.

"I'll be right back." And then he opens the door and disappears.

I wear one of Lo's baggy black shirts. I catch myself biting my nails that sting. The moment I drop my hand, Lo returns, and I perk up as I see who he's brought with him.

Maximoff Hale. Our baby, dressed in a red onesie that says: *Avenger in Training*. His little tufts of dark brown hair are smoothed down, and he sleeps in Lo's arms with his mouth open. We no longer poke at him to ensure that he's alive.

Lo is holding our son. The baby that we created together. Half of him and half of me.

It's the most beautiful image my brain has ever received. And I'm afraid of turning it into something dirtier. So I swiftly roll onto my stomach and hide beneath the comforter.

"Lily," Lo chides. The bed undulates beneath his weight, and he rests beside me. "Come out, love."

"I'm not coming anywhere," I say immediately, the red rash of embarrassment hot and cruel.

Lo yanks off the comforter. "You're not hiding in the bathroom or beneath the covers. You're scared that Moffy isn't safe in the nursery tonight. So he's sleeping between us."

I gape and turn on my side, meeting his narrowed amber eyes. "Lo, I . . ." *I'm afraid.* Of myself.

"You'll be fine, love." He gently rests Moffy on the mattress between our bodies. And tears prick my eyes. He's content, happy, and quiet. As all babies should be.

I relax and touch his little hand, his fingers clasping around my pinky in his sleep. Maybe I can do this. I exhale and look up at Lo. He's studying me, charting mental notes of all my urges. I shift a little and cross my ankles. But they're starting to subdue along with my anxiety.

The distraction is nice.

I watch Moffy sleep, and Lo eases back onto his pillow. He's going to have Lo's cheekbones. I can tell. Besides the dark hair, he looks a lot how Lo did in his baby pictures.

"What if I squash him?" I ask Lo.

"I'm going to put him in his crib when you fall asleep," he says.

I nod at this plan.

"Shut your eyes, love."

With only a smidgen of reluctance, I close my eyes. My mind

rolls onward as I think one thing: I will always have bad days. It's a fact that I've come to terms with. "Lo," I say softly.

"Yeah?"

"An addict will always be an addict?" There is no changing that, I think. He's so quiet that I end up peeking at him with one eye.

He stares at me with such intensity, stealing my breath. "Did you ever dream that we'd be cured or something?" he asks.

My other eye opens. "No," I whisper. "Did you?"

He shakes his head. "I knew from the beginning that we'd be addicted after all." His amber eyes bore straight through me. "I just didn't know whether we'd be in a better place than we were before."

We are. I don't even have to say the words. He knows the answer too. We're in the best place we've ever been, reaching a stasis together. It's beautiful up here, and even if I fear falling, it's nice to know I've been down that road before. And I can always walk to the top again.

Lo leans over our son to kiss me tenderly on the lips, a chaste kiss, but one full of lifelong promise. I let it guide me to sleep.

Sixty-five

Lily Calloway

Rose passes me and Daisy hot chocolate mugs before she settles on the brand-new tufted love seat beside Connor, Jane on his lap. Ryke and Daisy have claimed the tufted beige *couch* next to them. My sisters and I are all bundled in blankets; a cold front swept in this morning.

I cup my mug with one hand, a fuzzy purple throw around my shoulders. I sit between Lo's legs while he rests his back on the white stone fireplace, one hand on Moffy's bouncer. None of us slept all that well, but we're less focused on our babies and more focused on my little sister.

"What happened to the couch?" Daisy finally asks as she crosses her legs. Ryke has an arm wrapped around her waist, dark circles beneath his eyes. He has to take Daisy's mug before she spills the hot chocolate on her lap.

Rose wavers, a bad liar. "It's not important."

Daisy twists a strand of her brown hair around her finger. She looks younger with her natural color, I realize. She looks more her age, more innocent. "I know you all are waiting for me to make a big speech . . ." She twiddles her fingers, and my stomach hurts watching her restless quirks. I'm not so sure they're healthy parts of her anymore. I'm not sure they ever were. "But I don't have one that really describes what I felt last night."

"Dais, it's okay," Ryke says. "You don't have to say a fucking thing if you don't want to."

She uncrosses her legs and then crosses them back. "I need to, I think." Her green eyes flit between me and Rose. "These past ten months living with you have been some of the best of my life. Being the youngest, I've always felt left out, and you both managed to include me, even when you were having babies." She smiles, a sad smile. "I want you both to know that I love you so much."

I wipe my eyes and glance at Rose. Her gaze is all glassy, even if she's not crying yet. This sounds like a very sad goodbye. I'm not ready for it. I thought we'd all be living together way longer than this.

I enjoy waking up in the morning to my little sister breezing around the kitchen with blueberries. Like a ball of sunshine, helping Ryke cook pancakes for the house. I love when she skateboards in the living room, reciting her theories on life and love. And when she proposes water balloon fights in the dead heat of summer.

There was a time when I had no idea who Daisy Calloway was. But I know her now. She's my exuberant little sister, and I've grown to love her more than blood. I love her as a friend, and I selfishly don't want to let her go.

Daisy continues, silent tears rolling down her face, "In some ways, I feel like I've regressed. But then I remember all the hours I've spent with you both." She looks right at me. "And I think I would've missed all those moments had I been somewhere else." She sniffs. "I gained something here. And it's not something I want to lose."

I use the edge of my blanket to dry my eyes. "You won't," I say, my voice scratchy. "Whatever happens, you won't."

"We'll always be your sisters," Rose tells her. And that's when her tears fall. She rolls her eyes at the sight of them.

Daisy nods a few times. "I've realized that no matter where I go, I'm going to be afraid. I can travel all the way to Costa Rica and scare myself."

Ryke goes rigid at that. He rests his hand on Daisy's head in comfort.

"And even if I've been a little more out of it than usual, you've all made me happier," she declares. "So I'm staying."

"We both are," Ryke announces, and he messes Daisy's hair with a rough hand. She smiles up at him.

I gape. "Really?" I practically cry.

She laughs, rubbing her reddened eyes. "Really, really."

"This is the best news." I turn to Rose, expecting a similar reaction.

Her tears have dried, and she now *glares* at our little sister. "You could've spared me the swollen eyes by prefacing with *I'm staying*."

Lo cuts in, "She unthawed your heart with sentimental things. Don't bitch at her for it."

"I revoke that word from your vocabulary," Rose retorts, crossing her arms. Connor grins into his sip of coffee.

"Oh look at that, she put a spell on me," Lo says dryly. He nods to Connor. "How does it feel when she bewitches you? Do you go all dead inside?"

"Just the opposite," Connor replies, even playing into *magic* banter, which he usually shuts down. My smile hurts my cheeks.

Lo grimaces. "Christ. Sorry I asked."

"Speaking of you two," Ryke chimes in, gesturing between Connor and Rose. "I got a text from Lily last night saying that she convinced you to join social media. What the fuck?"

"I was already on Twitter," Connor reminds him. "She only had to convince Rose."

I perk up at the new topic. "Everyone should do it."

Ryke shoots me a dirty (the nonsexual kind of dirty) look.

"Please tell me that wasn't your high school fucking motto." This is protective Ryke coming forth. (The nonsexual kind of coming.)

I scrunch my nose as I contemplate this. "No, that's more Daisy. She's the one who tries to rally people into doing crazy things." I point at her. "Like walking the roof ledge of an apartment building."

"Yeah, bro," Lo says with a smile. "You're dating that one."

Ryke raises his brows at his girlfriend.

Daisy smiles so wide that it brightens the whole room. Tension extinguished. "I figure I have about thirty more years left of crazy things, so hey, I might as well do them with as many people as I can." She nudges his side. "Even if it's just you."

Ryke is about to full-on make out with her. I know that lusty look in his eyes. I wear it on too many occasions, I think. He ends up kissing her head and focuses back on all of us. "I thought we agreed no social media?"

"That was until last night," Connor says. "Lily tweeted that everyone was safe after the break in, and dozens of news stations credited that tweet as a legitimate source."

For the first time, our voice was truly heard. No twisting of our words. No bad editing or misplaced quotes.

"We're taking some control back," Rose adds.

Lo is new to this situation like Ryke and Daisy. Lines wrinkle his forehead as he digests this info. "And with what username are you taking control back?" he asks her. "@Callowitch, hashtag spank me?"

I smack Lo's chest.

"What?" he whispers to me.

"That was mean."

Connor isn't smiling, which means that this one definitely stung Rose.

She inhales strongly. "You just insulted both of my sisters, considering I'm Rose *Cobalt*. And hashtag, I *loathe* you."

Lo raises his hands. "All I'm saying, Rose *Cobalt*, is that no matter how much we go on social media, there'll still be people criticizing us. This isn't going to fix that."

I look up at him. "I know that, Lo." He's worried about me—that I've put all my faith in social media as a big solution. "We'll always have haters. But we'll have fans too. And I'd like to keep those."

Lo's shoulders relax, and he nods at me. "Okay."

"Rose's username is RoseCCobalt," I tell him. "It was the only free one."

"So I'm guessing Loren Hale is taken?" he asks me.

I nod. "Yep."

"Wait, how can someone take our names?" Ryke frowns.

Oh jeez. He's the only one not up to speed on the ways of Twitter. Daisy shows him her phone. "I'll create one for you."

"We're really doing this?" he asks, hesitating.

"Just be yourself," Connor tells him. "I know you probably fail at written word, but in person, you usually ace being who you are."

"I'm going to ignore the part where you fucking insulted me."

Connor grins. "Why? Those are the best parts."

Ryke flips him off.

"How about 'rykefuckmeadows' as a username?" Daisy asks, typing into her phone. "Oh wait . . . that's already taken too."

"Seriously?" Ryke says, sounding impressed. He leans over her to check the screen.

"Just do it backward," Lo says, "MeadowsRyke. He won't care."

"Yeah, that's fine with me," Ryke agrees.

"Got it," Daisy tells us. In the next few minutes, we spout off multiple ideas for Daisy's and Lo's usernames. And I steal Lo's phone to type in prospects.

"What's yours?" Lo asks Connor, forgetting Connor's verified Twitter account.

"My name, no breaks," Connor replies.

@ConnorCobalt. It's not surprising that he was able to snag that username. He had it before he even met us.

Lo peers over my shoulder as I zone in on a Twitter discussion between our fans. "Missed opportunity, Connor," Lo says with a growing smile.

"What's that?"

"One of your fans has the username: ConnorCockbalt." Lo tilts his head at him. "Hate to tell you this, but it's better than yours, love."

Connor's grin envelops his face. "I don't disagree with you."

I'm sucked into the Twitter discussion, my eyes glazing over the usernames. My hearts swells at each one.

@lorenhale
@rykemeadows
@ConnorCockbalt
@lilycalloways
@rosescalloway
@runcalloway
@callowaysisters
@lilocalloway
@coballoway
@cobaltscalloway

The people behind them mean something to me the way all fandoms do.

"That's pretty cool," Lo whispers in my ear. He's returned to the screen, peering behind me at the rest of the usernames.

"Yeah," I say with a bigger smile. "It's pretty cool."

"Try lorenhellion," he breathes. I do, and a green checkmark shows that it's available. Daisy chooses @daisyonmeadows, a silly pun that's also a little flirtatious. It suits her.

"So what does us being on social media fucking mean exactly?" Ryke asks. I think he knows. He just wants someone to say it.

I speak up first. "We can't try to hide anymore." I nod resolutely. It's ironic coming from the girl who used to be a hermit, who shied away from attention and cameras. By using social media, we're now cementing a future in the public eye.

No takebacks.

But if we're going to be under a spotlight, I'd much rather do it on *my* terms than someone else's. Maybe then we'll have a fighting chance at protecting Maximoff and Jane as they grow older. We all have a bigger voice now.

No one can steal that from us.

Sixty-six

Loren Hale

Ryke pops a bagel into a toaster. "Don't fucking say it," he tells me.

I must wear a mocking smile. "I wasn't going to say anything." While the girls talk quietly in the living room, we refill coffees in the kitchen.

Connor examines the expiration date on the milk. "I'll say it."

"Do it," I prod.

"Daisy Meadows," Connor puts it out there. The username she chose stirred old memories for us. We ream Ryke all the time about that possibility. Marrying her. Before, I'd shut him down. Now, it's fun to watch him roll his eyes and tell me to fuck off.

Ryke looks incensed as he waits for his breakfast to cook. "You two are fucking hilarious."

"I thought we were more predictable than hilarious," Connor says easily, trashing the milk. "But I accept both."

I lean against the stove. "Are you going to name your kids Wild or Pony?"

"Shut the fuck up," Ryke says lightly, but even he laughs. "Pony Meadows, really?"

"It's nature." I theatrically gasp like Daisy always does. "Nature is amazing."

"You fucking suck at mimicking her."

"Yeah, that was weak." I watch Connor pour his coffee in a mug. He combs his hand through his wavy hair, flattening some of the thicker strands. "Hey . . ." My blood ices, and I hesitate to say what's popped in my head.

But he spins around and sets his deep blue eyes on me. Waiting for me to finish.

I haven't asked him about the article in a while, the one involving my son. It hasn't cropped up on the internet. I assumed it was taken care of, but I'd sleep easier hearing it from him. I ask, "Did you and my dad work things out?"

"We're not going to be best friends any time soon, but we've set aside our differences for now." He takes a sip of coffee. "Turns out we have something in common." I read his gaze that's more open than usual, the answer clear.

They both love me.

That's not even the strangest part. What's crazy is that I feel *worthy* of love.

"So how'd you bury the article?" I ask with a frown. "Whatever it cost, I can write a check—"

"Don't worry about it," he says, his defenses rising, his emotions padlocked.

"Connor—"

"Lo," he says smoothly, "trust me when I tell you that it's taken care of. This isn't a part of your story anymore."

Ryke grabs his popped bagel. "Just take the easy fucking win, Lo. We all dodged a shit storm."

Not every situation has to be a full-on, dragged-out battle, and if this one is easier, yeah, I'll take it. "Thanks," I tell Connor.

"For you, anything."

This time when he says it, I recognize the depth to his words. I'm not sure what he did for me. With someone as guarded as Connor, I doubt I'll ever find out. But I'm sure that it was more than I could ever give.

Sixty-seven

Lily Calloway

The register is pretty simple, or if you'd rather man the espresso and coffee makers, you're welcome to do that. I thought the comics would be more up your alley though." I open some of the blinds on the Superheroes & Scones storefront windows. We're closed for another two hours, but I'm guiding Willow around, Maya in tow.

"I probably shouldn't be near hot liquids," Willow says softly. "I can be a klutz when I'm nervous." She adjusts the straps of her jean backpack on her arm. She still carries it around like a safety vest.

"Good to know," I say, watching her scan the empty store, as though it's her first time in here. Maybe as a future employee, it is. "If you don't want a job—"

"No, I do," she tells me quickly. "I really do. I'm just taking it all in." She pushes up her glasses. "It's my first time on my own . . ."

"Lo mentioned that to me." I've never been on my own. I've always had him, and I can't imagine being seventeen and deciding to journey off to another state in pursuit of happiness. It's something Daisy would've done, if she grew the courage.

Willow says she's not adventurous like my little sister, but this seems like a pretty big adventure to me.

"Your mom said that you can always go home. She left that door open for you, right . . . ?" I trail off, distracted by a *Celebrity Crush* tabloid on the counter. An employee must've left it behind. Normally, I'd itch to read a couple of headlines and flip through.

I pick up the magazine and go to trash it, doing the sensible thing. I think Ryke would be the proudest of all.

"Yeah." Willow nods. "It's always open."

"That's good," I say, a little absentminded as I toss the magazine in the trash. Ha! Take that, Wendy Collins, staff writer, and my arch nemesis. Before I close the lid, I do accidentally catch a peek of one headline: *Lily Calloway & Loren Hale Wedding Rumors!*

Nope. I refuse to believe they've leaked. We're keeping everything private and under wraps. This one peaceful day can't be ruined. I shut the trash lid and raise my chin like Rose would. I feel confident, but I'm sure I look silly.

Near me, Maya slips behind the register, counting the cash. "Roomie, come. Let me teach you, young wise one."

Willow smiles a little more as she follows Maya, her new roommate. Lo offered our house to his half-sister. We have plenty of extra rooms, but she didn't want to intrude. I think it's overwhelming. There are so many of us, and she's still trying to get used to a new place.

Maya is only twenty, and her old roommate just left for California, so it all worked out. Now Willow will finish her senior year here, and I suppose contemplate college. Normal stuff. Life doesn't stop when you take a new road. It always finds a way to go on.

A loud knock on the glass door jolts me awake. Especially as Garth emerges from the break room at the sound. My big-boned bodyguard hovers close to my side. I squint, distinguishing the face behind the glass door, the *closed* sign dangling near him.

My throat tightens.

It's the hoodie guy, the one that Lo said was named Garrison.

I bite my nail, hesitating to let him in. He knocks harder, and his narrowed eyes meet mine. They're not full of terror and rage. He apprehensively shifts his body weight from one foot to the other.

I look up at Garth. "Maybe I should just hear him out?"

Garth, a very diplomatic man, nods and says, "Whatever you want."

Okay. I trudge forward and tentatively unlock the door. When I peek my head out, Garrison draws his hoodie back, revealing his brown hair and boyish face.

He hesitantly glances over my shoulder. "Is Loren here?"

"No." I don't add that he's at our house, preparing for the final Hale Co. meeting this afternoon, where the board chooses the new CEO.

Garrison notices my bodyguard, and he lets out a short, pained laugh. "Forget it. This was a mistake." He's about to turn around and leave.

"Wait," I say quickly.

He freezes by the door, halfway turned.

"What do you want?"

He grinds his teeth like he has trouble producing the words. "Your boyfriend . . . he offered me and my friends a job." Garrison rolls his eyes. "It's fucking stupid anyway. Everything is."

"Lo told me about that," I say, swinging the door wider open. "Do you want to come in?" My stomach does this nervous flip thing, but it stops the minute his reddened, surprised eyes lock on mine.

"What?" he says in disbelief.

"If you want a job, you have to come into the store," I tell him. "Although . . ." A light bulb flickers in my brain. "It'd be kinda cool if we had a superhero mascot out front. Do you want to be a mascot?"

"No." He shakes his head like I'm half-crazy and half a godsend. No one has really ever looked at me like that—the *godsend* half. I've been plenty crazy before.

He slowly walks inside, his hands in his jean pockets, more nervous, I think.

Garth blocks him though. "I need to pat you down."

I think Garrison is going to put up a fight. But he spreads his arms out, and Garth pats his pockets and checks the hoodie pouch. When he finishes, Garth nods to me like *he's good.*

"So, you want a job?" I can't believe he's taking Lo's offer. I honestly didn't think any of them would bite.

Garrison can't stop staring at me, his emotions surfacing, ones that he probably meant to suppress. "You're not even going to ask me where I was that night? Or what happened?"

Oh. Maybe I was supposed to start with that. I just didn't want to scare him off, after I saw how much it took for him to come here. "Where were you?" I ask, reluctant to hear his answer.

He stares up at the ceiling in thought, shaking his head. "I'm not a good guy. I never told them to stop. I knew that they planned to break in and scare everyone, and I didn't do anything. I just let them leave." He chokes on another laugh. "And now they're all looking at a year in prison. And I'm standing free."

He doesn't look free to me. "What made you stay back?"

His gaze drops to the carpeted floor. "Everything your boyfriend said . . . fuck, I don't know. It just didn't feel right, scaring girls and babies . . . I know one of you has PTSD . . ."

I go rigid, and my mouth falls. "Wha . . . ?" That has been a fact we've all kept secret from the public.

"I didn't tell anyone," he says quickly. "I promise. I can't even remember who let it slip. Either Ryke or Loren shouted it at me. No one else was around." He hangs his head again. "I think . . . you should know that I planned to go with my friends."

He bites his lips to keep more emotions at bay. A lump lodges in my throat. I see my best friend, a young Loren Hale who has so many muddled and warring sentiments swirling around him. The pain of living. It's in Garrison's eyes.

"I literally could not move my stupid feet," he finally says. "And there's a part of me that wishes I was with them. That I got caught too."

It's just guilt. I swallow hard and say, "You did the right thing."

"Did I?" he asks and shakes his head again. "I can't even say *I'm sorry* because it feels fucking stupid. Like . . ." He runs a hand through his hair. "Like it's not enough, you know? It's not at all."

"This was enough," I tell him softly. "I promise, it was." I can't even imagine Lo finding his way here at seventeen, saying these guttural, painful things to absolve himself.

Loren Hale walked in agony for another half decade.

He'd be happy to learn that he saved someone from that today.

Garrison rubs his eyes with the sleeve of his black hoodie and then exhales deeply and scans the store like Willow had previously done.

"Here, I'll introduce you to Maya, the store manager. She'll have a better idea what positions need to be filled." I lead him over to the counter where Lo's little sister and Maya stand behind the register.

"Hey," Garrison greets the girls with a head nod.

As soon as Willow hears the male voice, she somehow knocks into the cash tray. It overturns and clatters to the floor.

"I'm *so* sorry," she says, her skin paling. The opposite of my embarrassed red flush. She sheepishly smiles at me, avoiding direct eye contact with Garrison. She bends down to collect the money while Maya fiddles with the computer.

"I can help," Garrison says, squatting to gather dollar bills and quarters.

Oh jeez. I watch the way he furtively glimpses at Willow while she clumsily scoops the cash. I know that look. It's one that says *you're pretty and interesting and I want to get to know you* all wrapped in one.

Before any flirting occurs, I do what Lo would want and slip between them. "Okay, now you've met Willow and, Willow, you've met Garrison. Meet and greet has ended." I'll have to text Lo to see if I should put them on separate shifts.

While I'd like Superheroes & Scones to be a geeky matchmaking facility, Willow is off-limits. Lo said to keep an eye on any "creepy guys" and mentioned that if a Captain America fanatic hits on her, he's clearly not good enough. Willow deservers Scott Summers and above.

It was the most overprotective, cutest superhero reference he's used in a while.

"Are you new here?" Garrison makes small talk.

No small talk. That's off-limits too. "Yep. Yep, everyone's new," I say rapidly. "Willow, can you get my purse from the break room?" I didn't bring a purse, so it'll take her some time. Smart thinking. I internally pat myself on the shoulder.

"Sure." She struggles to fit the cash tray back into the register.

"I can do it," Maya tells her, taking over.

Willow leaves to the break room, but she stops midway like she lost something. "My backpack . . ."

Garrison finds it on the ground before I do. "This?" He picks up the old jean backpack and carries it to her.

Their fingers brush as he passes it to Willow. "Thanks," she says, as pale as a ghost.

I give up. Maybe in another life, I was cupid and foretold every relationship there ever was. I smile at that thought. I prophesied them all except my very own.

Sixty-eight

Loren Hale

Y ou ready?" I ask Ryke as we step into the Hale Co. eleva-
tors that'll bring us to the board room. His unkempt hair
is barely combed, the sleeves of his white button-down rolled
to his forearms. He even ditched a suit jacket.

I thought for sure I'd be meeting someone besides my brother
today. I'd come face-to-face with the Ryke Meadows that's been
buttoning his shirts to the collar, tying wide ties, riding to the offices in a car, not a motorcycle.

"I usually ask you that," he says under his breath, quiet enough
that I don't comment on it.

I try to ignore the tension and punch the button. "You look like
yourself today." I gesture to his hair. "Just rolled out of bed, grabbed
the first thing on the floor." I'm about to joke more, but he's not
smiling or laughing.

His shoulders remain strict. We're about to cement one of our
futures, and Ryke believes neither is good. I don't know anymore.
This elevator doesn't seem like a ride to hell or to a cage. Somewhere from the beginning to now, I've changed.

"Ryke—"

"I tried to be different so I could beat you at this," he suddenly
says. "To help you. And I could barely stomach it."

"For what it's worth," I say, "I'm glad you changed back."

He nods repeatedly, staring at the floor while we stand side by side. The elevator doors have already closed, and we've begun to rise. "I need to tell you something," he breathes. He turns his head to me. "I got tested, at the hospital."

My brows pull together. "To see if you can donate?"

"Yeah." He waits a second, struggling to explain himself. "I'm a match."

I open my mouth, not sure what to say.

"Crazy, right?" he says roughly. "Who would've fucking thought that I'd be Dad's one chance at life?"

"You don't have to do anything," I remind him, my stomach at my knees.

Ryke runs his fingers through his hair, not confused or uncertain. "Regardless of what happens today," he says, "I've made a decision about the transplant surgery."

"Yeah?" I frown. I can't place what I hope he'll say. I just want everyone to live, but the cost of my dad living is high.

Then he stares right at me, with that stubborn self-confidence Ryke possesses, and he says, "I'm not doing this for him. I'm fucking doing this for *me*." He points at his chest. "Because I can't live with myself knowing that I could've helped him and I did *nothing*."

I'm surprised but then I'm not. He's the most compassionate person I've ever met. Without asking, he helped me stay sober for years on end. He became friends with a lonely girl who needed one. He watched over her when no one else did.

He will always be the biggest hero in my world. "I'll be there," I tell him. "Every step of the way."

Relief floods his dark features, no fight between us. "Good," he says, "because I'm going to be bored shitless in recovery."

I laugh once, then reach out, clasp his hand, pulling him closer for a hug. I pat his back. I'm about to say *thanks* or maybe *you can always back out if you need to.* It barely hits me that our dad might be able to watch my kid grow up. Ryke's too, if he has any.

But Ryke draws back, his hand firmly on my shoulder as he says, "It's a long process, but it's fucking happening. Sometime after your wedding, I'm thinking." His lips lift in a fraction of a smile. "When I made this choice, it felt fucking right. So, I'm doing it."

I can't talk him out of it, he's saying. Not that I can talk Ryke out of anything. "Should I buy board games? Operation?" I flash a wry smile.

He messes my hair with a full-blown grin, reminding me that I'm the little brother again.

And then the elevator stops. The doors slide open, and our smiles fade. Reality just a foot away. The meeting room down the hall in sight.

"I'm right behind you," Ryke tells me.

I take the first step onto the seventy-fifth floor of Hale Co.

This is it.

Sixty-nine

Loren Hale

Ryke and I sit on either end of the long table, seven board members on one side, seven on the other. While passing around sandwiches and coffee, they've been going over Hale Co.'s financial reports and business relations, no mention of the CEO title yet.

They've finally reached the end of their laundry list of topics. Focusing on the one that's haunting me.

Daniel Perth rises from his seat and buttons his suit. "We appreciate how much work you've both put in toward heading this company." He looks to Ryke. "As you've come to respect us, so have we to you. You're multilingual, quick to understand our approaches, and very receptive to new ideas. Your father boasted about you. He said you were too smart for your own good."

The board members collectively chuckle. Daniel smiles. "That's a decent compliment from Jonathan Hale. He doesn't give many."

Ryke stays quiet, but his eyes flicker to me more than once. We're far away from each other, separated by the length of the long wooden table.

My muscles bind the longer I sit here without answers. God, I want this. For so many reasons. My foot jostles, and I rub my lips. Waiting.

Then Daniel turns to me. "When we first met you, we weren't sure if you'd want to be involved with this company. Through your initiative, you've proven to us that you do." He pauses. "You're a lot like your father, but you're not him."

I clench my teeth, and I can feel my jaw sharpening. Right. I break eye contact, staring out at the floor-length window. The one that overlooks Philadelphia on a muggy afternoon. In the silence, I say, "What were you expecting exactly?"

"Let's see," Daniel says, "the son of Jonathan Hale: what he'd call a *little shit*. What Jonathan is. Someone who'd throw a bottle of wine at a wall, toss papers around, yell in an employee's face if the job didn't go as planned. Degrade a person so he'd feel better."

I frown and meet his face again.

"Don't look so shocked. We know the terrible parts of your father. We've been around him long enough. And we're all more than impressed to see that you didn't inherit his *habits*."

I did though. I inherited all of those things.

I stare dazedly at the table. My therapist told me something once.

He said, "*Sometimes the person we think we'll become is the person we already are, and the person we truly become is the person we least expect.*"

I'd been terrified of becoming my father for years. It's why I never wanted to take Hale Co. It's why I pulled against everything he threw at me.

And all that time, I was already him.

But I'm not my father anymore. I've become a better version of the person I once was. Someone I can stand to be around, someone I can live with.

Yeah. *It took long enough.* "Have you decided then?" I ask Daniel.

"We've voted, but ultimately, we realized that the decision should be left with you two. We want someone who truly *wants* to run this company. If that's both of you, then we'll be damn happy to have the Hale brothers as the face of Hale Co."

Hale brothers. Ryke's jaw hardens. He considers himself a Meadows, not a Hale.

"You want us to be CEOs together?" I ask.

"*Only* if that's what you want," he emphasizes.

I lock eyes with Ryke, and I lean forward, cupping my hands on the table. I'd do this with him, if he's up to it. But I still doubt he'd enjoy this life. I doubt he even wants it.

"Just tell me one thing," Ryke says to me, the board overhearing. But I block out their stern expressions. It's only me and my brother. "Will you be happy?"

My smile stretches my face. I can't contain it. "I already am." I've proven to *myself* that I could reach this point without a crutch. I'm sober. I'm healthy. I'm so goddamn alive.

Ryke smiles back like he's proud of me. "It's yours, little brother. I believe in you."

For months, those last four words are all I've ever wanted to hear. From Ryke, they mean everything to me.

Seventy

Lily Calloway

While I'm seated at the vanity in a hotel suite, Rose clips the front strands of my hair back into a diamond barrette. My three sisters and my mom flutter around me like bluebirds in *Cinderella*. I never thought I'd be a princess of any fairy tale. I'm more like the pumpkin that lies sadly on the wet pavement.

"What if he says no?" I suddenly spout my billionth fear of the morning.

"I'll rip off his penis," Rose says flatly as I stand up from the vanity bench. That is *not* something I'd enjoy. I love Loren Hale's cock, very much so.

Our mom rolls her eyes and then rests a hand on my shoulder. "Don't listen to your sister."

I never thought I'd be on speaking terms with my mom for my wedding day, but we are. We really are.

"He'll say yes," Poppy chimes in as she straightens out my white tulle skirt and silk fitted top. It's not a traditional wedding dress. I tried on almost all styles: mermaid, ballgown, A-line, empire. It wasn't until I found the skirt and shortened top combo that I felt like myself.

Daisy nudges my side. "And not because he knows his manhood is on the line."

"That'll only be two percent of the reason," Rose butts in. She splays the rest of my straight brown hair on my shoulders and glances at the clock on the hotel nightstand. "We should head to the roof."

Now? I must be a deer caught in headlights because everyone starts spouting encouragements at once. My mind whirls in a thousand different directions. I haven't seen Lo all day, and maybe that's what scares me about this impending ceremony. What if I arrive and he's not there? What if it starts raining? What if lightning strikes a guest down?

"*Lily*." Rose snaps her fingers in my face. She's standing right in front of me. My high-octane maid of honor. She lifts my chin so I meet her eyes and says, "He's waiting for you. Don't be afraid."

I inhale a strong breath. I'm about to marry my best friend. If I repeat it too many times, I start crying. So I pocket that thought, and I follow my sisters out of the hotel room and to the elevator. They're all my bridesmaids, dressed in lavender one-shoulder gowns. What Rose called Grecian-inspired.

As we rise to the rooftop, she passes me my bouquet of purple flowers, the fancy name for them escaping my mind.

I am flooded with thousands upon thousands of memories that contain Loren Hale. In each one, some part of our bodies touch. Our hands. Our legs. Our hearts. Subconsciously, he guides me to the rooftop where he waits.

I hear the violins through the hallway door. Poppy, the last bridesmaid, just pushed through, leaving me in the Philly high-rise with my father.

"Is Maximoff outside?" I press him for information, maybe to prolong the mystery behind the door.

My dad avoids the answer. "We're next." He places his hand on my back. "Ready, Lily?"

Am I ready to marry the man who has my entire soul?

The nervous anxiety subsides. I am. But it's not until my dad opens the door that I fully believe I'm marrying him. That this is my wedding day. October 10th.

On our terms.

At long, long last.

The skyline glitters in the sunlight, the air crisp and cool. And my sisters, in their purple Grecian dresses, stand in a diagonal line by an ivy arch. White flowers blooming around the structure. Their smiles could light the sun.

Purple petals decorate the aisle. White wooden chairs on either side. Our few family members turn their heads at my entrance. My mom with Jane, Willow, and Jonathan.

The dapper men beside the arch stand tall and poised: Sam, on the end, and Ryke, who cradles my son. Maximoff dressed in a red superhero cape and onesie, the letter M embroidered in black. Tears nearly burst forth, but I try my hardest to suppress them.

Make it to Loren Hale.

Make it to Loren Hale.

I repeat the mantra with each step forward. Connor stands behind Loren, officiating the wedding, but I focus solely on my best friend, shutting out the surroundings for an extended moment.

In a perfectly fitted tux, Lo waits at the end of the aisle for me, his hands cupped in front of his body. Those intoxicating amber eyes never diverge from mine, never break or part or leave me.

He is ice and scotch, sharp and dizzying—breathtakingly gorgeous. And when he looks at me, I see those thousands of memories course through his gaze. Seven-year-olds performing a backyard ceremony. Nine-year-olds racing around his father's mansion.

Fifteen-year-olds flipping through comic books on his bed.

We have consumed each other from day one. And we truly never let go.

Only a few paces from Lo, my dad kisses my cheek, returns to his seat next to my mom. Rose collects the bouquet from me, and I'm whisked by my own feet to Lo's side.

Magnetically, we cling together, his hand slipping into mine, our legs knocking as they find each other. We stand so close, like we fear someone else pulling us apart. I subconsciously tune out the music, and Lo cups my face, his eyes dancing across my features.

Mine fly across his.

I'd like to skip ahead to the part when we kiss. Lo must read me well. His smile suddenly dimples his cheeks, and he whispers, "Soon."

Soon. I like that.

"Lily, Lo," Connor says, attempting to deter my gaze. It works after he calls my name a second time. And I plant them on the well-dressed, impeccably styled Connor Cobalt. He's a billion dollars, and the perfect officiator for our wedding.

Lo told him nothing formal for the ceremony, something short and sweet.

"Before you each say a few words to each other," Connor tells us, "there's something we all want to say to you."

My brows scrunch and I look to Lo. He shakes his head at me like he wasn't warned about this plan. I scan my family in the audience, and my mom's already dabbing her eyes with tissues. Jonathan is beaming with pride, and my sisters . . . I turn to them, and they've sincerely lost it. Daisy is passing a tissue box down the line.

They're crying before I am.

What's going on?

Connor picks up where he left off. "I speak for everyone here today," he tells us, "when I say that you two—Lily and Loren—are the strongest people we've all ever had the honor to meet."

My eyes well. *What?* Lo squeezes my hand.

Connor remains stoic, his grin genuine and heartfelt. "You both have spent years praising all of us for our talents and our strengths, but you were too blinded by your own foibles to even realize how much we've revered you. For years, we've watched you fight for this future, for each other, and you've conquered a larger battle in your lifetime than most of us will ever come to see."

I feel the tears roll down my cheeks, my chin trembling. I never ever believed someone could say something like that to us. This is a dream, but I know it's not. Because Lo squeezes my hand again, his eyes misted too.

And Connor says, "You are our heroes, and today, we are grateful to celebrate your love and your life together."

Lo wipes his eyes with his sleeve. "Goddamn, Connor."

Everyone lets out tearful, emotional laughs. I do too, and Lo uses his thumb to dry off my face.

"You two have the floor," Connor tells us, taking a step back.

Our turn. I look up at Lo again, one of his hands on my hip, the bare skin where my skirt meets my top.

"First or second?" he asks me.

We didn't write down vows. We told each other to just say whatever hits us in the moment. I knew that if I tuned out the audience, his groomsmen, my bridesmaids—I'd be able to accomplish the task without stage fright. It's already begun. The last figure I see in my peripheral is Maximoff Hale, my smiling, happy superhero son.

"First," I whisper. "I'll go first."

His fingers are lost in my hair, his large hand encasing my cheek. I think back to days upon days with him. And I begin, "If someone ever asks how long we've spent together, I'd say for as long as my mind stretches back. I can't tell you the day that I fell in love with you because there wasn't a single day that I didn't." My voice shakes with more joy than I've ever known. "You have the purest parts of my heart, and I'm certain that in every alternate universe, I'm always, always in love with you."

His chest rises with mine, our breath matched. Exhale for exhale. Inhale for inhale. He leans close like he aches to kiss me. His arms wrap around my waist. And in his sweetly edged voice, he tells me, "Nearly every day of our lives you've wondered one thing."

Sex darts into my brain.

And a smile lights up his face, knowing full-well the dirty paths of my mind. "You've wondered when your superpowers will kick in."

His words flush my thoughts, and I focus on his intense, passionate gaze. "Have they?" I ask softly.

"According to your timeline," he says, "they've been present as far as your mind stretches back." His lips rise. "Lily Calloway . . . all this time, your superpower has been loving me." Tears cloud my eyes, and they don't stop, especially as he adds, "And you'll be happy to know that I'm not mortal."

"You aren't?" I choke.

"No." He shakes his head, brushing away the wetness beneath my eyes. "Because my superpower is the love that I have for you. It's out of this world, extraordinary, incomprehensible kind of love. And no one and nothing on this earth comes close to it."

My heart is so full that I can hardly breathe.

Our lips meet at the same moment, expressing the words we've spoken. Our bodies attract like magnets that've met for an unquantifiable time.

In the very happiest moment of my life, I learn three things:

I am strong.

I have powers.

And my soul meets Loren Hale's in every kiss. When the curtains on my universe close, he will still be with me. That, I'm sure of.

Epilogue

Loren Hale

Ghosts, witches, and zombie kids skip along the street at 5 p.m. on Halloween night. The sun hasn't even dropped yet, and they're already crazy for candy. I hop into my new car, another black Audi, with Connor in the passenger seat and Ryke in the back.

"Don't speed," Ryke says, buttoning his plaid flannel shirt, his plain Halloween costume. I still have no clue what he's dressed as, other than himself. "There's too many fucking kids out."

Connor checks his Rolex watch. "At least go ten over."

I glance at my mirror as I pull onto the street, ignoring comments from the peanut gallery.

Ryke says, "Your worst nightmare is being late to your own fucking party. Isn't it, Cobalt?"

"Only if the people attending matter," Connor replies. "If the party was full of carbon copies of you, I'd purposely be two hours late."

Ryke leans back in his seat. "You'd be the only one at that fucking party because versions of me wouldn't even go."

"That's rude," Connor says. "But if we're being realistic here, I wouldn't even invite one of you to my party. I like my guests to be potty trained."

They're giving me a migraine. "You both remember when I asked, 'hey, who wants to come with me to buy a couple bags of ice at the gas station?' *This* . . ." I take a hand off the wheel and gesture between the two of them. ". . . isn't what I had in mind." I could've been on my honeymoon this week, but Lily and I decided not to have one. We've spent years alone together, and the moments when we're living with our friends, with the people we love, with our son—those are the ones that feel like something special. We don't need to be in an exotic country or on the ocean to experience that.

We just need to be home.

"I wanted out of the fucking house," Ryke reminds me. Party planning isn't his thing. We're entertaining some of the kinder neighbors and their kids in our backyard, as well as our families tonight. Lily had a whole shopping list from Rose, and she forgot the ice.

Rose said the guest list was about fifty. The decorations remind me of parties the Calloways would throw. Fog machines, pumpkins, scarecrows, spider webs, face painting, and apple bobbing.

Connor says lightly, "Should we sing 'Happy Birthday' instead?"

"That depends . . ." I switch lanes and turn into the gas station. "Does it also come with a lap dance?"

Connor grins. "I only give those to people I truly love."

I park the car and turn toward him. "What lucky bastards."

He unbuckles his seatbelt. "Only one bastard," he corrects. "I'll grab the ice. You two stay here." He leaves me and my brother, shutting the car door behind him.

Ryke climbs up from the backseat to the passenger, a silver plastic bottle of Ziff: River Rush in hand. He drinks the last of the translucent green liquid in one gulp. It's the number one selling sports drink to date, a flavor that Ryke helped choose after Greg asked.

My brother notices me staring at the bottle. "Blue Squall is being taken off the market in November," he says. "It's still fucking strange that I'm the face of anything."

"You mean after you went to jail?" He was dropped from plenty of sponsorships after the statutory rape rumors, but it was all false.

He nods, setting the bottle in the cup holder.

"It's been a year," I remind him. "People forget."

"Even if we don't." His dark eyes rise to mine. "Do you ever think about four years ago, the night we met?"

"The Halloween party?" I vaguely recall. The memory is blurry, some of it black from booze. I can piece apart scenes, but the ones that contain Ryke are practically all shadowed.

"Yeah, the one that Connor invited you to."

"Sometimes." My hand falls off the steering wheel. "I can't remember a lot of it." I know I fought with guys on the Penn track team because I stole their family's alcohol. Someone punched me, and Ryke, dressed as Green Arrow, intervened at one point.

Ryke rests his head back. "I think about it almost every fucking day."

My brows furrow. "What about?"

He looks at me again. "I think about what would've happened if I just left you there."

"I'll tell you, bro, so you can stop torturing yourself." I don't break his gaze. "I would've woken up the next morning, kick-started the day with some Baileys, then switched to whiskey and bourbon. Every hour, every damn day, and I would've taken down the only girl I've ever loved with me."

His nose flares as he restrains his emotion.

"You saved me, and the way I see it, Rose saved Lily." In rehab, the counselors told me that I was a real asshole—that I said unconscionable things to people and that *no one* should be around me when they're in a bad place. But I needed someone. Without support, it'd be too hard to stand up and too easy to fall down.

Ryke's one decision changed my world.

"When I think back to that day, or what I can remember," I tell

Ryke, "I don't usually think about what a fucking asshole I was. I'm just grateful for the kind of guy you were then and the one you are now." I flash him a half-smile. "I love you, man."

"Fuck you," he says lightly, his lips lifting.

Connor knocks on the passenger window, two bags of ice in hand. I pop the trunk, and after he sets the bags in there, he returns to the passenger window.

"He wants his seat back," I tell Ryke.

Ryke flips off Connor though and says, "Fuck off."

Two seconds later, he opens the back door and slides in. "I thought you enjoyed the backseat," Connor tells him. "You have two windows to stick your head out of instead of one."

"You're getting him confused with Daisy," I chime in, remembering a road trip with just the three of us and her. Every time Connor and I manned the wheel, our anxiety hit the roof, and we almost forced Ryke to drive the whole way.

"And she's fucking cooler than both of you," Ryke retorts while I drive back home.

Connor's brow arches. "I take your opinion on the matter with low regard."

"I'm not a dog, Cobalt."

"But you are fucking Daisy Calloway," he replies easily. "Logically, you'd believe that she's about a blow job or two cooler than us."

I switch lanes again. "You better add more hand jobs to that," I tell him. "Lily said that Daisy hates giving head."

Ryke pinches his eyes with his fingers. "I fucking hate you both."

I glance at my brother beside me. "It'll pass, bro. And if it makes you feel any better, Rose apparently hates blow jobs too."

"Because she can't take all of me in her mouth and it aggravates her," Connor clarifies.

Ryke glares. "For fuck's sake, you couldn't let me bask in that for at least two seconds, could you?"

"I speak the whole truth. Someone has to." Connor plasters on one of his fake grins that actually says, *half of what I say is bullshit.* He digs into a plastic bag at his feet and opens a package of vampire teeth. He mentioned how he didn't have time to go all out on a costume because he's been working since five this morning. He wears his usual suit and tie.

I'm in a gray wool sweater. Beneath that is a white button-down and a green tie. A green and black scarf lies on my neck. I drive up to the guards at the neighborhood gate and verify who I am. Half a minute later, I pull into our driveway and park in the garage.

We split up to find the girls, and I carry both bags of ice inside. "Where's my 'puff?!" I shout as I kick the door open to the kitchen.

Lily looks up from a giant vat of punch, stirring the chunks of fruit with a spatula. I find myself slowing my pace, just to engrain this image of Lily: her cheeks rosy-red as she exerts extra effort, her gangly arms hidden beneath a black sweater and robe, her yellow tie peeking out by the collar.

"Me?" she asks, her nose crinkling in confusion. Christ, I want to kiss her. Wrap my arms around her.

I near Lil, setting the ice on the counter. Then I mockingly check over my shoulder. "Is there another Hufflepuff in the house, love?"

"Maximoff could be Hufflepuff one day," she points out. "We don't know yet."

I don't have to search far for him. He's right beside Lily, in his bouncer on the floor. He sleeps in his black wizard robe. We thought about dressing him as Harry Potter with the scar, but he hated the plastic glasses.

"Or he could be Slytherin," she notes, not leaving out my Hogwarts House. He could be almost anything, and I'd still be proud to call him my son.

There are small moments where I still fear for him. Struggles he may face, mistakes I know he'll make, but I just remind myself something that I never even considered a year ago.

I remind myself that he has us. And back then, I would've pitied him for landing a shit like me. But I'm not a shit. I'm not worthless or pathetic. If my son ever trips, I have no doubt that I can carry him as far as he needs to go. I love my child unconditionally, the way that I love my wife, and I will praise him. I will cherish him. And I will adore him.

I'll give him everything that we were starved of.

"If he's Gryffindor," Lily muses, "does that mean he's cooler than us?"

"No way," I tell her. "Ryke is in that house and we're a million times cooler than him. He started off tweeting one-word tweets for a full *week*." I couldn't believe the amount of people that retweeted his tweet that said: *Wednesday*. That's it. Wednesday.

"That was lame," she ponders, wrapping her arms around the bowl. Why the hell is she hugging the punch? "But he climbs rocks with his bare hands."

"Yeah? And I can make you come a dozen times in one night. Who is more impressive?"

Her cheeks redden and her lips part, all breathy. "You." And then she concentrates on the punch, and I realize she's trying to lift the giant bowl in her thin arms.

"Lily Hale." I give her a look.

"It's a temperamental bowl."

"Use one of your spells to move it, little puffy," I tease.

She crinkles her nose again. "I can't."

"Lost your wand?"

Her eyes flit to my lips. And a smile pulls my face. She's turned on by wizard jokes. God, I fucking love her. I step near to help her, but she raises her hand.

"Stay back."

"That's not a spell."

"You're too attractive right now." She crosses her ankles and then glances at the oven clock.

I already hear people arriving in the backyard, so it's not like we can have a quickie in the closet. And it's not like she's ever yearning for a two-second fuck anyway.

"Mess up your hair," she orders.

I rake my fingers through my longer strands of hair on the top.

Her eyes comically pop out of her head. "Dontdothat," she slurs, her breathing heavy in need.

"How about," I say, prying the punch bowl from her, "we go outside with Moffy."

She nods repeatedly like I just read the Declaration of Independence.

"You first," I tell her. She picks up our three-and-a-half-month-old son, perching him on her side, and leads the way.

The sliding glass door is open, people walking in and out. The backyard is full of kids in Halloween outfits, parents, and festive decorations. Apples even float in the pool, the water orange from the colored light. The neighborhood party is an olive branch. A start to a safe and normal life here.

I place the punch bowl on the long table of assorted Halloween treats, and I take a cookie for Lily and a couple Fizz Lifes. She sits on a hay bale with Moffy, a perfect people-watching seat.

Before I reach Lil, her older sister cuts me off, glowering at me. "You couldn't have chosen a more appropriate costume," I tell Rose, popping the tab of my drink.

"Do you even know what I am?" she retorts, her hands haughtily placed on her hips. I scan her costume: a black tutu, black paint over her eyes, and her hair in a bun.

"A devil. Oh wait, that's not your costume. That's just you." Clearly, she's dressed as the Black Swan, pulling off a Natalie Portman look.

"If I was a devil, my trident would be halfway up your ass by now." She pokes my chest with her finger. "I gave you my sketches *last week* and they're still unopened."

"Calloway Couture Babies will survive if I take a couple extra days to look through them," I remind her. "And really, you don't need my approval."

"Yes, I do," she retorts. "We're business partners."

I laugh. "That's the scariest thing I've heard all day."

Her lips twitch in a smile. "Just look at them."

I nod. "I will."

She flips her hair with her hand and her yellow-green eyes land on her husband, chatting with the neighbors. He wears a fake smile, even with the vampire teeth. And he cradles his daughter in his arms, who's dressed in a white tutu and headband.

Before she can march over to him, Connor notices her approaching and breaks away from his conversation with the neighbors. Rose narrows her eyes at the fake teeth in his mouth. "Those probably make you slur and yet you're still schmoozing."

"It's what I'm good at," Connor says, *clearly*. Her eyes turn to fire and he only grins wider. Jesus. "Assumptions are what you aren't good at, darling"

"I'm better at them than you, and that's all that matters." She holds out her hands for Jane. "Come here, little gremlin. We're matching. You don't need to be in the hands of an egotistical vampire."

Connor beams and when they stare at each other it's like two dominant personalities equalizing out. Impossible. But somehow right. I shake my head and leave their sides just as they turn their conversation to French.

I finally make it back to Lily, sliding next to her. I hand her the cookie and then lift Moffy in my arms.

"Have you seen Daisy?" Ryke suddenly asks us, coming over with a plate of chips and spinach dip. "I can't fucking find her."

"Check the moon," I tell him.

He gives me a weird look.

My lips pull in a dry smile. "That's where she claims she goes in her answering machine message."

"Hilarious." He pops a chip in his mouth.

Moffy squirms, waking from his nap. He tries to suck on my finger, and before I ask, Lil passes me his bottle. I press it to his lips, and he eagerly grips the sides as he drinks.

Then Lily makes a gasping noise.

"What?" I quickly look up at her, but she's not focused on Moffy.

"You don't see it," she says, trying to cover my eyes. Hers are planted on something by the apple bobbing tub.

"Too late," I tell her, my gaze narrowing at Garrison dressed as *nothing*. He just wears all black. And he fixes my sister's wet hair off her forehead, her costume: Vega from *Street Fighter*. His hand brushes her hip, and she lets out a nervous laugh.

I like him. But I like her more. Willow is *my* responsibility while she lives in Philly, and his track record is shit.

"They're cute," Lily reminds me.

I shake my head and grimace the longer I watch this young romance unfold. I wonder if we were that love sick growing up.

Ryke tells Lily, "He's a fucking hormonal teenage guy with anger issues. It's not cute."

Lily swallows a bite of cookie. "I was a hormonal teenage girl. Minus the teenage part, I still kind of am . . ."

"And you're adorable," I tell Lily, kissing her temple.

"*Anger issues*," Ryke emphasizes, licking his fingers.

Garrison slings his arm around Willow's waist. Great. Quickly, I press a hand to Moffy's ear and shout, "Hey! You two!"

Willow's and Garrison's heads whip over to the hay bales across the pool. It takes a single Hale death-glare for them to break apart like a bomb exploded at their feet.

"That was mean," Lily tells me.

Ryke butts in, "You wouldn't think it was mean if you knew the shit he said about you."

"What?" She frowns.

I'm not close enough to slap the back of my brother's head, but I'd like to. "He has no filter," I remind her. "He's working on it." Hopefully. I've talked to him a lot at Superheroes & Scones. He's still a dick, but he's less of a dick now than he was before.

Ryke has a hard time forgiving any guy who degrades women—except maybe me. I called his own mom a word that he can't even say . . . and at the time, I thought she was my mother. It's fucked up. *I* was fucked up. So I get that guy. More than anyone probably will.

"Ca-caw!" someone shouts from up high. We all follow the noise to the roof of the house. "Ca-caw!" Daisy, wearing an antler headband and a brown shirt, sits on the shingles. Her gaze is pinned right on my brother. "Hunt me."

She might as well have said *fuck me*. I try to tune them out and feed my kid, but it's hard not to overhear.

"Deer don't ca-caw, Calloway," Ryke deadpans.

She gasps. "How'd you know I was a deer?" Her smile brightens as she swings her legs off the ledge. Her hair is pulled back in a braid, her long scar visible across her face.

Lily slaps my arm repeatedly. "Nerd star alert," she tells me.

Jesus Christ, I don't have the mental stability to watch both couples at the same time. My brain will implode on impact. I purposefully just train my focus on my brother if I have to choose one. I missed his reply to Daisy, but he trashes his plate and heads to her.

Instead of entering the house, he climbs up the drainpipe, using his upper-body strength. Making it look like he's taking the fucking stairs to reach Daisy. When he sits his ass on the shingles and kisses her, more than a few people clap and cheer.

But all I see is a guy who'll be bedridden for a month and a half after a high-risk surgery. And even if he's okay after that, I see a guy who's willing to climb four-thousand-foot cliffs with no rope to catch him.

My brother's lifespan is shorter than mine. I know it. And I hate it.

He deserves to outlive me and every goddamn person here.

Never in my life did I think having a brother would change me. Make me better than who I am. But there's something about siblings that pushes you to thrive in ways that a parent can't.

"Hey, Lil," I breathe, putting Moffy's bottle down.

"Hmm?" She's fixated on Connor and Rose, a giddy smile on her face. Her sister saved her. I said that to Ryke earlier, and it's the fucking truth. Rose took care of Lily when I was in rehab; she was there when I should've been. When I *couldn't* be.

And the words just leave me. "Someday," I say, "I want another kid."

She freezes and very slowly turns to face me, stunned in disbelief. I've never professed this or even let it linger for longer than a second. "What . . . ?"

I lick my lips. "I *believe* that we can raise more than one kid. It doesn't have to be in a year or two or even three. But someday, I want to meet Luna and whoever else. I don't want Maximoff to be an only child like I was growing up."

I've lived both versions: no siblings, siblings. For me, there's no question which one I'd choose again.

I wait for Lily's response, but her facial expression hasn't shifted past shocked.

"Unless . . . you don't . . ." I trail off, watching her chin quake.

And then she breaks into a smile, tears rolling down her cheeks. That's a yes. She's wanted this, I realize. But she didn't entertain it—for me.

"You thought one and done?" I ask with a rising smile.

She nods, rubbing her forearms across her cheeks, drying her tears. "I know you love him," she sniffs. "So much. But you never talked about it."

I tuck a piece of hair behind her ear. "I never told you this but having a kid, it affected me." I exhale these strong sentiments that propel me forward. "And I'm not saying it's been easy or it's been this magic solution to my problems. Sometimes it made things worse, overwhelmed me, but . . . it shook me. It woke me up." I pause. "And somewhere in my head, I tightened the things that'd been coming loose. I know they can always unscrew again. I know that I could relapse down the line. But I'm not looking at the worst parts of my life anymore. I'm focusing on the best things I have. And there are a whole hell of a lot of those."

Lily's eyes say *I love you*. So many of them that my chest rises in sync with hers. Moffy in my arms, she inches closer and rests her cheek on my chest.

I hug her against me and kiss the outside of her lips. She's not crossing her legs or squirming. She's not pleading for sex. Tears squeeze through the creases of her eyes, this gorgeous, happy smile playing at her lips.

"I'm supposed to give you presents on your birthday," she murmurs, "not the other way around."

"You've given me enough to last a hundred more birthdays, love." At twenty-five, I am in desperate love with a girl who desperately loves me back. There is nothing more that I want than to experience life with her.

She touches Moffy's tiny fingers, and she skims his cheek with a gentle, caring brush of her thumb.

My family. My wife. My son.

Never did I think I'd be the recipient of fragile, precious things.

Every single part of me is alive today. And it'll be tomorrow. I'm not dying in my own body anymore. I am truly living. Peace courses through me. It's the quiet that I never thought existed. And the heaven that I never believed was meant for me.

Lily and I—we may have started our relationship as pretend.

But for as long as I can remember, our love has always been real.

ACKNOWLEDGMENTS

So many people have made the Addicted series special to us. In ways that we can't justly articulate. It's been a whirlwind and a dream, and to know that this is a reality that we can share with you—there is nothing more powerful for us and so we want to begin by saying thank you.

To our mom—our very own Rose Calloway—thank you for your constant, unwavering love. You've taught us about family and loyalty, and given us a great deal of confidence, all while wearing heels. You're one of the most generous human beings, and we only hope to grow up with a fraction of your heart. At twenty-three, we have a long way to go, but we're ready, thanks to you.

To our dad and brother—thanks for always believing in us. It has made standing up and moving forward after any tumbles and falls so much easier. We love you both.

And to the Fizzle Force, fans of the Addicted series—you mean much more to us than just fans. You're all our friends. Whether we've met you, whether you're anonymous, whether the most you've done is read our work. You have changed us. You've made us better writers. You've made us push ourselves. And we can look fondly at Lily and Lo in peace.

Thank you for sticking with us. Thank you for standing behind these characters. You're the Wampa cap to our Lily. The high heels to our Rose. And the sunshine to our Daisy. Without you, this series wouldn't be what it is now.

Have hope. Stay strong. We'll see you again.

As Lily would say, *thankyouthankyouthankyou.*

BONUS SCENE:

Lily's 24th Birthday Questionnaire

Lily Calloway

I like watching Loren Hale sleep.

Without thinking much else that sounds creepy, but I promise I had more thoughts coming—not *that* kind of coming.

"Lil?" Lo squints in the darkness, his arm beneath his pillow. And I wonder if the power of my thoughts woke him. I kind of like this superpower, but I should wield it wisely.

"Lo," I whisper back, turning on my side in bed, our noses close. "Do you think I'm creepy?"

"No, love." He kisses the tip of my nose. "Go back to sleep."

I sit up on my elbows against his wishes and grab my phone off the end table. "We're supposed to take a video for our fandom on my birthday. I told them I'd be live five minutes ago. I meant to wake you but . . ." *you looked so peaceful.* We don't get much sleep with a newborn these days. I open a social media app and lean against our headboard.

"It's four a.m.," he mutters and checks the clock before sitting up next to me, his light brown hair messy until he runs a hand through the strands.

"I know. I can't wait." I couldn't sleep much, and instead of scrolling through gossip sites, this seems healthier and more fun. But maybe not at the cost of Lo's sleep. "You can go back to—"

"You're not doing this without me, Lily Calloway." My name sounds raspy in his slowly waking state. It's sexy, but I try to concentrate on my phone while Lo scoots closer to me. His slowly rising smile is also too attractive and makes me smile too.

Okay, this was a really good idea. One of my best, maybe. He leans against me to fit in the frame of the camera, and my heart thumps.

It's dark on my phone, so I reach over and flick on my lamp. Then I hesitate for a second. "Do you think they can tell we're in bed?" I glance down at my outfit. I'm in one of Lo's black shirts with just panties. My bottom half is hidden from sight, and Lo is completely shirtless, the start of his toned abs just making the frame.

I find my legs tangling with his, and part of me—a large part—would like to spend a minute or two touching him . . .

But we're still on a strict *no sex* schedule since I had our baby, so I don't start what I won't want to end.

"Not unless you accidentally drop the phone." Lo raises my arm that has begun to droop.

"I'm not good at this," I realize.

Lo takes the phone and holds it for me. He immediately starts recording the live video before I adjust—I needed to mentally prepare to greet hundreds or thousands or even possibly *millions* of viewers. I needed to take a sip of water, fix my bed hair, and make sure I don't have a booger. These are important things!

"Lo!" I descend halfway down the blankets, my mouth and nose hidden. And in one hasty moment, I've given the entire world the answer to where we're filming. I'm officially horrible at greeting fans.

Lo stares into the camera, much better at this than me. "Lily woke up at four a.m. on our time to say hi to all of you—"

"And answer questions," I add, my voice muffled beneath the blanket.

Lo's lips rise a fraction. "It's my best friend's birthday today. She's kind of camera shy, even when it's her own camera. Bear with us."

In the live comments, someone asks: *how old is your best friend turning?*

"My best friend is turning twenty-four," Lo answers. "I've recently discovered that she's part blanket monster."

I attempt to rouse a glare his way.

Lo flashes me a smile, not one of his dry ones. A genuine, heartfelt *I love you* smile. "Aw, look the blanket monster is squinting at me." He turns the camera in my direction, and I disappear beneath our champagne comforter, arms clung around his waist.

He feigns surprise. "Shit, now we're going to have three more months of summer."

I slide onto his body, already halfway splayed on him anyway, and then I rest my chin on his chest. He pulls the top of the comforter down, exposing my head. The phone's camera is pointed at us again, and I make out a question in the comments.

"'*What is your favorite memory of a past birthday?*'" I read. "I liked my ninth birthday. My dad rented out the roller rink for me."

Lo frowns as he remembers this moment in our history. Of course he was there too. "You never even made it onto the rink."

"It was slick," I refute. "And I saw Michael Rosen *fall* four times. He was athletic. I'm not athletic."

Lo tilts his head. "There has to be a better memory than one that involves Michael 'I'm-going-to-turn-into-a-douche-bag-lacrosse-player' Rosen."

"Not that we dislike him!" I shout at the camera. "I'm sure if you're listening, Michael Rosen, you turned out to be awesome."

"*I* don't like him," Lo tells me more than the viewers. "He's a douchebag."

"*Was*," I clarify. "People can change, Lo."

Lo makes a face.

"And I like that birthday," I try to explain. "You helped me skate on the carpet by the benches. It was fun."

Lo begins to smile. "If you say so." He looks back at the questions. "'*What superhero show or movie would you like to be a part of and why?*'" He pauses for a millisecond. "*X-Men: First Class.* In that timeline, social media wouldn't exist, and I wouldn't have to talk to all of you." He flashes a bitter half-smile.

"Lo!" I sit up, straddling his waist.

He angles the camera right at me.

"I apologize for him," I say to everyone. "He didn't mean it."

Lo flips the camera back to his face. "Yes I did." He gives the crowd another dry smile, and the comments explode with heart-eye emojis. Fans love him the most out of everyone, even when his sarcasm is so thick you can't tell what he truly means.

Lo reads another question, "'*What kind of words of advice would you give to the Lily Calloway of five years ago?*'" He spins the camera back on me, and in those amber eyes—calm and happy—I'm reminded of how far we've come from the beginning. Where we weren't even really together.

Now here we are, and we've tried so, so hard to be better for ourselves and each other. I never want to stop trying.

I could dish out cerebral words to the viewers, ones that I've said in therapy and mulled over in my head for years, but they feel almost too tender and vulnerable right now. I want to keep this lighter.

I look more at Lo than the phone. "I would say, 'Lily, stop masturbating.'"

His cheekbones are suddenly as sharp as ice. "Huh, well, I'd tell my younger self to make sure *you* don't give that advice to your younger self."

I narrow my eyes. "Then I'd destroy the time machine on my way to the past."

Lo doesn't look amused. "Then how are you going to get home?"

"A Time Turner."

Lo lets out a short laugh. "Tell Hermione Granger I said hi."

"I'm serious." I scoot closer to his chest, still straddling his waist. I press my palms to his abs. His shoulders remain against the headboard.

"And I'm seriously doubting you'd be friends with a Gryffindor, little 'puff." He acts like he's going to kiss my lips, and then he sticks his tongue in my ear.

"Lo!" I push his chest, not really shoving him away—I don't want to do that. The phone flops onto the bed, and he's unconcerned as he retrieves our poorly recorded video from the comforter. I point a nonthreatening finger at him. "Daisy and Ryke are Gryffindors."

He wears an irritated look. "You're in bed with a Slytherin, love. Snakes don't get along with lions." Even as he says it, I know it's not true. He loves his brother and looks up to him. It's a cemented truth.

When I focus on the phone, I notice we're only gaining new viewers, not losing them. The comments are mostly nice too.

Omg you two are so freaking cute!!!!
I want Lo to love me like he loves you!
What comics would you recommend??
I can't. This is the cutest thing ever.
What's your favorite superhero movie?
Did he wake up just for her? 😍

I try to glance over any negative ones (they unfortunately do exist but thankfully in small quantities) and I pick the next question. "*'If you had a time machine, what moment in time would you choose to go back to and live again?'*"

Before I even think of a response, Lo interjects, "Nowhere. Our time machine is destroyed."

I nod once, agreeing on this. No time machines for us. I want the ability to reach home with Lo and the rest of my family.

Lo turns the phone towards himself. "*What is something you'd put in a time capsule to dig up twenty years from now?*"

"Condoms," I say automatically. Then my neck roasts, and I can feel the red flush rise to my cheeks.

Lo is staring at me with love in his eyes, but I have to clarify. I can't leave the public hanging without an explanation.

"What if in twenty years there's a shortage of condoms? They'd be useful."

"I can always pull out," Lo teases, knowing I hate when he does that.

I shake my head slowly. In the back of my head, I remember we're on a live video, but I don't want to be ashamed. I can do this.

"No?" he wonders. "You'd rather my—"

I cover his mouth with two hands. "This is a PG show!" I can do this to an extent! There might be kids watching. I drop my hands, thinking he won't bring this to a dirty territory.

Then he says, "We're an R-rated couple."

I blush. "Nowearent," I slur together in haste.

"We aren't?" He feigns confusion. "I could've sworn last night I made you—"

I cover his mouth again. "He's been banned!" I'm smiling more than anything, and I feel his lips rise against my palms.

His hands are on my butt beneath the covers. *Yes.*

No!

I don't know . . . I like birthday groping. He knows I like it too because my body is hot all over. It's just . . . this must end soon, before I accidentally start grinding on Lo's dick. That will *not* be happening on camera.

Ever.

I read the next question. "*If you knew you were going to die tomorrow, what would you do today?*" I answer quickly, "This.

Only Moffy would be with us." A wave of comments asks *where is he??* "He's sleeping, and no, we're not getting him." It took so long for him to finally fall asleep, and we're trying to stick to a schedule.

"*'What is the best gift Lo has ever given you?'*" I read, and I feel his smile against my hands again. I want to say *sex*, especially since Lo has given me the best sex I've ever had and the world should know—but my first reaction isn't the true one. "Being there for me whenever I've reached a low," I say honestly. We might've enabled each other, but we've also spent so long making up for our mistakes.

He clasps my wrists and lowers my hands. His eyes have softened, and that says it all.

"Andthemindblowingsex," I say so quickly.

"The important part," he teases and kisses the corner of my lips. I want him so much closer, but I restrain myself from basically clinging to him like a koala to a tree. I don't want to smother him so much.

He glances at the screen in his hand. He's doing a good job of making sure the viewers don't get an intimate tour of our bedroom. "*'What's the worst birthday gift you've ever received?'*"

"A crayon," I tell him.

"I was twelve," he says, outing the fact that the crayon was a gift from *him*. Being twelve isn't really an excuse either. We weren't in kindergarten. Twelve isn't a *here's a crayon, will you be my friend* age.

I stare blankly.

"And that was Purple Mountain Majesty," he defends. "Your favorite crayon."

"You forgot my birthday."

He grimaces only a little. "I'd also discovered hard liquor. You should be happy I remembered the rest of your birthdays."

I'll take what I can get.

Mostly, I'm surprised he mentioned his entrance into liquor at such a young age over the video, but he's not that tense. We're both relaxing into just being ourselves.

I read, "*Birthday wish that you've had that you badly want to happen.*" I don't have to ponder this for too long. "A one-on-one visit with Mr. Peter Pan."

"You want a boy in green tights to break into your window?"

I gawk. "You love Peter Pan too. Don't act like you hate him." And then I add, "He reminds me of you a little." He opens his mouth, but I add again, "But no one could possibly compare to you—and if anyone broke into my window, I'd want it to be Loren Hale."

He waits patiently, and I let out a breath. "Done?" he asks.

I nod.

"Good, because I was going to say I don't hate him. He's just an asshole." He flashes a dry smile right at the camera. "Like me."

Oh jeez. "Next question." I clear my throat and peek at the phone screen again. "*If you were a superhero, what would your name and superpower be?*" I pause. "This will take some thought and a list."

Lo groans. "No lists. I'm sick of lists." Having a baby has forced us to be more organized. He reads, "*Are you a fan of surprise birthday parties?*"

Hmm. I always get anxious if my mom wants to throw a surprise party, so I know this question has lots of stipulations. "If they include other kinds of surprises . . . maybe." My thighs instinctively tighten around his waist.

Lo lifts me higher, and I can tell he's trying to stifle arousal.

I tuck a strand of my messy hair behind my ear. "Now they're asking quickfire questions." I point at the screen. "*Magic or mutant powers?*"

"Both," Lo cheats.

I nod, definitely cheating with him.

"*'Hogwarts or Xavier's School for the Gifted Youngsters?'*" I answer, "We'd spend four years at Hogwarts—before the Dark Lord does serious damage—and then head over to Xavier's."

"Smart thinking, love."

I smile and read, "*'Stalia or Stydia?'*"

"Stydia," Lo says. We're both in agreement on this *Teen Wolf* ship. We've had hour-long discussions about it.

"*'Comic series TV show or movie adaptation?'*" I read.

"Marvel movies," Lo says instantly.

"I like the DC shows though."

Lo gives me the side-eye with an added glare. He's so pro-Marvel, it's actually cute. He sets a hand on my forehead.

"I'm not sick."

"You're definitely coming down with something. DC-itis."

I swat his hand and then read the next one. "*'Vampire or werewolf?'*"

"Vampire," we say in unison.

"*'Wampa cap or X-Men Wolverine watch?'*" I read. Oh this is tough. "Wampa."

Lo stays quiet. I know he wants to align with *X-Men* paraphernalia, but the *Star Wars* hat has meant a lot to me over the years—so he can't choose.

He reads, "*'Cereal or pizza?'* Pizza. The ones who'd choose cereal are in the basement."

"Raisy is alive!" I promote my favorite ship.

Lo just shakes his head like I truly am falling under some sort of "itis"—but I'd like to think it's the best kind of illness, something that perpetuates good news, good feelings, and only good days.

"*'Lover or fighter?'*" I ask.

Lo gives me a *what the hell?* look.

"It's a real question." I point at the screen before the comment disappears.

I think he's about to say "lover"—or maybe it's just me believing Loren Hale is a lover before he's a fighter—but a baby's cry resounds through the monitor on the end table.

"And that's our cue to leave," Lo says. He nods at the camera. "Thanks, whoever's watching. You managed to lure out the blanket monster. Any last words?" He spins the camera to me.

"Thankyouthankyou!" I say quickly and wave, feeling a little silly but proud. My cheeks redden, but I'm smiling.

He shuts off the video, closes social media, and then climbs out of bed. He comes around to my side and tugs my arm so I reach the edge. "Want a ride?"

I respond by climbing onto his back, arms around his collar and legs wrapped loosely around his waist. He mostly supports me with his arms beneath by knees.

Moffy's only crying a little, so my heart isn't clenching like it sometimes does.

When we're in the hallway, I point at the nursery and say, "To the Batmobile, Robin."

He drops me instantly, and I thud on my butt. "Hey."

"Hey, what?" He crosses his arms, and even though he purposefully dropped me, I'm staring up at the best-looking face the universe has ever seen. And he belongs to me.

"It's my birthday," I remind him.

"Really? I don't recall carrying my best friend to a damn *batmobile* on her birthday. I'd never give her such a shitty present."

I contemplate this. "Then where are we going, Loren Hale?"

He squats in front of me, our lips a breath apart. My chest rises in a strong inhale.

And he says softly, "To Neverland."

He lifts me in a front piggyback, our eyes locked together, my heart bursting. He walks down the hall, to Neverland, silently hoping to fulfill the one birthday wish that I've wanted badly. My one-on-one with Peter Pan.

I know it's already come true. I've spent nearly all my life with the boy who can fly, and I plan to spend the rest of it with him too.

BONUS SCENE:

Rose's 26th Birthday at Cobalt Diamonds

Rose Cobalt

Delicate diamonds sit in glass display cases. Necklaces, earrings, bracelets, rings, watches, pendants, broaches—anything and everything hits me like a sudden gasp.

I'm not *literally* gasping.

At least not in the presence of my husband. It's already enough that he caught me smiling when his limo driver dropped us off at the Cobalt Diamonds storefront in New York City. And Connor hasn't let it go.

"You smile like that only around me," he gloats, our baby nestled against his chest. Jane is absolutely revolting in the most adorable baby way. I swear if any harm *ever* comes to her, I'd scorch the earth and never sleep until the enemy is gutted. Slowly.

She deserves nothing less.

I also didn't expect how much I'd love seeing Connor cradle our daughter. He holds Jane so confidently and protectively. The image tries to defrost the ice in my veins.

He's even dressed in a dapper suit today. *He looks handsome.* I can't deny it. Not as he stands poised and self-assured by the register. The store is only open for today, a special request for my twenty-sixth birthday.

I scoff at him and scan a display case with vintage-inspired jewelry. I zero in on the gorgeous white gold, diamond waterfall earrings as they call out to me.

He sidles over to the case, his larger-than-life presence vacuuming oxygen from the room and my lungs. "Those are Canadian diamonds."

A conflict-free source. All the diamonds sold here are harvested in a responsible, legitimate manner and ethically sourced, and some are even lab grown. It's important to both of us.

I know I'll eventually choose those earrings, but I find myself prolonging the entire moment. I tear my gaze off the case and pin it onto my husband.

"I was smiling because I was standing beneath a sign that said *diamonds*," I rebut. "It had nothing to do with you."

Do not let Connor Cobalt win.

This is practically written in our marriage license, right below the line that belongs to him: *Accept every challenge that Rose Calloway Cobalt gives you.*

The rest of our lives will be anything but boring.

Connor's grin is rising to extraordinary proportions. "You were also standing beneath a sign that said *Cobalt*."

"A name that also belongs to me," I retort.

His grin only grows. "Oui. You were smiling over our name."

I narrow my yellow-green eyes, piercing a hole in his forehead. "Over *diamonds*." I'm not giving in this easily. "I didn't even see the word *Cobalt*."

His eyes flit down my body. "Then I'd suggest glasses—"

"Says the man who had trouble reading the scoreboard at a Model UN conference." I think I've finally shot down his ego.

His lips fall into a line, and then he laughs. "George Browning had the worst handwriting I've ever seen. It's not a fault of mine but his." He makes a note of saying his name, *George*.

I can only remember so many small and insignificant details.

His brain is a library filled with thousands of dusted books, ready to be consumed all over again.

I cross my arms over my chest, my Chanel diaper bag hanging on the crook of my arm. I'm about to call him out, but Jane stirs in his arms, drawing my attention to our daughter. She lets out little puffs of breath in her sleep.

She's beautiful, my gremlin.

When I think about how she's a piece of him and a piece of me, together, my eyes begin to well. She softens me sometimes; I know it, and I don't even hate it, not even a little.

I love her, sleeping and awake.

Connor walks closer to me. "As beautiful as our daughter is, she's not a diamond. If you want one, you might want to look at them. Unless you'd like another child."

I let out a short laugh and shift my blazing stance. He'd just *love* to give me that kind of birthday present.

His humored eyes do not match my combative glare. I start feeling more like melted ice pretending to be frozen solid today, but I think Connor loves me all the same.

"I could just be checking on you," I tell him. "To make sure you're not close to dropping our daughter." I uncross my arms and plant them on my hips, making a point to raise my chin.

He closes the distance between us with another step.

It unravels me a little, my pulse escalating.

"I'm more than capable of holding our baby."

"Mmm," I muse, almost embarrassed at my lack of response. Air catches in my throat, and I swallow it. Then I collect my hair over one shoulder. His hot gaze trails across the bareness of my neck—and it almost pushes me to cover my skin again.

I don't though. I like watching his desire, as much as I like letting him work to obtain mine.

"Can you give her to me?" I ask, my sudden request intriguing him.

His brow arches. "Why?"

"I don't want to stain her dress when I tear out your jugular and feed it to the wolves," I say in the flattest voice. I expect him to step *backward*.

He steps *forward*.

I glower.

He grins.

Ugh. God.

My statement would scare 99.9 percent of the population, but I don't tell him this—that he's *rare* and *unique*. He'd be the first to award himself those titles.

"You want to touch my neck, Rose?" he asks, his voice smooth like the surface of a lake.

"To do harm to your neck, Richard."

"You'd never do harm to me."

"You don't know that," I refute.

"I do," he says. "You love me."

I snort, but I can't refute—I do love him. More than I've ever loved a man. My phone buzzes in my pocket, and I'm thankful for the distraction at first.

Less when I see who messaged me.

Emailed you a list of fan questions for your birthday. Lily and Loren did this via social media with positive public reception. I've pitched this idea to the publicity team for you. Your answers will be published in an article on a reputable site tonight. Please email them back as soon as you can. Publicist needs to send them to the journalist asap.
—Mom

An uneasy feeling clenches my stomach. I text her quickly. *No. I'm not interested in competing with Lily. EVER.* I'm pursing my lips and practically grinding my teeth. Does *EVER* in all capital letters seem too hostile? Yes. Should I erase it?

Probably.

I begin to delete.

No, screw this—I'm retyping it. I hit send.

She responds even faster.

> Don't be so dramatic. —Mom

I roll my eyes.

"Your mother?" Connor assumes.

"She's insufferable." I explain what's happening when another text vibrates my phone.

> It's not the same as Lily. Yours will be published in an article. Hers was via social media. It wasn't even professional. The publicity team all agreed this is a great opportunity for you. You need good publicity. —Mom

Back when I made the horrendous decision to sign Scott Van Wright's contract to film *Princesses of Philly*, I would've done almost anything to be publicly praised and save my struggling fashion line. Now, however, Calloway Couture isn't on the brink of failure. I'm not as desperate for good publicity.

And how can she not see that she's usurping Lily's idea?

Another incoming text.

> Your sister won't care. A lot of work went into this for you, Rose. —Mom

"I'm texting Lily," I tell Connor. Quickly, I ask my sister for permission. In two seconds, she answers saying she truly doesn't care. So I agree to this article questionnaire, just to get my mother off my back.

I slip my phone in the diaper bag.

I'm aware that there was no *happy birthday* message in any text my mom sent. Though I can't be bitter since I had a joint party with Lily on the third. Maybe she thinks my birthday celebrations have ended, even if August fifth hasn't.

I selfishly love my birthday too much to just let this day pass without any indication that it belongs to me. I realize the day is not literally mine, but I'd at least like *some* recognition, a little praise, and maybe, yes, adoration.

I thought Connor might forget about me today, just say *happy birthday* in the morning since we had the party on the third. Taking me here to pick out anything I like—it's already made the day perfect. More so because he remembered me. And he knows what I love.

I set the diaper bag on the display case. "Is there a computer here?" I ask Connor. "I have to answer these fan questions. I'll pick a piece of jewelry afterwards." I'd type on my phone, but it's easier to make a typo.

"The office has one," he says.

I follow Connor toward the back of the store. He passes me a sleepy Jane before he unlocks the door.

"Shh," I tell her, stroking her soft arm as her eyes try to open. I kiss her head and murmur, "Go back to sleep, my little gremlin."

I can feel her heart beating slowly, and her eyes shut completely at my last word.

"Rose," Connor says, opening the door more.

I begin to walk inside the office, but I stop in the doorway, stunned for a moment. I process the room.

Red roses.

Everywhere.

Vases line the desk, petals on the floor. Flickering lights create the illusion of candles on the windowsill, New York City beautiful at night.

On the coffee table, a champagne bottle rests in ice, already opened. Two glasses filled.

It's intimate. And beyond perfect.

I didn't expect this at all.

Connor takes Jane out of my arms again, and he places her in a soft baby carrier by the couch, a Scrabble game set up on the coffee table.

"You planned this," I practically whisper, so shocked and grateful. I head farther into the office.

"It's your birthday," he replies. "I was going to take you to Skaneateles, but I thought you'd prefer to be closer to home with Jane today."

He's right, and yet those words stick in the back of my throat. I produce ones that are sometimes just as rare. "Thank you," I say. He hates the entire concept of birthdays, and yet, he always plays into mine.

Translation: *I love you, darling.*

He walks closer and closer. I grip the edge of the desk, breath locked in my lungs. And I think he's going to pull me in his arms and kiss the nape of my neck. He takes his charm, his poise, and his arrogance and slips past me, claiming the only office chair at the desk.

I glare. "Never mind."

"Never mind . . . what?" He knows what. He begins typing on the keyboard, bringing up the home screen.

"Never mind my *thank you*," I clarify. "I'm retracting it."

"You can't retract what's already been said. It's physically impossible."

I growl a little, and his lips rise as he focuses on the screen.

I feel like we're teenagers, preparing for day two of Model UN, both hogging the computer in a conference room—the one used for PowerPoint presentations. We'd take five-minute shifts, refusing to let each other have access for too long.

"Let me sit down." I try it this way. "It's my birthday. Don't you love me, Richard?"

His grin is obnoxious, and I wonder if he's thinking the same as me: *as teenagers I would've never been able to use this line. A marriage and a baby later, look at us now.*

"I'm not prohibiting you from sitting down." He clicks into my email. He knows my passcodes only because I know his.

"What are you talking about?" I snap back. "There's only one chair."

He pats his leg, telling me I can sit on his *lap*.

No.

Absolutely *not*. I steel my gaze. "In your dreams, Richard."

"This is my reality."

"A queen doesn't share her throne."

"I wouldn't share mine either," he says smoothly. "Not with anyone but you." He meets my eyes, and this time, love and challenge are in them. *You didn't marry a pushover*, he's told me many times before.

I like that he's this way. I like that he's not gentle and that he doesn't always bend to my will. I love that he takes charge *more* than me.

I accept the challenge. *Fine*. I tug down the hem of my black dress that hugs my curves, and I sit on his lap. He immediately pulls my back against his chest, until my ass is positioned right on the bulge in his black slacks.

I try to ignore his cock and the way he still seems to dominate me, even though I'm on *him*. It pricks my nerve endings. I attempt to lean forward and begin typing, but he keeps my back to his chest, his head still above mine as he stares down at me. Six-foot-four—he will *always* tower and command.

"I can't reach the keyboard," I note.

He scoots forward in the chair, my chest coming close to the lip of the desk. I'm rigid and stiff, an unoiled Tin Man. I mechanically touch the keys, the document already popped open.

1. What is your favorite memory of a past birthday?

His closeness is so distracting; I can hardly concentrate. Where are his hands? I blink a couple times and then type, *All of them*.

I feel his laugh against my back. "How descriptive."

"I like all of my birthdays," I snap.

This isn't true.

Loren Hale has ruined probably eight or nine of them, but I always wanted him there—because then it assured that Lily would come.

I raise a hand at Connor like *shut up*. Of course I can't see his face since he's behind me.

I move on to question number two.

2. What do you think Connor would say are his five favorite things about you?

His hands are on my ass. *My ass*, I type.

"Your intelligence," he states.

My hair, I add.

"Your temper."

My legs.

"Your confidence."

My lungs. I can practically feel him grinning behind me.

"Your exaggerations."

My eyes. I slam the last key.

"I do adore your eyes," he says. "We should add some truths because now it sounds like you married a pig." He reaches out to change my answer, and I swat his hand from the keyboard.

"This is my duty," I say dramatically.

He tries hard not to laugh because I turn my head and *glare* at him so hard. "Your duty is to lie to the world about me?"

"I speak only truths, Richard."

"Another lie, *Rose*."

I huff. "Fine." I delete *legs* and *hair* and type in *intelligence* and *confidence*. I'm too distracted to find better words.

3. If you could only see three people for the rest of your life, who would they be?

My fingers freeze on the keyboard. His hands are on my thighs, slowly sliding up the hem of my dress. "Richard," I warn.

"Focus, Rose."

"I'm trying," I retort.

"I can give you the answers."

My face tightens. "I don't need a cheat sheet from *you* on my own opinions." I begin to type, roused like a gathering fire. *Connor. Jane. My sisters.*

"I didn't realize a group of people is now considered one individual."

I raise a hand for him to be quiet. I cannot choose between my sisters. It's like asking me to saw a pair of heels in half. It cripples me inside.

Connor suddenly clasps my hand, and with his grip on my thigh, he spins me around so I'm straddling his waist. My back faces the computer, and now my gaze is boring fatally into him. I can't type like this. I can't even see the computer screen.

He scoots closer to the computer, until my back presses against the edge of the desk.

"Connor," I say, nervous about what he plans to do.

"Trust me," he says in a strong voice that reminds me of who he is. I can give up control to my husband in intimate situations, but typing this email is something I'd do *outside* the bedroom. The mix of the two is heady and unnerving.

His arms extend beneath mine, reaching the keyboard easily. My lips are near the base of his jaw, and part of me wants him to look at me and kiss me . . .

His gaze falls in knowing, and he retracts one hand from the keyboard. His thumb skims my bottom lip. My body shudders and begins to pulse.

"I have to answer . . ." I'm so distracted. I shake my head, as if tearing through the cobwebs of my mind.

"I think you want my lips on your lips, Rose," he says deeply. "Just like I want mine on yours." And then he kisses me, so fully that my whole body seems to meet his more than it already has. My arms hang loosely by the chair. Then I clutch on to his biceps.

His tongue parts my lips once, enough to melt my mind and loosen my joints. His thumb replaces his tongue, and my breath hitches, a moan tickling my throat.

He reads the next question to me, "*Lily and Daisy are drowning. Who would you save first and why?*"

I choke on his thumb, and he immediately removes it, concern flickering in his blue eyes. He watches me for a second, and I shake my head vehemently this time. "I'm *not* choosing. I can't choose, don't you dare type anything else or I'll—"

"I won't," he says, hand tenderly on my cheek. "I promise."

It calms me immediately.

He removes his hand to type a response. He takes a little longer than I expect, and I still can't believe I'm letting him do this.

And then I can believe it. I take deeper inhales, feeling better and less anxious by sharing this task. Some days I obsess over emails, taking *hours* to send them. I'll reread, fix little words or the sentence structure, reread again—it goes on and on. Connor has been a force in my life that helps me stop and breathe.

He reads, "*What is one quality you possess that you hope will pass on to the little one?*"

"Definitely not your narcissism," I say.

He grins. "Loving yourself is a great quality."

"Loving yourself *too* much is a flaw."

"I disagree."

"Then maybe you should name your firstborn son *Narcissus*."

He almost laughs. "*Our* firstborn," he amends. "And it's a little presumptuous. If he's not a narcissist and he has that name, then he becomes an oxymoron. I don't like it."

I wouldn't have allowed it anyway. "Independence," I tell him. "I'd love for Jane to be independent, above everything, I think."

"You think?"

It sounds wishy-washy, so unlike me to attach an "I think" on the end. "I know," I retort, taking my hands off his waist. I cross them over my chest.

He looks entirely aroused by my haughtiness. That's on him. He should cower, not pull me closer. I listen to him type on the keyboard, our gazes locked as he does so. Connor only drifts away when he reads the next question.

"'*This or that,*'" he tells me. "'*Neck kisses or forehead kisses from me?*'"

I glare. "Is this real?" I try to peek over my shoulder at the form, but he quickly stops me, his hand against my cheek. I drill a fiercer look on him. "Richard."

"Answer the question, Rose."

"Neither."

His lips press against my neck, and I intake a sharp breath. In the most fluid transition, his lips rise to my forehead, leaving a warm imprint, scalding me. I shudder again, my thighs involuntarily quivering.

He gives me a carnal once-over. "Forehead kisses," he breathes, removing his hands and probably typing *that*. I don't refute because it's the answer.

"'*Dior or Versace?*'" he asks.

I've barely regrouped, but I quickly answer, "Dior," to show that I am *not* undone or unraveled.

"*'Building a snowman or doing snow angels?'*"

What the fuck kind of question is this? I start cringing at the idea of rolling around in snow and soaking my coat. "Snowman."

He types fast. "*'Hair in a ponytail or braid?'*"

"Pony."

"*'Working with me or with Ryke for the day?'*"

Part of me wants to push Connor's buttons. Ones that rarely, if at all, are ever pushed. Some could even claim he has no hot-tempered buttons or raging bone in his body, but I know he isn't immune to jealousy or wrath.

He feels just like the rest of us.

I'm just not sure choosing Ryke over Connor would do much. If I pick Loren's brother, it'd be a bald-faced lie, and Connor would sniff it out like a bloodhound.

His typing stops midway, maybe realizing that I'm hesitating. "What would he offer you that I don't?"

"He talks less."

"And you can listen to him use unclever variations of the word *fuck* for three hours."

I groan. "You're incorrigible."

"I'm honest."

So am I. "I'd work with you," I tell him. *Because I trust you and love you most.* I actually end with this, "Even if you annoy me most."

He pushes my ass harder, and I dig into him, *oh God.* He whispers French in the pit of my ear, but I'm too aroused to untangle the words.

"*'Camping or hiking?'*" he asks in that smooth voice before kissing the base of my neck. I shut my eyes.

"Hiking."

His hands dive beneath my dress, rising up the bareness of my inner-thighs. "*'Hugs or cuddles?'*" he asks.

I grimace at the word *cuddle*. How soft and awful it sounds. Yet, hugs seem far worse. "Cuddles," I breathe, my chest collapsing as he sucks on my neck. I clutch his arms and stifle a moan that wants to escape.

He clutches the back of my head with one hand and whispers in my ear, "*'Painting or drawing?'*"

"Drawing." I tremble.

Every word sounds more seductive and visceral from his lips. "*'Reading or writing?'*" His mouth trails across my collar.

"Reading."

And then his lips find mine, kissing me powerfully, with such command that I'm left loose in his arms, ones that catch me as I fall against the edge of the desk.

He pulls me into his body, gripping my hair, tugging. *Connor.* I moan into the next kiss, and then stop suddenly, my mind more vivid—on the questions . . .

"You never typed my answers," I breathe heavily, my lips reddened from the kiss.

He combs his fingers through my hair with affection. "I already did."

"How . . . ?" I glare. "Did you even read me the right questions?" He wasn't staring at the computer. I suddenly spin around to look. On the screen, every question is what he asked, accompanied with the correct responses that I'd given him.

"I memorized the questions," he explains.

With one glance, most likely. I don't mean to underestimate his intellect. Sometimes I truly am shocked by how smart he is. He filled out everything about me before I'd even told him. And it was all correct.

He knows me too well, and there is real comfort in this fact.

I reach forward and hit send to my mother, a weight rising off my chest. Then I face Connor again, happy that he's my husband and that I'm here today with him and Jane.

Once we're both on our feet, standing together, and his hand finds mine, Connor says, "Let's toast."

"To what?" I ask as he passes me a champagne flute.

He raises his glass. "To my beautiful, intelligent, confident, and madly independent wife." He pauses with a gorgeous, rising grin that I love to hate. "Happy birthday, darling."

I'm about to take a sip of my bubbly champagne, but he doesn't sip his yet. He's an unemotional man, who rarely lets anyone see through his brick wall. Right now, the wall has vanished. Completely. He stares at me with more love, more heart in his eyes than he ever allows to pass through.

It sweeps me back, leaving me overwhelmed and breathless.

And he says softly, "Je t'aime."

I love you.

BONUS:

Ryke Meadows's 26th
Birthday Interview

Here's what happened: *Corbin Nery, the Calloway family's publicist, tried to contact Ryke to answer fan questions for his birthday on September 19th. Ryke never answered a single one of Nery's calls or texts. Nery was left to send the questions to Loren Hale in order to deliver them to Ryke. Loren told Nery,* "I can give these to him, but he's in a foul fucking mood, so don't expect a goddamn novel from my brother." *The "mood" that Loren is referring to points toward Ryke's recent break from rock climbing. And in a manner of speaking, Ryke is pissy.*

Ryke emailed these fan questions back five minutes after he received them. These are his answers.

Q: What is your favorite memory of a past birthday?
A: Rock climbed in Borneo at 9 with Adam Sully.

Q: What would be your ideal scenario for a day spent with Connor Cobalt on a lonely island?
A: Setting off on a fucking hike. Away from him.

Q: Name five extra things you'd pack on an adventurous trip to the wilderness when all the necessities like flashlight, tent, etc., are already packed.
A: A fucking book.

Q: If you could change one thing in the world, what would it be?
A: For addiction to never fucking exist.

Q: If you had the opportunity to be different, what would you change about yourself?
A: Less stubborn.

Q: If you had a time machine, what moment in time would you pick to go back to and live again?
A: Any moment with Daisy.

Q: Greatest adventure you've ever had?
A: Being in love with Dais.

Q: Greatest wish for yourself?
A: Live the fullest life.

Q: What is the most dangerous and adventurous thing you would ever do with Daisy?
A: El Encierro. (Running of the Bulls in Pamplona.)

Q: What is a language that you would want to learn for yourself?
A: Portuguese.

Q: What was the strangest birthday gift you've been given?
A: A dog collar. I'll give you one fucking guess to figure out who gave it to me.

Q: What is the next place you'd like to take Daisy to?
A: Too many places to name.

THIS OR THAT

Q: Cupcakes or chocolate cake?
A: Either.

Q: Red Hot Chili Peppers or Arctic Monkeys?
A: RHCP.

Q: Daisy's hair up or down?
A: I love her hair any fucking way.

Q: California or Florida?
A: CA.

Q: Lakes or rivers?
A: Both.

Q: Piercings or tattoos?
A: Tattoos.

Q: Rock climbing or running?
A: Climbing.

Q: Wall sex or shower sex?
A: Wall sex in the shower.

Q: Couch or table?
A: What the fuck.

Q: Run errands with Rose or with Lily?
A: Both and neither.

Q: Go scuba diving or skydiving?
A: Skydiving.

Q: Ice cream or frozen yogurt?
A: Frozen yogurt.

BONUS: TEXT MESSAGE THREAD

LILY: Hey. Say someone was going to get you a birthday present. Would you appreciate a tiny mountain statue with your face carved on it (like Mt. Rushmore) or would you prefer a tiny mountain statue with a tiny man statue that looks like you on top?

LILY: Be honest.

RYKE: Don't get me a fucking birthday present. Problem solved.

LILY: It wasn't a problem! It was just a question. One you have to answer.

RYKE: The better question is how the fuck are you going to get a mini-sculpture of my face onto a mini-mountain. What the fuck, Lily?

LILY: I know people.

LILY: Okay, Connor knows people. Mini-mountain sculpting people. So which one????

RYKE: Buy me new carabiners.

LILY: That's not any fun.

RYKE: Neither is staring at my face on a mountain.

BONUS: PLAYLIST

"All Comes Down" by Kodaline

"I'm Gonna Be (500 Miles)" by Sleeping At Last

"There Goes Our Love Again" by White Lies

"Someday" by LP

"Like Real People Do" by Hozier

"Say My Name (feat. Zyra)" by ODESZA

"Fury Oh Fury" by Nico Vega

"Come a Little Closer" by Cage The Elephant

"Sheep In Wolves Clothes" by Little Hurricane

"White Lies—EP Version" by Max Frost

"Outro" by M83

**KEEP READING FOR AN EXCERPT
FROM THE NEXT NOVEL
IN THE ADDICTED SERIES**

Fuel the Fire

Rose Cobalt

Take directions from your husband, Rose Cobalt.

Who, *who* fated me with this night? *You, Rose.* A sour taste fills my mouth. I am partly to blame, I'll admit. I refused to let him drive. I thought if I was behind the wheel, he'd tell me where we're headed.

Instead, he's given me the barest of directions. I'm driving blindly, at his will.

Take directions from Connor Cobalt, outside of the bedroom. I'd rather drown myself in hot, bubbling magma.

"Turn left at the light," Connor says, his fingers to his lips. I catch his smug smile, illuminated in the blue glow of the dashboard.

I itch to do the opposite, to take a sharp *right*, but wherever we're going, I want to be there as much as him. The endgame—which I am privy to—means more to me than starting a fresh rivalry with my husband. So I suck up my overwhelming pride and whip my Escalade left.

I can feel him gloating. "The more you grin like I'm giving you a quickie in a disgusting public bathroom, the more my ovaries wither and *die*," I tell him. "So just think about all of our future children you're annihilating, Richard."

He outstretches his arm behind my headrest. "I'm so extraordinary that my mere grin can make you infertile?"

"I was insulting you," I retort, my eyes flickering to him.

His brow arches with more satisfaction. "It was partially a compliment and partially erroneous."

I scoff. "Erroneous?"

"Illogical, irrational, senseless—"

"I *know* what erroneous means. I just want to cut off your tongue for using it against me." He may be right. It's not a rational statement, but I would hope my ovaries would stand with me and not firmly on his side.

"You forget that I use my tongue for your pleasure—turn right."

I swing the car to the right. "I don't need your tongue," I refute. "I have other means of pleasuring myself." Though masturbating isn't quite as good or substantial, but I'm avoiding another compliment toward a man who finds them in insults.

His fingers drum the headrest. "Are these means battery-operated?"

I shoot him a sharp look, not denying the truth.

His thumb brushes my cheek, and I actually relax some. "Your argument lacks evidence, darling. Turn left after this light."

I roll to a stop, the red light gleaming along the nearly deserted street. It's 10 p.m. on Thanksgiving night, everyone eating pie with their families indoors. Not gallivanting across the back roads of Philadelphia on a bizarre mission.

"Where are we going?" I ask for the fourth time.

"A parking lot," he says again.

"I've passed about thirty of them already." I motion to the empty one beside a dimly lit gas station. "Will that one not suffice?"

"A *specific* parking lot," Connor amends. One that he had to

Google on his phone, the device clutched in his palm. "We're almost there. Do you think your ovaries will survive until then?"

"Do you plan on impregnating me in this parking lot?" I glare, spinning fully toward him while we wait for the green light. He wears a blue button-down and suit jacket, tailored perfectly for his six-foot-four frame. Connor Cobalt is as classy as he is conceited. Both attract me.

Both annoy me.

I'm a paradox. And maybe that's why he loves me.

"I plan on impregnating you seven more times," he declares, "but not tonight." He cups my face, and his thumb brushes my bottom lip in a slow, measured line.

My chest falls shallowly, especially as his eyes flit to my mouth. He wants eight kids. An *empire*. We already have one child together, but there are stipulations that we haven't discussed in full detail yet if we want more. For another time. Another day. We have too many crises to stir another one.

"You're taking too much pleasure in this," I say a bit quieter than I intended. I'm not even sure what I'm referring to: our proposed empire, him controlling our destination, or turning me on?

"You're the one out of breath," Connor says calmly, but I hear the humor behind his voice. After being married for almost two and a half years, I've learned the subtlety in his tones. Either that or he's decided to ease off the façade for me. I like to think it's a little of both.

But I doubt I'll ever know.

"It's green," he announces without breaking my gaze.

I turn my head, and his hand drops. I drive to "wherever the hell he directs me to"—which is my least favorite destination.

After another five minutes, he tells me to slow down and turn right into a parking lot. I pick my foot off the gas and the car lolls.

"Right here." He gestures ahead of us.

I swerve into the empty parking lot and digest my surroundings:

the front of a closed fabric store, lights off, the building as dark as the starless sky.

I park my Escalade in the third row and switch off the ignition, my heart thudding against my tight rib cage. The quiet blankets us, the reality of our choices starting to catch up to my head.

Connor watches me, not speaking. Maybe he thinks I'll back out. I won't.

I understand who and what this is for.

"Let's just do this quick." I unbuckle and swivel around to face him. "Before anyone realizes we're gone." We slipped out of my parents' house after apple pie. I set my six-month-old daughter in my mother's arms and left her there for a couple hours. That was harder than this will be.

I pull my glossy brown hair back into a sleek pony, snapping the band violently before I focus on Connor in the passenger seat. His brows are pinched, lines across his forehead, his enjoyment depleting with mine.

My spine is at a stiff ninety-degree angle, and I struggle to un-cross my ankles. "What now?" I ask, though I'm fairly certain I know what happens next.

"You want instructions?" He gives me a pointed look like, *you've been arguing with me for the past hour for giving them.*

My eyes flame. "When it comes to your penis, I would like in-structions, yes." I've yet to master blowing him, and the whole ordeal gives me an anxious heat that I almost never wear.

Blowing him in a public parking lot—I never imagined I'd do something so juvenile. But when it comes to protecting the people I love, my list of *don'ts* decreases dramatically.

He unclips his seatbelt. "Lean against the door and spread your legs open." My eyes grow in surprise.

"What?"

"Lean against the door—"

"I heard you the first time," I retort. "I just . . ." I have to read between his words. *Spread your legs open.* I dazedly shake my head.

Translation: *You're not blowing me, darling.*

He waits for me to accept this switch.

I hesitate, only because I like following the rules. "Connor, they told me to give you oral." If we really wanted, I could even *pretend* to blow him. We just need to act like we're doing it close to the windows.

He slides near me and reaches down, gripping my ankle. He slips off my black, five-inch heels before I can protest. And then he lifts my feet on the seat, so I'm forced to lean against the door like he previously requested. I need the support anyway, blood rushing through my veins at his strong, assured movements.

With my ankles still in his grasp, he splits my legs apart. I tug down the hem of my pleated black dress, shrouding my lacy black panties from his view—but more importantly the view of someone outside.

A determined look pulses in his blue eyes, ambition and confidence that's harder and better than a slap on the ass.

He kneels on the seat and reaches beneath my dress, his fingers skimming my panties.

"Connor," I warn. All I can think—if we don't do this right, to their liking, then we're screwing everything on day one.

"Ils jouent notre jeu. On ne joue pas le leur." *They play our game. We don't play theirs.* He adds in French, "Ensemble." *Together.*

We do this together or not at all.

I'm more in love with him, conquering the world by his side, than I ever was as his competition. He was ready to be my teammate the minute I graduated prep school, but I put the brakes on that, choosing a different college than him. I wasn't ready to be something more. We stayed rivals. He didn't want to wait for my cap and gown, for our entrance into adulthood, and so when the opportunity arose, he asked me out.

We dated. We married.

We had a baby.

Together, we're a force of nature to be reckoned with. That's not my hubris speaking. It's just the truth.

I nod once, power pouring through me. "Ensemble." *Together.*

He kisses my ankle as he raises my leg, slipping off my panties. I keep yanking at my dress, the side of my ass exposed. Though I'm not sure how much someone can spot through the windows.

Connor sets my panties on the dashboard and then places his hand on mine, shielding more of my body from view. He lifts my left leg over his shoulder, his body hovering over the middle console.

He whispers, "Lean back and shut your eyes."

I do as told, even if I'm not in the bedroom, this is a bedroom activity. And I'd rather not be in control.

I rest against the car door and close my eyes, trying not to think about anyone lurking outside.

Connor grips my hips and scoots me closer to him, so my back is at a better angle, only my shoulders braced against the door handle.

In the quiet moment, a distant car honk sounds closer, and my eyes snap open. I try to straighten and peer out the windshield.

Connor grips my face, rotating my head to him. "Focus on me. Or would you rather suck my cock?"

I glare. "Would *you* like to switch?" I challenge, even though I *in no way* want to be photographed with my head above his pants. Not if there's an alternative.

His head in my crotch. I approve.

"You know what I find mildly irritating?" he asks, his voice calm, collected, but I hear the tightness of his words, as though annoyance, a hidden emotion, fists each syllable.

"Your voice," I rebut.

He withholds a grin. "Answering a question with a question." His clutch is still forceful on my jaw. My body is in his complete possession. "This is how you answer a question, Rose."

I listen closely.

"No," he says, "I do not want to switch places with you. They believe we're their marionettes. We'll show them the strings, but we will *always* move on our own accord." He pauses, his eyes flitting to my mouth again. "But most importantly, you believe my tongue is expendable." His face nears mine, which he grasps, and I breathe so heavily as he whispers, "You're going to remember, Rose, why it's *absolutely* essential."

I feel myself clench.

"Now close your eyes," he commands.

I have no problem listening to him now, blocking out our surroundings—or at least my imagination that is doing more harm than good.

I shut my eyes again, and as he lowers his head between my legs, his hand travels from my jaw to my neck. He's reaching up and choking me with the right amount of force. *Oh God*. His tongue and mouth kiss my heat—I shudder and grip the leather, the back of my head hitting the glass window, shoulders digging into the handle.

"Please," I cry deeply, feeling him adjust his fingers around my neck, gripping slightly harder so I can't speak. My head lightens . . . *God yes*.

The sensitivity that his tongue plays with—it's better than any of my toys. It shocks each nerve and flames my core, my skin flushed. I only hear my staggered breaths in the silence of the car.

I open my eyes. Just to see his head disappeared between my legs. One of his hands is up my dress, clutching the side of my ass. And his other long, outstretched arm lies against my body as he steals my oxygen.

That arm builds my arousal as much as everything else, my toes beginning to curl. *Connor* . . .

I hold on to his forearm and touch his large hand that wraps around the majority of my neck. And then his phone buzzes by the gearshift, threatening to tumble beneath the depths of my seat.

He removes his hand off my ass to grab it, but he continues pleasuring me, a second cry in my throat at the way he hits a nerve.

He passes me the phone, reminding me that we're a team here. His fingers loosen on my neck, only a little to reorient my head. I keep the cell low and open his lock screen with his password: 0610.

It was a text message.

> Where the hell did you and Rose
> go? —Loren

I try to stifle a cringe, hating to think about Loren Hale while I'm with Connor like this. Actually, thinking about him at all is about as low on my to-do list as setting myself on fire. (Setting myself on fire ranks higher.)

Though, that's not entirely accurate seeing as how we're new business partners. I never thought that'd happen. I'm not wholly happy about it but I'm not disappointed either. Besides Connor, my relationship with Loren is the most complex one I have.

Before I can even tell Connor about the text, another one buzzes.

And this time, I have a hard time reading the words. Connor suddenly fills me with his fingers, and my back arches and my head tips to the side, my eyes tightening shut, too many heightened emotions overtaking me in a hot, electric wave. My body is his in this moment. He could do whatever he wanted to me, and I'd let him, willingly.

"Please," I beg. I used to hate the sound of my voice when I was with him in bed. How weak and wanting it was—but now I love that I can give myself to someone else this way. I'm allowed to be vulnerable too.

He pumps his fingers deeper into me, simultaneously flicking my clit with his tongue. He squeezes my neck, and I reach a blinding climax, my lips parting. No noise escapes, too breathless to create a moan. My hips rise and my muscles constrict. He leaves his fingers inside of me while I pulse around them.

Connor raises his head, watching me catch my breath, his own desire washing over his features. He stares at me like he'd rather fuck me at our house than return to my parents'. If we didn't have responsibilities like friends and a daughter, then maybe that'd be possible.

But I like the way our life is. Minus a couple large kinks that we need to smooth down before Jane reaches a certain age. Before we decide to have more children.

These are the kind of kinks that have deadlines. If we don't iron them by a certain point, it's over for us. The Cobalt family will just consist of Jane, Connor, and me.

I want Jane to have a sister, more than anything else. The best parts of my childhood consisted of Lily, Daisy, and Poppy. And I can't imagine her growing up without one.

Connor looks at me as though he's reading my innermost thoughts, with reverence and intrigue. I touch his hand around my neck and he laces my fingers with his.

He sits up, kneeling.

I check his phone again.

> What the fuck are you doing?
> Samantha just opened photo albums.
> We're going to be stuck here for
> another three fucking hours if you
> don't come back. —Ryke

"It seems we're wanted."

"We're always wanted," he says, pulling my arm so I straighten up against the seat. His lips linger near my neck. "We're the oldest, smartest, and most responsible of our roommates."

I turn my head to call him conceited and maybe note that his ego is choking me more than his hand.

The minute I swing in his direction, he kisses me, not for long, but enough that my insult disappears. He bites my lip gently before he releases.

I swallow, and as I clench between my legs, I suddenly remember something. I am not wearing panties. And I'm sitting on a leather seat. *My* leather seat. And I'm aroused and wet and—I push away from him and snatch my panties from the dashboard. I try to examine the damage I caused to my beautiful leather seat, and how gross it must be, for me, to sit here while we drive back.

"You're not that wet, Rose," he says.

I smack his chest. "Shut up—"

He clasps my hand again and lifts me onto his lap so I can see the seat. No stains, but I contemplate whether or not I should have the leather properly—

"I'll have it cleaned tomorrow," Connor tells me, easing my concerns. I nod and he slips my panties on my legs, dressing me. He reaches over and opens the passenger door before climbing out, setting me on *his* chair. When he walks around the Escalade to the driver's side, his cell vibrates in my palm.

Got the photo. You'll see it
tomorrow. —WA

My shoulders relax. "They accepted the switch."

Connor hears me as he shuts the door, the corners of his lips rising. He was certain they wouldn't have a problem. His confidence in life and his choices are unparalleled.

He turns the car on with a much wider grin. "'Look like the innocent flower, but be the serpent under it.'"

I tilt my head at him. "*Macbeth.*" The quote from Shakespeare is very familiar to me.

He wears that billion-dollar grin again. We won round one of a much larger game tonight. At least that's what it feels like.

At the end of the day, we're still in bed with the media. And no one knows this but Connor and me.

People look to Connor to fix their problems, to solve things greater than them, and usually he says no. If there's no benefit for him, he sees no point to help, to take that risk.

But there was one exception.

I saw it happen. That day. Weeks ago. Connor came into our bedroom and told me that he had to bury an article. He said the only way to do it was to make a deal with the press. Me and him. If we feed a tabloid scandalous photos or a headline every so often, then they'd agree to never print this one defaming editorial.

"Is it about Jane?" I asked, my eyes flaming. I was ready to raise hell at the *Celebrity Crush* offices, to march to New York and stick a finger in the face of a journalist and shout and scream. I even grabbed my purse off my vanity stool.

Connor stopped me, and I read his gaze well enough.

It wasn't about our daughter.

The article was about someone else. He explained how *Celebrity Crush* was going to run a story on Lily and Loren's son, my sister and my brother-in-law. How the tabloid was going to claim their paternity test a forgery, citing Maximoff's deep chocolate brown hair as evidence of being Ryke's son. Ryke, as in Loren's half-brother.

Lo has light brown hair. His birth mother's hair color. Not

dark brown, the shade that Ryke, their father, and now Moffy all share.

The article is a stretch, a false claim. But one that would rock Lily and Loren's world. After fighting for so long, they deserved a win.

Their son deserves to *never* doubt his parentage.

"I have to help Lo," Connor said, his brows cinching at his own words. He knew. He knew that what he was doing was so out of his character. Because here was a man that always weighs opportunity cost. This, in no way, benefited him. In fact, it cost him.

And for the first time, in probably his entire life, he's choosing a price with no reward for himself.

"You know when you asked me to do this with you?" I say softly while he drives back to my childhood house.

He nods once.

"I think I fell in love with you all over again," I admit. This is something I would have chosen. Without a second thought. To protect the people I love. Years ago, Connor would have laughed at those words.

Love. It meant nothing to him.

Now it's guiding his choices.

Krista and Becca Ritchie are *New York Times* and *USA Today* bestselling authors and identical twins—one a science nerd, the other a comic book geek—but with their shared passion for writing, they combined their mental powers as kids and have never stopped telling stories. They love superheroes, flawed characters, and soul mate love.

VISIT KRISTA AND BECCA RITCHIE ONLINE

KBRitchie.com
KBMRitchie

Ready to find
your next great read?

Let us help.

Visit prh.com/nextread

Penguin
Random
House